GIRDED IN NEW ARMOR...
NAKED TO NEW WORLDS

"The fighting suit is the deadliest personal weapon ever built, and with no weapon is it easier for the user to kill himself through carelessness. Turn around, Sergeant.

"Case in point." He tapped a large square protuberance between the shoulders. "Exhaust fins. As you know, the suit tries to keep you at a comfortable temperature no matter what the weather's like outside. Therefore, these fins get *hot*—especially hot, compared to darkside temperatures—as they bleed off the body's heat.

"All you have to do is lean up against a boulder of frozen gas...and in about one-hundredth of a second, you have the equivalent of a hand grenade going off right below your neck. You'll never feel a thing..."

—from Joe Haldeman's "Hero"

EDITED BY JOE HALDEMAN
WITH CHARLES G. WAUGH AND
MARTIN HARRY GREENBERG

BODY ARMOR: 2000

ACE SCIENCE FICTION BOOKS
NEW YORK

BODY ARMOR: 2000

An Ace Science Fiction Book/published by arrangement with
the editors

PRINTING HISTORY
Ace Science Fiction edition/April 1986

ISBN: 0-441-06976-2

Ace Science Fiction Books are published by The Berkley Publishing Group,
200 Madison Avenue, New York, New York 10016.
PRINTED IN THE UNITED STATES OF AMERICA

Contents

INTRODUCTION

Joe Haldeman

Surely there has been personal armor for as long as men have fought. When European adventurers sailed out to conquer primitive cultures, they found all odd sorts of it: the Aztecs' quilted vests, Micronesian rope armor; shirts and skirts of leather and rattly conglomerations of wooden slats, shells, bone—all generally useless against gunpowder, and much of it probably more of symbolic than actual value even against the autochthones' own primitive weapons.

Which is not to say you have to be an ignorant primitive to find your armor suddenly irrelevant, or even a liability. Interlocked shields did nothing against Archimedes' catapulted burning pitch. Heavy mail proved transparent to the English longbow. Articulated plate armor wouldn't deflect the matchlock's ball. The effectiveness of any kind of armor has to serve as a goad to ingenuity: if SWAT teams are protected by Kevlar undershirts, then criminals buy Teflon-coated bullets, or shoot for the head.

My personal acquaintance with body armor is limited to the flak jacket we were occasionally issued in Vietnam. This was a bulky but fairly lightweight armored vest, with plates of some tough substance (a ceramic-plastic composite, I think) sewn in pockets all around. It wasn't part of our regular issue, since my outfit of combat engineers spent most of its time walking around in the woods, and you couldn't wear a rucksack over the armored vest. But they sometimes were handed out when we settled in one place for a while.

The soldiers' attitude toward the vests was perhaps predictable. It was awkward to do any kind of real labor hobbled by them—and for engineers, frontline combat is continual chain-gang labor relieved by occasional terror—and they got clammy with sweat and chafed. It was common knowledge (whether actually true or not) that the flak jackets would stop small pieces of shrapnel, but not big killing pieces, and not bullets. So why wear them? The big chunk or the bullet would kill you anyhow, and the minor wound the vest might deny you could be good for a week's vacation and a Purple Heart. Maybe even a transfer to the rear or a trip home. So wearing the vest, especially when we weren't actually under fire, became a sign of inexperience or cowardice, or at least eccentricity.

(An interesting inversion of this attitude surfaces in the Marine Corps' published history of the Battle for Khe Sanh—arguably the grittiest, most sustained battle in the Vietnam War. The fight for Hill 861A was particularly desperate, ground fog and darkness reducing both sides to hand-to-hand combat and point-blank blasting: "Since the fighting was in such close quarters," the official history says, "both sides used hand grenades at extremely short range. The Marines had the advantage of their armored vests and they would throw a grenade, then turn away from the blast, hunch up, and absorb the fragments in their flak jackets and the backs of their legs. On several occasions [they] 'blew away' enemy soldiers at less than 10 meters." The history does not record whether it crossed anybody's mind that a piece of shrapnel in the butt could be a ticket out of Khe Sanh.)

Anyhow, since I had illusions of surviving Vietnam to come back and become a rich and famous writer, I ignored public opinion and did wear a flak jacket whenever they were issued. I would like to be able to report that the vest saved me from death or serious injury, but it didn't—except in that it seemed to be a good-luck charm; I was never hit while wearing one, save for a dramatic but painless bullet in the canteen. Furthermore, when I did finally buy a ticket out of the jungle, none of the nine or ten most serious wounds I sustained was above the waist or below the shoulders; the only wounds I got that would have been stopped by a flak jacket were no more serious than shaving nicks.

So from my experience, the best kind of futuristic body armor would be something that was one hundred percent effective in increasing the wearer's *luck*. Might as well make it lightweight and unobtrusive—hell, invisible—and not usable by the enemy. Just some little device to make sure the enemy always misses. People have been experimenting along these lines for a long time, with religious amulets and rabbits' feet and so forth, and a certain amount of anecdotal evidence has accrued attesting to their effectiveness, perhaps only because when such a device fails, the person using it can no longer be an informant. At any rate, anecdotal evidence is untrustworthy. A friend of mine in Vietnam took a sniper's bullet in the back but his life was saved, at least for the time being, by his inability to spell: the bullet lodged in the dictionary he kept in his rucksack to help with letters home. The incident was written up in the Pacific *Stars and Stripes,* but somehow the dictionary had become a Bible; it was over his heart, not his spine; and the bullet had stopped on the word "peace."

So we'll fall back on the traditional assumption that one makes one's own luck. What features would you incorporate into personal armor to maximize your chances of coming back alive?

One factor to consider is that offense and defense tend to merge in combat, so a good way to protect yourself is to deliver such a withering field of fire that the enemy dares not peek out to aim. (Von Clausewitz said "the best defense is a rain of blows.") There are two problems with this strategy. The obvious one is that you only have a finite amount of ammunition, whether you're shooting bullets or photons. You may need some of it to soldier with. The other problem is less obvious: you don't want blatantly to be the most dangerous thing around. Ask any trooper who's led a combat assault with a flame-thrower, if you can find one still alive. The roaring blossom of flame is painfully conspicuous, and becomes every enemy soldier's first-priority target.

The route writers usually follow in science fiction is to equip *every* soldier so he's about as lethal as the Golden Horde. Robert Heinlein took this principle to its apotheosis with his Mobile Infantry in *Starship Troopers*—tactical nukes and death rays, able to leap tall mountains in a single bound—and he did such a good and thorough job of it that it's hard to write a science-fiction war story without showing his influence.

When I was writing *The Forever War* (of which "Hero" in this collection is the beginning), a friend read the first seventy or so pages and said, hey, you're writing an answer to *Starship Troopers*. That hadn't occurred to me; I thought Dickson and Harrison had answered the book's politics quite well (*Naked to the Stars* and *Bill the Galactic Hero,* respectively) without any help from me. The only formal plan I had in mind for the novel was to address certain aspects of the Vietnam War in science-fiction metaphor. But look at this, my friend said—you've stolen Heinlein's fighting suits! To which I wearily replied, what do you expect? They're fighting in conditions that might be hard vacuum and close to absolute zero, or might be a hot desert planet or one with a corrosive atmosphere.... I should have them fighting in their underwear? Suits of mail?

He was right, though; I *was* affected by Heinlein's 1959 book (which I had read at least twice), even though I wasn't thinking about it consciously. I was also affected by dozens of earlier science-fiction war tales, less memorable ones, that I'd absorbed back in the years when I was ignoring school and reading a couple of novels a day. Who knows, maybe Heinlein read those, too.

So I was not surprised, when the stories for this anthology came in, to find that many of the body armor schemes were reminiscent of Heinlein—even if they were written before *Starship Troopers*. It's interesting, though, that in these stories the armor is often more trouble than it's worth, which seems to be a consistent irony with military hardware: most of the things that are truly effective against the enemy tend to be effective against the user as well, if he trips or sneezes or forgets to put on the safety before he scratches his ear with the muzzle. (You think that doesn't happen?)

Here they are, then, all these armored heroes and antiheroes, victims and villains. Thrill to their trials and, if you're like me, be glad that you can face your own battles with no more protection than a three-piece suit and a new haircut.

CONTACT!

David Drake

Something shrieked over the firebase without dipping below the gray clouds. It was low and fast and sounded so much like an incoming rocket that even the man on Golf Company's portable latrine flattened instantly. Captain Holtz had knocked over the card table when he hit the dirt. He raised his head above the wreckage in time to see a bright blue flash in the far distance. The crash that rattled the jungle moments later sent everyone scrabbling again.

"Sonic boom," Major Hegsley, the fat operations officer, pontificated as he levered himself erect.

"The hell you say," Holtz muttered, poised and listening. "Paider, Bayes," he grunted at the two platoon leaders starting to pick up their bridge hands, "get to your tracks."

Then the klaxon on the tactical operations center blatted and everyone knew Holtz had been right again. The captain kicked aside a lawn chair blocking his way to his command vehicle. The radioman scuttled forward to give his powerful commander room in front of the bank of radios. "Battle six, Battle four-six," the tanker snapped as he keyed the microphone. "Shoot." Thirty seconds of concentrated information spat out of the speaker while Holtz crayoned grid coordinates in on an acetate-

5

covered map. "Roger, we'll get 'em." Turning to the radioman he ordered, "Second platoon stays for security here—get first and third lined up at the gate and tell Speed I'll be with him on five-two." While the enlisted man relayed the orders on the company frequency, Holtz scooped up a holstered .45 and his chicken vest and ran for his tank.

Golf Company was already moving. Most of the drivers had cranked up as soon as they heard the explosion. Within thirty seconds of the klaxon, the diesels of all nine operable tracks were turning over while the air still slapped with closing breechblocks. Tank 52 jingled as Hauley, its driver, braked the right tread and threw the left in reverse to swing the heavy war machine out of its ready position. Holtz ran up to the left side, snapping his vest closed at the shoulder. He was one of the few men in the squadron who wore a porcelain-armored chicken vest without discomfort, despite its considerably greater weight than the usual nylon flak jacket. In fact, Holtz was built much like one of his tanks. Though he was taller than average, his breadth made him look stocky at a distance and simply gigantic close up. He wore his black hair cropped short, but a thick growth curled down his forearms and up the backs of his hands.

Speed, a weedy, freckled staff sergeant with three years' combat behind him, grasped his captain by the wrist and helped him swing up on five-two's battered fender. As frail as he looked, Speed was probably the best track commander in the company. He was due to rotate home for discharge in three days and would normally have been sent to the rear for stand-down a week before. Holtz liked working with an experienced man and had kept him in the field an extra week, but this was Speed's last day. "You wanna load today, Captain?" he asked with an easy smile. He rocked unconcernedly as Hauley put the tank in gear and sent it into line with a jerk.

Holtz smiled back but shook his head. He always rode in the track commanders' position, although in a contact he could depend on Speed to fight five-two from the loader's hatch while he directed the company as a whole. Still smiling, the big officer settled heavily onto the hatch cover behind the low-mounted, fifty-caliber machinegun and slipped on his radio helmet.

"OK, listen up," he said on the company frequency, ignoring commo security as he always did when talking to his unit. He had a serene assurance that his gravelly voice was adequate identification—and that his tanks were a certain answer to any dinks who tried to stop him. His boys were as good and as deadly as any outfit in 'Nam. "Air Force claims they zapped a bird at high altitude and it wasn't one of theirs. We're going to see whose it was and keep Charlie away till C-MEC gets a team out here. Four-four leads, west on the hardball to a trail at Yankee Tango five-seven-two, three-seven-nine: flyboys think the bird went down around seventy-forty, but keep your eyes open all the way—Charlie's going to be looking too."

Holtz's track was second in line with the remaining five tanks of the first and third platoons following in single file. As each one nosed out of the firebase its TC flipped a switch. Electric motors whined to rotate the turrets 30 degrees to one side or the other and lower the muzzles of the 90mm main guns. The big cannon were always loaded, but for safety's sake they were pointed up in the air except when the tanks prowled empty countryside. Otherwise, at a twitch of the red handle beside each track commander a wall or a crowd of people would dissolve in shattered ruin.

"Well, you think we're at war with China now?" Holtz shouted to Speed over the high jangle of the treads. "Hell, I told you you didn't want to go home—what do you bet they nuked Oakland five minutes ago?" Both men laughed.

The path from the firebase to the highway was finely divided muck after three days of use. The tanks, each of them burdened with fifty tons of armor and weaponry, wallowed through it. There was nothing laughable in their awkwardness. Rather, they looked as implacably deadly as tyrannosaurs hunting in a pack. On the asphalt hardball, the seven vehicles accelerated to thirty-five miles an hour, stringing out a little. Four-four had all its left-side torsion bars broken and would not steer a straight line. The tank staggered back and forth across the narrow highway in a series of short zigzags. From the engine gratings on its back deck, a boy with a grenade launcher stared miserably back at the CO's track while the rough ride pounded his guts to jelly.

Holtz ignored him, letting his eyes flick through the vegetation to both sides of the roadway. Here along the hardball the land was in rubber, but according to the map they would have to approach the downed aircraft through broken jungle. Not the best terrain for armor, but they'd make do. Normally the tanks would have backed up an air search, but low clouds had washed the sky gray. Occasionally Holtz could hear a chopper thrumming somewhere, above him but always invisible. No air support in a contact, that was what it meant. Maybe no medevac either.

Ahead, four-four slowed. The rest of the column ground to a chattering halt behind it. Unintelligible noises hissed through Holtz's earphones. He cursed and reached down inside the turret to bring his volume up. Noise crackled louder but all sense was smothered out of it by the increased roar of static. Four-four's TC, Greiler, spoke into the ear of his grenadier. The boy nodded and jumped off the tank, running back to five-two. He was a newbie, only a week or two in the field, and young besides. He clambered up the bow slope of the tank and nervously blurted, "Sir, Chick says he thinks this is the turn-off but he isn't sure."

As far as Holtz could tell from the map, the narrow trail beside four-four should be the one they wanted. It led south, at any rate. Hell, if the MiG was what had gone howling over the firebase earlier the flyboys were just guessing for location anyway. The overcast had already been solid and the bird could have fallen anywhere in III Corps for all anybody knew.

"Yeah, we'll try it," Holtz said into his helmet mike. No reaction from four-four. "God damn it!" the captain roared, stabbing his left arm out imperiously. Four-four obediently did a neutral steer on the hardball, rotating 90 degrees to the left as the treads spun in opposite directions. Clods of asphalt boiled up as the road's surface dissolved under incalculable stresses. "Get on the back, son," Holtz growled at the uncertain newbie. "You're our crew for now. Speed!" he demanded. "What's wrong with our goddam radio? It worked OK at the firebase."

"Isn't the radio," Speed reported immediately, speaking into his own helmet microphone. "See, the intercom works, it's something screwing up off the broadcast freeks. Suppose the dinks are jamming?"

"Crap," Holtz said.

The trail was a half-abandoned jeep route, never intended for anything the width of a tank. They could shred their way through saplings and the creepers that had slunk across the trail, of course, and their massive rubber track blocks spewed a salad of torn greenery over their fenders. But full-sized trees with trunks a foot or more thick made even the tanks turn: grunting, clattering; engines slowing, then roaring loudly for torque to slue the heavy vehicles. Holtz glanced back at the newbie to see that he was all right. The boy's steel pot was too large for him. It had tilted forward over his eyebrows, exposing a fuzz of tiny blond hairs on his neck. The kid had to be eighteen or they wouldn't have let him in the country, Holtz thought, but you sure couldn't tell it by looking at him.

A branch whanged against Holtz's own helmet and he turned around. The vegetation itself was a danger as well as a hiding place for unknown numbers of the enemy. More than one tanker had been dusted off with a twig through his eye. There were a lot of nasty surprises for a man rolling through jungle twelve feet in the air. But if you spend all your time watching for branches, you missed the dink crouched in the undergrowth with a rocket launcher—and he'd kill the hell out of you.

Sudden color in the sky ahead. Speed slapped Holtz on the left shoulder, pointing, but the CO had already seen it. The clouds covered the sky in a dismal ceiling no higher than that of a large auditorium. While both men stared, another flash stained the gray momentarily azure. There was no thunder. Too brightly colored for lightning anyway, Holtz thought. The flashes were really blue, not just white reflected from dark clouds.

"That can't be a klick from here, Chief," Speed's voice rattled. Holtz glanced at him. The sergeant's jungle boots rested on the forward rim of his hatch so that his bony knees poked high in the air. Some people let their feet dangle inside the turret, but Speed had been around too long for that. Armor was great so long as nothing penetrated it. When something did—most often a stream of molten metal blasted by the shaped explosive of a B-41 rocket—it splashed around the inner surface of what had been protection. God help the man inside then. 'Nam offered enough ways to die without looking for easy ones.

The officer squinted forward, trying to get a better idea of the brief light's location. Foliage broke the concave mirror of the clouds into a thousand swiftly dancing segments. Five-two was jouncing badly over pot holes and major roots that protruded from the coarse, red soil as well.

"Hey," Speed muttered at a sudden thought. Holtz saw him drop down inside the tank. The earphones crackled as the sergeant switched on the main radio he had disconnected when background noise smothered communications. As he did so, another of the blue flashes lit up the sky. Static smashed through

Holtz's phones like the main gun going off beside his head.

"Jesus Christ!" the big officer roared into the intercom. "You shorted the goddam thing!"

White noise disappeared as Speed shut off the set again. "No, man," he protested as he popped his frame, lanky but bulbous in its nylon padding, back through the oval hatch. "That's not me—it's the lightning. All I did was turn the set on."

"That's not lightning," Holtz grunted. He shifted his pistol holster slightly so that the butt was handy for immediate use. "Hauley," he said over the intercom to the driver, "that light's maybe a hair south of the way we're headed. If you catch a trail heading off to the left, hold it up for a minute."

Speed scanned his side of the jungle with a practiced squint. Tendons stood out on his right hand as it gripped the hatch cover against the tank's erratic lurches. "Good thing the intercom's on wires," he remarked. "Otherwise we'd really be up a creek."

Holtz nodded.

On flat concrete, tanks could get up to forty-five miles an hour, though the ride was spine-shattering if any of the torsion bars were broken. Off-road was another matter. This trail was a straight as what was basically a brush cut could be—did it lead to another section on the plantation that flanked the hardball?—but when it meandered around a heavy tree bole the tanks had to slow to a crawl to follow it. Black exhaust boiled out of the deflector plates serving four-four in place of muffler and tail pipe. The overgrown trail could hide a mine, either an old one long forgotten or a sudden improvisation by a tankkiller team that had heard Golf Company moving toward it. The bursts of light and static were certain to attract the attention of all the NVA in the neighborhood.

That was fine with Holtz. He twitched the double handgrips of his cal-fifty to be sure the gun would rotate smoothly. He wouldn't have been in Armor if he'd minded killing.

The flashes were still intermittent but seemed to come more frequently now: one or two a minute. Range was a matter of guesswork, but appreciably more of the sky lighted up at each pulse. They must be getting closer to the source. The trail was taking them straight to it after all. But how did a MiG make the sky light up that way?

Speed lifted his radio helmet to listen intently. "AK fire," he said. "Not far away either," Holtz scowled and raised his own helmet away from his ears. As he did so, the air shuddered with a dull boom that was not thunder. The deliberate bark of an AK-47 chopped out behind it, little muffled by the trees.

Speed slipped the cap from a flare and set it over the primed end of the foot-long tube. "We can't get the others on the horn," he explained. "They'll know what a red flare means."

"Charlie'll see it too," Holtz argued.

"Hell, whoever heard of a tank company sneaking up on anybody?"

The captain shrugged assent. As always before a contact, the sweat filming the inner surface of his chicken vest had chilled suddenly.

Speed rapped the base of the flare on the turret. The rocket streaked upward with a liquid *whoosh!* that took it above the cloud ceiling. Moments later the charge burst and a fierce red ball drifted down against the flickering background. Holtz keyed the scrambler mike, calling, "Battle six, Battle six; Battle four-six calling." He held one of the separate earphones under his radio helmet. The only response from it was a thunder of static and he shut it off again. Remembering the newbie on the back deck, he turned and shouted over the savage rumble of the engine, "Watch it, kid, we'll be in it up to our necks any time now."

In the tight undergrowth, the tracks had closed up to less than a dozen yards between bow slope and the deflector plates of the next ahead. Four-four cornered around a clump of three large trees left standing to the right of the trail. The tank's bent, rusted fender sawed into the bark of the outer tree, then tore free. Hauley swung five-two wider as he followed.

A rocket spurted from a grove of bamboo forty yards away where the trail jogged again. The fireball of the B-41 seemed to hang in the air just above the ground, but it moved fast enough that before Holtz's thumbs could close on his gun's butterfly trigger the rocket had burst on the bow slope of four-four.

A great splash of orange-red flame enveloped the front of the tank momentarily, looking as if a gasoline bomb had gone off. The flash took only a split second but the roar of the explosion echoed and re-echoed in the crash of heavy gunfire. Four-four shuddered to a halt. Holtz raked the bamboo with a cal-fifty, directing the machinegun with his left hand while his right groped for the turret control to swing the main gun. Beside him, Speed's lighter machinegun chewed up undergrowth to the left of the trail. He had no visible targets, but you almost never saw your enemy in the jungle.

The muzzle brake of the 90mm gun, already as low as it could be aimed, rotated onto the bamboo. A burst of light automatic fire glanced off five-two's turret from an unknown location. Holtz ignored it and tripped the red handle. The air split with a sharp crack and a flash of green. The first round was canister and it shotgunned a deadly cone of steel balls toward the unseen rocketeer, exploding bamboo into the air like a tangle of broom straw. Brass clanged in the turret as the cannon's breech sprang open automatically and flung out the empty case. Speed dropped through the reeking white powder smoke evacuated into the hull.

Holtz hadn't a chance to worry about the newbie behind him until he heard the kid's grenade launcher chunk hollowly. Only an instant later its shell burst on a tree limb not thirty feet from the tank. Wood disintegrated in a puff of black and red; dozens of segments of piano wire spanged off the armor, one of them ripping a line down the captain's blue jowl. "Not so goddam close!" Holtz shouted, just as a slap on his thigh told him Speed had reloaded the main gun.

The second rocket hissed from a thicket to the right of five-two lighting up black-shrouded tree boles from the moment of ignition. Holtz glimpsed the Vietnamese huddled in the brush with the launching tube on his shoulder but there was no time to turn his machinegun before the B-41 exploded. The world shattered. Even the fifty tons of steel under Holtz's feet staggered as the shaped charge detonated against five-two's turret. A pencil stream of vaporized armor plate jetted through the tank. The baggy sateen of the officer's bloused fatigues burst into flame across his left calf where the metal touched it. Outside the tank the air rang with fragments of the rocket's case. Holtz, deafened by the blast, saw the newbie's mouth open to scream as the boy spun away from the jagged impacts sledging him. Somehow he still gripped his grenade launcher, but its fat aluminum barrel had flowered with torn metal as suddenly as red splotches had appeared on his flak jacket.

Holtz's radio helmet was gone, jerked off his head by the blast. Stupid with shock, the burly captain's eyes followed the wires leading down into the interior of the tank. Pooled on the floor-plate was all that remained of Speed. The gaseous metal had struck him while his body was bent. The stream had entered above the collarbone and burned an exit hole through the seventh rib near the spine. The sergeant's torso, raised instantly to a temperature of over a thousand degrees, had exploded. Speed's head had not been touched. His face was turned upward, displaying its slight grin, although spatters of blood made him seem more freckled than usual.

The clouds were thickly alive with a shifting pattern of blue fire and the air hummed to a note unconnected to the rattle of gunfire all along the tank column. The third tank in line, four-six, edged forward, trying to pass Holtz's motionless vehicle on the left. A medic hopped off the deck of four-six and knelt beside the newbie's crumpled body, oblivious to the shots singing off nearby armor.

Hauley jumped out of the driver's hatch and climbed back to his commander. "Sir!" he said, gripping Holtz by the left arm.

Holtz shook himself alert. "Get us moving," he ordered in a thick voice he did not recognize. "Give four-six room to get by."

Hauley ducked forward to obey. Holtz glanced down into the interior of the track. In fury he tried to slam his fist against the hatch coaming and found he no longer had feeling in his right arm. Where the sleeve of his fatigue shirt still clung to him, it was black with blood. Nothing spurting or gushing, though. The main charge of shrapnel that should have ripped through Holtz's upper body had impacted numbingly on his chicken vest. Its porcelain plates had turned the fragments, although the outer casing of nylon was clawed to ruin.

Five-two rumbled as Hauley gunned the engine, then jerked into gear. A long burst of AK fire sounded beyond the bamboo from which the first B-41 had come. A muffled swoosh signaled another rocket from the same location. This time the target, too, was hidden in the jungle. Holtz hosed the tall grass on general principles and blamed his shock-sluggish brain for not understanding what the Vietnamese were doing.

With a howl more like an overloaded dynamo than a jet engine, a metallic cigar shape staggered up out of the jungle less than a hundred yards from five-two's bow. It was fifty feet long, blunt-ended and featureless under a cloaking blue nimbus.

Flickering subliminally, the light was less bright than intense. Watching it was similar to laying a bead with an arc welder while wearing a mask of thick blue glass instead of the usual murky yellow.

As the cigar hovered, slightly nose down, another rocket streaked up at it from the launcher hidden in the bamboo. The red flare merged with the nimbus but instead of knifing in against the metal, the missile slowed and hung roaring in the air several seconds until its motor burned out. By then the nimbus had paled almost to nonexistence and the ship itself lurched a yard or two downward. Without the blinding glare Holtz could see gashes in the center section of the strange object, the result of a Communist rocket detonating nearby or some bright flyboy's proximity-fused missile. MiG, for Chrissake! Holtz swore to himself.

A brilliant flash leaped from the bow of the hovering craft. In the thunderclap that followed, the whole clump of bamboo blasted skyward as a ball of green pulp.

To Holtz's left, the cupola machinegun of four-six opened fire on the cigar. Either Roosevelt, the third tank's TC, still thought the hovering vessel was Communist or else he simply reacted to the sudden threat of its power. Brass and stripped links bounded toward Holtz's track as the slender black sent a stream of tracers thundering up at a flat angle.

The blue nimbus splashed and paled. Even as he swore, Holtz's left hand hit the lever to bring the muzzle of his main gun up with a whine. The blue-lit cigar shape swung end on to the tanks, hovering in line with the T-shaped muzzle brake of the cannon. Perhaps a hand inside the opaque hull was reaching for its weapons control, but Holtz's fingers closed on the red switch first. The ninety crashed, bucking back against its recoil stop while flame stabbed forward and sideways through the muzzle brake. Whatever the blue glow did to screen the strange craft, it was inadequate to halt the pointblank impact of a shell delivering over a hundred tons of kinetic energy. The nimbus collapsed like a shattered light bulb. For half a heartbeat the ship rocked in the air, undisturbed except for a four-inch hole in the bare metal of its bow.

The stern third of the craft disintegrated with a stunning crack and a shower of white firedrips that trailed smoke as they fell. A sphincter valve rotated in the center of the cigar. It was half opened when a second explosion wracked the vessel.

Something pitched out of the opening and fell with the blazing fragments shaken from the hull. Magnesium roared blindingly as the remainder of the ship dropped out of the sky. It must have weighed more than Holtz would have guessed from the way the impact shook the jungle and threw blazing splinters up into the clouds.

The tanks were still firing but the answering chug-chug-chug of AK-47's had ceased. Holtz reached for the microphone key, found it gone with the rest of his radio helmet. His scrambler phone had not been damaged by the shaped charge, however, and the static blanket was gone. "Zipper one-three," he called desperately on the medical evacuation frequency, "Battle four-six. Get me out a dust-off bird, I've got men down. We're at Yankee Tango seven-oh, four-oh. That's Yankee Tango seven-oh, four-oh, near there. There's clear area to land a bird, but watch it, some of the trees are through the clouds."

"Stand by, Battle four-six," an impersonal voice replied. A minute later it continued, "Battle four-six? We can't get a chopper to you now, there's pea soup over the whole region. Sorry, you'll have to use what you've got to get your men to a surgeon."

"Look, we need a bird," Holtz pressed, his voice tight. "Some of these guys won't make it without medevac."

"Sorry, soldier, we're getting satellite reports as quick as they come in. The way it looks now, nobody's going to take off for seven or eight hours."

Holtz keyed off furiously. "Hauley!" he said. "C'mere."

The driver was beside him immediately, a dark-haired Pfc who moved faster than his mild expression indicated. Holtz handed him the phones and mike. "Hold for me. I want to see what's happened."

"Did you tell about the, the . . ." Hauley started. His gesture finished the thought.

"About the hole in the jungle?" Holtz queried sarcastically. "Hell, you better forget about that right now. Whatever it was, there's not enough of it left to light your pipe." His arms levered him out of the hatch with difficulty.

"Can I—" Hauley began.

"Shut up. I can make it," his CO snapped. His left leg was cramped. It almost buckled under him as he leaped to the ground. Holding himself as erect as possible, Holtz limped over the four-six. Roosevelt hunched questioningly behind his gunshield, then jumped out of his cupola and helped the officer onto the fender.

"Quit shouting," Holtz ordered irritably as the loader sprayed a breeze-shaken sapling. "Charlie's gone home for today. Lemme use your commo," he added to the TC, "mine's gone."

He closed his eyes as he fitted on the radio helmet, hoping his double vision would clear. It didn't. Even behind closed eyelids a yellow-tinged multiple afterimage remained. The ringing in his ears was almost as bad as the static had been, but at least he could speak. "Four-six to Battle four," Holtz rasped. "Cease firing unless you've got a target, a real target."

The jungle coughed into silence. "Now, who's hurt? Four-four?"

"Zack's bad, sir," Greiler crackled back immediately. "That rocket burned right through the bow and nigh took his foot off. We got the ankle tied, but he needs a doc quick."

Half to his surprise, Holtz found that four-four's driver and the newbie blown off the back of his own track were the only serious casualties. He ignored his own arm and leg; they seemed to have stopped bleeding. Charlie had been too occupied with the damaged cigar to set a proper ambush. Vaguely, he wondered what the Vietnamese had thought they were shooting at. Borrowing the helmet from four-six's loader, the officer painfully climbed off the tank. His left leg hurt more every minute. Heavily corded muscle lay bare on the calf where the film of blood had cracked off.

Davie Womble, the medic who usually rode the back deck of four-six, was kneeling beside the newbie. He had laid his own flak jacket under the boy's head for a cushion and wrapped his chest in a poncho. "Didn't want to move him," he explained to Holtz, "but that one piece went clean through and was sucking air from both sides. He's really wasted."

The boy's face was a sickly yellow, almost the color of his fine blond hair. A glitter of steel marked the tip of a fragment which had zigzagged shallowly across his scalp. It was so minor compared to other damage that Womble had not bothered to remove it with tweezers. Holtz said nothing. He stepped toward four-four, whose loader and TC clustered around their driver. The loader, his M-16 tucked under his right arm, faced out in to the jungle and scanned the pulverized portion. "Hey," he said, raising his rifle. "Hey! We got one!"

"Watch it," the bloodied officer called as he drew his .45. He had to force his fingers to close around its square butt. Greiler, the track commander, was back behind his cal-fifty in seconds, leaping straight onto the high fender of his tank and scrambling up into the cupola. The loader continued to edge toward the body he saw huddled on the ground. Twenty yards from the tank he thrust his weapon out and used the flash suppressor to prod the still form.

"He's alive," the loader called. "He's—oh my God, oh my *God!*"

Holtz lumbered forward. Greiler's machinegun was live and the captain's neck crawled to think of it, hoping the TC wouldn't bump the trigger. The man on the ground wore gray coveralls of a slick, rubbery-appearing material. As he breathed, they trembled irregularly and a tear above the collarbone oozed dark fluid. His face was against the ground, hidden in shadow, but there was enough light to show Holtz that the man's outflung hand was blue. "Stretcher!" he shouted as he ran back toward the tracks.

Hauley wore a curious expression as he held out the scrambler phone. Holtz snatched and keyed it without explanation. "Battle six, Battle four-six," he called urgently.

"Battle four-six, this is Blackhorse six," the crisp voice of the regimental commander broke in unexpectedly. "What in hell is going on?"

"Umm, sir. I've got three men for a dust-off and I can't get any action out of the chopper jockeys. My boys aren't going to make it if they ride out of here on a tank. Can you—"

"Captain," the cool voice from Quan Loi interrupted, "it won't do your men any good to have a medevac bird fly into a tree in these clouds. I know how you feel, but the weather is the problem and there's nothing we can do about that. Now, what happened?"

"Look," Holtz blurted, "there's a huge goddam clearing here. If they cruise at five hundred we can guide them in by—"

"God damn it, man, do you want to tell me what's going on or do you want to be the first captain to spend six months in Long Binh Jail?"

Holtz took a deep breath that squeezed bruised ribs against the tight armored vest. Two troopers were already carrying the blue airman back toward the tanks on a litter made of engineer stakes and a poncho. He turned his attention back to the microphone and, keeping his voice flat, said, "We took a prisoner. He's about four feet tall, light build, with a blue complexion. I guess he was part of the crew of the spaceship the Air Force shot down and we finished off. He's breathing now, but the way he's banged up I don't think he will be long."

Only a hum from the radio. Then, "Four-six, is this some kind of joke?"

"No joke. I'll have the body back at the firebase in four, maybe three hours, and when they get a bird out you can look at him."

"Hold right where you are," the colonel crackled back. "You've got flares?"

"Roger, roger." Holtz's face regained animation and he began daubing at his red cheek with a handkerchief. "Plenty of flares, but the clouds are pretty low. We can set a pattern of trip flares on the ground, though."

"Hold there: I'm going up freek."

It was getting dark very fast. Normally Holtz would have moved his two platoons into the cleared area, but that would have meant shifting the newbie—Christ, he didn't even know the kid's name! If they'd found the captive earlier, a chopper might have already been there. Because of the intelligence value. Christ, how those rear echelon mothers ate up intelligence value.

"Four-six? Blackhorse six."

"Roger, Blackhorse six." The captain's huge hand clamped hard on the sweat-slippery microphone.

"There'll be a bird over you in one-oh, repeat one-oh, mikes. Put some flares up when you hear it."

"Roger. Battle four-six out." On the company frequency, Holtz ordered. "Listen good, dudes, there's a dust-off bird coming by in ten. Any of you at the tail of the line hear it, don't pop a flare but tell me. We want it coming down here, not in the middle of the jungle." He took off the helmet, setting it beside him on the turret. His head still buzzed and, though he stared into the jungle over the grips of the cal-fifty, even the front sight was a blur. Ten minutes was a long time.

"I hear it!" Roosevelt called. Without waiting for Holtz's order, he fired the quadrangle of trip flares he had set. They lit brightly the area cleared by the alien's weapon. While those ground flares sizzled to full life, Greiler sent three star clusters streaking into the overcast together. The dust-off slick, casting like a coonhound, paused invisibly. As a great gray shadow it drifted down the line of tanks. Its rotor kicked the mist into billows, flashing dimly.

Gracelessly yet without jerking the wounded boy, Womble and a third-platoon tanker pressed into service as stretcher-bearer rose and started toward the bird. As soon as the slick touched down, its blades set to idle, the crew chief with his Red Cross armband jumped out. Holtz and the stretcher with the newbie reached the helicopter an instant after the two nearer stretchers.

"Where's the prisoner?" the crew chief shouted over the high scream of unloaded turbines.

"Get my men aboard first," Holtz ordered briefly.

"Sorry, Captain," the air medic replied, "with our fuel load we only take two this trip and I've got orders to bring the prisoner back for sure."

"Stuff your orders! My men go out first."

The crew chief wiped sweat from the bridge of his nose; more trickled from under his commo helmet. "Sir, there's two generals and a bird colonel waiting on the pad for me; I leave that—" he shook his head at the makeshift stretcher—"that back here and it's a year in LBJ if I'm lucky. I'll take one of you—"

"They're both dying!"

"I'm sorry but . . ." The medic's voice dried up when he saw what Holtz was doing. "You can't threaten me!" he shrilled.

Holtz jacked a shell into the chamber of the .45. None of his men moved to stop him. The medic took one step forward as the big captain fired. The bullet slammed into the alien's forehead, just under the streaky gray bristles of his hairline. Fluid spattered the medic and the side of the helicopter behind him.

"There's no prisoner!" Holtz screamed over the shuddering thunder inside his skull. "There's nothing at all, do you hear? Now get my men to a hospital!"

Hauley tried to catch him as he fell, but the officer's weight pulled them both to the ground together.

The snarl of a laboring diesel brought him out of it. He was on a cot with a rolled flak jacket pillowed under his head. Someone had removed his chicken vest and bathed away the crusts of dried blood.

"Where are we?" Holtz muttered thickly. His vision had cleared and the chipped rubber of the treads beside him stood out in sharp relief.

Hauley handed his CO a paper cup of coffee laced with something bitter. "Here you go. Lieutenant Paider took over and we're gonna set up here for the night. If it clears, we'll get a chopper for you too."

"But that . . . ?" Holtz gestured at the twilit bulk of a tank twenty feet away. It grunted to a halt after neutral-steering a full 360 degrees.

"That? Oh, that was four-four," Hauley said in a careless voice. "Greiler wanted to say thanks—getting both his buddies dusted off, you know. But I told him you didn't want to hear about something that didn't happen. And everybody in the company'll swear it didn't happen, whatever some chopper jockey thinks. So Greiler just moved four-four up to where the bird landed and did a neutral steer . . . on nothing at all."

"Nothing at all," Holtz repeated before drifting off. He grinned like a she-tiger gorging on her cubs' first kill.

THE WARBOTS

Larry S. Todd

*The history of armored war
from 1990 to 17,500 A.D.*

With the improvement of lethal weapons, soldiers on a battle-field have shown great and understandable interest in staying out of the line of fire. In early wars, where sticks, stones, and lances and bows were the main medium of battlefield commerce, this goal could be accomplished by hiding behind any bulky object, or through desertion. However, as time went on this became increasingly difficult. Either the bulky objects were not as strong as they had been once or the weapons used were less aware of said barriers. Some soldiers adopted a rigid code of martial etiquette and tin suits, but the effectiveness of the knight grew limited when gunpowder was invented.

In the twentieth century great powered suits of armor, called "tanks," came into common use. They required a concentrated barrage to stop them and definitely provided their pilots and crew a more salubrious environment within than they could expect to find without. Nonetheless, a tank still had a great deal of vulnerable places, was far too heavy and noisy, and had limited mobility. In the 1990's the tanks which were covered with borosilicate fiber plates were much lighter and more mobile than their predecessors, but still lacked ideal conditions for operation. They could not wade through swamps nor avoid being attacked from behind any more easily than the old tanks, nor could they retreat very fast. Clearly, there had to be something better.

The General Motors Terrain Walker
ca. 1995

Originally developed for construction work and back-echelon packhorsing, the GM Walker was quickly accepted by the armies of America, Earth, when it was proved that the machine could carry a gun. Standing twelve feet tall and weighing eight tons, the Walker could stride down a highway at 30 mph and do 20 mph on rough terrain, such as burnt-out slums. Nuclear powered, it required little servicing and often powered its weapons directly from its own power system. Great hydraulic pistons operated its arms and legs, which followed every movement made by the pilot. The pilot was strapped in a control cradle that translated every motion to the Walker, and he had a clear view fore and aft through a plexiglass bubble. The Walker was equipped with a wide range of sensory devices, among them snooperscopes, radar, amplified hearing, some primitive smell-detection devices and tactile pads on the hands and feet, all of which were wired to the pilot.

It was equipped to retreat fast, attack faster and explode when hit, with a satisfying nuclear blast. When this was commonly learned, there were very few enemy soldiers who were willing to harm the things, which made them extremely effective in clearing out potential battlefields. But it also made getting them to a battlefield to begin with a touchy proposition. Few soldiers liked sitting on an atomic bomb, even though it would only go off if they were killed, and a Geneva Convention in 1992 declared them formal nuclear weapons.

However, with the turmoil of the late twentieth and early twenty-first centuries growing out of hand, they were used with increasing frequency.

In October, 2000, an armed insurrection in Harlem City, America, caused Walkers to be brought out into the streets. Patrolling the city with squads of armed soldiers (and their

GENERAL MOTORS TERRAIN WALKER

HEIGHT: 4.5 M   ARMAMENT: NONE   SENSORIES: CCLR, IR, MIDAR, SLODAR
MASS: 7500 kg   ON BOARD CREW: 1   MAINTENANCE CREW: 17
POWER OUTPUT: 2500 HP   COST: ₩14,000,000 NEOBUCKS
CONSTRUCTION: METAL, CERMETS, COMPOSITES, PLASTIC, RUBBER, SILICONITE
SPEED: 50 KPH
LIFTING STRENGTH: 3500 kg
CARRYING STRENGTH: 2500 kg

GENERAL MOTORS CORPORATION
DETROIT FREE STATE, NEOMERICA

CIRCUM-CORNER LOOKING RADAR (CCLR)
MICROWAVE RANGING SENSOR
SUNROOF
RADIO MAST
HELICOPTER LIFT RINGS
REARVIEW MIRROR
WIPERS
TURN SIGNALS
AIR INTAKE
HEADS UP DISPLAY
SHOULDER SOCKET JOINT SYSTEM
ERGONOMETRIC HARNESS
90° ROTATION COLLAR
SLEEVED VANE JOINT
2" THICK LEXAN PANEL
WEAPONS ATTACHMENT SOCKETS
LOWER HEADLIGHTS
ROTATION COLLAR
SYSTEMS ACCESS PANEL
90° THIGH ROTATION COLLAR
SLEEVED VANE JOINT
HARDSHELLED HANDS WITH PRESSURE SENSITIVE PADS
ANKLE ATTITUDE CONTROL PISTONS
ARTICULATED FOOT

nuclear explosion capacities secretly damped), they effectively cleared the rioters out of the burning city, and into a large prison combine, where they were kept until their tempers were drowned in rainy weather. Of fifty Walkers shipped in, only two were disabled. One had a department store, its pilot had rashly pushed over, fall in on it; the other had broken legs from a kamikaze automobile.

In November, 2000, the great series of civil wars in China were formally entered by the United States of America, Earth, and Walkers painted with ominous designs marched through the burning cities and villages, panicking those Chinese who would be panicked and nuking those who felt compelled to fight back. Four nuclear explosions in Peking were enough to show the Red Chinese that fighting the things was useless, so they were given a wide berth and finally succeeded in bottling ninety per cent of the Red Chinese army in a small part of Manchuria, Earth.

In February, 2002, there were massive earthquakes all over the globe. Japan sank beneath the sea; California followed suit; the coastline of Europe would never be the same, and America's east coast was washed clean by tsunami.

A few months later the Mississippi Valley collapsed, creating an inland sea in America. With three-fifths of the human race wiped out, the remainder lost all further interest in conflict and turned to more immediate and peaceful pursuits, such as cleaning up after the party.

The Walkers were instrumental in assisting in heavy construction. They rebuilt the foundations of cities, realigned the world's power conduits, built dams and, in one fierce burst of zealous activity, built almost a hundred thousand miles of beautiful roadway in four years. Three years after that commercial aircars were produced in profusion. The new roads were ignored and slowly cracked while approaching obsolescence.

The McCauley Walker
ca. 2130

2130 was an eventful year. The first complete cities were incorporated on Mars; the moon formally declared independence of the Four Nations of Earth; the first non-government spon-

McCAULEY WALKER (AMBULANT)

HEIGHT: 4.9 m
MASS: 5900 kg
POWER OUTPUT: 3000 hp
CONSTRUCTION: CERMET, SKINLON, COMPOSOL, PARAPRENE, GLASAL
SPEED: 55 kph
LIFTING STRENGTH: 10,000 kg
CARRYING STRENGTH: 4,000 kg

ARMAMENT: NONE   SENSORIES: MFO, MFA, SOC, SLR, CCLR
ONBOARD CREW: 1   MAINTENANCE CREW: 12
COST: Cr 2,000,000
DESIGN: AMBULANT DIVISION,
McCAULEY INDUSTRIES,
DEXATRON ISLAND, L5

EARCELL

REAR AND FRONT LOOKING
MULTIFREQUENCY BINOCULARS
(MFO)

RUNNING LIGHTS

HOLOGRAPHIC
LIGHTING SOURCES

OPTIC CELLS

GULLWING
HATCH

90°
ROTATION
COLLAR

OPTIC
CELL

RECOIL
SOCKET
FOR
RAILGUN

FAT
BOY

120°
ROTATION
COLLAR

RAILGUN

18° ARM
EXTENSION
HYDRAULICS

HEADLIGHTS

AMMUNITION
CASSETTE

90°
ROTATION
COLLAR

ACCESS
TO FOOT
COMPRESSORS

LOADING
CLAMP

ENTIRE UNIT COVERED
WITH SEMI-SOFT
"FRIENDLY ARMOR"
SKIN TO PREVENT
LOUD IMPACTS AND
JARRING RECOIL

RECOIL
PISTON
AND
TRIGGER

AIR EXHAUST

INDEPENDENTLY
POWER-PRESSURIZED RUBBER TOE "TIRES"

sored spaceship lines went into business, and a new Walker was released to the antiriot squads.

Called "pinheads" because of its set of electric binoculars (which could see from electricity up through the spectrum to X-rays) which functioned as a head, the McCauley Walker had far more flexibility than the GM. Nearly sixteen feet of tempered aluminum and borosilicates, yet weighing only four tons, the McCauley could duplicate all human movements except those requiring bending in the trunk or waist. It could run 55km/hr, was able to lift objects of up to ten tons and turned out to be a massive failure.

The McCauley Walker was a total weapon, designed for optimum placement of components in the least space. The structural members were cast or electroblown around the defense systems, so that it was impossible to deactivate them. The defense systems were inexorably bound with the machine's own conscious battlefield computers. To activate the Walker meant it would at once be at top fighting condition, ready to blast out with weapons which could not be removed from its hull without expenditures of twice its original cost. This did not make it a noteworthy construction machine. Its one experiment in this use had it firing lasers at bulldozers, graders, solidifiers and road crews. The unions kicked up a fuss. It was obviously not a very good construction machine.

Ten thousand of them were built at a cost of two million credits apiece, and it cost four thousand credits to maintain each per year, whether or not they were used. A fortune was spent on the hundred acres of sheds outside of Indianapolis in which they were housed, and it was here that the Walkers remained for eighty years, unused except for occasional exercises to keep them from rusting or whatever it was they did. But there were no wars. Riots were fairly common, but rarely large enough for Walkers to be brought out for them, and never located close enough to an airport to have Walkers in on them before they were effectively over.

In 2210 the Martian Colonial Government declared formal independence of the Four Nations of Earth and confiscated all Four Nation military property to see that their constitution was respected. It wasn't however, for the Four Nations were full of people who would suffer great financial losses if Mars became free. So the First Interplanetary War was begun.

Terran troop transports landed four hundred Walkers on the Syrtis Greenspot, where they were jeered and mocked by a

large army of Martian colonists. Following the Martians out
across the desert, the Walkers made rapid progress on them
until the old plastic sleeves that kept dirt and abrasives out of
the leg joints began to crack from age. Martian sand got in and
jammed the joints, and the Martian Colonial Armor walked a
safe distance around the field of immobile Walkers, attacked
the Terran positions from behind and won their independence.
It was never disputed again.

The Burton Damnthing
ca. 2680

There seemed to be little reason for the development of more
advanced power armor until about 2680, for the solar system
enjoyed a period of unparalleled peace, productivity and lei-
sure. With great space vessels over a mile in diameter, powered
by nuclear inertial drives, men traveled near the speed of light
and colonized the near stars, where they found a surprising
profusion of planets. In 2548 the Helium Distant Oscillator was
developed, making instant interstellar communication possible,
even though actual travel still took objective years. From the
device, the human colonies could reap instant benefit from
discoveries made years of travel away. Many of the great C-
jammers, as the huge interstellar vessels were known, were
dismantled and sold after this, till only about seventy were
being used, mostly for carrying great big things which weren't
likely to change much in coming years. Terraforming tools,
multiforges (the all-purpose manufacturing tool of the day),
great generators for increasing or decreasing gravitation of
planets and moons, even little C-jammers—and colonists—
were the major items of trade, with a few luxury items thrown
in for balancing the tapes.

On the fourth planet of Procyon there dwelt a race of intelligent lizards, the Kezfi, who were in their early atomic age
when the human colony was set upon the seventh planet. Moss,
the colony, was a difficult world to tame, and the Kezfi were
more than delighted to trade labor for the secrets of making
spaceships. This went on from 2570 to 2680, when Moss had
a population of nearly ten million, three terraformed moons
and several rocks in the nearby asteroid belt that replaced a
sixth planet. The Kezfi were becoming quite avid colonizers

BURTON DAMNTHING

HEIGHT: 5 m   ARMAMENT: 6×10 GRENADES, 10⁸ WATT LASER, BATTLERAFT
MASS: 4500 kg   ONBOARD CREW: 1 MAINTENANCE CREW: 4
POWER OUTPUT: 1900 kw   COST: 6,000,000 ETU
CONSTRUCTION: METALS, CERMETS, ARMORSKIN, AM____ ID, PLASTAL, PARAPRENE
SPEED: 65 km/hr
LIFTING STRENGTH: 1800 kg   DESIGN: MARY DANYEL BURTON
CARRYING STRENGTH: 1000 kg   MANUFACTURER: KARNAK MULTIFORGE, INC.

MAIN SENSORY CLUSTER
SENTRY CLUSTER
GRENADE LAUNCHER
ROTATING TURRET
AERIAL LIFT HOOK
BATTLERAFT
BATTLERAFT STATION
HEAD-TO-HEAD DISPLAY
CLAM SHELL HATCH
TENTACLE SEAT BELTS WITH NEURAL PICKUPS
MAIN LOGIC CENTER
AMORPHOID MAIN BEARINGS
120° ROTATION COLLAR
ELBOW SLEEVE
HOLOGRAPHIC LIGHTING SOURCE
120° ROTATION COLLAR
120° ROTATION COLLAR
ACCESS PANEL
KNEE SLEEVE
"SOFT-TOUCH" MECHANICAL HAND
"RELATIVISTIC" B-B GUN
INFLATED RUBBER FEET

and rather sophisticated in the ways of space. They began to have reservations about the presence of humans in their solar system, for these humans were of another star and were occupying a planet which otherwise would have been Kezfic. A war began, and the Mossists needed a weapon which could be used effectively against the Kezfi.

The Burton Damnthing was a sophisticated instrument. Its shoulder and hip joints were friction free, being cast of amorphoid iron. Just as a toy magnet will cause a piece of thin iron to twist and bend without actual contact, amorphoid iron could twist and contort itself on a massive scale, controlled by banks of magnets and topological distorters, yet lose none of its strength and hardness. However, due to the size of the magnet banks, its use was restricted to the major joints, the elbows and knees being cloth-sleeved mechanical joints.

Unlike the two previous models, the Burton Damnthing did not use a control cradle for the pilot. Instead, the man sat in a large padded seat, strapped into assorted nerve-induction pickups. It was as though the Damnthing was his own body.

On Armageddon, Alpha Centauri II, animals with multiple heads had been discovered. Due to the violent ecology, they had been forced to develop a sense of perception that extended in all directions, to warn the major head about potential danger. Called Cohen's Battlefield Sense, it was brought into the Damnthing to detect lurking Kezfi. The lizards squawked when found out and never could quite understand how their hiding places were located, since they were self-admitted experts at camouflage.

On the right shoulder of the Damnthing there was a large socket to contain a device called a battlecraft. It was a small, condensed version of the offensive weapons of the Damnthing, floating on inertial and antigravity drives, powered by a fusion pack and controlled by a specially educated chimpanzee brain in aspic. Since the battlecraft was as effective five hundred miles from the Damnthing as five hundred feet, it removed some of the intimacy from death. This rightly concerned the Kezfi, who liked a personal confrontation with their assassin, on the logic that he might be taken with them. Not being able to enjoy the Kezfi's Honorable Death at the hands of these dirty fighters from another star, the lizards decided to call it quits. And, not being proud or anything, they decided further to let them have Moss and its moons, and they would stick to what they had been allotted.

The Christopher Warbot
ca. 3250

The Kezfi, as has been said and is probably known by most readers who have known them, preferred to die the Kezfi's Honorable Death and could not understand the sending of men into war in armor. They assumed these things must be robots, then, since they had never been able to get one intact enough to study, so they built their own teams of war robots, called them and the human armor "warbots" and by 3250 decided they had grown weary enough of resident humans to start another war.

At the battle of Granite Rock, in the Procyon Asteroids, the Kezfi first learned about the new Christopher Warbot. They also learned the ineffectiveness of sending remote control robots into battle against manned craft.

After a number of crushing defeats, and a few surprising victories, the final blow was put on the second war of Procyon when the C-jammer Brass Candle, massing fifty-five million kilotons and traveling at .92C, smacked violently into their major colony of Daar es Suun, killing over a billion Kezfi. After this impressive disaster, nobody, Kezfi or human, was very willing to press his point further.

The Christopher Warbot had no legs, but floated on inertial-antigrav pods which enabled it to work as effectively in space as on the ground. On its back was a complete service and repairs center for the battlecraft, and on its front, on either side of the entrance hatch, it bore twin electric cannon. The study of amorphics had developed to the point where an entire arm could be made of amorphoid, though it was limited to bending at the appropriate places a human arm would bend. Since nobody was quite sure how to go about bending the artificial arm where there were no joints in their own, this did not disturb anyone deeply.

The only nerve pickups were those in the seat cushions and the helmet, but the soldier had better-than-ever control over the machine. The entire surface area was sheathed so that it could feel pain and pressure from bullet strikes, and thus Cohen's Battlefield Sense was implemented by another protection

device. The head, now attached through a long tentacle, held eyes, ears, and other senses, and the mobility of the Christopher Warbot was such that it replaced most other forms of heavy armor. War was becoming less burdened down by killing machines.

Greedy Nick's Warbot
ca. 4721

In 3579 a stardrive was finally developed, and humanity emerged from the Slowboat Age to the Age of Expansion. Most of the C-jammers were outfitted with drives and used to set up enormous colonies in one blow, and since a light-year could be covered in somewhat less than two days, colonization went on rather rapidly. In 3900 the Cuiver Foundation went far beyond borders of human space and established the Antarean League among the ninety-four planets of Antares, the seventeen planets of Antares's Green Companion star and assorted dwarf stars in the adjoining locality. Since Antares was a dynastic monarchy, nobody paid it much attention.

In 4718 a scoutship of Antares came scuttling back to the League bearing great tidings of war, with a race of tall, rust-red crustaceans called Peolanti, who had established a small empire near Antares. The delightful ruler of Antares, Pantocrator Nicholas Cuiver the Greedy, immediately threw a complete travel silence around the League, from 4718 to 4723, at the end of which Greedy Nick announced that the Antarean League now controlled a globe of space forty light-years in diameter. The Peolanti liked to fight from gigantic spaceships, huge portable fortresses, and mobile asteroids, which dictated definite limits to their mobility. Greedy Nick did away with using battleships other than to transport the warbots to the battlespaces, and let the Peolanti try and find them with their poor radar nets. They couldn't compete, or even begin to. A laser beam can be used with fair effectiveness against a big battleship, for at least you know where it is, but little dinky hard knots of mayhem could neither be seen nor be hit very often.

Greedy Nick's Warbot boasted triple mayhem converters, a nasty weapon which could spit laser beams all the way up and

CUIVER (GREEDY NICK) WARBOT

HEIGHT: 1.9 m   ARMAMENT: 3 MEGAWATT MCs, 1 CT CANNON, 12 1gr CT BOMBS, 2 XRASORS
MASS: 2300 kg   SENSORIES: MFO, MONITOR SENSE, AP,
POWER OUTPUT: 35 kw   ONBOARD CREW: 1
POWER SOURCE: MICROKERNEL   SUPPORT CREW: 1/5 WARBOTS
CONSTRUCTION: AMORPHOID, INCRALSTEN, SHORMAN, ICTITE I, II, III, SHIBIUCHI, SHAKUDO, CERMET
SPEED: TO 10,000 km/hr.
LIFTING STRENGTH: 2000 kg   DESIGN: ARBOL 4 (A1)
CARRYING STRENGTH: 2000 kg   MANUFACTURE: CUIVER MACROFABER, ANTARES VERT

AMORPHOID
EXTRUSION
HOUSING

BATTLECRAFT IN CARRYING
POSITION

HEAD IN CARRYING
POSITION

FLOWER-PETAL
CONTROL HELMET

AMORPHOID
EXTRUSION
HEAD

MULTIBAND
ECTOSPHERE
MONITOR
SENSE
ANTENNAE

MFO

HIGH RESOLUTION
ECTOSPHERE
ANTENNAE

ANTI
MATTER
CANNON

XRASORS

DOCKING
FIXTURE
FOR
HEAD

LASERCOM
OPTIC
CELLS
(LOC)

HATCH & HEAD
SADDLE
(QUORCELAIN WITH
SOLID SHAKUDO
ORNAMENTAL INLAY)

MAYHEM
CONVERTORS
(CONNECTED TO
QUANTUM HYPERVASS
IN POWER SYSTEM)

AMORPHOID
ARM

ORNATE SHELL OF
STABILIZED SHAKUDO
& SHIBIUCHI METALS

down the spectrum, pull tricks with gravity that resulted in
atomic bonds falling apart, heat or freeze things by time-
induction, a side effect of the discovery of the chronogravitic
spectrum. The head was no longer connected to the body, but
floated freely and had its own complement of weapons. The
battlecraft was harder than ever to detect and destroy, being
controlled by a brain taken from an Armageddon animal more
vicious than a tyrannosaur and of near-human intelligence.

Amorphics had developed a tentacle which could stretch ten
times its length for an arm, retract to a wrinkly nubbin, and
yet be perfectly controllable by the pilot. He sat in his cabin
which was padded both by cushions and paragravity, free from
being bounced around, wearing a helmet and sitting in the lotus
position of meditation. In order to properly control a warbot,
a soldier had to be an accomplished Yogi.

The Warbots at Critter's Gateway
ca. 7200

While all manner of advances were made in the warbots since
the Peolanti wars, and several smaller wars were fought with
them, there were no significant changes in their appearance
until the discovery of Critter's Universe.

Eleven light-years from Antares there was a small dust cloud
which emitted a healthy amount of radio waves. These clouds
were not uncommon, so little attention beyond marking it as
a navigation hazard was paid to it. Then Jorj Critter, a pro-
spector looking for natural rubies, flew into it. It turned out to
be an area in which space had formed a side-bubble, where
physical laws were somewhat different. The periodic table of
Critter's Universe held but four elements, a solid, a gas, a
plasma and a liquid, promptly dubbed Earth, Air, Fire and
Water. While perfectly stable in their own little universe, sub-
jecting any object made of them to our physical laws caused
destabilization of the Fire content, which caused the whole
mass to oscillate into pure energy. Since Critter found it was
very simple to control this attempt to justify itself to our physical laws, he told Andrew the Meditator, the current Pantocrator
of Antares, about this new power source.

Critter's Universe, which is only about a hundred light-years

CRITTER'S GATEWAY WARBOT

HEIGHT: 2.2m   ARMAMENT: UP TO 15 DIFFERENT SIMULTANEOUS MANIFESTATIONS
MASS: 2900 kg   SENSORIES: MFO, MONITOR SENSE, AP, OTHERS IN MEMORY BANKS
POWER OUTPUT: 75 kw   ONBOARD CREW: 1 SUPPORT CREW: 0
POWER SOURCE: MICROKERNEL/ANTIMATTER
CONSTRUCTION: AMORPHOID, DURO CERMA, PLASTENES, ICTITE II, III, IV, STEN CAROM,
SPEED: TO 5,000 km/hr
LIFTING STRENGTH: 2000 kg   DESIGN: HUBLEY INSTITUTE, R & D DIVISION
CARRYING STRENGTH: 2000 kg   MANUFACTURE: CUIVER MACROFABER, A.VERT

MONITOR "SPINNER"
MFO "TUNING FORK"
LASERCOM OPTIC CELLS (7)
MONITOR CELL
MFO
X RASORS (2)

NEURO INTERFACIAL RECEPTOR
SENSORY FACILITATOR

COMFORT SYSTEMS (GALLEY, RECYCLER, BEVERAGE DISPENSER, ETC.)
MFO
MONITOR CELLS (2)
X RASORS (2)
AUDIO GRILL
AUXILIARY CRAFT CONTROL ANTENNA

BATTLERAFT IN FLUX STATE
DORSAL AMORPHOID EXTRUSION HEAD

STARBOARD AMORPHOID EXTRUSION HEAD

HATCH
LASERCOM OPTIC CELLS
PORT AMORPHOID EXTRUSION HEAD

"EXTRUDED" AMORPHOID HAND

MAIN AND SECONDARY SENSORY BLISTERS

in diameter, did coexist with a large section of the Terran Organization of Star States, who, having learned about this, decided they should own it. The TOSS went to war with Antares, the focal point of the war being around the little nebula, Critter's Gateway. TOSS battlewagons and mobile asteroids faced over a million warbots of Antares and soon discovered that they could not possibly defeat such a swarm of tiny adversaries. The TOSS never got within a billion miles of the actual gateway, and would have lost regardless of whether or not the League pulled another trick from a hat.

For several thousand years, Green Companion of Antares had been known as a tempestuous stellar bastard, constantly filling all space around it with radiation clouds and fouling up communications. It had several dozen planets which could be very pleasant if the sun were calmed down somewhat, so the Hubley University extension at Antares Vert had been established in 6200 to seek ways of controlling the star. Shortly before the war, they found the first major advance of macromechanics, how to blow a star into a nova. It worked as well on stable, main-sequence stars as on the huge, wasteful monsters like Rigel, upon which it was demonstrated. The TOSS now realized that the League could seed their stars through Critter's Universe and blow them all to perdition before anything could be done. Hastily withdrawing their forces from the Gateway, the TOSS began cultivating good feelings with forced urgency.

The warbot used at Critter's Gateway was a very capable little vessel, as much spaceship as groundcraft. The soldier, sitting in lotus, was freed of his helmet. From an amorphoid plate at the top of the warbot, he could extrude a battleraft or a head; from two plates at the side he could extrude any of an arsenal of two hundred weapons. The circuitry of these amorphic devices was mostly magnetic and gravitic domains, which could not be altered by any amount of twisting and contorting, so they could be extruded whenever needed, otherwise remaining placid as a puddle of quicksilver in their storage tanks.

Antares, while again the little empire of space, was also the most powerful, for they had over a million of these things strutting back and forth through space.

The Quicksilver Kid
ca. 10,000

By the Eodech (10,000 A.D.) amorphics had developed a warbot made of nothing but amorphoid metals, memory plastics, solid liquids, contact fields and other prodigies of science. Normally a simple near-globe eight feet big, the Quicksilver Kid looked very much like a glob of mercury when in action. Hands, head, battlecraft and whatnot could be extruded from whatever part of the surface area they would seem to be most useful, and the weapons system had an additional development.

Hidden in the block-circuitry of the hull was a memory center containing records of every science applicable to military purposes, as well as a mechanical design center, so that a soldier need merely size up the situation and inform his warbot to create a weapon equal to it, and hammer away. Powered by antimatter breakdown, the warbot had more than enough power to see this done. No longer were warbots shuttled about by other spacecraft, but had a speed of about one light-year per hour to make its rounds.

In the Early Eodechtic centuries the Sophisticate Age had come about. In known space, a flattened sphere roughly five thousand light-years in diameter, there were seventy major human empires, twenty-two joint human-nonhuman Leagues, one hundred ninety nonhuman empires and fourteen weird things which defied description, save that they seemed to be sociological systems of order originally cooked up by something which could have been intelligent but more likely was something else, the exact nature of which was even more difficult to ascertain. But they never did make any trouble, probably because they found each other and intelligent life even more impossible than we found them.

There were many wars in the Eodechtic centuries, but none of them especially large on the grand scale. But warbots were used in all of them. For example, the Korel Empire Collapse.

The Korel were human adaptations, two feet tall and looking like toy dolls (behaving much like them, too. Korel were well known for their immaturity). They had a little empire flourishing until 10590, when one of their kings went insane on the

QUICKSILVER WARBOT

HEIGHT: 2.5 m   ARMAMENT: CONSISTANT WITH NORTHING TREATY OF CETUS, T.O.S.S.
MASS: 4500 kg   SENSORIES: MOR, SR, AIO, CPI, AP, SPIGRAM RED, SPIGRAM BLUE
POWER OUTPUT: 1,000,000 hp
POWER SOURCE: 'LITTLE BANG'
CONSTRUCTION: AMORPHOID 1,2,3,4,5, POLYMOL, SILDIN, WHITESTONE, REDSTONE, BLACKSTONE
SPEED: TO 10,000 km/sec   DESIGN: SHARDEI OF SIGRIL, SUBTAN INSTITUTE
LIFTING STRENGTH: ?   MANUFACTURER: SIGRIL OF CETUS, DULL WORLD
CARRYING STRENGTH: ?

throne and attacked the Palaric States, which were then growing into importance. The Korel had a few worthy weapons, which aided in their conquering several planets, and then an ally, the Karpo Regime, a race of hideous gray frogs who had been waiting on the sly for some way to build a little empire. As soon as the Korel had done as much as they could, the Karpo turned on them and soon had a very effective little empire, as well as a full-time occupation in scaring the border stars of the Pale (Palaric States).

An approaching fleet of warbots, after having been ordered to sum up the situation, performed a maneuver which was historical because of its originality. A hundred thousand warbots came together and fused their masses into a thousand medium-sized battleships, which attacked the Karpo fleets. The Karpo fired a salvo at them and broke them all into monolithic chunks of wreckage, which they then went in to investigate. Twisted wreckage, once it surrounded the Karpo fleet, suddenly turned quicksilver, returned to a hundred thousand intact warbots, and destroyed forever the Karpo Regime.

The Korel were chastised mildly. One could never expect much from them in the way of wisdom.

The First Alakar
ca. 11,000

By 11,000, enough was known about forcefields to expect a soldier sheathed in them to have as much, if not more, protection than an amorphoid shell could provide. The shell was done away with, except for the helmet, and the battlecraft was equipped with everything that had previously been reserved for the warbot itself. Since the new soldier appeared to be a man, wearing a small belt and carrying an outlandish rifle, with a battlecraft at heel and a small scrap of amorphoid called a "steel pimple" floating about his head, he could no longer be called a warbot. From Antarean mythology the name "Alakar," meaning war-god, was lifted. It seemed appropriate.

The methods of battle were now entirely different. The soldier could fly in free space, though they now returned to the use of spaceships. His forcefields could protect him from the heat of a sun, could be totally impenetrable, or set to pass

2ND ALAKAR (POWER ARMOR)

HEIGHT: ADJUSTABLE   ARMAMENT: CONSISTANT WITH ANTAREAN WAR OFFICE SPECIFICATIONS
MASS: 400 kg   SENSORIES: SPIGRAM III, MOR, MONITOR, AP
POWER OUTPUT: 10,000 hp
POWER SOURCE: ANTIMATTER
CONSTRUCTION: AMORPHOID 1,2,3,4,5,6,7, WHITESTONE SERIES, CLEVER IRON, PRIMORDIUM, GLISTINE, LINK
SPEED: TO 5000 km/sec
LIFTING STRENGTH: 500 kg
CARRYING STRENGTH: 500 kg   DESIGN: ENGRILAY SOTMOR, LINK RESEARCH INSTITUTE
                                 MANUFACTURE: ANY AMORPHOID PROGRAMMING SYSTEM

BATTLERAFT IN
STANDARD FORM

SENSORY INPUT PLATE (SPIGRAM, MOR)

TRANSMUTATION INPUT SOURCE

STEEL PIMPLE

MONITOR ANTENNAE

CLAMSHELL CUIRASS

BELLY PLATE with MAGNESENSE

EFFORT AMPLIFIER (ELBOW)

GIRDLE

BATTLERAFT IN HANDWEAPON FORM

"7 PARSEC BOOTS"

EFFORT AMPLIFIER (KNEE)

DRIVE CARTRIDGES

either matter or energy, but refuse the other.

His body was operated on to the extent of surgical placement of wires which increased his native strength and reflex speed immensely as well as enabled him to rigidify himself for space travel.

An example of fighting methods could be taken from the uprising of Murmash Krodd, on the Chembal Starstrand, 11211.

Here a fleet of Kroddic ships attacked a small neighboring democracy, and the Humanity Soldiers were requested in. The Krodds saw the human fleet approaching, but it vanished before their eyes, and they could not understand what had become of it until they were recalled quickly by Murmash Krodd himself, who had seen them fall from his skies and subjugate his city in ten minutes.

The method was this: when the Kroddic Fleet was sure to have seen the Humanity Soldiers approach, they snapped on their helmets, activated their fields and took to free space. The ships broke apart in thousands of brick-sized chunks of amorphoid, each reorganized to contain its own drives and control systems. The Alakars and ships did not rejoin until in orbit of Kesal of Murmash Krodd, when they rained down from the sky and forced the fat crustacean to order his fleet back, lest they destroy the planets of Murmash Krodd. When the Kroddic ships were all grounded, the Alakars set solar-phoenix to them, and they burned to radioactive ashes.

The Second Alakar
ca. 14500

The sleek Alakar of the 14500's was respected as being the most capable fighter in space. He controlled six battlecrafts, each a featureless egg until ordered to think up a weapon to cover a situation. He commanded three steel pimples, which contained all of his forcefield equipment, and, being strictly defensive weapons, never left his vicinity. His uniform was made of bioplastic with layer upon layer of sensory-defector pseudocells, which kept his brain flooded with such an amount of information that an Alakar had to be trained for five years. The helmet, often decorated with fanciful sculpture, feather crests, and back-curtains, could lock every atom of his body to a field that intensified the interatomic bond-strength to a point where he could withstand a nuclear barrage in the flesh, as well as do all the reflex-speedups he needed. Being an Alakar was much like being a superman under LSD, save that the hallucinations were very real displays of actual conditions, which could be interpreted usefully.

The hand weapons were now losing their physical structure with alarming rapidity, the great gaps between parts being filled in with a curious substance called Link. Research in chrono-gravitics had led to the discovery of how to replace the sub-atomic bonds of matter, which were an effect of space, with something that was a side-effect of time. This new matter was completely undetectable and very impalpable except by a certain set of rules.

If Link were made of pure carbon, one could not force pure carbon through it; it might as well be a brick wall. Carbon compounds moved slowly through it, growing warm as they did so. Things which had no carbon content moved through without resistance, except with the extremely unlikely possibility that two nuclei might collide, which they certainly did not do very much.

Link had curious properties of conduction and insulation which made it particularly desirable as a weapon component, in addition to the fact that it didn't take up much room.

The Second Alakar was used in several conflicts, among them the most noticeable being the Haak Wars of 14696. The Haak, centipedean creatures from some obscure place in the galactic center, had stretched their empire out in a most curious fashion. Most races preferred to expand in a globe, the center being their planet of origin. The Haak expanded in a straight line thirty light-years across. They had a science of teleportation which could get a Haak on the outside border of his empire, twenty thousand light-years to the center, in two years. They did not do very much work with spaceships, beyond sending robot probes to land colonization reception booths. When the first booths of Haak began landing on human planets in the distant Lace Pattern, the alarm went out. The Lace Pattern was occupied by a large number of little human and non-human empires, none very large, and because it was four years of travel from the Palaric States, the nearest really organized culture, it never heard much from the main body of civilization, except from wandering ships of Alakars. In fact, it was not generally known that all those marvelous myths of Antares, and TOSS, and Pale, and so on, were *not* fairy tales. Few of the Alakars who wandered through the region had ever been anywhere near the Civilization.

The entire war, though it dragged on for ten years, was hardly eighth-page news back in Antares.

The Final Alakar
ca. 17500

Even though Civilization of Humankind (which included almost every alien race that had ever heard of Terra or Antares Imperator) was a growing concern, it had still not explored more than ten per cent of the stars in its own dominion. In some space which both the TOSS and Antares claimed, a new race had come up and were doing some exploration and state-building on their own. The TOSS was willing to put up with it only as long as Antares gave them no assistance, but when the Pantocrator, out of the goodness of his heart or whatever, started to assist them with technological gifts, it was too much.

Minor races of the TOSS who felt endangered immediately went to war, minor allies of Antares resisted them, until by 17485 both big empires were ready to blow their cookies and have it out at one another. The race that had started the brouhaha had long since had their fill of imperialism, and were perfectly willing to settle for what they had, but now it was a matter of interstellar pride, and neither the TOSS nor the League was going to be bested. It was a marvelous war.

Antares, who had always seemed to have the last thing to say insofar as weapons advances were concerned, finally sent a squad of Ultimate Alakars onto the field of the war.

The Alakar himself wore no weapons, though he carried a few hand weapons of negligible presence (mostly fashioned from Link), wore no helmet and had six steel pimples which performed all the functions of the helmet, as well as being able to operate as battlecrafts. The Alakar, upon landing on a planet which had not been invaded, would immediately alert the civilians to go to the public shelters hundred of miles beneath the planetary crust and take all personal valuables with them. They were given twenty-four hours, but during this time, since the Alakar was almost sure to be under attack, he would certainly be occupied. His steel pimples would head for the nearest masses of amorphoid, often automobiles and private spacecraft, and perform a virus-function. Whatever the amorphoid had been previously would be erased; the pimples would realign and combine all available amorphoid into great robot fortresses, fleets of battlecrafts and orbiting platforms, and would infect normal metals with amorphic domain, causing entire communications networks to start converting into amorphoid weapons. If it went on mainly unchecked, within fifty hours of commence-attack, the military command centers buried in the centers of the planets could expect their control panels to swim like quicksilver and turn into atomic bombs.

The planetary defenses would initiate their own amorphic conversions, trying to fight back, and would cause the comm networks to fight back at ground level. Flotillas of planetary steel pimples would commandeer as much amorphoid as possible, until the entire war began to resemble the attack of a viral disease upon a protoplasmic organism. If the planetary defense won, the Alakar was killed or forced to retreat, and the mass-computer would return every bit of registered amorphoid on the surface to its original state (unregistered amorphoid, such as kitchen appliances, generally kept firing away until told to desist. Registered amorphoid, which had a certain key-pattern built in, instantly reverted).

If the Alakar won, the same thing would be done, except that he would now control the planet and invite his forces into orbit. Since the governments of Antares and the TOSS were very similar, in basic policies, the civilians rarely cared too much who held the upper hand, so long as they were not too often changed.

Naturally, this being a war, damage was done. A wrecked city stayed quite wrecked, though there was rarely any loss of life. But recovery from an attack took several years, and when Antares finally bested the TOSS, they found that they had a tremendous financial responsibility to rebuild what they had undone.

The Ten Years' War left both empires quite at a loss as what to do, so finally they just got their hands dirty, devalued their currency and rebuilt. But it had been a tremendous war while it lasted.

THE SCAPEGOAT

C.J. Cherryh

I

DeFranco sits across the table from the elf and he dreams for a moment, not a good dream, but recent truth: all part of what surrounds him now, a bit less than it was when it was happening, because it was gated in through human eyes and ears and a human notices much more and far less than what truly goes on in the world—

—the ground comes up with a bone-penetrating thump and dirt showers down like rain, over and over again; and deFranco wriggles up to his knees with the clods rattling off his armor. He may be moving to a place where a crater will be in a moment, and the place where he is may become one in that same moment. There is no time to think about it. There is only one way off that exposed hillside, which is to go and keep going. DeFranco writhes and wriggles against the weight of the armor, blind for a moment as the breathing system fails to give him as much as he needs, but his throat is already raw with too much oxygen in three days out. He curses the rig, far more intimate a frustration than the enemy on this last long run to the shelter of the deep tunnels....

He was going home, was John deFranco, if home was still there, and if the shells that had flattened their shield in this zone had not flattened it all along the line and wiped out the base.

The elves had finally learned where to hit them on this weapons system too, that was what; and deFranco cursed them one and all, while the sweat ran in his eyes and the oxy-mix tore his throat and giddied his brain. On this side and that shells shocked the air and the ground and his bones; and not for the first time concussion flung him bodily through the air and slammed him to the churned ground bruised and battered (and but for the armor, dead and shrapnel-riddled). Immediately fragments of wood and metal rang off the hardsuit, and in their gravity-driven sequence clods of earth rained down in a patter mixed with impacts of rocks and larger chunks.

And then, not having been directly in the strike zone and dead, he got his sweating human limbs up again by heaving the armor-weight into its hydraulic joint-locks, and desperately hurled fifty kilos of unsupple ceramics and machinery and ninety of quaking human flesh into a waddling, exhausted run.

Run and fall and run and stagger into a walk when the dizziness got too much and never waste time dodging.

But somewhen the jolts stopped, and the shell-made earth-quakes stopped, and deFranco, laboring along the hazard of the shell-cratered ground, became aware of the silence. His staggering steps slowed as he turned with the awkward foot-planting the armor imposed to take a look behind him. The whole smoky valley swung across the narrowed view of his visor, all lit up with ghosty green readout that flickered madly and told him his eyes were jerking in panic, calling up more than he wanted. He feared that he was deaf; it was that profound a silence to his shocked ears. He heard the hum of the fans and the ventilator in the suit, but there would be that sound forever, he heard it in his dreams; so it could be in his head and not coming from his ears. He hit the ceramic-shielded back of his hand against his ceramic-coated helmet and heard the thump, if distantly. So his hearing was all right. There was just the smoke and the desolate cratering of the landscape to show him where the shells had hit.

And suddenly one of those ghosty green readouts in his visor jumped and said **000** and started ticking off, so he lumbered about to get a look up, the viewplate compensating for the sky in a series of flickers and darkenings. The reading kept up, ticking away; and he could see nothing in the sky, but base was still there, it was transmitting, and he knew what was happening. The numbers reached **Critical** and he swung about again and looked toward the plain as the first strikes came in and the smoke went up anew.

He stood there on the hillcrest and watched the airstrike he had called down half an eternity ago pound hell out of the plains. He knew the devastation of the beams and the shells. And his first and immediate thought was that there would be no more penetrations of the screen and human lives were saved. He had outrun the chaos and covered his own mistake in getting damn near on top of the enemy installation trying to find it.

And his second thought, hard on the heels of triumph, was that there was too much noise in the world already, too much death to deal with, vastly too much, and he wanted to cry with the relief and the fear of being alive and moving. Good and proper. The base scout found the damn firepoint, tripped a trap and the whole damn airforce had to come pull him out of the fire with a damn million credits worth of shells laid down out there destroying ten billion credits' worth of somebody else's.

Congratulations, deFranco.

A shiver took him. He turned his back to the sight, cued his locator on, and began to walk, slowly, slowly, one foot in front of the other, and if he had not rested now and again, setting the limbs on his armor on lock, he would have fallen down. As it was he walked with his mouth open and his ears full of the harsh sound of his own breathing. He walked, lost and disoriented, till his unit picked up his locator signal and beaconed in the Lost Boy they never hoped to get back.

"You did us great damage then," says the elf. "It was the last effort we could make and we knew you would take out our last weapons. We knew that you would do it quickly and that then you would stop. We had learned to trust your habits even if we didn't understand them. When the shelling came, towers fell; and there were over a thousand of us dead in the city."

"And you keep coming."

"We will. Until it's over or until we're dead."

DeFranco stares at the elf a moment. The room is a small and sterile place, showing no touches of habitation, but all those small signs of humanity—a quiet bedroom, done in yellow and green pastels. A table. Two chairs. An unused bed. They have faced each other over this table for hours. They have stopped talking theory and begun thinking only of the recent past. And deFranco finds himself lost in elvish thinking again. It never quite makes sense. The assumptions between the lines are not human assumptions, though the elf's command of the language is quite thorough.

At last, defeated by logicless logic: "I went back to my base," says deFranco. "I called down the fire; but I just knew the shelling had stopped. We were alive. That was all we knew. Nothing personal."

There was a bath and there was a meal and a little extra ration of whiskey. HQ doled the whiskey out as special privilege and sanity-saver and the scarcity of it made the posts hoard it and ration it with down-to-the-gram precision. And he drank his three days' ration and his bonus drink one after the other when he had scrubbed his rig down and taken a long, long bath beneath the pipe. He took his three days' whiskey all at once because three days out was what he was recovering from, and he sat in his corner in his shorts, the regs going about their business, all of them recognizing a shaken man on a serious drunk and none of them rude or crazy enough to bother him now, not with congratulations for surviving, not with offers of bed, not with a stray glance. The regs were not in his command, he was not strictly anywhere in the chain of command they belonged to, being special ops and assigned there for the reg CO to use when he had to. He was 2nd Lt. John R. deFranco if anyone bothered and no one did here-abouts, in the bunkers. He was special ops and his orders presently came from the senior trooper captain who was the acting CO all along this section of the line, the major having got hisself lately dead, themselves waiting on a replacement, thank you, sir and ma'am; while higher brass kept themselves cool and dry and safe behind the shields on the ground a thousand miles away and up in orbit.

And John deFranco, special op and walking target, kept his silver world-and-moon pin and his blue beret and his field-browns all tucked up and out of the damp in his mold-proof plastic kit at the end of his bunk. The rig was his working uniform, the damned, cursed rig that found a new spot to rub raw every time he realigned it. And he sat now in his shorts and drank the first glass quickly, the next and the next and the next in slow sips, and blinked sometimes when he remembered to.

The regs, male and female, moved about the underground barracks in their shorts and their T's like khaki ghosts whose gender meant nothing to him or generally to each other. When bunks got double-filled it was friendship or boredom or outright desperation; all their talk was rough and getting rougher, and their eyes when real pinned-down-for-days boredom set in were hell, because they had been out here and down here on this world for thirty-seven months by the tally on bunker 43's main entry wall; while the elves were still holding, still digging in and still dying at unreasonable rates without surrender.

"Get prisoners," HQ said in its blithe simplicity; but prisoners suicided. Elves checked out just by *wanting* to die.

"Establish a contact," HQ said. "Talk *at* them—" meaning by any inventive means they could; but they had failed at that for years in space and they expected no better luck onworld. Talking to an elf meant coming into range with either drones or live bodies. Elves cheerfully shot at any target they could get. Elves had shot at the first human ship they had met twenty years ago and they had killed fifteen hundred men, women, and children at Corby Point for reasons no one ever understood. They kept on shooting at human ships in sporadic incidents that built to a crisis.

Then humanity—all three humanities, Union and Alliance and remote, sullen Earth—had decided there was no restraint possible with a species that persistently attacked modern human ships on sight, with equipage centuries less advanced—*Do we have to wait,* Earth's consensus was, *till they do get their hands on the advanced stuff? Till they hit a world?* Earth worried about such things obsessively, convinced of its paramount worldbound holiness and importance in the universe. The cradle of humankind. Union worried about other things—like breakdown of order, like its colonies slipping loose while it was busy: Union pushed for speed, Earth wanted to go back to its own convolute affairs, and Alliance wanted the territory, preferring to make haste slowly and not create permanent problems for itself on its flank. There were rumors of other things too, like Alliance picking up signals out this direction, of something other than elves. Real reason to worry. It was at least sure that the war was being pushed and pressed and shoved; and the elves shoved back. Elves died and died, their ships being no match for human-make once humans took after them in earnest and interdicted the jump-points that let them near human space. But elves never surrendered and never quit trying.

"Now what do we do?" the joint command asked themselves collectively and figuratively—because they were dealing out bloody, unpalatable slaughter against a doggedly determined and underequipped enemy, and Union and Earth wanted a quick solution. But Union as usual took the Long View: and on this single point there was consensus. "If we take out every ship they put out here and they retreat, how long does it take before they come back at us with more advanced armaments? We're dealing with lunatics."

"Get through to them," the word went out from HQ. "Take them out of our space and carry the war home to them. We've got to make the impression on them now—or take options no one wants later." ·

Twenty years ago. Underestimating the tenacity of the elves. Removed from the shipping lanes and confined to a single world, the war had sunk away to a local difficulty; Alliance still put money and troops into it; Union still cooperated in a certain measure. Earth send adventurers and enlistees that often were crazier than the elves: Base culled those in a hurry.

So for seventeen years the matter boiled on and on and elves went on dying and dying in their few and ill-equipped ships, until the joint command decided on a rougher course; quickly took out the elves' pathetic little space station, dropped troops onto the elvish world, and fenced human bases about with antimissile screens to fight a limited and on-world war—while elvish weaponry slowly got more basic and more primitive and the troops drank their little measures of imported whiskey and went slowly crazy.

And humans closely tied to the elvish war adapted, in humanity's own lunatic way. Well behind the lines that had come to exist on the elves' own planet, humans settled in and built permanent structures and scientists came to study the elves and the threatened flora and fauna of a beautiful and earthlike world, while some elvish centers ignored the war, and the bombing went on and on in an inextricable mess, because neither elves nor humans knew how to quit, or knew the enemy enough to know how to disengage. Or figure out what the other wanted.

And the war could go on and on—since presumably the computers and the records in those population centers still had the design of starships in them. And no enemy which had taken what the elves had taken by now was ever going to forget.

There were no negotiations. Once, just once, humans had tried to approach one of the few neutral districts to negotiate and it simply and instantly joined the war. So after all the study and all the effort, humans lived on the elves' world and had no idea what to call them or what the world's real name was, because the damn elves had blown their own space station at the last and methodically destroyed every record the way they destroyed every hamlet before its fall and burned every record and every artifact. They died and they died and they died and sometimes (but seldom nowadays) they took humans with them, like the time when they were still in space and hit the base at Ticon with ¾-cee rocks and left nothing but dust. Thirty thousand dead and not a way in hell to find the pieces.

That was the incident after which the joint command decided to take the elves out of space.

And nowadays humanity invested cities they never planned to take and they tore up roads and took out all the elves' planes, and they tore up agriculture with non-nuclear bombs and shells trying not to ruin the world beyond recovery, hoping eventually to wear the elves down. But the elves retaliated with gas and chemicals which humans had refrained from using. Humans interdicted supply and still the elves managed to come up with the wherewithal to strike through their base defense here as if supply were endless and they not starving and the world still green and undamaged.

DeFranco drank and drank with measured slowness, watching regs go to and fro in the slow dance of their own business. They were good, this Delta Company of the Eighth. They did faithfully what regs were supposed to do in this war, which was to hold a base and keep roads secure that humans used, and to build landing zones for supply and sometimes to go out and get killed inching humanity's way toward some goal the joint command understood and which from here looked only like some other damn shell-pocked hill. DeFranco's job was to locate such hills. And to find a prisoner to take (standing orders) and to figure out the enemy if he could.

Mostly just to find hills. And sometimes to get his company

into taking one. And right now he was no more damn good, because they had gotten as close to this nameless city as there were hills and vantages to make it profitable, and after that they went onto the flat and did what?

Take the place inch by inch, street by street and discover every damn elf they met had suicided? The elves would do it on them, so in the villages south of here they had saved the elves the bother, and got nothing for their trouble but endless, measured carnage, and smoothskinned corpses that drew the small vermin and the huge winged birds—(they've been careful with their ecology, the Science Bureau reckoned, in their end-less reports, in some fool's paper on large winged creatures' chances of survival if a dominant species were not very careful of them—)

(—or the damn birds are bloody-minded mean and tougher than the elves, deFranco mused in his alcoholic fog, knowing that nothing was, in all space and creation, more bloody-minded than the elves.)

He had seen a young elf child holding another, both stone dead, baby locked in baby's arms: they love, dammit, they love—And he had wept while he staggered away from the ruins of a little elvish town, seeing more and more such sights—because the elves had touched off bombs in their own town center, and turned it into a firestorm.

But the two babies had been lying there unburned and no one wanted to touch them or to look at them. Finally the birds came. And the regs shot at the birds until the CO stopped it, because it was a waste: it was killing a non-combatant lifeform, and that (O God!) was against the rules. Most of all the CO stopped it because it was a fraying of human edges, because the birds always were there and the birds were the winners, every time. And the damn birds like the damn elves came again and again, no matter that shots blew them to puffs of feathers. Stubborn, like the elves. Crazy as everything else on the planet, human and elf. It was catching.

DeFranco nursed the last whiskey in the last glass, nursed it with hands going so numb he had to struggle to stay awake. He was a quiet drunk, never untidy. He neatly drank the last and fell over sideways limp as a corpse, and, tender mercy to a hill-finding branch of the service the hill-taking and road-building regs regarded as a sometime natural enemy—one of the women came and got the glass from his numbed fingers and pulled a blanket over him. They were still human here. They tried to be.

"There was nothing more to be done," says the elf. "That was why. We knew that you were coming closer, and that our time was limited." His long white fingers touch the table-surface, the white, plastic table in the ordinary little bedroom. "We died in great numbers, deFranco, and it was cruel that you showed us only slowly what you could do."

"We could have taken you out from the first. You knew that." DeFranco's voice holds an edge of frustration. Of anguish. "Elf, couldn't you ever understand that?"

"You always gave us hope we could win. And so we fought, and so we still fight. Until the peace. My friend."

"Franc, Franc—" —it was a fierce low voice, and deFranco came out of it, in the dark, with his heart doubletiming and the instant realization it was Dibs talking to him in that low tone and wanting him out of that blanket, which meant wire-runners or worse, a night attack. But Dibs grabbed his arms to hold him still before he could flail about. "Franc, we got a move out there, Jake and Cat's headed out down the tunnel, the lieutenant's gone to M1 but M1's on the line, they want you out there, they want a spotter up on hill 24 doublequick.

"Uh." DeFranco rubbed his eyes. "Uh." Sitting upright was brutal. Standing was worse. He staggered two steps and caught the main shell of his armor off the rack, number 12 suit, the lousy stinking armor that always smelled of human or mud or the purge in the ducts and the awful sick-sweet cleaner they wiped it out with when they hung it up. He held the plastron against his body and Dibs started with the clips in the dim light of the single 5-watt they kept going to find the latrine at night— "Damn, damn, I gotta—" He eluded Dibs and got to the toilet, and by now the whole place was astir with shadow-figures like a scene out of a gold-lighted hell. He swigged the stinging mouthwash they had on the shelf by the toilet and did his business while Dibs caught him up from behind and finished the hooks on his left side. "Damn, get him going," the sergeant said, and: "Trying," Dibs said, as others hauled deFranco around and began hooking him up like a baby into his clothes, one piece and the other, the boots, leg and groin-pieces, the sleeves, the gloves, the belly clamp and the backpack and the power-

on—his joints ached. He stood there swaying to one and another tug on his body and took the helmet into his hands when
Dibs handed it to him.

"Go, go," the sergeant said, who had no more power to
give a special op any specific orders than he could fly; but HQ
was in a stew, they needed his talents out there, and deFranco
let the regs shove him all they liked: it was his accommodation
with these regs when there was no peace anywhere else in the
world. And once a dozen of these same regs had come out into
the heat after him, which he never quite forgot. So he let them
hook his weapons-kit on, then ducked his head down and put
the damned helmet on and gave it the locking half-twist as he
headed away from the safe light of the barracks pit into the
long tunnel, splashing along the low spots on the plastic grid
that kept heavy armored feet from sinking in the mud.

"Code: *Nightsight*," he told the suit aloud, all wobbly and
shivery from too little sleep; and it read his hoarse voice patterns
and gave him a filmy image of the tunnel in front of him.
"Code: *ID*," he told it, and it started telling the two troopers
somewhere up the tunnel that he was there, and on his way.
He got readout back as Cat acknowledged. "**la-6yg-p30/30**,"
the green numbers ghosted up in his visor, telling him Jake and
Cat had elves and they had them quasi-solid in the distant-
sensors which would have been tripped downland and they
themselves were staying where they were and taking no chances
on betraying the location of the tunnel. He cut the ID and Cat
and Jake cut off too.

They've got to us, deFranco thought. *The damned elves got
through our screen and now they've pushed through on foot,
and it's going to be hell to pay—*

Back behind him the rest of the troops would be suiting up
and making a more leisurely prep for a hard night to come.
The elves rarely got as far as human bunkers. They tried. They
were, at close range and with hand-weapons, deadly. The dying
was not all on the elves' side if they got to you.

A cold sweat had broken out under the suit. His head ached
with a vengeance and the suit weighed on his knees and on his
back when he bent and it stank with disinfectant that smelled
like some damn tree from some damn forest on the world that
had spawned every human born, he knew that, but it failed as
perfume and failed at masking the stink of terror and of the

tunnels in the cold wet breaths the suit took in when it was not on self-seal.

He knew nothing about Earth, only dimly remembered Pell, which had trained him and shipped him here by stages to a world no one bothered to give a name. Elfland, when High HQ was being whimsical. Neverneverland, the regs called it after some old fairy tale, because from it a soldier never never came home again. They had a song with as many verses as there were bitches of the things a soldier in Elfland never found.

> *Where's my discharge from this war?*
> *Why, it's neverneverwhere, my friend.*
> *Well, when's the next ship off this world?*
> *Why, it's neverneverwhen, my friend.*
> > *And time's what we've got most of,*
> > *And time is what we spend,*
> > *And time is what we've got to do*
> > *In Neverneverland.*

He hummed this to himself, in a voice jolted and crazed by the exertion. He wanted to cry like a baby. He wanted someone to curse for the hour and his interrupted rest. Most of all he wanted a few days of quiet on this front, just a few days to put his nerves back together again and let his head stop aching. . . .

. . . Run and run and run, in a suit that keeps you from the gas and most of the shells the elves can throw—except for a few. Except for the joints and the visor, because the elves have been working for twenty years studying how to kill you. And air runs out and filters fail and every access you have to Elfland is a way for the elves to get at you.

Like the tunnel openings, like the airvents, like the power plant that keeps the whole base and strung-out tunnel systems functioning.

Troopers scatter to defend these points, and you run and run, belatedly questioning why troopers want a special op at a particular point, where the tunnel most nearly approaches the elves on their plain.

Why me, why here—because, fool, HQ wants close-up reconnaissance, which was what they wanted the last time they sent you out in the dark beyond the safe points—twice, now, and they expect you to go out and do it again because the elves missed you last time.

Damn them all. (With the thought that they will use you till the bone breaks and the flesh refuses. And then a two-week rest and out to the lines again.)

They give you a medical as far as the field hospital; and there they give you vitamins, two shots of antibiotic, a bottle of pills and send you out again. "We got worse," the meds say then.

There always are worse. Till you're dead.

DeFranco looks at the elf across the table in the small room and remembers how it was, the smell of the tunnels, the taste of fear.

II

So what're the gals like on this world?
Why, you nevernevermind, my friend.
Well, what're the guys like on this world?
Well, you neverneverask, my friend.

"They sent me out there," deFranco says to the elf, and the elf—a human might have nodded but elves have no such habit—stares gravely as they sit opposite each other, hands on the table.

"You alway say 'they,'" says the elf. "We say 'we' decided. But you do things differently."

"Maybe it *is* we," deFranco says. "Maybe it is, at the bottom of things. We. Sometimes it doesn't look that way."

"I think even now you don't understand why we do what we do. I don't really understand why you came here or why you listen to me, or why you stay now— But we won't understand. I don't think we two will. Others maybe. You want what I want. That's what I trust most."

"You believe it'll work?"

"For us, yes. For elves. Absolutely. Even if it's a lie it will work."

"But if it's not a lie—"

"Can you make it true? *You* don't believe. That—I have to

find words for this—but I don't understand that either. How
you feel. What you do." The elf reaches across the table and
slim white hands with overtint like oil on water catch at brown,
matte-skinned fingers whose nails (the elf has none) are broken
and rough. "It was no choice to you. It never was even a choice
to you, to destroy us to the heart and the center. Perhaps it
wasn't to stay. I have a deep feeling toward you, deFranco. I
had this feeling toward you from when I saw you first; I knew
that you were what I had come to find, but whether you were
the helping or the damning force I didn't know then, I only
knew that what you did when you saw us was what humans
had always done to us. And I believed you would show me
why."

DeFranco moved and sat still a while by turns, in the dark, in
the stink and the strictures of his rig; while somewhere two
ridges away there were two nervous regs encamped in the entry
to the tunnel, sweltering in their own hardsuits and not running
their own pumps and fans any more than he was running his—
because elvish hearing was legendary, the rigs made noise, and
it was hard enough to move in one of the bastards without
making a racket: someone in HQ suspected elves could pick
up the running noises. Or had other senses.

But without those fans and pumps the below-the-neck part
of the suit had no cooling and got warm even in the night. And
the gloves and the helmets had to stay on constantly when
anyone was outside, it was the rule: no elf ever got a look at
a live human, except at places like the Eighth's Gamma Company. Perhaps not there either. Elves were generally thorough.

DeFranco had the kneejoints on lock at the moment, which
let him have a solid prop to lean his weary knees and backside
against. He leaned there easing the shivers and the quakes out
of his lately-wakened and sleep-deprived limbs before he rattled
in his armor and alerted a whole hillside full of elves. It was
not a well-shielded position he had taken: it had little cover
except the hill itself, and these hills had few enough trees that
the fires and the shells had spared. But green did struggle up
amid the soot and bushes grew on the line down on valley level
that had been an elvish road three years ago. His nightsight
scanned the brush in shadow-images.

Something touched the sensors as he rested there on watch,
a curious whisper of a sound, and an amber readout ghosted

up into his visor, dots rippling off in sequence in the direction the pickup came from. It was not the wind: the internal computer zeroed out the white sound of wind and suit-noise. It was anomalies it brought through and amplified; and what it amplified now had the curious regular pulse of engine-sound.

DeFranco ordered the lock off his limbs, slid lower on the hill and moved on toward one with better vantage of the road so it came up from the west—carefully, pausing at irregular intervals as he worked round to get into position to spot that direction. He still had his locator output off. So did everyone else back at the base. HQ had no idea now what sophistication the elves had gained at eavesdropping and homing in on the locators, and how much they could pick up with locators of their own. It was only sure that while some elvish armaments had gotten more primitive and patchwork, their computer tech had nothing at all wrong with it.

DeFranco settled again on a new hillside and listened, wishing he could scratch a dozen maddening itches, and wishing he were safe somewhere else: the whole thing had a disaster-feeling about it from the start, the elves doing something they had never done. He could only think about dead Gamma Company and what might have happened to them before the elves got to them and gassed the bunker and fought their way into it past the few that had almost gotten into their rigs in time—

Had the special op been out there watching too? Had the one at bunker 35 made a wrong choice and had it all started this way the night they died?

The engine-sound was definite. DeFranco edged higher up the new hill and got down flat, belly down on the ridge. He thumbed the magnification plate into the visor and got the handheld camera's snake-head optics over the ridge on the theory it was a smaller target and a preferable target than himself, with far better nightsight.

The filmy nightsight image came back of the road, while the sound persisted. It was distant, his ears and the readout advised him, distant yet, racing the first red edge of a murky dawn that showed far off across the plain and threatened daylight out here.

He still sent no transmission. The orders were stringent. The base either had to remain ignorant that there was a vehicle coming up the road or he had to go back personally to report it; and lose track of whatever-it-was out here just when it was getting near enough to do damage. Damn the lack of specials to team with out here in the hot spots, and damn the lead-footed regs: he had to go it alone, decide things alone, hoping Jake and Cat did the right thing in their spot and hoping the other regs stayed put. And he hated it.

He edged off this hill, keeping it between him and the ruined, shell-pocked road, and began to move to still a third point of vantage, stalking as silently as any man in armor could manage.

And fervently he hoped that the engine-sound was not a decoy and that nothing was getting behind him. The elves were deceptive as well and they were canny enemies with extraordinary hearing. He hoped now that the engine-sound had deafened them—but no elf was really fool enough to be coming up the road like this, it was a decoy, it had to be, there was nothing else it could be; and he was going to fall into it nose-down if he was not careful.

He settled belly-down on the next slope and got the camera-snake over the top, froze the suit-joints and lay inert in that overheated ceramic shell, breathing hard through a throat abused by oxygen and whiskey, blinking against a hangover headache to end all headaches that the close focus of the visor readout only made worse. His nose itched. A place on his scalp itched behind his ear. He stopped cataloging the places he itched because it was driving him crazy. Instead he blinked and rolled his eyes, calling up readout on the passive systems, and concentrated on that.

Blink. Blink-blink. Numbers jumped. The computer had come up with a range as it got passive echo off some hill and checked it against the local topology programmed into its memory. Damn! Close. The computer handed him the velocity. 40 KPH with the 4 and the 0 wobbling back and forth into the 30's. DeFranco held his breath and checked his hand-launcher, loading a set of armor-piercing rounds in, quiet, quiet as a man could move. The clamp went down as softly as long practice could lower it.

And at last a ridiculous open vehicle came jouncing and whining its way around potholes and shell craters and generally making a noisy and erratic progress. It was in a considerable hurry despite the potholes, and there were elves in it, four of them, all pale in their robes and one of them with the cold glitter of metal about his/her? person, the one to the right of the driver. The car bounced and wove and zigged and zagged up the hilly road with no slackening of speed, inviting a shot for all it was worth.

Decoy?

Suicide?

They were crazy as elves could be, and that was completely. They were headed straight for the hidden bunker, and it was possible they had gas or a bomb in that car or that they just planned to get themselves shot in a straightforward way, whatever they had in mind, but they were going right where they could do the most damage.

DeFranco unlocked his ceramic limbs, which sagged under his weight until he was down on his belly; and he slowly brought his rifle up, and inched his way up on his belly so it was his vulnerable head over the ridge this time. He shook and he shivered and he reckoned there might be a crater where he was in fair short order if they had a launcher in that car and he gave them time to get it set his way.

But pushing and probing at elves was part of his job. And these were decidedly anomalous. He put a shot in front of the car and half expected elvish suicides on the spot.

The car swerved and jolted into a pothole as the shell hit. It careened to a stop; and he held himself where he was, his heart pounding away and himself not sure why he had put the shot in front and not into the middle of them like a sensible man in spite of HQ's orders.

But the elves recovered from their careening and the car was stopped; and instead of blowing themselves up immediately or going for a launcher of their own, one of the elves bailed out over the side while the helmet-sensor picked up the attempted motor-start. Cough-whine. The car lurched. The elvish driver made a wild turn, but the one who had gotten out just stood there—*stood,* staring up, and lifted his hands together.

DeFranco lay on his hill; and the elves who had gotten the car started swerved out of the pothole it had stuck itself in and lurched off in escape, not suicide—while the one elf in the robe with the metal border just stood there, the first live prisoner anyone had ever taken, staring up at him, self-offered.

"You damn well stand still," he yelled down at the elf on outside com, and thought of the gas and the chemicals and thought that if elves had come up with a disease that also got to humans here was a way of delivering it that was cussed enough and crazy enough for them.

"Human," a shrill voice called up to him. "Human!"

DeFranco was for the moment paralyzed. An elf knew what to call them: an elf *talked*. An elf stood there staring up at his hill in the beginnings of dawn and all of a sudden nothing was going the way it ever had between elves and humankind.

At least, if it had happened before, no human had ever lived to tell about it.

"Human!" the same voice called—*uu-mann,* as best high elvish voices could manage it. The elf was not suiciding. The elf showed no sign of wanting to do that; and deFranco lay and shivered in his armor and felt a damnable urge to wipe his nose which he could not reach or to get up and run for his life, which was a fool's act. Worse, his bladder suddenly told him it was full. Urgently. Taking his mind down to a ridiculous small matter in the midst of trying to get home alive.

The dawn was coming up the way it did across the plain, light spreading like a flood, so fast in the bizarre angle of the land here that it ran like water on the surface of the plain.

And the elf stood there while the light of dawn grew more, showing the elf more clearly than deFranco had ever seen one of the enemy alive, beautiful the way elves were, not in a human way, looking, in its robes, like some cross between man and something spindly and human-skinned and insectoid. The up-tilted ears never stopped moving, but the average of their direction was toward him. Nervous-like.

What does he want, why does he stand there, why did they throw him out? A target? A distraction?

Elvish cussedness. DeFranco waited, and waited, and the sun came up; while somewhere in the tunnels there would be troopers wondering and standing by their weapons, ready to go on self-seal against gas or whatever these lunatics had brought.

There was light enough now to make out the red of the robes that fluttered in the breeze. And light enough to see the elf's hands, which looked—which looked, crazily enough, to be tied together.

The dawn came on. Water became an obsessive thought. DeFranco was thirsty from the whiskey and agonized between the desire for a drink from the tube near his mouth or the fear one more drop of water in his system would make it impossible to ignore his bladder; and he thought about it and thought about it, because it was a long wait and a long walk back, and relieving himself outside the suit was a bitch on the one hand and on the inside was damnable discomfort. But it did get worse. And while life and death tottered back and forth and his fingers clutched the launcher and he faced an elf who was surely up to something, that small decision was all he could think of clearly—it was easier to think of than what wanted thinking out, like what to do and whether to shoot the elf outright, counter to every instruction and every order HQ had given, because he wanted to get out of this place.

But he did not—and finally he solved both problems: took his drink, laid the gun down on the ridge like it was still in his hands, performed the necessary maneuver to relieve himself outside the suit as he stayed as flat as he could. Then he put himself back together, collected his gun and lurched up to his feet with small whines of the assisting joint-locks.

The elf never moved in all of this, and deFranco motioned with the gun. "Get up here. . . ."—not expecting the elf to understand either the motion or the shout. But the elf came, slowly, as if the hill was all his (it had been once) and he owned it. The elf stopped still on the slant, at a speaking distance, no more, and stood there with his hands tied (*his*, deFranco decided by the height of him). The elf's white skin all but glowed in the early dawn, the bare skin of the face and arms against the dark, metal-edged red of his robe; and the large eyes were set on him and the ears twitched and quivered with small pulses.

"I am your prisoner," the elf said, plain as any human; and deFranco stood there with his heart hammering away at his ribs.

"Why?" deFranco asked. He was mad, he was quite mad and somewhere he had fallen asleep on the hillside, or elvish gas had gotten to him through the open vents—he was a fool to have gone on open circulation; and he was dying back there somewhere and not talking at all.

The elf lifted his bound hand. "I came here to find you."

It was not a perfect accent. It was what an elvish mouth could come up with. It had music in it. And deFranco stood and stared and finally motioned with the gun up the hill. "Move," he said, "walk."

Without demur his prisoner began to do that, in the direction he had indicated.

· · ·

"What did I do that humans always do?" deFranco asks the elf, and the grave sea-colored eyes flicker with changes. Amusement, perhaps. Or distress.

"You fired at us," says the elf in his soft, songlike voice. "And then you stopped and didn't kill me."

"It was a warning."

"To stop. So simple."

"God, what else do you think?"

The elf's eyes flicker again. There is gold in their depths, and gray. And his ears flick nervously. "DeFranco, deFranco, you still don't know why we fight. And I don't truly know what you meant. Are you telling me the truth?"

"We never wanted to fight. It was a warning. Even animals, for God's sake—understand a warning shot."

The elf blinks. (And someone in another room stirs in a chair and curses his own blindness. Aggression and the birds. Different tropisms. All the way through the ecostructure.)

The elf spreads his hands. "I don't know what you mean. I never know. What can we know? That you were there for the same reason I was? Were you?"

"I don't know. I don't even know that. *We never wanted a war*. Do you understand that, at least?"

"You wanted us to stop. So we told you the same. We sent our ships to hold those places which were ours. And you kept coming to them."

"They were ours."

"Now they are." The elf's face is grave and still. "DeFranco, a mistake was made. A ship of ours fired on yours and this was a mistake. Perhaps it was me who fired. What's in this elf's mind? Fear when a ship will not go away? What's in this human's mind? Fear when we don't go away? It was a stupid thing. It was a mistake. It was our region. Our—"

"Territory. You think you owned the place."

"We were in it. We were there and this ship came. Say that I wasn't there and I heard how it happened. This was a frightened elf who made a stupid mistake. This elf was surprised by this ship and he didn't want to run and give up this jump-point. It was ours. You were in it. We wanted you to go. And you stayed."

"So you blew up an unarmed ship."

"Yes. I did it. I destroyed all the others. You destroyed ours.

Our space station. You killed thousands of us. I killed thousands of you."

"Not me and not you, elf. That's twenty years, dammit, and you weren't there and I wasn't there—"

"I did it. I say I did. And you killed thousands of us."

"We weren't coming to make a war. We were coming to straighten it out. Do you understand that?"

"We weren't yet willing. Now things are different."

"For God's sake—why did you let so many die?"

"You never gave us defeat enough. You were cruel, de-Franco. Not to let us know we couldn't win—that was very cruel. It was very subtle. Even now I'm afraid of your cruelty."

"Don't you understand yet?"

"What do I understand? That you've died in thousands. That you make long war. I thought you would kill me on the hill, on the road, and when you called me I had both hope and fear. Hope that you would take me to higher authority. Fear—well, I am bone and nerve, deFranco. And I never knew whether you would be cruel."

The elf walked and walked. He might have been on holiday, his hands tied in front of him, his red robes a-glitter with their gold borders in the dawn. He never tired. *He* carried no weight of armor; and deFranco went on self-seal and spoke through the mike when he had to give the elf directions.

Germ warfare?

Maybe the elf had a bomb in his gut?

But it began to settle into deFranco that he had done it, he had done it, after years of trying he had himself a live and willing prisoner, and his lower gut was queasy with outright panic and his knees felt like mush. *What's he up to, what's he doing, why's he walk like that— Damn! they'll shoot him on sight, somebody could see him first and shoot him and I can't break silence—maybe that's what I'm supposed to do, maybe that's how they overran Gamma Company—*

But a prisoner, a prisoner speaking human language—

"Where'd you learn," he asked the elf, "where'd you learn to talk human?"

The elf never turned, never stopped walking. "A prisoner."

"Who? Still alive?"

"No."

No. Slender and graceful as a reed and burning as a fire
and white as beach sand. *No*. Placidly. Rage rose in deFranco,
a blinding urge to put his rifle butt in that straight spine, to
muddy and bloody the bastard and make him as dirty and as
hurting as himself; but the professional rose up in him too, and
the burned hillsides went on and on as they climbed and they
walked, the elf just in front of him.

Until they were close to the tunnels and in imminent danger
of a human misunderstanding.

He turned his ID and locator on; but they would pick up
the elf on his sensors too, and that was no good. "It's deFranco,"
he said over the com. "I got a prisoner. Get HQ and get me a
transport."

Silence from the other end. He cut off the output, figuring
they had it by now. "Stop," he said to the elf on outside audio.
And he stood and waited until two suited troopers showed up,
walking carefully down the hillside from a direction that did
not lead to any tunnel opening.

"Damn," came Cat's female voice over his pickup. "Da-
amn." In a tone of wonder. And deFranco at first thought it
was admiration of him and what he had done, and then he
knew with some disgust it was wonder at the elf, it was a
human woman looking at the prettiest, cleanest thing she had
seen in three long years, icy, fastidious Cat, who was picky
what she slept with.

And maybe her partner Jake picked it up, because: "Huh,"
he said in quite a different tone, but quiet, quiet, the way the
elf looked at their faceless faces, as if he still owned the whole
world and meant to take it back.

"It's Franc," Jake said then into the com, directed at the
base. "And he's right, he's got a live one. Damn, you should
see this bastard."

III

So where's the generals in this war?
Why, they're neverneverhere, my friend.
Well, what'll we do until they come?
Well, you neverneverask, my friend.

"I was afraid too," deFranco says. "I thought you might have a bomb or something. We were afraid you'd suicide if anyone touched you. That was why we kept you sitting all that time outside."

"Ah," says the elf with a delicate move of his hands. "Ah. I thought it was to make me angry. Like all the rest you did. But you sat with me. And this was hopeful. I was thirsty; I hoped for a drink. That was mostly what I thought about."

"We think too much—elves and humans. We both think too much. *I'd have given you a drink of water, for God's sake.* I guess no one even thought."

"I wouldn't have taken it."

"Dammit, why?"

"Unless you drank with me. Unless you shared what you had. Do you see?"

"Fear of poison?"

"No."

"You mean just my giving it."

"Sharing it. Yes."

"Is pride so much?"

Again the elf touches deFranco's hand as it rests on the table, a nervous, delicate gesture. The elf's ears twitch and collapse and lift again, trembling. "We always go off course here. I still fail to understand why you fight."

"Dammit, I don't understand why you can't understand why a man'd give you a drink of water. Not to hurt you. Not to prove anything. For the love of God, *mercy,* you ever learn that word? Being decent, so's everything decent doesn't go to hell and we don't act like damn animals!"

The elf stares long and soberly. His small mouth has few expressions. It forms its words carefully. "Is this why you pushed us so long? To show us your control?"

"No, dammit, to hang onto it! So we can find a place to stop this bloody war. It's all we ever wanted."

"Then why did you start?"

"Not to have you push *us!*"

A blink of sea-colored eyes. "Now, now, we're understanding. We're like each other."

"But you won't stop, dammit it, you wouldn't stop, you haven't stopped yet! People are still dying out there on the front, throwing themselves away without a thing to win. Nothing. *That*'s not like us."

"In starting war we're alike. But not in ending it. You take years. Quickly we show what we can do. Then both sides know. So we make peace. You showed us long cruelty. And we wouldn't give ourselves up to you. What could we expect?"

"Is it that easy?" DeFranco begins to shiver, clenches his hands together on the tabletop and leans there, arms folded. "You're crazy, elf."

"Angan. My personal name is Angan."

"A hundred damn scientists out there trying to figure out how you work and it's that damn simple?"

"I don't think so. I think we maybe went off course again. But we came close. We at least see there was a mistake. That's the important thing. That's why I came."

DeFranco looked desperately at his watch, at the minutes ticking away. He covers the face of it with his hand and looks up. His brown eyes show anguish. "The colonel said I'd have three hours. It's going. It's going too fast."

"Yes. And we still haven't found out why. I don't think we ever will. Only you share with me now, deFranco. Here. In our little time."

The elf sat, just sat quietly with his hands still tied, on the open hillside, because the acting CO had sent word no elf was setting foot inside the bunker system and no one was laying hands on him to search him.

But the troopers came out one by one in the long afternoon and had their look at him—one after another of them took the trouble to put on the faceless, uncomfortable armor just to come out and stand and stare at what they had been fighting for all these years.

"Damn," was what most of them said, in private, on the com, their suits to his suit; "damn," or variants on that theme.

"We got that transport coming in," the reg lieutenant said when she came out and brought him his kit. Then, unlike herself: "Good job, Franc."

"Thanks," deFranco said, claiming nothing. And he sat calmly, beside his prisoner, on the barren, shell-pocked hill by a dead charcoal tree.

Don't shake him, word had come from the CO. Keep him real happy—don't change the situation and don't threaten him and don't touch him.

For fear of spontaneous suicide.

So no one came to lay official claim to the elf either, not even the captain came. But the word had gone out to Base and to HQ and up, deFranco did not doubt, to orbiting ships, because it was the best news a frontline post had had to report since the war started. Maybe it was dreams of leaving Elfland that brought the regs out here, on pilgrimage to see this wonder. And the lieutenant went away when she had stared at him so long.

Hope. DeFranco turned that over and over in his mind and probed at it like a tongue into a sore tooth. Promotion out of the field. No more mud. No more runs like yesterday. No more, no more, no more, the man who broke the Elfland war and cracked the elves and brought in the key—

—to let it all end. For good. *Winning*. Maybe, maybe—

He looked at the elf who sat there with his back straight and his eyes wandering to this and that, to the movement of wind in a forlorn last bit of grass, the drift of a cloud in Elfland's blue sky, the horizons and the dead trees.

"You got a name?" He was careful asking anything. But the elf had talked before.

The elf looked at him. "Saitas," he said.

"Saitas. Mine's deFranco."

The elf blinked. There was no fear in his face. They might have been sitting in the bunker passing the time of day together.

"Why'd they send you?" DeFranco grew bolder.

"I asked to come."

"Why?"

"To stop the war."

Inside his armor deFranco shivered. He blinked and he took a drink from the tube inside the helmet and he tried to think about something else, but the elf sat there staring blandly at him, with his hands tied, resting placidly in his lap. "How?" deFranco asked, "how will you stop the war?"

But the elf said nothing and deFranco knew he had gone further with that question than HQ was going to like, not wanting their subject told anything about human wants and intentions before they had a chance to study the matter and study the elf and hold their conferences.

"They came," says deFranco in that small room, "to know what you looked like."

"You never let us see your faces," says the elf.

"You never let us see yours."

"You knew everything. Far more than we. You knew our world. We had no idea of yours."

"Pride again."

"Don't you know how hard it was to let you lay hands on me? That was the worst thing. You did it again. Like the gunfire. You touch with violence and then expect quiet. But I let this happen. It was what I came to do. And when you spoke to the others for me, that gave me hope."

In time the transport came skimming in low over the hills, and deFranco got to his feet to wave it in. The elf stood up too, graceful and still placid. And waited while the transport sat down and the blades stopped beating.

"Get in," deFranco said then, picking up his scant baggage, putting the gun on safety.

The elf quietly bowed his head and followed instructions, going where he was told. DeFranco never laid a hand on him, until inside, when they had climbed into the dark belly of the transport and guards were waiting there— "Keep your damn guns down," deFranco said on outside com, because they were light-armed and helmetless. "What are you going to do if he moves, shoot him? Let me handle him. He speaks real good." And to the elf: "Sit down there. I'm going to put a strap across. Just so you don't fall."

The elf sat without objection, and deFranco got a cargo strap and hooked it to the rail on one side and the other, so there was no way the elf was going to stir or use his hands.

And he sat down himself as the guards took their places and the transport lifted off and carried them away from the elvish city and the frontline base of the hundreds of such bases in the world. It began to fly high and fast when it got to safe airspace, behind the defense humans had made about themselves.

There was never fear in the elf. Only placidity. His eyes traveled over the inside of the transport, the dark utilitarian hold, the few benches, the cargo nets, the two guards.

Learning, deFranco thought, still learning everything there was to learn about his enemies.

"Then I was truly afraid," says the elf. "I was most afraid that they would want to talk to me and learn from me. And I would have to die then to no good. For nothing."

"How do you do that?"

"What?"

"Die. Just by wanting to."

"Wanting is the way. I could stop my heart now. Many things stop the heart. When you stop trying to live, when you stop going ahead—it's very easy."

"You mean if you quit trying to live you die. That's crazy."

The elf spreads delicate fingers. "Children can't. Children's hearts can't be stopped that way. You have the hearts of children. Without control. But the older you are the easier and easier it is. Until someday it's easier to stop than to go on. When I learned your language I learned from a man named Tomas. He couldn't die. He and I talked—oh, every day. And one day we brought him a woman we took. She called him a damn traitor. That was what she said. Damn traitor. Then Tomas wanted to die and he couldn't. He told me so. It was the only thing he ever asked of me. Like the water, you see. Because I felt sorry for him I gave him the cup. And to her. Because I had no use for her. But Tomas hated me. He hated me every day. He talked to me because I was all he had to talk to, he would say. Nothing stopped his heart. Until the woman called him traitor. And then his heart stopped, though it went on beating. I only helped. He thanked me. And damned me to hell. And wished me health with his drink."

"Dammit, elf."

"I tried to ask him what hell was. I think it means being still and trapped. So we fight."

("He's very good with words," someone elsewhere says, leaning over near the monitor. "He's trying to communicate something but the words aren't equivalent. He's playing on what he does have.")

"For God's sake," says deFranco then, "is that why they fling themselves on the barriers? Is that why they go on dying? Like birds at cage bars?"

The elf flinches. Perhaps it is the image. Perhaps it is a thought. "Fear stops the heart, when fear has nowhere to go. We still have one impulse left. There is still our anger. Everything else has gone. At the last even our children will fight you. So I fight for my children by coming here. I don't want to talk about Tomas any more. The birds have him. *You* are what I was looking for."

"Why?" DeFranco's voice shakes. "Saitas—Angan—I'm scared as hell."

"So am I. Think of all the soldiers. Think of things important to you. I think about my home."

"I think I never had one. —This is crazy. It won't work."

"Don't." The elf reaches and holds a brown wrist. "Don't leave me now, deFranco."

"There's still fifteen minutes. Quarter of an hour."

"That's a very long time . . . here. Shall we shorten it?"

"No," deFranco says and draws a deep breath. "Let's use it."

At the base where the on-world authorities and the scientists did their time, there were real buildings, real ground-site buildings, which humans had made. When the transport touched down on a rooftop landing pad, guards took the elf one way and deFranco another. It was debriefing: that he expected. They let him get a shower first with hot water out of real plumbing, in a prefabbed bathroom. And he got into his proper uniform for the first time in half a year, shaved and proper in his blue beret and his brown uniform, fresh and clean and thinking all the while that if a special could get his field promotion it was scented towels every day and soft beds to sleep on and a life expectancy in the decades. He was anxious, because there were ways of snatching credit for a thing and he wanted the credit for this one, wanted it because a body could get killed out there on hillsides where he had been for three years and no desk-sitting officer was going to fail to mention him in the report.

"Sit down," the specials major said, and took him through it all; and that afternoon they let him tell it to a reg colonel and lieutenant general; and again that afternoon they had him tell it to a tableful of scientists and answer questions and questions and questions until he was hoarse and they forgot to feed him lunch. But he answered on and on until his voice cracked and the science staff took pity on him.

He slept then, in clean sheets in a clean bed and lost touch with the war so that he waked terrified and lost in the middle of the night in the dark and had to get his heart calmed down before he realized he was not crazy and that he really had gotten into a place like this and he really had done what he remembered.

He tucked down babylike into a knot and thought good

thoughts all the way back to sleep until a buzzer waked him and told him it was day in this windowless place, and he had an hour to dress again—for more questions, he supposed; and he thought only a little about his elf, *his* elf, who was handed on to the scientists and the generals and the AlSec people, and stopped being his personal business.

"Then," says the elf, "I knew you were the only one I met I could understand. Then I sent for you."

"I still don't know why."

"I said it then. We're both soldiers."

"You're more than that."

"Say that I made one of the great mistakes."

"You mean at the beginning? I don't believe it."

"It could have been. Say that I commanded the attacking ship. Say that I struck your people on the world. Say that you destroyed our station and our cities. We are the makers of mistakes. Say this of ourselves."

"I," the elf said, his image on the screen much the same as he had looked on the hillside, straight-spined, red-robed—only the ropes elves had put on him had left purpling marks on his wrists, on the opalescing white of his skin, "I'm clear enough, aren't I?" The trooper accent was strange coming from a delicate elvish mouth. The elf's lips were less mobile. His voice had modulations, like singing, and occasionally failed to keep its tones flat.

"It's very good," the scientist said, the man in the white coveralls, who sat at a small desk opposite the elf in a sterile white room and had his hands laced before him. The camera took both of them in, elf and swarthy Science Bureau xenologist. "I understand you learned from prisoners."

The elf seemed to gaze into infinity. "We don't want to fight anymore."

"Neither do we. Is this why you came?"

A moment the elf studied the scientist, and said nothing at all.

"What's your people's name?" the scientist asked.

"You call us elves."

"But we want to know what you call yourselves. What you call this world."

"Why would you want to know that?"

"To respect you. Do you know that word, respect?"

"I don't understand it."

"Because what you call this world and what you call your-selves *is* the name, the right name, and we want to call you right. Does that make sense?"

"It makes sense. But what you call us is right too, isn't it?"

"Elves is a made-up word, from our homeworld. A myth. Do you know *myth?* A story. A thing not true."

"Now it's true, isn't it?"

"Do you call your world Earth? Most people do."

"What you all it is its name."

"We call it Elfland."

"That's fine. It doesn't matter."

"Why doesn't it matter?"

"I've said that."

"You learned our language very well. But we don't know anything of yours."

"Yes."

"Well, we'd like to learn. We'd like to be able to talk to you your way. It seems to us this is only polite. Do you know *polite?*"

"No."

A prolonged silence. The scientist's face remained bland as the elf's. "You say you don't want to fight anymore. Can you tell us how to stop the war?"

"Yes. But first I want to know what your peace is like. What, for instance, will you do about the damage you've caused us?"

"You mean reparations."

"What's that mean?"

"Payment."

"What do you mean by it?"

The scientist drew a deep breath. "Tell me. Why did your people give you to one of our soldiers? Why didn't they just call on the radio and say they wanted to talk?"

"This is what you'd do."

"It's easier, isn't it? And safer."

The elf blinked. No more than that.

"There was a ship a long time ago," the scientist said after a moment. "It was a human ship minding its own business in a human lane, and elves came and destroyed it and killed everyone on it. Why?"

"What do you want for this ship?"

"So you do understand about payment. Payment's giving something for something."

"I understand." The elvish face was guileless, masklike, the long eyes like the eyes of a pearl-skinned buddha. A saint. "What will you ask? And how will peace with you be? What do you call peace?"

"You mean you don't think our word for it is like your word for it?"

"That's right."

"Well, that's an important thing to understand, isn't it? Before we make agreements. Peace means no fighting."

"That's not enough."

"Well, it means being safe from your enemies."

"That's not enough."

"What is enough?"

The pale face contemplated the floor, something elsewhere.

"What *is* enough, Saitas?"

The elf only stared at the floor, far, far away from the questioner. "I need to talk to deFranco."

"Who?"

"DeFranco." The elf looked up. "DeFranco brought me here. He's a soldier; he'll understand me better than you. Is he still here?"

The colonel reached and cut the tape off. She was SurTac. Agnes Finn was the name on her desk. She could cut your throat a dozen ways, and do sabotage and mayhem from the refinements of computer theft to the gross tactics of explosives; she would speak a dozen languages, know every culture she had ever dealt with from the inside out, integrating the Science Bureau and the military. And more, she was a SurTac *colonel*, which sent the wind up deFranco's back. It was not a branch of the service that had many high officers; you had to survive more than ten field missions to get your promotion beyond the ubiquitous and courtesy-titled lieutenancy. And this one had. This was Officer with a capital O, and whatever the politics in HQ were, this was a rock around which a lot of other bodies orbited: *this* probably took her orders from the joint command, which was months and months away in its closest manifestation. And that meant next to no orders and wide discretion, which was what SurTacs did. Wild card. Joker in the deck.

There were the regs; there was special ops, loosely attached; there were the spacers, Union and Alliance, and Union regs were part of that; beyond and above, there was AlSec and Union intelligence; and that was this large-boned, red-haired woman who probably had a scant handful of humans and no knowing what else in her direct command, a handful of SurTacs loose in Elfland, and all of them independent operators and as much trouble to the elves as a reg base could be.

DeFranco knew. He had tried that route once. He knew more than most what kind it took to survive that training, let alone the requisite ten missions to get promoted out of the field, and he knew the wit behind the weathered face and knew it ate special ops lieutenants for appetizers.

"How did you make such an impression on him, Lieutenant?"

"I didn't try to," deFranco said carefully. "Ma'am, I just tried to keep him calm and get in with him alive the way they said. But I was the only one who dealt with him out there, we thought that was safest; maybe he thinks I'm more than I am."

"I compliment you on the job." There was a certain irony in that, he was sure. No SurTac had pulled off what he had, and he felt the slight tension there.

"Yes, ma'am."

"Yes, ma'am. There's always the chance, you understand, that you've brought us an absolute lunatic. Or the elves are going an unusual route to lead us into a trap. Or this is an elf who's not too pleased about being tied up and dumped on us, and he wants to get even. Those things occur to me."

"Yes, ma'am." DeFranco thought all those things, face to face with the colonel and trying to be easy as the colonel had told him to be. But the colonel's thin face was sealed and forbidding as the elf's.

"You know what they're doing out there right now? Massive attacks. Hitting that front near 45 with everything they've got. The Eighth's pinned. We're throwing air in. And they've got somewhere over two thousand casualties out there and airstrikes don't stop all of them. Delta took a head-on assault and turned it. There were casualties. Trooper named Herse. Your unit."

Dibs. O God. "Dead?"

"Dead." The colonel's eyes were bleak and expressionless. "Word came in. I know it's more than a stat to you. But that's what's going on. We've got two signals coming from the elves. And we don't know which one's valid. We have ourselves an alien who claims credentials—*and* comes with considerable effort from the same site as the attack."

Dibs. Dead. There seemed a chill in the air, in this safe, remote place far from the real world, the mud, the bunkers. Dibs had stopped living yesterday. This morning. Sometime. Dibs had gone and the world never noticed.

"Other things occur to the science people," the colonel said. "One which galls the hell out of them, deFranco, is what the alien just said. *DeFranco can understand me better.* Are you with me, Lieutenant?"

"Yes, ma'am."

"So the Bureau went to the secretary, the secretary went to the major general on the com; all this at fifteen hundred yesterday; and *they* hauled me in on it at two this morning. You know how many noses you've got out of joint, Lieutenant? And what the level of concern is about that mess out there on the front?"

"Yes, ma'am."

"I'm sure you hoped for a commendation and maybe better, wouldn't that be it? Wouldn't blame you. Well, I got my hands into this, and I've opted you under my orders, Lieutenant, because I can do that and high command's just real worried the Bureau's going to poke and prod and that elf's going to leave us on the sudden for elvish heaven. So let's just keep him moderately happy. He wants to talk to you. What the Bureau wants to tell you, but I told them *I'd* make it clear, because they'll talk tech at you and I want to be sure you've got it—it's just real simple: you're dealing with an alien; and you'll have noticed what he says doesn't always make sense."

"Yes, ma'am."

"Don't yes ma'am me, Lieutenant, dammit; just talk to me and look me in the eye. We're talking about communication here."

"Yes—" He stopped short of the ma'am.

"You've got a brain, deFranco, it's all in your record. You almost went Special Services yourself, that was your real ambition, wasn't it? But you had this damn psychotic fear of taking ultimate responsibility. And a wholesome fear of ending up with a commendation, posthumous. Didn't you? It washed you out, so you went special ops where you could take orders from someone else and still play bloody hero and prove something to yourself—am I right? I ought to be; I've got your psych record over there. Now I've insulted you and you're sitting there turning red. But I want to know what I'm dealing with. We're in a damn bind. We've got casualties happening out there. Are you and I going to have trouble?"

"No. I understand."

"Good. Very good. Do you think you can go into a room with that elf and talk the truth out of him? More to the point, can you make a decision, can you go in there knowing how much is riding on your back?"

"I'm not a—"

"I don't care what you *are,* deFranco. What I want to know is whether *negotiate* is even in that elf's vocabulary. I'm assigning you to guard over there. In the process I want you to sit down with him one to one and just talk away. That's all you've got to do. And because of your background maybe you'll do it with some sense. But maybe if you just talk for John deFranco and try to get that elf to deal, that's the best thing. You know when a government sends out a negotiator—or anything like—that individual's not average. That individual's probably the smartest, canniest, hardest-nosed bastard they've got, and he probably cheats at dice. We don't know what this bastard's up to or what he thinks like, and when you sit down with him you're talking to a mind that knows a lot more about humanity than we know about elves. You're talking to an elvish expert who's here playing games with us. Who's giving us a real good look-over. You understand that? What do you say about it?"

"I'm scared of this."

"That's real good. You know we're not sending in the brightest, most experienced human on two feet. And that's exactly what that rather canny elf has arranged for us to do. You understand that? He's playing us like a keyboard this far. And how do you cope with that, Lieutenant deFranco?"

"I just ask him questions and answer as little as I can."

"Wrong. You let him talk. You be real *careful* what you ask him. What you ask is as dead a giveaway as what you tell him. Everything you do and say is cultural. If he's good he'll drain you like a sponge." The colonel bit her lips. "Damn, you're *not* going to be able to handle that, are you?"

"I understand what you're warning me about, Colonel. I'm

not sure I can do it, but I'll try."

"Not sure you can do it. *Peace* may hang on this. And several
billion lives. Your company, out there on the line. Put it on
that level. And you're scared and you're showing it, Lieutenant;
you're too damned open, no wonder they washed you out. Got
no hard center to you, no place to go to when I embarrass the
hell out of you, and *I'm* on your side. You're probably a damn
good special op, brave as hell, I know, you've got commend-
ations in the field. And that shell-shyness of yours probably
makes you drive real hard when you're in trouble. Good man.
Honest. If the elf wants a human specimen, we could do worse.
You just go in there, son, and you talk to him and you be your
nice self, and that's all you've got to do."

"We'll be bugged." DeFranco stared at the colonel deliberately, trying to dredge up some self-defense, give the impression he was no complete fool.

"Damn sure you'll be bugged. Guards right outside if you
want them. But you startle that elf I'll fry you."

"That isn't what I meant. I meant—I meant if I could get
him to talk there'd be an accurate record."

"Ah. Well. Yes. There will be, absolutely. And yes, I'm a
bastard, Lieutenant, same as that elf is, beyond a doubt. And
because I'm on your side I want you as prepared as I can get
you. But I'm going to give you all the backing you need—
you want anything, you just tell that staff and they better jump
to do it. I'm giving you carte blanche over there in the Science
Wing. Their complaints can come to this desk. You just be
yourself with him, watch yourself a little, don't get taken and
don't set him off."

"Yes, ma'am."

Another slow, consuming stare and a nod.

He was dismissed.

IV

So where's the hole we're digging end?
Why, it's neverneverdone, my friend.
Well, why's it warm at the other end?
Well, hell's neverneverfar, my friend.

"This colonel," says the elf, "it's her soldiers outside."

"That's the one," says deFranco.

"It's not the highest rank."

"No. It's not. Not even on this world." DeFranco's hands open and close on each other, white-knuckled. His voice stays calm. "But it's a lot of power. She won't be alone. There are others she's acting for. They sent me here. I've figured that now."

"Your dealing confuses me."

"Politics. It's all politics. Higher-ups covering their—" DeFranco rechooses his words. "Some things they have to abide by. They have to do. Like if they don't take a peace offer— that would be trouble back home. Human space is big. But a war—humans want it stopped. I know that. With humans, you can't quiet a mistake down. We've got too many separate interests. . . . We got scientists, and a half dozen different commands—"

"Will they all stop fighting?"

"Yes. My side will. I know they will." DeFranco clenches his hands tighter as if the chill has gotten to his bones. "If we can give them something, some solution. You have to understand what they're thinking of. If there's a trouble anywhere, it can grow. There might be others out there, you ever think of that? What if some other species just—wanders through? It's happened. And what if our little war disturbs them? We live in a big house, you know that yet? You're young, you, with your ships, you're a young power out in space. God help us, we've made mistakes, but this time the first one wasn't ours. We've been trying to stop this. All along, we've been trying to stop this."

"You're what I trust," says the elf. "Not your colonel. Not your treaty words. Not your peace. You. Words aren't the belief. What you do—that's the belief. What you do will show us."

"I can't!"

"I can. It's important enough to me and not to you. *Our little war.* I can't understand how you think that way."

"Look at that!" DeFranco waves a desperate hand at the room, the world. Up. "It's so big! Can't you see that? And one planet, one ball of rock. It's a little war. Is it worth it all? Is it worth such damn stubbornness? Is it worth dying in?"

"Yes," the elf says simply, and the sea-green eyes and the white face have neither anger nor blame for him.

DeFranco saluted and got out and waited until the colonel's orderly caught him in the hall and gave his escort the necessary authorizations, because *no one* wandered this base without an escort. (But the elvès are two hundred klicks out *there*, de-Franco thought; and who're we fighting anyway?) In the halls he saw the black of Union elite and the blue of Alliance spacers and the plain drab of the line troop officers, and the white and pale blue of the two Science Bureaus; while everywhere he felt the tenuous peace—damn, maybe we *need* this war, it's keeping humanity talking to each other, they're all fat and sleek and mud never touched them back here— But there was haste in the hallways. But there were tense looks on faces of people headed purposefully to one place and the other, the look of a place with something on its collective mind, with silent, secret emergencies passing about him— *The attack on the lines,* he thought, and remembered another time that attack had started on one front and spread rapidly to a dozen; and missiles had gone. And towns had died.

And the elvish kids, the babies in each others' arms and the birds fluttering down; and Dibs—Dibs lying in his armor like a broken piece of machinery—when a shot got you, it got the visor and you had no face and never knew it; or it got the joints and you bled to death trapped in the failed shell, you just lay there and bled: he had heard men and women die like that, still in contact on the com, talking to their buddies and going out alone, alone in that damn armor that cut off the sky and the air—

They brought him down tunnels that were poured and cast and hard overnight, *that* kind of construction, which they never got out on the Line. There were bright lights and there were dry floors for the fine officers to walk on; there was, at the end, a new set of doors where guards stood with weapons ready—

—against *us?* DeFranco got that sense of unreality again, blinked as he had to show his tags and IDs to get past even with the colonel's orders directing his escort.

Then they let him through, and further, to another hall with more guards. AlSec MPs. Alliance Security. The intelligence and Special Services. The very air here had a chill about it, with only those uniforms in sight. *They* had the elf. Of course they did. He was diplomatic property and the regs and the generals had nothing to do with it. He was in Finn's territory. Security and the Surface Tactical command, that the reg command only controlled from the top, not inside the structure. Finn had a leash, but she took no orders from sideways in the structure. Not even from AlSec. Check and balance in a joint command structure too many light-years from home to risk petty dictatorships. He had just crossed a line and might as well have been on another planet.

And evidently a call had come ahead of him, because there were surly Science Bureau types here too, and the one who passed him through hardly glanced at his ID. It was his face the man looked at, long and hard; and it was the Xenbureau interviewer who had been on the tape.

"Good luck," the man said. And a SurTac major arrived, dour-faced, a black man in the SurTac's khaki, who did not look like an office-type. *He* took the folder of authorizations and looked at it and at deFranco with a dark-eyed stare and a set of a square, well-muscled jaw. "Colonel's given you three hours, Lieutenant. Use it."

"We're more than one government," says deFranco to the elf, quietly, desperately. "We've fought in the past. We had wars. We made peace and we work together. We may fight again but everyone hopes not and it's less and less likely. War's expensive. It's too damn open out here, that's what I'm trying to tell you. You start a war and you don't know what else might be listening."

The elf leans back in his chair, one arm on the back of it. His face is solemn as ever as he looks at deFranco. "You and I, you-and-I. The world was whole until you found us. How can people do things that don't make sense? The *whole* thing makes sense, the parts of the thing are crazy. You can't put part of one thing into another, leaves won't be feathers, and your mind can't be our mind. I see our mistakes. I want to take them away. Then elves won't have theirs and you won't have yours. But you call it a little war. The lives are only a few. You have so many. You like your mistake. You'll keep it. You'll hold it in your arms. And you'll meet these others with it. But they'll see it, won't they, when they look at you?"

"It's crazy!"

"When we met you in it we assumed *we*. That was our first great mistake. But it's yours too."

DeFranco walked into the room where they kept the elf, a luxurious room, a groundling civ's kind of room, with a bed and a table and two chairs, and some kind of green and yellow pattern on the bedclothes, which were ground-style, free-hanging. And amid this riot of life-colors the elf sat crosslegged on the bed, placid, not caring that the door opened or someone came in—until a flicker of recognition seemed to take hold and grow. It was the first humanlike expression, virtually the only expression, the elf had ever used in deFranco's sight. Of course there were cameras recording it, recording everything. The colonel had said so and probably the elf knew it too.

"Saitas. You wanted to see me."

"DeFranco." The elf's face settled again to inscrutability.

"Shall I sit down?"

There was no answer. DeFranco waited for an uncertain moment, then settled into one chair at the table and leaned his elbows on the white plastic surface.

"They treating you all right?" deFranco asked, for the cameras, deliberately, for the colonel— *(Damn you, I'm not a fool, I can play your damn game, Colonel, I did what your SurTacs failed at, didn't I? So watch me.)*

"Yes," the elf said. His hands rested loosely in his red-robed lap. He looked down at them and up again.

"I tried to treat you all right. I thought I did."

"Yes."

"Why'd you ask for me?"

"I'm a soldier," the elf said, and put his legs over the side of the bed and stood up. "I know that you are. I think you understand me more."

"I don't know about that. But I'll listen." The thought crossed his mind of being held hostage, of some irrational violent behavior, but he pretended it away and waved a hand at the other chair. "You want to sit down? You want something to drink? They'll get it for you."

"I'll sit with you." The elf came and took the other chair, and leaned his elbows on the table. The bruises on his wrists showed plainly under the light. "I thought you might have gone back to the front by now."

"They give me a little time. I mean, there's—"

(Don't talk to him, the colonel had said. Let him talk.)

"—three hours. A while. You had a reason you wanted to see me. Something you wanted? Or just to talk. I'll do that too."

"Yes," the elf said slowly, in his lilting lisp. And gazed at him with sea-green eyes. "Are you young, deFranco? You make me think of a young man."

It set him off his balance. "I'm not all that young."

"I have a son and a daughter. Have you?"

"No."

"Parents?"

"Why do you want to know?"

"Have you parents?"

"A mother. Long way from here." He resented the questioning. Letters were all Nadya deFranco got, and not enough of them, and thank God she had closer sons. DeFranco sat staring at the elf who had gotten past his guard in two quick questions and managed to hit a sore spot; and he remembered what Finn had warned him. "You, elf?"

"Living parents. Yes. A lot of relatives?"

Damn, what trooper had they stripped getting that part of human language? Whose soul had they gotten into?

"What are you, Saitas? Why'd they hand you over like that?"

"To make peace. So the Saitas always does."

"Tied up like that?"

"I came to be your prisoner. You understand that."

"Well, it worked. I might have shot you; I don't say I would've, but I might, except for that. It was a smart move, I guess it was. But hell, you could have called ahead. You come up on us in the dark—you looked to get your head blown off. Why didn't you use the radio?"

A blink of sea-green eyes. "Others ask me that. Would you have come then?"

"Well, someone would. Listen, you speak at them in human language and they'd listen and they'd arrange something a lot safer."

The elf stared, full of his own obscurities.

"Come on, they throw you out of there? They your enemies?"

"Who?"

"The ones who left you out there on the hill."

"No."

"Friends, huh? *Friends* let you out there?"

"They agreed with me. I agreed to be there. I was most afraid you'd shoot them. But you let them go."

"Hell, look, I just follow orders."

"And orders led you to let them go?"

"No. They say to talk if I ever got the chance. Look, me, personally, I never wanted to kill you guys. I wouldn't, if I had the choice."

"But you do."

"Dammit, you took out our ships. Maybe that wasn't personal on your side either, but we sure as hell can't have you doing it as a habit. All you ever damn well had to do was go away and let us alone. You hit a world, elf. Maybe not much of one, but you killed more than a thousand people on that first ship. Thirty thousand at that base, good God, don't sit there looking at me like that!"

"It was a mistake."

"Mistake." DeFranco found his hands shaking. No. Don't raise the voice. Don't lose it. (Be your own nice self, boy. Patronizingly. The colonel knew he was far out of his depth. And he knew.) "Aren't most wars mistakes?"

"Do you think so?"

"If it is, can't we stop it?" He felt the attention of unseen listeners, diplomats, scientists—himself, special ops, talking to an elvish negotiator and making a mess of it all, losing everything. (Be your own nice self— The colonel was crazy, the elf was, the war and the world were and he lumbered ahead desperately, attempting subtlety, attempting a caricatured simplicity toward a diplomat and knowing the one as transparent as the other.) "You know all you have to do is say quit and there's ways to stop the shooting right off, ways to close it all down and then start talking about how we settle this. You say that's what you came to do. You're in the right place. All you have to do is get your side to stop. They're killing each other out there, do you know that? You come in here to talk peace. And they're coming at us all up and down the front. I just got word I lost a friend of mine out there. God knows what by now. It's no damn sense. If you can stop it, then let's stop it."

"I'll tell you what our peace will be." The elf lifted his face placidly, spread his hands. "There is a camera, isn't there? At least a microphone. They do listen."

"Yes. They've got camera and mike. I know they will."

"But your face is what I see. Your face is all human faces to me. They can listen, but I talk to you. Only to you. And this is our peace. The fighting will stop, and we'll build ships again and we'll go into space, and we won't be enemies. The mistake won't exist. That's the peace I want."

"So how do we do that?" (Be your own nice self, boy—DeFranco abandoned himself. Don't see the skin, don't see the face alien-like, just talk, talk like to a human, don't worry about protocols. *Do* it, boy.) "How do we get the fighting stopped?"

"I've said it. They've heard."

"Yes. They have."

"They have two days to make this peace."

DeFranco's palms sweated. He clenched his hands on the chair. "Then what happens?"

"I'll die. The war will go on."

(God, now what do I do, what do I say? How far can I go?) "Listen, you don't understand how long it takes us to make up our minds. We need more than any two days. They're dying out there, your people are killing themselves against our lines, and it's all for nothing. Stop it now. Talk to them. Tell them we're going to talk. Shut it down."

The slitted eyes blinked, remained in their buddha-like abstraction, looking askance into infinity. "DeFranco, there has to be payment."

(Think, deFranco, think. Ask the right things.)

"What payment? Just exactly who are you talking for? All of you? A city? A district?"

"One peace will be enough for you—won't it? You'll go away. You'll leave and we won't see each other until we've built our ships again. You'll begin to go—as soon as my peace is done."

"Build the ships, for God's sake. And come after us again?"

"No. The war is a mistake. There won't be another war. This is enough."

"But would everyone agree?"

"Everyone does agree. I'll tell you my real name. It's Angan. Angan Anassidi. I'm forty-one years old. I have a son named Agaita; a daughter named Siadi; I was born in a town named Daogisshi, but it's burned now. My wife is Llaothai Sohail, and she was born in the city where we live now. I'm my wife's only husband. My son is aged twelve, my daughter is nine.

They live in the city with my wife alone now and her parents and mine." The elvish voice acquired a subtle music on the names that lingered to obscure his other speech. "I've written— I told them I would write everything for them. I write in your language."

"Told who?"

"The humans who asked me. I wrote it all."

DeFranco stared at the elf, at a face immaculate and distant as a statue. "I don't think I follow you. I don't understand. We're talking about the front. We're talking about maybe that wife and those kids being in danger, aren't we? About maybe my friends getting killed out there. About shells falling and people getting blown up. Can we do anything about it?"

"I'm here to make the peace. Saitas is what I am. A gift to you. I'm the payment."

DeFranco blinked and shook his head. "Payment? I'm not sure I follow that."

For a long moment there was quiet. "Kill me," the elf said. "That's why I came. To be the last dead. The saitas. To carry the mistake away."

"Hell, no. No. We don't shoot you. Look, elf—all we want is to stop the fighting. We don't want your life. Nobody wants to kill you."

"DeFranco, we haven't any more resources. We want a peace."

"So do we. Look, we just make a treaty—you understand *treaty?*"

"I'm the treaty."

"A treaty, man, a treaty's a piece of paper. We promise peace to each other and not to attack us, we promise not to attack you, we settle our borders, and you just go home to that wife and kids. And I go home and that's it. No more dying. No more killing."

"No." The elf's eyes glistened within the pale mask. "No, deFranco, no paper."

"We make peace with a paper and ink. We write peace out and we make agreements and it's good enough; we do what we say we'll do."

"Then write it in your language."

"You have to sign it. Write your name on it. And keep the terms. That's all, you understand that?"

"Two days. I'll sign your paper. I'll make your peace. It's

nothing. Our peace is in me. And I'm here to give it."

"Dammit, we don't kill people for treaties."

The sea-colored eyes blinked. "Is one so hard and millions so easy?"

"It's different."

"Why?"

"Because—because—look, war's for killing; peace is for staying alive."

"I don't understand why you fight. Nothing you do makes sense to us. But I think we almost understand. We talk to each other. We use the same words. DeFranco, don't go on killing us."

"Just you. Just you, is that it? Dammit, that's crazy!"

"A cup would do. Or a gun. Whatever you like. DeFranco, have you never shot us before?"

"God, it's not the same!"

"You say paper's enough for you. That paper will take away all your mistakes and make the peace. But paper's not enough for us. I'd never trust it. You have to make my peace too. So both sides will know it's true. But there has to be a saitas for humans. Someone has to come to be a saitas for humans. Someone has to come to us."

DeFranco sat there with his hands locked together. "You mean just go to your side and get killed."

"The last dying."

"Dammit, you are crazy. You'll wait a long time for that, elf."

"You don't understand."

"You're damn right I don't understand. Damn bloody-minded lunatics!" DeFranco shoved his hands down, needing to get up, to get away from that infinitely patient and not human face, that face that had somehow acquired subtle expressions, that voice which made him forget where the words had first come from. And then he remembered the listeners, the listeners taking notes, the colonel staring at him across the table. Information. Winning was not the issue. Questions were. Finding out what they could. Peace was no longer the game. They were dealing with the insane, with minds there was no peace with. Elves that died to spite their enemies. That suicided for a whim and thought nothing about wiping out someone else's life.

He stayed in his chair. He drew another breath. He collected his wits and thought of something else worth learning. "What'd you do with the prisoners you learned the language from, huh? Tell me that?"

"Dead. We gave them the cup. One at a time they wanted it."

"Did they."

Again the spread of hands, of graceful fingers. "I'm here for all the mistakes. Whatever will be enough for them."

"Dammit, elf!"

"Don't call me that." The voice acquired a faint music. "Remember my name. Remember my name. DeFranco—"

He had to get up. He had to get up and get clear of the alien, get away from that stare. He thrust himself back from the table and looked back, found the elf had turned. Saitas-Angan smelled of something dry and musky, like spice. The eyes never opened wide, citrine slits. They followed him.

"Talk to me," the elf said. "Talk to me, deFranco."

"About what? About handing one of us to you? It won't happen. It bloody won't happen. We're not crazy."

"Then the war won't stop."

"You'll bloody die, every damn last one of you!"

"If that's your intention," the elf said, "yes. We don't believe you want peace. We haven't any more hope. So I come here. And the rest of us begin to die. Not the quiet dying. Our hearts won't stop. We'll fight."

"Out there on the lines, you mean."

"I'll die as long as you want, here. I won't stop my heart. The saitas can't."

"Dammit, that's not what we're after! That's not what we want."

"Neither can you stop yours. I know that. We're not cruel. I still have hope in you. I still hope."

"It won't work. *We can't do it,* do you understand me? It's against our law. Do you understand law?"

"Law."

"Right from wrong. Morality. For God's sake, killing's wrong."

"Then you've done a lot of wrong. You have your mistake too. DeFranco. You're a soldier like me. You know what your life's value is."

"You're damn right I know. And I'm still alive."

"We go off the course. We lose ourselves. You'll die for war but not for peace. I don't understand."

"I don't understand. You think we're just going to pick some poor sod and send him to you."

"You, deFranco. I'm asking you to make the peace."

"Hell." He shook his head, walked away to the door, colonel-be-hanged, listeners-be-hanged. His hand shook on the switch and he was afraid it showed. End the war. "The hell you say."

The door shot open. He expected guards. Expected—

—It was open corridor, clean prefab, tiled floor. On the tiles lay a dark, round object, with the peculiar symmetry and ugliness of things meant to kill. Grenade. Intact.

His heart jolted. He felt the doorframe against his side and the sweat ran cold on his skin, his bowels went to water. He hung there looking at it and it did not go away. He began to shake all over as if it were already armed.

"Colonel Finn." He turned around in the doorway and yelled at the unseen monitors. "Colonel Finn—get me out of here!"

No one answered. No door opened. The elf sat there staring at him in the closest thing to distress he had yet showed.

"Colonel! *Colonel, damn you!"*

More of silence. The elf rose to his feet and stood there staring at him in seeming perplexity, as if he suspected he witnessed some human madness.

"They left us a present," deFranco said. His voice shook and he tried to stop it. "They left us a damn present, elf. And they locked us in."

The elf stared at him; and deFranco went out into the hall, bent and gathered up the deadly black cylinder—held it up. "It's one of yours, elf."

The elf stood there in the doorway. His eyes looking down were the eyes of a carved saint; and looking up they showed color against his white skin. A long nailless hand touched the doorframe as the elf contemplated him and human treachery.

"Is this their way?"

"It's not mine." He closed his hand tightly on the cylinder, in its deadliness like and unlike every weapon he had ever handled. "It's damn well not mine."

"You can't get out."

The shock had robbed him of wits. For a moment he was not thinking. And then he walked down the hall to the main door and tried it. "Locked," he called back to the elf, who had joined him in his possession of the hall. The two of them together. DeFranco walked back again, trying doors as he went.

He felt strangely numb. The hall became surreal, his elvish companion belonging like him, elsewhere. "Dammit, what have you got in their minds?"

"They've agreed," the elf said. "They've agreed, deFranco."

"They're out of their minds."

"One door still closes, doesn't it? You can protect your life."

"You still bent on suicide?"

"You'll be safe."

"Damn them!"

The elf gathered his arms about him as if he too felt the chill. "The colonel gave us a time. Is it past?"

"Not bloody yet."

"Come sit with me. Sit and talk. My friend."

"Is it time?" asks the elf, as deFranco looks at his watch again. And deFranco looks up.

"Five minutes. Almost." DeFranco's voice is hoarse.

The elf has a bit of paper in hand. He offers it. A pen lies on the table between them. Along with the grenade. "I've written your peace. I've put my name below it. Put yours."

"I'm nobody. I can't sign a treaty, for God's sake." De-Franco's face is white. His lips tremble. "What did you write?"

"Peace," said the elf. "I just wrote peace. Does there have to be more?"

DeFranco takes it. Looks at it. And suddenly he picks up the pen and signs it too, a furious scribble. And lays the pen down. "There," he says. "There, they'll have my name on it." And after a moment: "If I could do the other—O God, I'm scared. I'm *scared.*"

"You don't have to go to my city," says the elf, softly. His voice wavers like deFranco's. "DeFranco—here, here they record everything. Go with me. Now. The record will last. We have our peace, you and I, we make it together, here, now. The last dying. Don't leave me. And we can end this war."

DeFranco sits a moment. Takes the grenade from the middle of the table, extends his hand with it across the center. He looks nowhere but at the elf. "Pin's yours," he says. "Go on. You pull it, I'll hold it steady."

The elf reaches out his hand, takes the pin and pulls it, quickly.

DeFranco lays the grenade down on the table between them, and his mouth moves in silent counting. But then he looks up

at the elf and the elf looks at him. DeFranco manages a smile.
"You got the count on this thing?"

The screen breaks up.

The staffer reached out her hand and cut the monitor, and Agnes
Finn stared past the occupants of the office for a time. Tears
came seldom to her eyes. They were there now, and she chose
not to look at the board of inquiry who had gathered there.

"There's a mandatory inquiry," the man from the reg command said. "We'll take testimony from the major this afternoon."

"Responsibility's mine," Finn said.

It was agreed on the staff. It was pre-arranged, the interview,
the formalities.

Someone had to take the direct hit. It might have been a
SurTac. She would have ordered that too, if things had gone
differently. High command might cover her. Records might be
wiped. A tape might be classified. The major general who had
handed her the mess and turned his back had done it all through
subordinates. And he was clear.

"The paper, Colonel."

She looked at them, slid the simple piece of paper back
across the desk. The board member collected it and put it into
the folder. Carefully.

"It's more than evidence," she said. "That's a treaty. The
indigenes know it is."

They left her office, less than comfortable in their official
search for blame and where, officially, to put it.

She was already packed. Going back on the same ship with
an elvish corpse, all the way to Pell and Downbelow. There
would be a grave there onworld.

It had surprised no one when the broadcast tape got an elvish
response. Hopes rose when it got the fighting stopped and
brought an elvish delegation to the front; but there was a bit
of confusion when the elves viewed both bodies and wanted
DeFranco's. Only DeFranco's.

And they made him a stone grave there on the shell-pocked
plain, a stone monument; and they wrote everything they knew
about him. *I was John Rand DeFranco,* a graven plaque said.
*I was born on a space station twenty light-years away. I left
my mother and my brothers. The friends I had were soldiers
and many of them died before me. I came to fight and I died*

for the peace, even when mine was the winning side. I died at the hand of Angan Anassidi, and he died at mine, for the peace; and we were friends at the end of our lives.

Elves—*suilti* was one name they called themselves—came to this place and laid gifts of silk ribbons and bunches of flowers—flowers, in all that desolation; and in their thousands they mourned and they wept in their own tearless, expressionless way.

For their enemy.

One of their own was on his way to humankind. For humankind to cry for. *I was Angan Anassidi,* his grave would say; and all the right things. Possibly no human would shed a tear. Except the veterans of Elfland, when they came home, if they got down to the world—they might, like Agnes Finn, in their own way and for their own dead, in front of alien shrine.

THE LAST CRUSADE

George H. Smith

"Julius Caesar named this place 'Lutetia Parisiorum,' which means 'the mud town of the Parissii.' Later on people got around to calling it 'the city of light,'" Marty Coleman was saying.

"Well, Julius was sure as hell a lot closer to the truth than those others," I tell him. We was sitting in the mud in what's left of some big building and me and Joe White was listening to Marty, our Sergeant, talking like he always does. When I says the Sergeant was talking I mean he was talking over the C.C., the company communication circuit, because what with having our mecho-armor on and the other side raising a little hell, we couldn't of heard him any other way.

"Yeah, I guess you're right, Ward. There isn't much light around here anymore," Coleman admitted.

"The only light you ever see around here these days is a flare or a rocket going over," White says in that funny flat voice of his.

From time to time Coleman would lift the headpiece of his armor above the pile of rubble in front of us and take a quick look out over the big open square toward where the enemy was holed up on the other side. About half the time he'd draw small arms or automatic fire.

"Those birds must have infrared eyepieces too," he says as he sets down.

"Ah they ain't even got mecho-armor," I says.

"No, but they have body armor and helmets with quite a bit of stuff in them."

"I'll bet they ain't got anything like we got." I was feeling pretty fine right then thinking how much better off we was than the poor joes in the infantry. We don't just fight in our suits, we live in 'em. They ain't only a mechanized suit of armor, they're our barracks, messroom and latrine and all radiation and rain proof. We got more fire power than a company of infantry and more radio equipment than a tank.

"You know there's lots worse ways of fighting a war," I says. "You climb into one of these babies and they seal you up like a sardine but at least you're warm and dry and you don't even have to use your own feet to walk. You got a nice little atomic power pack to move you around."

"You couldn't move the legs of one of these things if you had to," the Sergeant says.

"It . . . it just seems like a kind of funny way to fight a war," White says, talking like he always did, as though he had to hunt for every word before he said it.

"What's funny about it? They been fighting it this way for ten years, haven't they?" I demands.

"I guess so . . . I don't know . . ."

"Yeah, ten years. And the last five of it we've spent crawling back and forth in what used to be Paris," the Sergeant was talking again. "Just think . . . in the old wars they used to call it Gay Paree."

"It's gay all right," I says, following a movement on my ground radar screen. A beep had shown up, indicating activity over where the enemy was. Their guns was silent now but across the mud pools came their voices, voices that from time to time cut in on our circuits and competed with the voices of our own side.

Suddenly a girl was talking, a girl with a soft voice that was like warm lips against your ear. "Hello there, you fellows across the line. It's not much fun being here is it? Especially when you know that some non-draft back in the hometown walked off with your girl a long time ago.

"Honey Chile," the voice went on, "this is your old gal, Sally May, and I know how you all feel 'cause I used to be on the same side myself until I found out how things are over here in the People's Federal Democratic Eastern Republics . . ." The bleat of a code message cut through the syrupy tones, tore at our ears for a few moments and faded away. Slowly the sweet music drifted back.

"Well, fellows, we're gonna play you some real homey music in a few minutes, but first we're gonna tell you all about our contest. We know you all Yankee boys like contests and this one is a real humdinger."

"This here contest is open to every GI over there in the mecho-units. And have we got prizes? Why, honey, we sure have! Listen to this big first prize: $100,000 in gold! And then we have an expense paid vacation in the scenic Crimea and a brand new factory special Stalin sportscar. And fellows, get this: A TV appearance on a nationwide hookup with a dinner date afterwards with glamorous Sonia Nickolovich, the famous ballerina.

"Now I guess you boys are wonderin' what you gotta do to win these wonderful prizes. Well, this is how easy it is. All you gotta do is write out a thousand word statement on 'How my mecho-armor works' and deliver it along with your armor to the nearest P.F.D.E.R. army unit. Now . . . isn't that easy? And this contest is open to everyone but agents of the P.F.D.E.R. and their relatives."

The soft voice faded away.

"Why . . . the dirty— What do they think we are?"

Just on general principles I sent a half-dozen 75 mm shells in the direction of their lines.

"I don't—think I—understand that at all. What are they trying to do?" White asks. "I thought the enemy was Reds."

"You're in pretty bad shape, ain't you buddy?" I laughs. "Can't you even remember who you're fighting?"

"Leave him alone, will you, Ward," the Sergeant orders. "If you had been brain washed as many times as he has you'd have trouble remembering things too."

"Whatta ya mean?"

Sarge swung the big headpiece of his armor around and looked at White through his electric eyes. "How many times have you been captured, Whitey?" he asks.

"I . . . I don't know, Sarge. I don't remember. Twice . . . I guess."

"That's two brain washings from the enemy and two re-washings from our own psycho units. Four electronic brain washings don't leave much in a man's brain."

"Well, I'll be damned. Which side was you on first, Whitey?" I asks.

"I don't know . . . I don't remember."

"Ah come on now, you must know. Was you a Russian or an American? Western Democratic People's Federal Republics or People's Federal Democratic Eastern Republics—which side?"

"I . . . don't know. All I know is that they ain't good and we got to fight them until we kill all of them."

"How do you know they ain't good?" I demands. "If you don't know which side you was on to start with, maybe you was shootin' at your own brothers this morning . . . or your mother."

"You better watch your mouth, Ward. There might be a Loyalty Officer tuned in on the band. You wouldn't want a probe, would you?" Coleman asks.

"Ah, they ain't listenin', Sarge. This guy gives me the willies. He don't know nothin' but how to run that damn armor and how to fight. He don't even know who he was to start with."

"I wish I did know . . . I wish I . . ."

"You know, Whitey, maybe you was a big shot on the other side. Maybe you was Joe Stalin's grandson or something."

"Remember!" an eager voice whispered in our ears. *"Remember what you are fighting for. In the W.D.P.F.R. there are more washing machines than in any place else in the world!"*

I had to laugh. "You ever seen a washing machine, Sarge?" I asks.

Coleman was looking back toward our lines. "Yeah. There used to be a place called Brooklyn that was full of 'em. You know, there's something going on back there. The whole company seems to be moving up. And there's a big armored crawler there with a smaller one parked beside it."

He sits back down with a clanking of armor. "Must be some big shots coming around to see how we're winning the war."

"I wish someone would use a can opener on me right now and take me out of this walking sardine can and plump me into a washing machine. I ain't been clean in five years," I says.

"Do they have washing machines on the other side?" Whitey wants to know.

"Naw. They ain't got nothin' like that, nothin' at all," I tells him. "Things like washing machines is reserved for us capitalists."

"If we got washing machines and they ain't, then what are we fighting for?" Whitey asks.

"You better ask the Sarge that. He's the intellectual around here. He reads all the comic books and things."

"Why do you think we're fighting, Whitey?" Coleman asks.

"Well, Sarge . . . I don't know. If I could just remember who I used to be, I'd know. Sometime I'm gonna remember. Every once in a while I can almost . . . but then I don't."

"Well, why do you *think* we're fighting?" I asks.

"Well . . . well . . . I guess it's that there's bad guys and good guys . . . just like in the comics or on the TV shows. We're the good guys and they're the bad guys. Is that right, Sarge?"

"I don't know, Whitey. That might be some of it but I kinda think that maybe it has something to do with when we won the last war or thought we won it. We thought we had finished with the Nazis but I guess maybe we got fooled. In Europe the Nazis all turned Communist and in America the Commies all turned Nazi. Either way people like them have always got the jump on the joes in between. In Europe they pointed at them and called them Nazis. In America they pointed at them and called them Reds. Pretty soon people didn't know the difference, except that it was better to be pointing than to be pointed at."

"Now, Sarge, you're the one that better be careful. You wouldn't want the Loyalty Officer to be hearing that sort of talk, would you?" I cuts in.

"Maybe you're right but I kinda think that's why . . ."

Just then the command circuit in our helmets opened up with orders for us to pull back and join the rest of the company. All the way back Whitey doesn't say anything so I figure he's trying to remember who he is. Well, we gets back to the command post without drawing more than a little small arms fire and a couple of rockets, but things is really popping there. The big crawler Coleman seen from our outpost is settin' there in the middle of the street and the whole company is gathered around it.

"What's goin' on?" I say as I sidle up beside Fred Dobshanski.

"Don't you guys know? There's a big drive comin' up. General Mac Williams is gonna talk to us himself."

Whitey was right beside me. He sure was a funny guy, always hanging around and asking questions. Sometimes I used to wonder what he looked like. You get used to not seeing any of the guys when you're in the forward areas. Sometimes for weeks or months at a time a whole area will be contaminated with bacteria or radiation and you don't open your suit at all. Even if you're wounded the mecho-armor gives you a shot and takes you back to a field hospital . . . that is, if it's still working. So you get used to not knowing what the guys look like and not caring much. But with Whitey it was different. His voice had such a dull someplace-else sound to it that you got to wondering if there was really anyone in that suit of armor or not. You got to wondering if maybe it just walked around by itself.

"Mac Williams? Who's he?" Whitey asks as if in answer to my thoughts.

"Hell, don't you know anything?" Fred says.

"I guess I don't. I . . . I . . . don't even know who I was. I sorta wish I knew who I used to be."

"Mac Williams is Fightin' Joe Mac Williams. He's going to talk to us. Look . . . there he is now."

I adjusted my eyepieces for direct vision and sure enough on the kind of balcony on the back of this big armored crawler was a guy. I mean to tell you he sure looked like something too. He was in full battle armor with scarlet trimmings and gold rivets. He was wearing a mother-of-pearl plated helmet with three stars set in rubies. Even the twin machine guns that were fitted to his armor instead of the 75 recoilless and 40 mm we had on ours was plated to look like silver.

"Gosh! Imagine a General coming 'way up here in all this mud and stuff. That guy must really have guts!" someone mutters on the company circuit.

"Yeah. I bet he's only got one swimming pool in that land yacht of his."

"Shut up! What's the matter with you? That ain't no way to talk. You a sub or something?"

"Say, did you guys see what I saw through the windows of that crawler? Dames!"

"Dames?"

"Who you kiddin'?"

"So help me. There was two of them. Two big, tall, willowy, blond WAC Captains!"

"Them's the General's aides."

"Yeah? What do they aid him at?"

"Shut up you guys," the Captain's voice cuts in. "The General is going to speak."

Well then he starts right in telling us about the great crusade we're engaged upon and how civilization is at stake. And how proud the home folks is of us. Of course, he admits we haven't had any direct word from the States since last year when we had those big cobalt bomb raids, but he just knows that they all love us. Right when he starts I know we're in for trouble, 'cause when the brass start talking about crusades, a lot of joes is gonna get killed.

He goes on with this for half an hour, and all the time the TV cameras is grinding away from this other crawler that is filled with newsers and video people. He mentions blood sixteen times and that ain't good. Sweat he says fourteen times and guts an even dozen. When it really looks bad, though, is when he calls the Major and the Captain up and pins a medal on each of the medal racks that officers wear on the front of their armor. When they start passing out the medals ahead of time, brother, it ain't good, it ain't good at all.

When he gets through with all this, the old boy retires into his crawler.

"I guess he's going to plan the battle," I says.

"Ha," says Sergeant Coleman's voice in my ear. "All the blood and guts in that speech wore him out so much he's got to retire to his bar for a few quick ones with them two aides of his."

"Now, Sarge," I says, "that ain't no way for a patriot to talk."

"My patriotism is at a very low ebb at the moment. Do you know what kind of a party we're going to have in the morning?"

"No," I says, "but I would be interested in finding out."

"You've seen that huge mile-long building that's across the square from us?"

"I've seen it and found little to like about it. The enemy has every kind of gun in there that's been invented."

"Well, the Captain says that that's it! Fighting Joe wants us to take it."

"Remember boys, remember that the way of life in the

*W.D.P.F.R. is better. Remember what you're fighting for—
hotdogs and new cars, electric refrigerators and apple pie,
sweethearts and mother. Don't let mother down boys!"*

A voice that used to sell us bath soap is selling us war.

"That kind of sounds like we're getting ready to move in,
don't it Sarge?" I says.

Sure enough a half hour later we starts to move up. The
whole company of thirty men is on its way with the rest of the
battalion close behind.

"Say, maybe there'll be some dames up ahead," Dobshanski
is saying.

"What do you want with dames? You got the Waiting Wife
and the Faithful Sweetheart on your TV, ain't you?" the Sergeant says.

"It ain't the same. It ain't the same at all," Dobshanski says.

I cuts in with, "Hey, did you guys hear what I heard? Pretty
soon we won't really need women anymore. Those new suits
of armor we're going to get have got Realie TV sets in 'em.
When a gal comes on it's just like she was in the suit with
you. Those suits is gonna take care of everything and I mean
everything."

"Ah, who ya kiddin'? Who ya handin' that line to?"

"Him and his inside dope!"

Twenty minutes later we're in position among the wrecked
buildings on our side of the square and several kinds of hell is
traveling back and forth across it. As is usual, the enemy seems
to have as good an idea as to what we're about as we have.

"Oh, brother," Coleman moans. "Did Mac Williams send
them a copy of his orders as soon as he got through writing
them?"

Heavy shells and rockets is plowing up the already plowed up
pavement all around us. Geysers of mud and water are being
lifted by shells on all sides. I see a couple of guys go down
and I stumbles over a tangled mess of armor and flesh as we
break from cover and start across the hundred yards or so of
the square.

Floater rockets are overhead, circling kind of lazy like and
lighting up the whole company as pretty as flares. It's real
comfortin' to see guys on all sides of you, but not so comfortin'
when you sees them fallin' right and left.

I know I'm running with the rest of the guys 'cause I can

hear my power pack rev up and feel the steel legs of my suit pounding along through the mud. I can feel the suit automatically swerving to avoid shell holes and to throw off the enemy aim. Not that they're really aiming, they're just tossing everything they got into that square and bettin' on the law of averages. The whole length of the big marble building we're after is lit up now, but not with lights, it's lit up with gun flashes.

The company and batallion radio bands is a mess. Even the command circuit is filled with guys yellin' and screamin', but there don't seem to be much point to orders right now anyway. I keep on goin' cause I don't know what else to do. Once or twice I recognize Coleman and White by the numbers on their armor and I get one glimpse of Fred Dobshanski just as half a dozen 70 mm shells tear his armor and him apart.

Then I'm almost at the building, and I'm being hit by point-blank light machine-gun fire. I'm blazing back with my 40 and 75, pouring tracers through the windows and being thankful my armor can take machine-gun fire even at close range.

There's other guys all around me now and we're smashing through doors and crashing over window sills into the building. The place is full of enemy joes and they're hitting us with everything they can throw. I take a couple of 40 mm shells that knock me off my feet, but Whitey blasts the gun crew two seconds later. We fight our way up a pair of marble stairways and they're really pouring it on us from up above, when suddenly they take a notion to rush us and come rushing down the steps . . . about three hundred of them.

What we did to them ain't pretty. That light plastic battle armor of theirs don't even look like stopping our stuff; and packed together like they are on those steps, it's murder. A lot of them get to the bottom, but there ain't much left of them when they get there.

It's all over then. Guys are yelling for the Medic robot and for the Ammo robots and others are just slumped down in their suits waiting for something else to happen . . . and it ain't long in happening. It can't be more than ten minutes after we chased the last Reds out the back of our objective before their heavy guns're trying to knock it down around our ears.

Armor or no armor, what's left of the battalion takes refuge in the cellars where a few hours before the Reds were playing possum from our guns. Coleman, Whitey and I find us a nice heavy beam and are standing under it. Coleman is talking, as usual, and Whitey is wondering who he is and I'm watching the Major and Captain take inventory. Our assets ain't what they used to be. There's about twenty guys left in our company and maybe about sixty-five in the whole battalion.

I guess that's why the Major ain't very friendly when some of the guys dig out a couple dozen women and children who've been hiding in the building.

"Well, I'll be damned! Look what's comin' in!" I says to Coleman. There's maybe twenty women and the rest is kids.

"Why do the kids always seem to outlast the rest of the people, Sarge?" I asks. "Every place we been in this town, there's always more kids left alive than older folks."

"I don't know, Ward. Maybe they make a smaller target."

They've already got the kids lined up and we've given 'em the candy bars wrapped in propaganda leaflets that we all carry. Like all foreigners, they ain't very polite or grateful. They can't even understand what I'm saying even when I turn up my outside amplifier full power.

"What's the matter with them punks? Don't they appreciate candy?" I asks the Sergeant who is muttering to one of them in some of their own gibberish.

"They say the Russians didn't give them anything but lumps of sugar and we don't give them anything but candy. They'd like something else."

"Now ain't that just like people like them," I says to White. "No gratitude to us for liberating them or for feedin' 'em."

"I think I would know what it's all about if I could just remember. You know, Sarge, for a few minutes up above there I almost remembered. Then the shelling started and . . . and . . . I don't know . . ." Whitey is still harping on his favorite subject so I turns back to the Sergeant and the kids he's talkin' to.

"What's with these punks? What they got to complain about? If it wasn't for us they wouldn't have no country."

"They say that the Russians was about to take them away to a camp and make soldiers out of them and they're afraid we'll do the same."

"Well . . . what in hell do they want to do? Spend the rest of their lives hiding in a hole while we do their fighting?"

"This youngster says he doesn't want to be brain washed. He doesn't want to be a soldier."

"He's right," Whitey pipes up. "He don't want to be like me. You know, I had a dream . . . or did I remember? Anyway in this ... dream ... of mine, I remembered that I had been an important person like you said, Ward. But not on the enemy side. I knew something and wanted to tell it to the whole army but they didn't want me to. That's why they sent me to the psycho machines. That's why they made me like I am."

"What was it you knew, White?" the Sergeant asks.

"I'm not sure. It was something ... something about there not being any more Western Federation or any Eastern Republics ... no more America ... no more Russia ... just two self-perpetuating armies ... like hordes of maggots crawling across the corpse of Europe."

"That's a funny sort of dream ... a very funny sort of dream," the Sergeant says.

"Why would you have any sort of crazy dream like that?" I demands. "You know we hear broadcasts about how things are getting along so fine back home all the time."

"How long's it been since you got a letter, Ward?" Coleman asks.

"Letter? I don't remember. Who'd write to me anyway? What's the matter with them kids? Do they want the Russians to come back and rape their mothers and sisters?"

"I'll ask them," Sarge says, and starts gibbering again through his outside amplifier to a skinny brat that's doing the talking for all of them. Pretty quick the kid gabbles back just like he understood.

"He says that their mothers and sisters have been raped so many times by both sides that it don't make any difference anymore."

"They ain't got no grat ..." I starts to say but the Major is yelling at the Captain so I stop to listen.

"Where are their men? Where are they hiding?" He shakes his fist under the noses of these French women and the Captain questions them.

"Why did they permit the Russians to hide out in this building? Don't they know that being here is collaborating with the enemy? Where are their men? I'll have them hung!" The Major is really hopping mad.

"I beg your pardon, sir." The Captain interrupts him. "This woman says that their men are on the second floor and ..."

"Good! Send six men up there and hang every one of them."

"Sir, they say that the Russians have already hung them. As American collaborationists, sir!"

"What! Humph! Well . . . send some men up there to cut them down and hang them again. No! Wait, Captain! We'll wait until the TV cameras get here."

It was just then that the word came for us to pull back, for us to give up this building and fall back to our old positions.

"My God! What's the matter with them?" Whitey asks. "After all the guys we lost taking this place, why do we have to give it up?"

"Maybe they want us to do it over again for the TV," the Sergeant says as we watch the other two companies pull out, herding the civilians before them.

"I don't want to go," Whitey says suddenly. "If I stay here I might remember."

"To hell with it, Whitey," Coleman tells him. "Maybe you wouldn't like it if you did remember. Maybe you're better off this way."

"I like it here. There used to be pictures up above . . . I found a piece of one during the fighting . . . it was . . . beautiful."

"Come on, Whitey! Let's get going! Don't you see what the Captain's doing?" I says. The others look and start moving fast. The Captain must have been mad about giving up our objective 'cause he'd set up a disruptor bomb on the floor and started a time fuse. Maybe you've never seen a disruptor bomb and maybe you wouldn't want to. In a way they're an improvement on the atomic bomb. They cause individual atomic explosions that keep blasting for hours after you start them. When the bomb gets through, there won't be anything left.

Pretty quick we're out in the open and running as fast as our mecho-legs can carry us. We're about halfway across the square when I see Whitey suddenly break away from Coleman and head back toward the building.

He gets there and is heading in the door just as the disruptor bomb lets loose. That building started doing a dance, a kind of strip tease I guess 'cause it's shedding roof and walls right and left.

Later on, when we're back in our lines, I'm sitting beside Coleman while our mecho-armor is whipping up some X-rations for us.

"Why did he do it, Sarge? Why'd Whitey go back?"

"I don't know. There was something about that building that he thought he remembered. It reminded him of something. That picture he found kind of set him off. He said maybe it was the last one there was in the world."

"Did . . . he remember who he was?"

"I guess at the last he did . . . or at least he remembered something."

"Did he remember his name?"

"I guess so."

"Well, what was it?"

"He didn't tell me. Maybe his name was Man."

"Man? That's a funny name. Well . . . his name sure is mud now."

"Maybe the two names are the same, Ward," he says. The Sergeant always was a funny guy.

HIRED MAN

Richard C. Meredith

The burning city was a hideously beautiful sight below them when Brand finally called a halt.

"Stop here for just a minute."

His breath was coming hard and for the first time in longer than he could remember he was conscious of the enormous mass of a fully armored combat suit.

"What for?" Davidson's voice came through Brand's earphones. But Davidson paused in his loping, reaction-pack-assisted run toward the crest looming above. "There's enough of them left to chase us."

"Let me catch my breath," Brand said, hating to hear himself admit fatigue.

"It can't be more than a couple of kilometers or so," Wisse said, having stopped a few meters beyond Davidson and remaining barely visible to Brand, a vaguely monstrous, ghostlike shape in the darkness and among wind-twisted trees of the mountainside.

"I know," Brand gasped.

The suit was too damned heavy. Something was wrong in the feedback. Something was wrong in this whole setup.

"Brand," Davidson blurted. "How do you read rendezvous?"

Brand dropped to one knee on the rocky mountainside,

turning away from the burning city below. He flashed a time reading on the inside of his helmet's faceplate.

"Three minutes," he said.

"Then let's get the hell out of here."

Brand sighed, knowing that there was no point in arguing. They had to make rendezvous or they were stuck on New Iowa for good. As trustworthy as he believed the Dravians to be, he knew they would not make two runs down to pick them up. If he, Davidson and Wisse—sole survivors of the raiding party that had hit the colonial city—did not make rendezvous they were on their own.

"Roger."

Brand could see the faint glow of Wisse's reaction pack as it assisted him in a six-meter leap up the mountain slope. Davidson, too, jump-jetted up the slope toward the plateau and the homing signal transmitted from the rendezvous site.

Brand paused and looked back down into the burning city below for longer than he should have. Better than half of New Iowa City was now aflame. Mildly Brand regretted what he and the others had had to do. They really had not planned on destroying more than a few essential places—power stations, water works, central communications, things like that. But neither had they counted on the kind of resistance the colonists had put up. The half-assed farmer-colonists from Old Earth had never shown much in the way of defenses in the past.

The homing transmitter flashed a reading on Brand's faceplate. Looking up the slope toward the crest, he found he could see neither Davidson nor Wisse. He had to catch up.

The reaction pack kicked at his back and his feet kicked at the earth below him. The force of his legs was amplified a dozen times by the suit and he moved cursing all New Iowans—and the particular one who had blown a building out from under him with an H.E. bomb he hadn't suspected that the colonists possessed. Well, they hadn't figured on the colonists' coming up with combat suits either. Still, he'd been hit harder than he thought. The damned suit had been damaged—read-outs told him so clearly enough—but not so badly that he couldn't get to the pickup site, even if he did have to work a little harder at it. He sure as hell wasn't going to let the Dravians take off without him—not with what they owed him.

It was kick and jet, kick and jet. Sluggish though it was, the combat suit carried him up the slope, over the rough, ancient boulders and angular outcroppings of rock, over and around the gnarled trees, up toward the safety of the plateau.

Another full minute had passed before he crested the plateau and landed again on level, solid earth. Snapping the night visor down with a twist of his head, through infrared he made out the dim figures of Davidson and Wisse no more than half a kilometer away. Few trees up here obscured the view and the ground itself was surprisingly level. An odd geological formation, some remote part of his mind commented—but somehow these mountains reminded him of home, the harsh beauty of Breakdown Heights where mere survival was something to be proud of. Not like the soft living the damned New Iowans had in the lush valleys below.

Where Davidson and Wisse stood had to be the place, Brand told himself. The image projected against his faceplate agreed. The homer was transmitting from straight ahead. And a time projection remained until rendezvous. The Dravian corvette ought to be coming into view any time.

Running, leaping, assisted by the reaction pack but still fighting the sluggishness of the suit, he crossed the distance to where his companions stood.

"You almost blew it," Davidson said sarcastically.

"We all almost blew it," Brand replied, remembering what had happened in the city below.

"They ought to be in sight," Davidson said, looking up into the night sky again. "Ought to be firing retros by now."

"Ought to be," Wisse repeated quietly. "Which way would they come?"

"From the north, I think," Brand replied, flashing a compass image on his faceplate and then looking into the sky in that direction.

"We ought to see 'em by now," Davidson said.

Brand read the time.

"They're due."

"More than due," Wisse said. "They're fifteen seconds late."

"Give them a chance," Davidson said. "They'll show up."

"Yeah, I know they will," Wisse half-heartedly agreed.

"Well, the Fuzzies never failed us before." Davidson's voice was almost angry.

"There's always a first time," Wisse said but apparently regretted it immediately.

He forced a laugh that did nothing to cheer Brand.

Neither Brand nor Davidson spoke. They just read the time, looked back at the sky, read the time again.

Davidson, with reddish-blonde hair and a florid face beneath the helmet of his combat suit, was the biggest of the three men. But even he was not tall when compared with most representatives of mankind. Breakdown Heights, with a gravity of nearly one-and-a-half Gs, was noted for the strength and endurance of its natives, not their height.

Brand was shorter than Davidson, though he made up for his lack of height by the width and massiveness of his shoulders. His face, too, was wide. His eyes were deep, dark pools behind the covering of his helmet. He was the loner of the group, a man with few friends, one whose quick temper did not encourage close relationships. Now he was doing an excellent job of keeping his temper in check. He knew he had to.

Wisse was shorter still than Brand and slighter of build— but still a man whose physical strength had been nurtured by the massive, desolate homeworld of the mercenaries. His thin face could barely be seen inside his helmet.

There was growing concern on it.

"A full minute," he said. "They've never been late for a pickup before." His voice was seriously worried.

"How far behind us do you think they were?" Davidson asked.

"Ten minutes maybe," Brand replied, feeling the concern beginning to grow within himself. "Parker slowed them down when he set off that mini A-bomb in the river."

"I hope he slowed them," Wisse said.

I do, too . . .

Brand remembered that Parker himself had died in the miniature nuclear blast that had widened the river into a new lake in the center of the city. Beyond that it was all a jumble in his mind now, what happened down there in New Iowa City. But it had clearly been an ambush—the New Iowans fitted out in combat suits as good as those of the raiders, coming out of doorways, leaping from roofs, moving with the precision of trained troops, in moments surrounding the raiders who had expected to meet no real resistance at all. The New Iowans had never known anything like that before, not when the mercenaries had hit the farms and smaller towns.

Some good men died there, he told himself. Twenty-seven of the hardest mercenaries in the galaxy had bought it before the

three of them—four, but Parker had not made it all the way—
fought their way out of the trap, throwing thermos and H.E.'s
and everything else they had in every direction and made it up
the mountain to the plateau and the rendezvous spot.

Dammit, I wish they'd hurry, Brand told himself.

"Two minutes," Davidson said, his voice a dead calm.

"What's wrong with them?" Wisse demanded.

"They'll come," Brand said. He was senior man now. He
ought to take command, if you could call it that. "Their timing's
just off, that's all."

He looked up at the sky again. Still nothing, still an absolute
nothing, unless you counted the brilliant stars of New Iowa's
sky, something you didn't when you were looking for a Dravian
corvette.

"Wisse," he said suddenly, "go back to the cliff and see if
the farmers really are following us."

"What if the Fuzzies come?" Wisse demanded.

"If they come, we'll make them wait."

"No, you go."

Brand swung up his right arm, the one whose sleeve housed
the rocket launcher. He leveled it at the chest of Wisse's suit.

"Go back and look."

Wisse did not speak but after a few moments and another
search of the sky he turned and loped back toward the edge of
the plateau.

"Wonder what's keeping them," Davidson muttered, apparently more to himself than to Brand.

"Bad timing."

"Nonsense. You ever heard of a Fuzzy being a second off?
I don't like none of this."

Turning toward the plateau's edge, Brand said through the
radio link, "See anything, Wisse?"

"They're coming up."

Panic was in the other man's voice.

Damn.

Brand wondered who had picked Wisse for a mercenary.
He ought to be a *klopak* fisherman, starting to break down at
the first little—and then he remembered the slaughter of the
city. The picture was damned near impossible—he didn't know
whether to be ashamed of the Breakdowners or whether to
admire the colonists. If they really were colonists—he pondered for a moment. But if not New Iowans, who then?

"How many?" he asked.

"Can't tell," said Wisse's voice in his earphones. "Couple of dozen."

"Can't be," Davidson said. "There couldn't have been so many of 'em left. Parker must've killed off a whole squad himself."

"Calm down and count them," Brand commanded. "They ought to be emitting enough infrared for that."

He checked the time. Five minutes. Hard to believe Dravians could be that far off schedule.

"Fourteen," Wisse's voice said after a while. "I clearly count fourteen of them in combat suits."

His voice was calmer now. He had regained control of himself.

"Too many," Davidson said. "We couldn't hold 'em."

"We might have to," Brand said. "They can't be much better off than we are."

"They haven't been under full power as long as we have," Davidson replied.

Brand nodded in agreement but said, "Better check all our systems." Then to Wisse: "How far away?"

"Less than halfway up the slope," the other replied. "It'll take them a good ten minutes to get up here."

And if the Fuzzies don't show up in another ten minutes . . .

Brand let his thoughts trail off.

"Come on back," he said.

While he waited for Wisse's return he made a quick readout of his suit systems and wished he hadn't. The suit was worse off than he thought. More than half of his all-important feedback circuits had already gone to backups and a few were out altogether. Ammunition was just about gone, as was the internal air supply, though he could switch to external if things didn't get too hot. Fuel for the reaction pack was next to nothing and his power cells—well, you could expect only so much out of the thumbnail-size cells these suits carried and he had been running hard ever since he hit the atmosphere just after the beginning of New Iowa's long night.

"How is it?" he asked Davidson.

"The suit? Still working but I don't have much power left. Hour or two."

You're ahead of me . . .

Brand read the time. The Dravians were an impossible seven-and-a-half minutes late.

Wisse was back and began to check out his own suit systems.

"You act like you're runnin' the show now, Brand," Davidson said. "How do you figure it?"

"I don't," Brand answered. "I just wait here until they come for us."

"And what if they don't come?" Wisse asked, that edge of panic returning to his voice.

Brand's voice was cold. "They will."

"How can you be so damn sure?" Davidson demanded. "They ain't people. How do you know what they decided to do. Hell, man, we don't even know why we're fightin' here."

"How long have we been working for the Fuzzies?" Brand asked.

"Nearly a standard," Davidson replied.

"Have they ever failed us yet?"

"Like Wisse said—"

"They'll show! In the meantime we'd better prepare a defensive position."

"You're out of your mind," Davidson said. "Wisse counted fourteen of 'em. We got no choice but to run." Obviously Davidson did not like to use the word but he used it. "We can carry the homer so the Fuzzies'll know where we are."

"The homer was for us," Brand said as matter-of-factly as he could. "They're not using it. They've got their own systems."

"Still, they could monitor it," Wisse said.

"They said they'd pick us up here," Brand said.

"Yeah, and they said they'd do it nine minutes ago."

The three men stood glaring at each other through the thick helmets of their combat suits. Maybe the others could run, Brand thought, for a little while. They had more reserve power than he had—their suits were in better shape. But he knew that his suit would not carry him more than a couple of kilometers. And when he did have to fight again he wanted some power for what weapons systems he had left.

"Ten minutes now," Davidson said, his voice oddly quiet. "In less than five they're going to come busting over that crest and those boys are mad. I ain't fool enough to stand around and wait for them."

"Wait five more minutes," Brand said, neither commanding nor begging. He no longer gave a damn what they did.

"No," Davidson said and looked to Wisse for agreement.

"We're taking the homer and we're heading for those peaks over to the east. Maybe if we get there we can hold them off."

"For how long?"

"A hell of a lot longer than we could from here."

Eleven minutes. Maybe the Dravians really aren't coming. They aren't human. How do you know what they're really thinking?

During those agonizing waits, memories flashed through Brand's mind—one of the Dravians coming to Breakdown Heights and hiring a troop of mercenaries to drive the colonists from Old Earth off Brahiban III, or New Iowa, as the colonists and Earth's federation called the planet. Mercenaries prided themselves on being what they were—why not fight against humans on the side of a bunch of stubby, red, six-legged Dravians? The Fuzzies paid in hard cash and what did the men of Breakdown Heights owe New Iowa, or even Earth?

Breakdowners had fought for and against just about every sentient race in the galaxy anyway. What did a little terrorism on New Iowa matter?

But what if the Dravians had decided not to pay off?

The eventuality seemed unlikely. The Fuzzies didn't work that way .

The Dravians would come. They had simply been delayed. By what?

Twelve minutes. At last Davidson spoke again.

"You comin' with us?"

"Take the homer. I'll stay here."

"You're a damned fool."

"We'll see."

Brand turned his attention away from the others and began to search for something that resembled a defensive position. He saw a few trees and a few boulders—and up ahead about half a kilometer or so was a sizable depression in the ground, as well sheltered as anything on the plateau.

"Brand," Davidson said suddenly after he had picked up the homing transmitter and tucked it under his arm. "Come with us. You don't stand a chance here."

"I don't have power enough to make it halfway to those peaks of yours," he said slowly, bitterly. "I'm better off here."

Thirteen minutes. The combat-suited and deadly furious New Iowans would be coming over the crest any time now.

"I guess you know what you're doing," Davidson said.

"I hope you do," Brand replied.

Brand could hear Davidson's snort through the earphones of his helmet but none of the three men spoke again.

Turning his back on his companions, Brand bit down on the switch that broke him from the radio link and, as quickly as he could, crossed the distance to the depression. By the time he reached it and turned to look back, Davidson and Wisse had vanished, moving toward the peaks some kilometers away. He wondered if they would make it and what they would do when they got there.

Settling back in what protection the broken earth, stone and few trees offered, he threw one more glance skyward. Nothing. No bright movement there to indicate the arrival of the Dravians.

His gaze dropped to the edge of the plateau, where the fourteen New Iowans would soon be arriving.

That some people might consider this a bad way to die never entered his mind. His father and his father before him had died on alien worlds, fighting other people's battles. He had always expected to go that way, too. But he had hoped for a few more visits to Breman's Planet before that time came. Well, he could remember the last visit—and that had been one hell of a time.

He shifted the energy rifle from his backpack, fitted it into the suit's shoulder socket, checked the weapon's internal power and was gratified to see that it still had a little charge. He could draw from his suit cells for the rifle but decided against it. He would need that power for other things.

Sighting the weapon along the plateau's horizon, he waited.

And while he waited he could not help but wonder about the sincerity of the aliens for whom he worked. They had never before given him any reason to doubt them. Now he could only wait a little longer, give them the benefit of his doubts and hope they would show up soon.

Then he saw, through his night visor, the infrared glow of a man's warm body and the heat of an operating combat suit. He felt no recoil as the energy rifle fired. The weapon's brilliant blaze was only partially dimmed by the night visor and the polarization of the helmet's filters. For an instant the combat-suit figure blazed with the same light—then exploded.

One down. Brand flashed a time reading on the inside of his helmet. The Fuzzies were a full fifteen minutes late.

No further movement came along the horizon for a while. When it did come it was hard to see, even with the night visor. The New Iowans had cut back on the infrared emission of their suits—damned good suits for a bunch of farmers.

They were almost invisible when they topped the crest, six or seven of them at once, and rushed forward.

Brand depressed the firing stud of the rifle, made a quick sweep across his field of fire and saw at least one man fall backward down the slope, his combat suit exploding flames. The others, though, fell forward, their arms arching above their heads as, suit-assisted, they threw.

Grenades shattered the earth and rocks of the plateau.

The colonists had had no time to get his position. They were throwing blind.

Brand licked the dryness of his lips, pulled at his suit's water nipple.

A dozen meters or less to his left a grenade exploded, showering him with broken stone, shaking the earth under him.

Brand replied in kind but he did not have to throw. A tube slid up over his left shoulder. He guided the grenade launcher with his left hand, aiming it, then triggering it to throw out its two remaining bombs. And he was not firing blindly. He had a damned good idea of where the colonists were.

The next explosions were more distant as his grenades fell near the plateau's edge. He thought he saw a twisted figure fly into the air but he was not sure, nor did he waste time concerning himself with it. He had too much to do.

The remaining colonists had crossed the crest. They had their own energy rifles, maybe ten or twelve of them. More than half were firing—and now they knew where he was.

His rifle blazed. He caught a rising man full in its glare and the man died in the flames.

Suddenly the colonists' weapons became still as an enormously amplified voice called out, "Cease firing."

Now what? Brand, too, stilled his weapon.

"Mercenary," the voice called out, "listen to me. This is Lieutenant Hamid of the Federation Marines."

Federation troops? Brand no longer wondered why his opposition had not behaved like farmers and clerks. By now he had pinpointed the exact location of the loudspeaker. He aimed the rifle. "Surrender, you fool," the marine officer's voice boomed across the plateau. "You're fighting your own kind. You don't know what you've gotten into. The Dravians are—"

But by now Brand had pressed the firing stud and the marine lieutenant would never speak another word. He died in an exploding combat suit.

Brand fired again, sweeping across the plateau with the energy rifle until he saw its blaze trickle down to a pale light, then fade out, its charge exhausted.

He shrugged, snapped the weapon from its socket, ignored its fall and launched a homing rocket from the sleeve of his right arm.

What were Federation Marines doing in this? He wondered. New Iowa was not in the federation.

Something exploded beside him, lifting him bodily into the air, throwing him back to the tortured earth. He fell on his left shoulder, his teeth grating in agony.

He rolled over and came up to his knees, trying to orient himself, and then, snapping back the night visor, he turned his eyes upward in one last frantic sweep of the sky in the hope that—there it was, a moving spot of light, too slow to be a meteor, coming down, still slowing.

He turned back toward his attackers—there seemed to be more than Wisse had counted—feeling the growing sluggishness of his suit, the growing weight of a left arm whose feedback circuits were hardly working. He tried to find the rendezvous spot, recognized it on the almost featureless plateau. The marines had not yet reached it.

He took no time to count his remaining rockets. He merely loosed them in a steady stream toward the marines until the magazine was empty and the plateau was a blaze of exploding missiles. For a few instants the marines were disorganized.

Brand came erect slowly. His suit was definitely failing. Circuits were damaged. Power was running low. Feedback was almost unresponsive at times. But he did get to his feet and he started running, snatching the unused slug-throwing pistol from his hip and firing explosive shells before him as he ran.

The marines took too little time to recover, to aim at the

running, leaping figure. An energy beam laced the earth before him, setting grass aflame. He jetted over it. Another beam lashed into his backpack, where something exploded. His gyros failed. He tumbled in mid-air, fell crashing to the earth, his back burned and blistered, his lips broken against the faceplate of the helmet.

He staggered to his feet, somewhere dimly between consciousness and unconsciousness. He stumbled, regained his footing, ran.

Now the flame in the sky had become a distinct object, a short, stubby, wingless Dravian corvette, and its crew had seen the battle below. Energy cannons, one from each side of the ship, fired toward the marines.

Brand sighed a grateful sob and fell to his knees.

One, two—perhaps a dozen shots were sent toward the corvette before the marines broke in panic, fell back toward the edge of the plateau. They knew they were not up to taking on the ship's cannon.

Somehow Brand was on his feet again. He fired a few meaningless shots after them. Then he awkwardly ran on toward the landing spot.

The corvette's final descent rockets fired. The ship hovered for a moment, then slowly, gently lowered itself to the ground.

It had hardly touched down when Brand reached its side, paused, searched for the airlock. He found it as it began to open. He staggered in and the air cycle began.

A single Dravian was waiting for him inside.

If a Terran mammal had tried to look like a spider but had forgotten to add the final two legs, it might have somewhat resembled a Dravian—but not much. The roughly egg-shaped body was mounted on six legs, each of which ended in an appendage that could function as a foot or a hand as the occasion required. Body and legs were covered with a short, reddish-bronze hair that rippled constantly, ventilating the skin below. Dravian features, half a dozen eyes, an equal number of nostrils, a wide, slack mouth, fringed hearing organs, were all fixed in the forward, smaller end of the egg. These were what faced Brand and spoke to him in astonishingly good Anglo-Terran.

"Where are the others?" the Dravian asked.

It took a few moments for the words to sink in. The suit's

audio receptors were working fine. Brand's mind was not.

"Dead, all but two of them," he replied at last, realizing how much that last sprint had taken from him.

"And the other two?"

"Up in the hills," Brand told him. "They were afraid you wouldn't come. You were late."

He could not read Dravian symbols, so he could not determine the alien's rank from the badges he wore on his back.

"Regrettable but unavoidable," the Dravian said. "Come with me."

The Dravian led him down the passageway to the area of the ship that had been adapted for human passengers.

"Go in," the Dravian said. "Administer to yourself and change clothing. The captain will wish to see you at once."

"Okay," Brand said, fighting the pain of his burned back and the fatigue that was washing over his body. "But about the others—"

"Do not concern yourself with them," the Dravian said and gently pushed him into the man-size air lock that led into the empty human quarters.

Less than ten minutes later Brand was out of the combat suit, had been treated by an auto-medic programmed for humans and had dressed himself in thermal coveralls. He slipped oxygen tanks and a cooler onto his back, a fishbowl helmet over his head and stepped back into the airlock, feeling a little more than half alive.

What bothered him most as he cycled back out through the airlock and into the corridor where the Dravian waited for him was the fact that the corvette was in flight and already out of New Iowa's atmosphere. He had felt the ship lift while he was changing, had heard the whistle of air along the hull as it thinned into the vacuum of space.

Stepping out of the lock, he could not help but feel a moment of almost irrational anger.

"Aren't you going to pick up my companions?" he demanded, wondering why he cared. They had deserted him.

"We have no time," the Dravian replied, pointing down the corridor and gesturing for Brand to walk in front of him. "We have a rendezvous to keep."

"They'll be killed down there," Brand said, annoyed at himself.

"We are sorry," the Dravian said in such a way that Brand knew there was no point in discussing it further.

A silence held between Brand and the Fuzzy until they reached a hatch that he was directed to enter alone. Ducking to pass through the hatch, Brand found himself in the suite of an alien whom he recognized, if only from the numerous badges on his back. This was the commander of the Dravian ship.

Between the Dravian captain and Brand stood a low table. On the table was a pile of silvery Kendalian exchange disks, money of value on any civilized planet in the known galaxy.

"You are the only survivor," the Dravian said. "The full payment is yours."

"There are two other survivors down there," Brand said. "You could still pick them up."

"No," the captain said, wriggling his body hair in a manner that seemed unusual. "As you humans say, 'It is out of my hands.' We are late and even now we will have difficulty rendezvousing with our fleet as scheduled."

In all honesty, Brand told himself, he was not greatly grieved over the loss of Davidson and Wisse. He had never particularly liked either of them.

"Okay," he said after a few moments, "if that's the way it is."

"Good," the Dravian captain said. "The exchange disks are yours." He paused before speaking again. "You and your companions were promised transportation to Breman's Planet upon the completion of your work."

"That's right," Brand replied, beginning to feel again that there was a lot going on that he did not understand.

"Would you care to take out another contract?"

"Now?"

"Yes, immediately," the captain replied. "The Dravian peoples find themselves at war with—another race. I will not go into details, except to say that this other race feels that we had infringed too frequently into a territory they consider to be theirs." The captain removed a sheet of permapape from a pouch under his body. "This contract is for the duration of the war—at three times your previous rate of pay."

Brand looked at the pile of disks on the table and things began to make sense—like why there were marines on New Iowa and why the corvette was late and why there was a fleet of Fuzzy ships and where they were going. He understood.

The whole business on New Iowa was probably just one small part of a whole series of provocations. He decided not to think beyond this.

His mind went back to the pile of exchange disks. He already had a small fortune, enough to lose himself in the ecstasy of Breman's Planet for months, maybe years.

"The war will be short," the captain was saying. "We have been preparing for it for a long time. Our enemies have not. Already our fleets are massed. Your job will consist of no more than mopping up the planet after we have destroyed its defenses. The conditions of the planet are ideal for your lifeform, by the way." A brief pause. "I guarantee you no more than six standard months and a bonus at least equal to this when we have finished."

Brand looked at the pile of disks again, visualizing it doubled. What did he owe anybody?

"Okay," he said. "Six months and then Breman's Planet."

"This is guaranteed," the Dravian said but there was something in that alien voice that Brand wondered about, some strange intonation that seemed to carry—was it disgust?

Brand took the offered contract, signed it and thumbed it without reading it and handed it back.

Seven standard months later Brand lay in the luxury of Breman's Planet, surrounded by all the sensual delights men had ever managed to devise. A girl's hand slipped a euphoric into his mouth, then roved across his body. He sighed. With the bundle he had he could live like this for the rest of his life—if only he could stop remembering, stop thinking.

But he couldn't. The once-beautiful planet had been a shambles. Its proud people were little more than slaves to the victorious Dravians. Its economic and political and moral power was finally and forever broken. For all practical purposes it was a planet as dead as its huge moon.

Brand had walked among its defeated people, a conqueror, and they, the beaten ones, had called him Judas, though he wasn't sure what that meant. Nor did he want to know.

He knew too much as it was. He shuddered inside himself and hated the Dravians—and wondered which planet was next on their list: Breakdown Heights, Cordoba, New California, Breman's Planet, which human world?

But he knew what he hated even more than the Dravians. And he would have to live with that—if he didn't pick up the pistol that lay a few centimeters from his hand and burn away his skull.

EARLY MODEL

Robert Sheckley

The landing was almost a catastrophe. Bentley knew his co-ordination was impaired by the bulky weight on his back; he didn't realize how much until, at a crucial moment, he stabbed the wrong button. The ship began to drop like a stone. At the last moment, he overcompensated, scorching a black hole into the plain below him. His ship touched, teetered for a moment, then sickeningly came to rest.

Bentley had effected mankind's first landing on Tels IV.

His immediate reaction was to pour himself a sizable drink of strictly medicinal scotch.

When that was out of the way, he turned on his radio. The receiver was imbedded in his ear, where it itched, and the microphone was a surgically implanted lump in his throat. The portable sub-space set was self-tuning, which was all to the good, since Bentley knew nothing about narrowcasting on so tight a beam over so great a distance.

"All's well," he told Professor Sliggert over the radio. "It's an Earth-type planet, just as the survey reports said. The ship is intact. And I'm happy to report that I did not break my neck in landing."

"Of course not," Sliggert said, his voice thin and emotion-

122

less through the tiny receiver. "What about the Protec? How does it feel? Have you become used to it yet?"

Bentley said, "Nope. It still feels like a monkey on my back."

"Well, you'll adjust," Sliggert assured him. "The Institute sends its congratulations and I believe the government is awarding you a medal of some sort. Remember, the thing now is to fraternize with the aborigines, and if possible to establish a trade agreement of some sort, any sort. As a precedent. We need this planet, Bentley."

"I know."

"Good luck. Report whenever you have a chance."

"I'll do that," Bentley promised and signed off.

He tried to stand up, but didn't make it on the first attempt. Then, using the handholds that had been conveniently spaced above the control board, he managed to stagger erect. Now he appreciated the toll that no-weight exacts from a man's muscles. He wished he had done his exercises more faithfully on the long trip out from Earth.

Bentley was a big, jaunty young man, over six feet tall, widely and solidly constructed. On Earth, he had weighed two hundred pounds and had moved with an athlete's grace. But ever since leaving Earth, he'd had the added encumbrance of seventy-three pounds strapped irrevocably and immovably to his back. Under the circumstances, his movements resembled those of a very old elephant wearing tight shoes.

He moved his shoulders under the wide plastic straps, grimaced, and walked to a starboard porthole. In the distance, perhaps half a mile away, he could see a village, low and brown on the horizon. There were dots on the plain moving toward him. The villagers apparently had decided to discover what strange object had fallen from the skies breathing fire and making an uncanny noise.

"Good show," Bentley said to himself. Contact would have been difficult if these aliens had shown no curiosity. This eventuality had been considered by the Earth Interstellar Exploration Institute, but no solution had been found. Therefore it had been struck from the list of possibilities.

The villagers were drawing closer. Bentley decided it was time to get ready. He opened a locker and took out his linguascene, which, with some difficulty, he strapped to his chest.

On one hip, he fastened a large canteen of water. On the other hip went a package of concentrated food. Across his stomach, he put a package of assorted tools. Strapped to one leg was the radio. Strapped to the other was a medicine kit.

Thus equipped, Bentley was carrying a total of 148 pounds, every ounce of it declared essential for an extraterrestrial explorer.

The fact that he lurched rather than walked was considered unimportant.

The natives had reached the ship now and were gathering around it, commenting disparagingly. They were bipeds. They had short thick tails and their features were human, but nightmare human. Their coloring was a vivid orange.

Bentley also noticed that they were armed. He could see knives, spears, lances, stone hammers and flint axes. At the sight of this armament, a satisfied smile broke over his face. Here was the justification for his discomfort, the reason for the unwieldy seventy-three pounds which had remained on his back ever since leaving Earth.

It didn't matter what weapons these aboriginals had, right up to the nuclear level. They couldn't hurt him.

That's what Professor Sliggert, head of the Institute, inventor of the Protec, had told him.

Bentley opened the port. A cry of astonishment came from the Telians. His linguascene, after a few seconds' initial hesitation, translated the cries as, "Oh! Ah! How strange! Unbelievable! Ridiculous! Shockingly improper!"

Bentley descended the ladder on the ship's side, carefully balancing his 148 pounds of excess weight. The natives formed a semicircle around him, their weapons ready.

He advanced on them. They shrank back. Smiling pleasantly, he said, "I come as a friend." The linguascene barked out the harsh consonants of the Telian language.

They didn't seem to believe him. Spears were poised and one Telian, larger than the others and wearing a colorful headdress, held a hatchet in readiness.

Bentley felt the slightest tremor run through him. He was invulnerable, of course. There was nothing they could do to him, as long as he wore the Protec. Nothing! Professor Sliggert had been certain of it.

• • •

Before takeoff, Professor Sliggert had strapped the Protec to Bentley's back, adjusted the straps and stepped back to admire his brainchild.

"Perfect," he had announced with quiet pride.

Bentley had shrugged his shoulders under the weight. "Kind of heavy, isn't it?"

"But what can we do?" Sliggert asked him. "This is the first of its kind, the prototype. I have used every weight-saving device possible—transistors, light alloys, printed circuits, pencil-power packs and all the rest. Unfortunately, early models of any invention are invariably bulky."

"Seems as though you could have streamlined it a bit," Bentley objected, peering over his shoulder.

"Streamlining comes much later. First must be concentration, then compaction, then group-function, and finally styling. It's always been that way and it will always be. Take the typewriter. Now it is simply a keyboard, almost as flat as a briefcase. But the prototype typewriter worked with foot pedals and required the combined strength of several men to lift. Take the hearing aid, which actually shrank pounds through the various stages of its development. Take the linguascene, which began as a very massive, complicated electronic calculator weighing several tons—"

"Okay," Bentley broke in. "If this is the best you could make it, good enough. How do I get out of it?"

Professor Sliggert smiled.

Bentley reached around. He couldn't find a buckle. He pulled inneffectually at the shoulder straps, but could find no way of undoing them. Nor could he squirm out. It was like being in a new and fiendishly efficient straitjacket.

"Come on, Professor, how do I get it off?"

"I'm not going to tell you."

"Huh?"

"The Protec is uncomfortable, is it not?" Sliggert asked. "You would rather not wear it?"

"You're damned right."

"Of course. Did you know that in wartime, on the battlefield, soldiers have a habit of discarding essential equipment because it is bulky or uncomfortable? But we can't take chances on you. You are going to an alien planet, Mr. Bentley. You will be exposed to wholly unknown dangers. It is necessary that you be protected at all times."

"I know that," Bentley said."I've got enough sense to figure out when to wear this thing."

"But do you? We selected you for attributes such as resourcefulness, stamina, physical strength—and, of course, a certain amount of intelligence. But—"

"Thanks!"

"But those qualities do not make you prone to caution. Suppose you found the natives seemingly friendly and decided to discard the heavy, uncomfortable Protec? What would happen if you had misjudged their attitude? This is very easy to do on Earth; think how much easier it will be on an alien planet!"

"I can take care of myself," Bentley said.

Sliggert nodded grimly. "That is what Atwood said when he left for Durabella II and we have never heard from him again. Nor have we heard from Blake, or Smythe, or Korishell. Can you turn a knife-thrust from the rear? Have you eyes in the back of your head? No, Mr. Bentley, you haven't—*but the Protec has!*"

"Look," Bentley had said,"believe it or not, I'm a responsible adult. I will wear the Protec at all times when on the surface of an alien planet. Now tell me how to get it off."

"You don't seem to realize something, Bentley. If only your life were at stake, we would let you take what risks seemed reasonable to you.But we are also risking several billion dollars' worth of spaceship and equipment. Moreover, this is the Protec's field test.The only way to be sure of the results is to have you wear it all the time. The only way to ensure *that* is by not telling you how to remove it. We want results. You are going to stay alive whether you like it or not."

Bentley had thought it over and agreed grudgingly. "I guess I might be tempted to take it off, if the natives were really friendly."

"You will be spared that temptation. Now do you understand how it works?"

"Sure," Bentley said."But will it really do all you say?"

"It passed the lab tests perfectly."

"I'd hate to have some little thing go wrong. Suppose it pops a fuse or blows a wire?"

"That is one of the reasons for its bulk," Sliggert explained patiently. "Triple everything. We are taking no chance of mechanical failure."

"And the power supply?"

"Good for a century or better at full load. The Protec is perfect, Bentley! After this field test, I have no doubt it will become standard equipment for all extraterrestrial explorers." Professor Sliggert permitted himself a faint smile of pride.

"All right," Bentley had said, moving his shoulders under the wide plastic straps. "I'll get used to it."

But he hadn't. A man just doesn't get used to a seventy-three-pound monkey on his back.

The Telians didn't know what to make of Bentley. They argued for several minutes, while the explorer kept a strained smile on his face. Then one Telian stepped forward. He was taller than the others and wore a distinctive headdress made of glass, bones and bits of rather garishly painted wood.

"My friends," the Telian said, "there is an evil here which I, Rinek, can sense."

Another Telian wearing a similar headdress stepped forward and said, "It is not well for a ghost doctor to speak of such things."

"Of course not," Rinek admitted. "It is not well to speak of evil in the presence of evil, for evil then grows strong. But a ghost doctor's work is the detection and avoidance of evil. In this work, we must persevere, no matter what the risk."

Several other men in the distinctive headdress, the ghost doctors, had come forward now. Bentley decided that they were the Telian equivalent of priests and probably wielded considerable political power as well.

"I don't think he's evil," a young and cheerful-looking ghost doctor named Huascl said.

"Of course he is. Just look at him."

"Appearances prove nothing, as we know from the time the good spirit Ahut M'Kandi appeared in the form of a—"

"No lectures, Huascl. All of us know the parables of Lalland. The point is, can we take a chance?"

Huascl turned to Bentley. "Are you evil?" the Telian asked earnestly.

"No," Bentley said. He had been puzzled at first by the Telians' intense preoccupation with his spiritual status. They hadn't even asked him where he'd come from, or how, or why. But then, it was not so strange. If an alien had landed on Earth during certain periods of religious zeal, the first question asked might have been, "Are you a creature of God or of Satan?"

"He says he's not evil," Huascl said.

"How would he know?"

"If he doesn't, who does?"

"Once the great spirit G'tal presented a wise man with three kdal and said to him—"

And on it went. Bentley found his legs beginning to bend under the weight of all his equipment. The linguascene was no longer able to keep pace with the shrill theological discussion that raged around him. His status seemed to depend upon two or three disputed points, none of which the ghost doctors wanted to talk about, since to talk about evil was in itself dangerous.

To make matters more complicated, there was a schism over the concept of the penetrability of evil, the younger ghost doctors holding to one side, the older to the other. The factions accused each other of rankest heresy, but Bentley couldn't figure out who believed what or which interpretation aided him.

When the sun drooped low over the grassy plain, the battle still raged. Then, suddenly, the ghost doctors reached an agreement, although Bentley couldn't decide why or on what basis.

Huascl stepped forward as spokesman for the younger ghost doctors.

"Stranger," he declared, "we have decided not to kill you."

Bentley suppressed a smile. That was just like a primitive people, granting life to an invulnerable being!

"Not yet, anyhow," Huascl amended quickly, catching a frown upon Rinek and the older ghost doctors. "It depends entirely upon you. We will go to the village and purify ourselves and we will feast. Then we will initiate you into the society of ghost doctors. No evil thing can become a ghost doctor; it is expressly forbidden. In this manner, we will detect your true nature."

"I am deeply grateful," Bentley said.

"But if you *are* evil, we are pledged to destroy evil. And if we must, we can!"

The assembled Telians cheered his speech and began at once the mile trek to the village. Now that a status had been assigned Bentley, even tentatively, the natives were completely friendly. They chatted amiably with him about crops, droughts and famines.

Bentley staggered along under his equipment, tired, but

inwardly elated. This was really a coup! As an initiate, a priest, he would have an unsurpassed opportunity to gather anthropological data, to establish trade, to pave the way for the future development of Tels IV.

All he had to do was pass the initiation tests. And not get killed, of course, he reminded himself, smiling.

It was funny how positive the ghost doctors had been that they *could* kill him.

The village consisted of two dozen huts arranged in a rough circle. Beside each mud-and-thatch hut was a small vegetable garden, and sometimes a pen for the Telian version of cattle. There were small green-furred animals roaming between the huts, which the Telians treated as pets. The grassy central area was common ground. Here was the community well and here were the shrines to various gods and devils. In this area, lighted by a great bonfire, a feast had been laid out by the village women.

Bentley arrived at the feast in a state of near-exhaustion, stooped beneath his essential equipment. Gratefully, he sank to the ground with the villagers and the celebration began.

First the village women danced a welcoming for him. They made a pretty sight, their orange skin glinting in the firelight, their tails swinging gracefully in unison. Then a village dignitary named Occip came over to him, bearing a full bowl.

"Stranger," Occip said, "you are from a distant land and your ways are not our ways. Yet let us be brothers! Partake, therefore, of this food to seal the bond between us, and in the name of all sanctity!"

Bowing low, he offered the bowl.

It was an important moment, one of those pivotal occasions that can seal forever the friendship between races or make them eternal enemies. But Bentley was not able to take advantage of it. As tactfully as he could, he refused the symbolic food.

"But it is purified!" Occip said.

Bentley explained that, because of a tribal taboo, he could eat only his own food. Occip could not understand that different species have different dietary requirements. For example, Bentley pointed out, the staff of life on Tels IV might well be some strychnine compound. But he did not add that even if he wanted to take the chance, his Protec would never allow it.

Nonetheless, his refusal alarmed the village. There were

hurried conferences among the ghost doctors. Then Rinek came over and sat beside him.

"Tell me," Rinek inquired after a while, "what do you think of evil?"

"Evil is no good," Bentley said solemnly.

"Ah!" The ghost doctor pondered that, his tail flicking nervously over the grass. A small green-furred pet, a mog, began to play with his tail. Rinek pushed him away and said, "So you do not like evil."

"No."

"And you would permit no evil influence around you?"

"Certainly not," Bentley said, stifling a yawn. He was growing bored with the ghost doctor's tortuous examining.

"In that case, you would have no objection to receiving the sacred and very holy spear that Kran K'leu brought down from the abode of the Small Gods, the brandishing of which confers good upon a man."

"I would be pleased to receive it," said Bentley, heavy-eyed, hoping this would be the last ceremony of the evening.

Rinek grunted his approval and moved away. The women's dances came to an end. The ghost doctors began to chant in deep, impressive voices. The bonfire flared high.

Huascl came forward. His face was now painted in thin black and white stripes. He carried an ancient spear of black wood, its head of shaped volcanic glass, its length intricately although primitively carved.

Holding the spear aloft, Huascl said, "O Stranger from the Skies, accept from us this spear of sanctity! Kran K'leu gave this lance to Trin, our first father, and bestowed upon it a magical nature and caused it to be a vessel of the spirits of the good. Evil cannot abide the presence of this spear! Take, then, our blessings with it."

Bentley heaved himself to his feet. He understood the value of a ceremony like this. His acceptance of the spear should end, once and for all, any doubts as to his spiritual status. Reverently he inclined his head.

Huascl came forward, held out the spear and—

The Protec snapped into action.

Its operation was simple, in common with many great inventions. When its calculator-component received a danger cue, the Protec threw a force field around its operator. This field rendered him invulnerable, for it was completely and absolutely impenetrable. But there were certain unavoidable disadvantages.

If Bentley had had a weak heart, the Protec might have killed him there and then, for its action was electronically sudden, completely unexpected and physically wrenching. One moment, he was standing in front of the great bonfire, his hand held out for the sacred spear. In the next moment, he was plunged into darkness.

As usual, he felt as though he had been catapulted into a musty, lightless closet, with rubbery walls pressing close on all sides. He cursed the machine's super-efficiency. The spear had not been a threat; it was part of an important ceremony. But the Protec, with its literal senses, had interpreted it as a possible danger.

Now, in the darkness, Bentley fumbled for the controls that would release the field. As usual, the force field interfered with his positional sense, a condition that seemed to grow worse with each subsequent use. Carefully he felt his way along his chest, where the button should have been, and located it at last under his right armpit, where it had twisted around to. He released the field.

The feast had ended abruptly. The natives were standing close together for protection, weapons ready, tails stretched stiffly out. Huascl, caught in the force field's range, had been flung twenty feet and was slowly picking himself up.

The ghost doctors began to chant a purification dirge, for protection against evil spirits. Bentley couldn't blame them.

When a Protec force field goes on, it appears as an opaque black sphere, some ten feet in diameter. If it is struck, it repels with a force equal to the impact. White lines appear in the sphere's surface, swirl, coalesce, vanish. And as the sphere spins, it screams in a thin, high-pitched wail.

All in all, it was a sight hardly calculated to win the confidence of a primitive and superstitious people.

"Sorry," Bentley said, with a weak smile. There hardly seemed anything else to say.

Huascl limped back, but kept his distance. "You cannot accept the sacred spear," he stated.

"Well, it's not exactly that," said Bentley. "It's just—well, I've got this protective device, kind of like a shield, you know?

It doesn't like spears. Couldn't you offer me a sacred gourd?"

"Don't be ridiculous," Huascl said. "Who ever heard of a sacred gourd?"

"No, I guess not. But please take my word for it—I'm not evil. Really I'm not. I've just got a taboo about spears."

The ghost doctors talked among themselves too rapidly for the linguascene to interpret. It caught only the words "evil," "destroy," and "purification." Bentley decided his forecast didn't look too favorable.

After the conference, Huascl came over to him and said, "Some of the others feel that you should be killed at once, before you bring some great unhappiness upon the village. I told them, however, that you cannot be blamed for the many taboos that restrict you. We will pray for you through the night. And perhaps, in the morning, the initiation will be possible."

Bentley thanked him. He was shown to a hut and then the Telians left him as quickly as possible. There was an ominous hush over the village; from his doorway, Bentley could see little groups of natives talking earnestly and glancing covertly in his direction.

It was a poor beginning for cooperation between two races.

He immediately contacted Professor Sliggert and told him what had happened.

"Unfortunate," the professor said. "But primitive people are notoriously treacherous. They might have meant to kill you with the spear instead of actually handing it to you. Let you have it, that is, in the most literal sense."

"I'm positive there was no such intention," Bentley said. "After all, you have to start trusting people sometime."

"Not with a billion dollars' worth of equipment in your charge."

"But I'm not going to be able to *do* anything!" Bentley shouted. "Don't you understand? They're suspicious of me already. I wasn't able to accept their sacred spear. That means I'm very possibly evil. Now what if I can't pass the initiation ceremony tomorrow? Suppose some idiot starts to pick his teeth with a knife and the Protec saves me? All the favorable first impression I built up will be lost."

"Good will can be regained," Professor Sliggert said sententiously. "But a billion dollars' worth of equipment—"

"—can be salvaged by the next expedition. Look, Professor,

give me a break. Isn't there some way I can control this thing manually?"

"No way at all," Sliggert replied. "That would defeat the entire purpose of the machine. You might just as well not be wearing it if you're allowed to rely on your own reflexes rather than electronic impulses."

"Then tell me how to take it off."

"The same argument holds true—you wouldn't be protected at all times."

"Look," Bentley protested, "you chose me as a competent explorer. I'm the guy on the spot. I know what the conditions are here. Tell me how to get it off."

"No! The Protec must have a full field test. And we want you to come back alive."

"That's another thing," Bentley said. "These people seem kind of sure they can kill me."

"Primitive peoples always overestimate the potency of their strength, weapons and magic."

"I know, I know. But you're certain there's no way they can get through the field? Poison, maybe?"

"Nothing can get through the field," Sliggert said patiently. "Not even light rays can penetrate. Not even gamma radiation. You are wearing an impregnable fortress, Mr. Bentley. Why can't you manage to have a little faith in it?"

"Early models of inventions sometimes need a lot of ironing out," Bentley grumbled. "But have it your way. Won't you tell me how to take it off, though, just in case something goes wrong?"

"I wish you would stop asking me that, Mr. Bentley. You were chosen to give the Protec a *full* field test. That's just what you are going to do."

When Bentley signed off, it was deep twilight outside and the villagers had returned to their huts. Campfires burned low and he could hear the call of night creatures.

At that moment, Bentley felt very alien and exceedingly homesick.

He was tired almost to the point of unconsciousness, but he forced himself to eat some concentrated food and drink a little water. Then he unstrapped the tool kit, the radio and the canteen, tugged defeatedly at the Protec, and lay down to sleep.

Just as he dozed off, the Protec went violently into action, nearly snapping his neck out of joint.

Wearily he fumbled for the controls, located them near his stomach, and turned off the field.

The hut looked exactly the same. He could find no source of attack.

Was the Protec losing its grip on reality, he wondered, or had a Telian tried to spear him through the window?

Then Bentley saw a tiny mog puppy scuttling away frantically, its legs churning up clouds of dust.

The little beast probably just wanted to get warm, Bentley thought. But of course it was alien. Its potential for danger could not be overlooked by the ever-wary Protec.

He fell asleep again and immediately began to dream that he was locked in a prison of bright red sponge rubber. He could push the walls out and out and out, but they never yielded, and at last he would have to let go and be gently shoved back to the center of the prison. Over and over, this happened, until suddenly he felt his back wrenched and awoke within the Protec's lightless field.

This time he had real difficulty finding the controls. He hunted desperately by feel until the bad air made him gasp in panic. He located the controls at last under his chin, released the field, and began to search groggily for the source of the new attack.

He found it. A twig had fallen from the thatch roof and had tried to land on him. The Protec, of course, had not allowed it. "Aw, come on now," Bentley groaned aloud. "Let's use a little judgment!"

But he was really too tired to care. Fortunately, there were no more assaults that night.

Huascl came to Bentley's hut in the morning, looking very solemn and considerably disturbed.

"There were great sounds from your hut during the night," the ghost doctor said. "Sounds of torment, as though you were wrestling with a devil."

"I'm just a restleess sleeper," Bentley explained.

Huascl smiled to show that he appreciated the joke. "My friend, did you pray for purification last night and for release from evil?"

"I certainly did."

"And was your prayer granted?"

"It was," Bentley said hopefully. "There's no evil around me. Not a bit."

Huascl looked dubious. "But can you be sure? Perhaps you should depart from us in peace. If you cannot be initiated, we shall have to destroy you—"

"Don't worry about it," Bentley told him. "Let's get started."

"Very well," Huascl said, and together they left the hut.

The initiation was to be held in front of the great bonfire in the village square. Messengers had been sent out during the night and ghost doctors from many villages were there. Some had come as far as twenty miles to take part in the rites and to see the alien with their own eyes. The ceremonial drum had been taken from its secret hiding place and was now booming solemnly. The villagers watched, chattered together, laughed. But Bentley could detect an undercurrent of nervousness and strain.

There was a long series of dances. Bentley twitched worriedly when the last figure started, for the leading dancer was swinging a glass-studded club around his head. Nearer and nearer the dancer whirled, now only a few feet away from him, his club a dazzling streak.

The villagers watched, fascinated. Bentley shut his eyes, expecting to be plunged momentarily into the darkness of the force field.

But the dancer moved away at last and the dance ended with a roar of approval from the villagers.

Huascl began to speak. Bentley realized with a thrill of relief that this was the end of the ceremony.

"O brothers," Huascl said, "this alien has come across the great emptiness to be our brother. Many of his ways are strange and around him there seems to hang a strange hint of evil. And yet who can doubt that he means well? Who can doubt that he is, in essence, a good and honorable person? With this initiation, we purge him of evil and make him one of us."

There was dead silence as Huascl walked up to Bentley.

"Now," Huascl said, "you are a ghost doctor and indeed one of us." He held out his hand.

Bentley felt his heart leap within him. He had won! He had been accepted! He reached out and clasped Huascl's hand.

Or tried to. He didn't quite make it, for the Protec, ever alert, saved him from the possibly dangerous contact.

"You damned idiotic gadget!" Bentley bellowed, quickly finding the control and releasing the field.

He saw at once that the fat was in the fire.

"Evil!" shrieked the Telians, frenziedly waving their weapons.

"Evil!" screamed the ghost doctors.

Bentley turned despairingly to Huascl.

"Yes," the young ghost doctor said sadly, "it is true. We had hoped to cure the evil by our ancient ceremonial. But it could not be. This evil must be destroyed! *Kill the devil!*"

A shower of spears came at Bentley. The Protec responded instantly.

Soon it was apparent that an impasse had been reached. Bentley would remain for a few minutes in the field, then override the controls. The Telians, seeing him still unharmed, would renew their barrage and the Protec would instantly go back into action.

Bentley tried to walk back to his ship. But the Protec went on again each time he shut it off. It would take him a month of two to cover a mile, at that rate, so he stopped trying. He would simply wait the attackers out. After a while, they would find out they couldn't hurt him and the two races would finally get down to business.

He tried to relax within the field, but found it impossible. He was hungry and extremely thirsty. And his air was starting to grow stale.

Then Bentley remembered, with a sense of shock, that air had not gone through the surrounding field the night before. Naturally—nothing could get through. If he wasn't careful, he could be asphyxiated.

Even an impregnable fortress could fall, he knew, if the defenders were starved or suffocated out.

He began to think furiously. How long could the Telians keep up the attack? They would have to grow tired sooner or later, wouldn't they?

Or would they?

He waited as long as he could, until the air was all but unbreathable, then overrode the controls. The Telians were sitting on the ground around him. Fires had been lighted and food was cooking. Rinek lazily threw a spear at him and the field went on.

So, Bentley thought, they had learned. They were going to starve him out.

He tried to think, but the walls of his dark closet seemed to be pressing against him. He was growing claustrophobic and already his air was stale again.

He thought for a moment, then overrode the controls. The Telians looked at him coolly. One of them reached for a spear.

"Wait!" Bentley shouted. At the same moment, he turned on his radio.

"What do you want?" Rinek asked.

"Listen to me! It isn't fair to trap me in the Protec like this!"

"Eh? What's going on?" Professor Sliggert asked, through the ear receiver.

"You Telians know—" Bentley said hoarsely—"you know that you can destroy me by continually activating the Protec. I can't turn it off! I can't get out of it!"

"Ah!" said Professor Sliggert. "I see the difficulty. Yes."

"We are sorry," Huascl apologized. "But evil must be destroyed."

"Of course it must," Bentley said desperately. "But not me. Give me a chance. *Professor!*"

"This is indeed a flaw," Professor Sliggert mused, "and a serious one. Strange, but things like this, of course, can't show up in the lab, only in a full-scale field test. The fault will be rectified in the new models."

"Great! But I'm here now! How do I get this thing off?"

"I *am* sorry," Sliggert said. "I honestly never thought the need would arise. To tell the truth, I designed the harness so that you could not get out of it under any circumstances."

"Why, you lousy—"

"Please!" Sliggert said sternly. "Let's keep our heads. If you can hold out for a few months, we might be able—"

"I can't! The air! Water!"

"Fire!" cried Rinek, his face contorted. "By fire, we will chain the demon!"

And the Protec snapped on.

Bentley tried to think things out carefully in the darkness. He would have to get out of the Protec. But how? There was a knife in his tool kit. Could he cut through the tough plastic straps? He would have to!

But what then? Even if he emerged from his fortress, the

ship was a mile away. Without the Protec, they could kill him with a single spear thrust. And they were pledged to, for he had been declared irrevocably evil.

But if he ran, he at least had a chance. And it was better to die of a spear thrust than to strangle slowly in absolute darkness.

Bentley turned off the field. The Telians were surrounding him with campfires, closing off his retreat with a wall of flame.

He hacked frantically at the plastic web. The knife slithered and slipped along the strap. And he was back in Protec.

When he came out again, the circle of fire was complete. The Telians were cautiously pushing the fires toward him, lessening the circumference of his circle.

Bentley felt his heart sink. Once the fires were close enough, the Protec would go on and stay on. He would not be able to override a continuous danger signal. He would be trapped within the field for as long as they fed the flames.

And considering how primitive people felt about devils, it was just possible that they would keep the fire going for a century or two.

He dropped the knife, used side-cutters on the plastic strap and succeeded in ripping it halfway through.

He was in Protec again.

Bentley was dizzy, half-fainting from fatigue, gasping great mouthfuls of foul air. With an effort, he pulled himself together. He couldn't drop now. That would be the end.

He found the controls, overrode them. The fires were very near him now. He could feel their warmth against his face. He snipped viciously at the strap and felt it give.

He slipped out of the Protec just as the field activated again. The force of it threw him into the fire. But he fell feet-first and jumped out of the flames without getting burned.

The villagers roared. Bentley sprinted away; as he ran, he dumped the linguascene, the tool kit, the radio, the concentrated food and the canteen. He glanced back once and saw that the Telians were after him.

But he was holding his own. His tortured heart seemed to be pounding his chest apart and his lungs threatened to collapse at any moment. But now the spaceship was before him, looming great and friendly on the flat plain.

He was going to just make it. Another twenty yards . . .

Something green flashed in front of him. It was a small, green-furred mog puppy. The clumsy beast was trying to get out of his way.

He swerved to avoid crushing it and realized too late that he should never have broken stride. A rock turned under his foot and he sprawled forward.

He heard the pounding feet of the Telians coming toward him and managed to climb on one knee.

Then somebody threw a club and it landed neatly on his forehead.

"Ar gwy dril?" a voice asked incomprehensibly from far off.

Bentley opened his eyes and saw Huascl bending over him. He was in a hut, back in the village. Several armed ghost doctors were at the doorway, watching.

"Ar dril?" Huascl asked again.

Bentley rolled over and saw, piled neatly beside him, his canteen, concentrated food, tools, radio and linguascene. He took a deep drink of water, then turned on the linguascene.

"I asked if you felt all right," Huascl said.

"Sure, fine," Bentley grunted, feeling his head. "Let's get it over with."

"Over with?"

"You're going to kill me, aren't you? Well, let's not make a production out of it."

"But we didn't want to destroy *you*," Huascl said. "We knew you for a good man. It was the devil we wanted!"

"Eh?" asked Bentley in a blank uncomprehending voice.

"Come, look."

The ghost doctors helped Bentley to his feet and brought him outside. There, surrounded by lapping flames, was the glowing great black sphere of the Protec.

"You didn't know, of course," Huascl said, "but there was a devil riding upon your back."

"Huh!" gasped Bentley.

"Yes, it is true. We tried to dispossess him by purification, but he was too strong. We had to force you, brother, to face that evil and throw it aside. We knew you would come through. And you did!"

"I see," Bentley said. "A devil on my back. Yes, I guess so."

That was exactly what the Protec would have to be, to them.

A heavy, misshapen weight on his shoulders, hurling out a black sphere whenever they tried to purify it. What else could a religious people do but try to free him from its grasp?

He saw several women of the village bring up baskets of food and throw them into the fire in front of the sphere. He looked inquiringly at Huascl.

"We are propitiating it," Huascl said, "for it is a very strong devil, undoubtedly a miracle-working one. Our village is proud to have such a devil in bondage."

A ghost doctor from a neighboring village stepped up. "Are there more such devils in your homeland? Could you bring *us* one to worship?"

Several other ghost doctors pressed eagerly forward. Bentley nodded. "It can be arranged," he said.

He knew that the Earth-Tels trade was now begun. And at last a suitable use had been found for Professor Sliggert's Protec.

IN THE BONE

Gordon R. Dickson

I

Personally, his name was Harry Brennan.

Officially, he was the *John Paul Jones,* which consisted of four billion dollars' worth of irresistible equipment—the latest and best of human science—designed to spread its four-thousand-odd components out through some fifteen cubic meters of space under ordinary conditions—designed also to stretch across light-years under extraordinary conditions (such as sending an emergency messenger-component home) or to clump into a single magnetic unit in order to shift through space and explore the galaxy. Both officially and personally—but most of all personally—he represents a case in point.

The case is one having to do with the relative importance of the made thing and its maker.

It was, as we know, the armored horseman who dominated the early wars of the Middle Ages in Europe. But, knowing this, it is still wise to remember that it was not the iron shell that made the combination of man and metal terrible to the enemy—but rather the essentially naked man inside the shell. Later, French knights depending on their armor went down before the cloth-yard shafts of unarmored footmen with bows, at Crécy and Poitiers.

And what holds true for armor holds true for the latest developments of our science as well. It is not the spacecraft or the laser on which we will find ourselves depending when a time of ultimate decision comes, but the naked men within and behind these things. When that time comes, those who rank the made thing before its maker will die as the French knights died at Crécy and Poitiers. This is a law of nature as wide as the universe, which Harry Brennan, totally unsuspecting, was to discover once more for us, in his personal capacity.

Personally, he was in his mid-twenties, unremarkable except for two years of special training with the *John Paul Jones* and his superb physical condition. He was five-eleven, a hundred seventy-two pounds, with a round, cheerful face under his brown crew-cut hair. I was Public Relations Director of the Project that sent him out; and I was there with the rest to slap him on the back the day he left.

"Don't get lost, now," said someone. Harry grinned.

"The way you guys built this thing," he answered, "if I get lost the galaxy would just have to shift itself around to get me back on plot."

There was an unconscious arrogance hidden in that answer, but no one marked it at the time. It was not the hour of suspicions.

He climbed into the twelve-foot-tall control-suit that with his separate living tank were the main components of the *John Paul Jones* and took off. Up in orbit, he spent some thirty-two hours testing to make sure all the several thousand other component parts were responding properly. Then he left the solar system.

He clumped together his components, made his first shift to orbit Procyon—and from there commenced his explorations of the stars. In the next nine weeks, he accumulated literally amazing amounts of new information about the nearby stars and their solar systems. And—this is an even better index of his success—located four new worlds on which men could step with never a spacesuit or even a water canteen to sustain them. Worlds so like Earth in gravity, atmosphere and even flora and fauna, that they could be colonized tomorrow.

Those were his first four worlds. On the fifth he encountered his fate—a fate for which he was unconsciously ripe.

The fact was the medical men and psychologists had overlooked a factor—a factor having to do with the effect of Harry's official *John Paul Jones* self upon his entirely human personal self. And over nine weeks this effect changed Harry without his ever having suspected it.

You see, nothing seemed barred to him. He could cross light-years by touching a few buttons. He could send a sensing element into the core of the hottest star, into the most poisonous planetary atmospheres or crushing gravities, to look around as if he were down there in person. From orbit, he could crack open a mountain, burn off a forest or vaporize a section of icecap in search of information just by tapping the energy of a nearby sun. And so, subtly, the unconscious arrogance born during two years of training, that should have been noted in him at take-off from Earth, emerged and took him over—until he felt that there was nothing he could not do; that all things must give way to him; that he was, in effect, master of the universe.

The day may come when a man like Harry Brennan may hold such a belief and be justified. But not yet. On the fifth Earthlike world he discovered—World 1242 in his records— Harry encountered the proof that his belief was unjustified.

II

The world was one which, from orbit, seemed to be the best of all the planets which he had discovered were suitable for human settlement; and he was about to go down to its surface personally in the control-suit, when his instruments picked out something already down there.

It was a squat, metallic pyramid about the size of a fourplex apartment building; and it was radiating on a number of interesting frequencies. Around its base there was mechanical movement and an area of cleared ground. Further out, in the native forest, were treaded vehicles taking samples of the soil, rock and vegetation.

Harry had been trained for all conceivable situations, including an encounter with other intelligent, spacegoing life. Automatically, he struck a specific button, and immediately a small torpedo shape leaped away to shift through alternate space and back to Earth with the information so far obtained. And a pale, thin beam reached up and out from the pyramid below. Harry's emergency messenger-component ceased to exist.

Shaken, but not yet really worried, Harry struck back instantly with all the power his official self could draw from the GO-type sun, nearby.

The power was funneled by some action below, directly into the pyramid itself; and it vanished there as indifferently as the single glance of a sunbeam upon a leaf.

Harry's mind woke suddenly to some understanding of what he had encountered. He reached for the controls to send the *John Paul Jones* shifting into the alternate universe and away.

His hands never touched the controls. From the pyramid below, a blue lance of light reached up to paralyze him, select the control-suit from among the other components and send it tumbling to the planetary surface below like a swatted insect.

But the suit had been designed to protect its occupant, whether he himself was operative or not. At fifteen hundred feet, the drag chute broke free, looking like a silver cloth candle-snuffer in the sunlight; and at five hundred feet the retro-rockets cut in. The suit tumbled to earth among some trees two kilometers from the pyramid, with Harry inside bruised, but released from his paralysis.

From the pyramid, a jagged arm of something like white lightning lashed the ground as far as the suit, and the suit's outer surface glowed cherry-red. Inside, the temperature suddenly shot up fifty degrees; instinctively Harry hit the panic button available to him inside the suit.

The suit split down the center like an overcooked frankfurter and spat Harry out; he rolled among the brush and fernlike ground cover, six or seven meters from the suit.

From the distant pyramid, the lightning lashed the suit, breaking it up. The headpiece rolled drunkenly aside, turning the dark gape of its interior toward Harry like the hollow of an empty skull. In the dimness of that hollow Harry saw the twinkle of his control buttons.

The lightning vanished. A yellow lightness filled the air about Harry and the dismembered suit. There was a strange quivering to the yellowness; and Harry half-smelled, half-tasted the sudden, flat bit of ozone. In the headpiece a button clicked without being touched; and the suit speaker, still radio-connected with the recording tank in orbit, spoke aloud in Harry's voice.

"Orbit . . ." it said. ". . . into . . . going . . ."

These were, in reverse order, the last three words Harry had recorded before sighting the pyramid. Now, swiftly gaining speed, the speaker began to recite backwards, word for word, everything Harry had said into it in nine weeks. Faster it went, and faster until it mounted to a chatter, a gabble, and finally a whine pushing against the upper limits of Harry's auditory register.

Suddenly, it stopped.

The little clearing about Harry was full of silence. Only the odd and distant creaking of something that might have been a rubbing branch or an alien insect came to Harry's ears. Then the speaker spoke once more.

"Animal . . ." it said flatly in Harry's calm, recorded voice and went on to pick further words from the recordings, ". . . beast. You . . . were an animal . . . wrapped in . . . made clothing. I have stripped you back to . . . animal again. Live, beast . . ."

Then the yellowness went out of the air and the taste of ozone with it. The headpiece of the dismembered suit grinned, empty as old bones in the sunlight. Harry scrambled to his feet and ran wildly away through the trees and brush. He ran in panic and utter fear, his lungs gasping, his feet pounding the alien earth, until the earth, the trees, the sky itself swam about him from exhaustion; and he fell tumbling to earth and away into the dark haven of unconsciousness.

When he woke, it was night, and he could not quite remember where he was or why. His thoughts seemed numb and unimportant. But he was cold, so he blundered about until he found the standing half-trunk of a lightning-blasted tree and crept into the burned hollow of its interior, raking frill-edged, alien leaves about him out of some half-forgotten instinct, until his own body-warmth in the leaves formed a cocoon of comfort about him; and he slept.

From then on began a period in which nothing was very clear. It was as if his mind had huddled itself away somehow like a wounded animal and refused to think. There was no past or future, only the endless now. If now was warm, it had always been warm; if dark—it had always been dark. He learned to smell water from a distance and go to it when he was thirsty.

He put small things in his mouth to taste them. If they tasted good he ate them. If he got sick afterwards, he did not eat them again.

Gradually, blindly, the world about him began to take on a certain order. He came to know where there were plants with portions he could eat, where there were small creatures he could catch and pull apart and eat and where there was water.

He did not know how lucky he was in the sheer chance of finding flora and fauna on an alien world that was edible—let alone nourishing. He did not realize that he had come down on a plateau in the tropical highlands, with little variation in day and night temperature and no large native predators which might have attacked him.

None of this, he knew. Nor would it have made any difference to him if he had, for the intellectual center of his brain had gone on vacation, so to speak, and refused to be called back. He was, in fact, a victim of severe psychological shock. The shock of someone who had come to feel himself absolute master of a universe and who then, in a few short seconds, had been cast down from that high estate by something or someone inconceivably greater, into the state of a beast of the field.

But still, he could not be a true beast of the field, in spite of the fact his intellectual processes had momentarily abdicated. His perceptive abilities still worked. His eyes could not help noting, even if incuriously, the progressive drying of the vegetation, the day-by-day shifting in the points of setting and rising of the sun. Slowly, instinctively, the eternal moment that held him stretched and lengthened until he began to perceive divisions within it—a difference between *now* and *was,* between *now* and *will be.*

III

The day came at last when he saw himself.

A hundred times he had crouched by the water to drink and, lowering his lips to its surface, seen color and shape rising to meet him. The hundredth and something time, he checked, a few inches above the liquid plane, staring at what he saw.

For several long seconds it made no sense to him. Then, at

first slowly, then with a rush like pain flooding back on someone rousing from the anesthesia of unconsciousness, he recognized what he saw.

Those were eyes at which he stared, sunken and dark-circled under a dirty tangle of hair. That was a nose jutting between gaunt and sunken cheeks above a mouth, and there was a chin naked only because once an ultrafine laser had burned out the thousand and one roots of the beard that grew on it. That was a man he saw—*himself.*

He jerked back like someone who has come face-to-face with the devil. But he returned eventually, because he was thirsty, to drink and see himself again. And so, gradually, he got used to the sight of himself.

So it was that memory started to return to him. But it did not come back quickly or all at once. It returned instead by jerks and sudden, partial relevations—until finally the whole memory of what had happened was back in his conscious mind again.

But he was really not a man again.

He was still essentially what the operator of the pyramid had broken him down into. He was still an animal. Only the memory and imaginings of a man had returned to live like a prisoner in a body that went on reacting and surviving in the bestial way it had come to regard as natural.

But his animal peace was broken. For his imprisoned mind worked now. With the control-suit broken up—he had returned to the spot of its destruction many times, to gaze beastlike at the rusting parts—his mind knew he was a prisoner, alone on this alien world until he died. To know that was not so bad, but remembering this much meant remembering also the existence of the someone or something that had made him a prisoner here.

The whoever it was who was in the pyramid.

That the pyramid might have been an automated, mechanical device never entered his mind for a moment. There had been a personal, directed, living viciousness behind the announcement that had condemned him to live as a beast. No, in that blank-walled, metallic structure, whose treaded mechanical servants still prospected through the woods, there was something alive—something that could treat the awesome power of a solar tap as a human treated the attack of a mosquito—but something *living.* Some being. Some Other, who lived in the pyramid, moving breathing, eating and gloating—or worse yet, entirely forgetful of what he had done to Harry Brennan.

And now that he knew that the Other was there, Harry began to dream of him nightly. At first, in his dreams, Harry whimpered with fear each time the dark shape he pursued seemed about to turn and show its face. But slowly, hatred came to grow inside and then outside his fear. Unbearable that Harry should never know the face of his destroyer. Lying curled in his nest of leaves under the moonless, star-brilliant sky, he snarled, thinking of his deprivation.

Then hate came to strengthen him in the daylight also. From the beginning he had avoided the pyramid, as a wild coyote avoids the farmyard where he was once shot by the farmer. But now, day after day, Harry circled closer to the alien shape. From the beginning he had run and hidden from the treaded prospecting machines. But now, slowly, he grew bolder, standing close enough at last to touch them as they passed. And he found that they paid no attention to him. No attention at all.

He came to ignore them in turn, and day by day he ventured closer to the pyramid. Until the morning came when he lay, silently snarling, behind a bush, looking out across the tread-trampled space that separated him from the nearest copper-colored face of the pyramid.

The space was roughly circular, thirty meters across, broken only by a small stream which had been diverted to loop inwards toward the pyramid before returning to its original channel. In the bight of the loop a machine like a stork straddled the artificial four-foot-wide channel, dipping a pair of long necks with tentacle-clustered heads into the water at intervals. Sometimes Harry could see nothing in the tentacles when they came up. Occasionally they carried some small water creature which they deposited in a tank.

Making a perfect circle about the tramped area, so that the storklike machine was guarded within them, was an open fence of slender wands set upright in the earth, far enough apart for any of the machines that came and went to the forest to pass between any two of them. There seemed to be nothing connecting the wands, and nothing happened to the prospecting machines as they passed through—but the very purposelessness of the wands filled Harry with uneasiness.

It was not until after several days of watching that he had a chance to see a small native animal, frightened by something in the woods behind it, attempt to bolt across a corner of the clearing.

As it passed between two of the wands there was a waveriness in the air between them. The small animal leaped high, came down and lay still. It did not move after that, and later in the day, Harry saw the indifferent treads of one of the prospecting machines bury it in the trampled earth in passing.

That evening, Harry brought several captive, small animals bound with grass up to the wand line and thrust them through, one by one at different spots. All died.

The next night he tried pushing a captive through a small trench scooped out so that the creature passed the killing line below ground level. But this one died also. For several days he was baffled. Then he tried running behind a slow-moving machine as it returned and tying a small animal to it with grass.

For a moment as the front of the machine passed through, he thought the little animal would live. But then, as the back of the machine passed the line, it, too, died.

Snarling, Harry paced around outside the circle in the brush until the sunset and stars filled the moonless sky.

In the days that followed, he probed every gap in the wand-fence, but found no safe way through it. Finally, he came to concentrate on the two points at which the diverted stream entered and left the circle to flow beneath the storklike machine.

He studied this without really knowing what he was seeking. He did not even put his studying into words. Vaguely, he knew that the water went in and the water came out again unchanged; and he also wished to enter and come out safely. Then, one day, studying the stream and the machine, he noticed that a small creature plucked from the water by the storklike neck's mass of tentacles was still wriggling.

That evening, at twilight, while there was still light to see, he waded up the two-foot depth of the stream to the point where the killing line cut across its watery surface and pushed some more of his little animals toward the line underwater.

Two of the three surfaced immediately, twitched and floated on limply, to be plucked from the water and cast aside on the ground by the storklike machine. But the third swam on several strokes before surfacing and came up living to scramble ashore, race for the forest and be killed by wands further around the circle.

Harry investigated the channel below the killing line. There was water there up to his mid-thigh, plenty to cover him completely. He crouched down in the water and took a deep breath.

Ducking below the surface, he pulled himself along with his fingertips, holding himself close to the bottom. He moved in as far as the tentacled ends. These grabbed at him, but could not reach far enough back to touch him. He saw that they came within a few inches of the gravel bottom.

He began to need air. He backed carefully out and rose above the water, gasping. After a while his hard breathing stopped, and he sat staring at the water for a long while. When it was dark, he left.

The next day he came and crept underwater to the grabbing area of the storklike machine again. He scooped out several handfuls of the gravel from under the place where the arms grabbed, before he felt a desperate need for air and had to withdraw. But that day began his labors.

IV

Four days later the bottom under the grasping tentacles was scooped out to an additional two feet of depth. And the fifth twilight after that, he pulled himself, dripping and triumphant, up out of the bend of the diverted stream inside the circle of the killing wands.

He rested and then went to the pyramid, approaching it cautiously and sidelong like a suspicious animal. There was a door in the side he approached through which he had seen the prospecting machines trundle in and out. In the dimness he could not see it; and when he touched the metallic side of the structure, his fingers, grimed and toughened from scrabbling in the dirt, told him little. But his nose, beast-sensitive now, located and traced the outline of the almost invisible crack around the door panel by its reek of earth and lubricant.

He settled down to wait. An hour later, one of the machines came back. He jumped up, ready to follow it in; but the door

opened just before it and closed the minute it was inside—nor
was there any room to squeeze in beside it. He hunkered down,
disappointed, snarling a little to himself.

He stayed until dawn and watched several more machines
enter and leave. But there was no room to squeeze inside, even
with the smallest of them.

During the next week or so he watched the machines enter
and leave nightly. He tied one of his small animals to an entering
machine and saw it pass through the entrance alive and scamper
out again with the next machine that left. And every night his
rage increased. Then, wordlessly, one daytime after he had
seen a machine deep in the woods lurch and tilt as its tread
passed over a rock, inspiration took him.

That night he carried through the water with him several
cantaloupe-sized stones. When the first machine came back to
the pyramid, in the moment in which the door opened before
it, he pushed one of the rocks before the right-hand tread. The
machine, unable to stop, mounted the rock with its right tread,
tilted to the left and struck against that side of the entrance.

It checked, backed off and put out an arm with the grasping
end to remove the rock. Then it entered the opening. But Harry
was already before it, having slipped through while the door
was still up and the machine busy pulling the stone aside.

He plunged into a corridor of darkness, full of clankings
and smells. A little light from the opening behind him showed
him a further, larger chamber where other machines stood
parked. He ran toward them.

Long before he reached them, the door closed behind him,
and he was in pitch darkness. But the clanking of the incoming
machine was close behind him, and the adrenalized memory
of a wild beast did not fail him. He ran, hands outstretched,
directly into the side of the parked machine at which he had
aimed and clambered up on it. The machine entering behind
him clanked harmlessly past him and stopped moving.

He climbed cautiously down in the impenetrable darkness.
He could see nothing; but the new, animal sensitivity of his
nose offered a substitute for vision. He moved like a hunting
dog around the chamber, sniffing and touching; and slowly a
clear picture of it and its treaded occupants built up in his mind.

He was still at this when suddenly a door he had not seen
opened almost in his face. He had just time to leap backwards

as a smaller machine with a boxlike body and a number of upward-thrusting arms entered, trundled to the machine that had just come back and began to relieve the prospecting machine of its sample box, replacing it with the one it carried itself.

This much, in the dim light from the open door, Harry was able to see. But then, the smaller machine turned back toward the doorway; and Harry, waking to his opportunity, ducked through ahead of it.

He found himself in a corridor dimly lit by a luminescent strip down the center of its ceiling. The corridor was wide enough for the box-collecting machine to pass him; and, in fact, it rolled out around him as he shrank back against one metal wall. It went on down the corridor, and he followed it into a larger room with a number of machines, some mobile, some not, under a ceiling lit as the corridor had been with a crossing translucent strip.

In this area all the machines avoided each other—and him. They were busy with each other and at other incomprehensible duties. Hunched and tense, hair erect on the back of his neck and nostrils spread wide, Harry moved through them to explore other rooms and corridors that opened off this one. It took him some little time; but he discovered that they were all on a level, and there was nothing but machines in any of them. He found two more doors with shallow steps leading up to them, but these would not open for him; and though he watched by one for some time, no machine went up the steps and through it.

He began to be conscious of thirst and hunger. He made his way back to the door leading to the chamber where the prospecting machines were parked. To his surprise, it opened as he approached it. He slipped through into darkness.

Immediately, the door closed behind him; and sudden panic grabbed him when he found he could not open it from this side. Then, self-possession returned to him.

By touch, smell and memory, he made his way among the parked machines and down the corridor to the outside door. To his gratification, this also opened when he came close. He slipped through into cool, fresh outer air and a sky already graying with dawn. A few moments later, wet but free, he was back in the woods again.

From then on, each night he returned. He found it was not necessary to do more than put any sizeable object before a returning machine. It would stop to clear the path, and he could enter ahead of it. Then, shortly after he was inside, a box-collecting machine would open the inner door.

Gradually, his fear of the machines faded. He came to hold them in a certain contempt. They always did the same thing in the same situation, and it was easy to trick or outmaneuver them.

But the two inner doors of the machine area with the steps would not open to him; and he knew the upper parts of the pyramid were still unexplored by him. He sniffed at the cracks of these doors, and a scent came through—not of lubricating medium and metal alone, but of a different musky odor that raised the hairs on the back of his neck again. He snarled at the doors.

He went back to exploring minutely the machine level. The sample boxes from the prospecting machines, he found, were put on conveyorbelt-like strips that floated up on thin air through openings in the ceiling—but the openings were too small for him to pass through. But he discovered something else. One day he came upon one of the machines taking a grille off the face of one of the immobile devices. It carried the grille away, and he explored the opening that had been revealed. It was the entrance to a tunnel or duct leading upward; and it was large enough to let him enter it. Air blew silently from it; and the air was heavy with the musky odor he had smelled around the doors that did not open.

The duct tempted him, but fear held him back. The machine came back and replaced the grille; and he noticed that it fitted into place with a little pressure from the outside, top and bottom. After the machine had left he pressed, and the grille fell out into his hands.

After a long wait, he ventured timorously into the tube—but a sudden sound like heavy breathing mixed with a wave of a strong, musky odor came at him. He backed out in panic, fled the pyramid and did not come back for two days.

When he came back, the grille was again neatly in place. He removed it and sat a long time getting his courage up. Finally, he put the grille up high out of reach of the machine which had originally removed it and crawled into the duct.

He crept up the tube at an angle into darkness. His eyes were useless, but the musky odor came strongly at him. Soon, he heard sounds.

There was an occasional ticking, then a thumping or shuffling sound. Finally, after he had crawled a long way up through the tube, there was a sound like a heavy puffing or hoarse breathing. It was the sound that had accompanied the strengthening of the musky odor once before; and this time the scent came strong again.

He lay, almost paralyzed with terror in the tube, as the odor grew in his nostrils. He could not move until sound and scent had retreated. As soon as they had, he wormed his way backwards down to the lower level and freedom, replaced the grille and fled for the outside air, once again.

But once more, in time, he came back. Eventually returned to explore the whole network of tubes to which the one he had entered connected. Many of the branching tubes were too small for him to enter, and the biggest tube he could find led to another grille from which the musky-smelling air was blasted with force.

Clearly it was the prime mover for the circulation of air through the exhaust half of the pyramid's ventilating system. Harry did not reason it out to himself in those intellectual terms, but he grasped the concept wordlessly and went back to exploring those smaller tubes that he could crawl into.

These, he found, terminated in grilles set in their floors through which he could look down and catch a glimpse of some chamber or other. What he saw was mainly incomprehensible. There were a number of corridors, a number of what could be rooms containing fixed or movable objects of various sizes and shapes. Some of them could be the equivalent of chairs or beds—but if so, they were scaled for a being plainly larger than himself. The lighting was invariably the low-key illumination he had encountered in the lower, machine level of the pyramid, supplied by the single translucent strip running across the ceiling.

Occasionally, from one grille or another, he heard in the distance the heavy sound of breathing, among other sounds, and smelled more strongly the musky odor. But for more than a week of surreptitious visits to the pyramid, he watched through various grilles without seeing anything living.

V

However, a day finally came when he was crouched, staring down into a circular room containing what might be a bed shape, several chair shapes and a number of other fixed shapes with variously spaced and depthed indentations in their surfaces. In a far edge of the circular room was a narrow alcove, the walls of which were filled with ranked indentations, among which several lights of different colors winked and glowed.

Suddenly, the dim illumination of the room began to brighten. The illumination increased rapidly, so that Harry cringed back from the grille, lifting a palm to protect his dimness-accustomed eyes. At the same moment, he heard approaching the sound of heavy breathing and sniffed a sudden increase in the musky odor.

He froze. Motionless above the grille, he stopped even his breathing. He would have stopped his heart if he could, but it raced, shaking his whole body and sounding its rapid beat in his ears until he felt the noise of it must be booming through the pyramid like a drum. But there was no sign from below that this was so.

Then, sliding into sight below him, came a massive figure on a small platform that seemed to drift without support into the room.

The aperture of the grille was small. Harry's viewpoint was cramped and limited, looking down directly from overhead. He found himself looking down onto thick, hairless brown-skinned shoulders, a thick neck with the skin creased at the back and a forward-sloping, hairless brown head, egg-shaped in outline from above, with the point forward.

Foreshortened below the head and shoulders was a bulging chinline with something like a tusk showing; it had a squat, heavy, hairless, brown body and thick short forearms with stubby claws at the end of four-fingered hands. There was something walruslike about the tusks and the hunching;—and the musky odor rose sickeningly into Harry's human nostrils.

The platform slid level with the alcove, which was too narrow for it to enter. Breathing hoarsely, the heavy figure on it heaved itself suddenly off the platform into the alcove, and the stubby hands moved over the pattern of indentations. Then, it turned and heaved itself out of the alcove, onto the flat bed surface adjoining. Just as Harry's gaze began to get a full-length picture of it, the illumination below went out.

Harry was left, staring dazzled into darkness, while the heavy breathing and the sound of the figure readjusting itself on the bed surface came up to his ears. After a while, there was no noise but the breathing. But Harry did not dare move. For a long time he held his cramped posture, hardly breathing himself. Finally, cautiously, inch-by-inch, he retreated down the tube, which was too small to let him turn around. When he reached the larger tubes, he fled for the outside and the safety of the forest.

The next day, he did not go near the pyramid. Or the next. Every time he thought of the heavy, brown figure entering the room below the grille, he became soaked with the clammy sweat of a deep, emotional terror. He could understand how the Other had not heard him or seen him up behind the grille. But he could not understand how the alien had not *smelled* him.

Slowly, however, he came to accept the fact that the Other had not. Possibly the Other did not have a sense of smell. Possibly . . . there was no end to the possibilities. The fact was that the Other had not smelled Harry—or heard him—or seen him. Harry was like a rat in the walls—unknown because he was unsuspected.

At the end of the week, Harry was once more prowling around back by the pyramid. He had not intended to come back, but his hatred drew him like the need of a drug addict for the drug of his addiction. He had to see the Other again, to feed his hate more surely. He had to look at the Other, while hating the alien, and feel the wild black current of his emotions running toward the brown and hairless shape. At night, buried in his nest of leaves, Harry tossed and snarled in his sleep, dreaming of the small stream backing up to flood the interior of the pyramid, and the Other drowning—of lightning striking the pyramid and fire racing through it—of the Other burning. His dreams became so full of rage and so terrible that he woke, twisting and with the few rags of clothing that still managed to cling unnoticed to him, soaked with sweat.

In the end, he went back into the pyramid.

Daily he went back. And gradually, it came to the point where he was no longer fearful of seeing the Other. Instead, he could barely endure the search and the waiting at the grilles until the Other came into sight. Meanwhile, outside the pyramid in the forest, the frill-edged leaves began to dry and wither and drop. The little stream sank in its bed—only a few inches, but enough so that Harry had to dig out the bottom of the streambed under the killing barrier in order to pass safely underwater into the pyramid area.

One day he noticed that there were hardly any of the treaded machines out taking samples in the woods any more.

He was on his way to the pyramid through the woods, when the realization struck him. He stopped dead, freezing in mid-stride like a hunting dog. Immediately, there flooded into his mind the memory of how the parking chamber for the treaded machines, inside the base of the pyramid, had been full of unmoving vehicles during his last few visits.

Immediately, also, he realized the significance of the drying leaves, the dropping of the water level of the stream. And something with the urgency of a great gong began to ring and ring inside him like the pealing of an alarm over a drowning city.

Time had been, when there had been no pyramid here. Time was now, with the year fading and the work of the collecting machines almost done. Time would be, when the pyramid might leave.

Taking with it the Other.

He began to run, instinctively, toward the pyramid. But, when he came within sight of it, he stopped. For a moment he was torn with indecision, an emotional maelstrom of fear and hatred all whirling together. Then, he went on.

He emerged a moment later, dripping, fist-sized rock in each hand, to stand before the closed door that gave the machines entrance to the pyramid. He stood staring at it, in broad daylight. He had never come here before in full daylight, but his head now was full of madness. Fury seethed in him, but there was no machine to open the door for him. It was then that the fury and madness in him might have driven him to pound wildly on the door with his stones or to wrench off one of the necks of the storklike machine at the stream and try to pry the door open. Any of these insane things he might have done and so have attracted discovery and the awesome power of the machinery and killing weapons at the command of the Other. Any such thing he might have done if he were simply a man out of his head with rage—but he was no longer a man.

He was what the Other had made him, an animal, although with a man locked inside him. And like an animal, he did not rave or rant, any more than does the cat at the mousehole, or the wolf waiting for the shepherd to turn in for the night. Instead, without further question, the human beast that had been Harry Brennan—that still called himself Harry Brennan, in a little, locked-away back corner of its mind—dropped on his haunches beside the door and hunkered there, panting lightly in the sunlight and waiting.

Four hours later, as the sun was dropping close to the treetops, a single machine came trundling out of the woods. Harry tricked it with one of his stones and, still carrying the other, ran into the pyramid.

He waited patiently for the small collecting machine to come and empty out the machine returned from outside, then dodged ahead of it, when it came, into the interior, lower level of the pyramid. He made his way calmly to the grille that gave him entrance to the ventilating system, took out the grille and entered the tube. Once in the system, he crawled through the maze of ductwork, until he came at last to the grille overlooking the room with the alcove and the rows of indentations on the alcove walls.

When he looked down through the grille, it was completely dark below. He could hear the hoarse breathing and smell the musky odor of the Other, resting or perhaps asleep, on the bed surface. Harry lay there for a number of slow minutes, smelling and listening. Then he lifted the second rock and banged with it upon the grille.

For a second there was nothing but the echoing clang of the beaten metal in the darkness. Then the room suddenly blazed with light, and Harry, blinking his blinded eyes against the glare, finally made out the figure of the Other rising upright upon the bed surface. Great, round, yellow eyes in a puglike face with a thick upper lip wrinkled over two tusks stared up through the grille at Harry.

The lip lifted, and a bubbling roar burst from the heavy fat-looking shape of the Other. He heaved his round body off the bed surface and rolled, waddling across the floor to just below the grille.

Reaching up with one blunt-clawed hand, he touched the grille, and it fell to the floor at his feet. Left unguarded in the darkness of the ductwork, Harry shrank back. But the Other straightened up to his full near six-and-a-half feet of height and reached up into the ductwork. His blunt clawed hand fastened on Harry and jerked. Off balance, Harry came tumbling to the floor of the chamber.

A completely human man probably would have stiffened up and broken both arms, if not his neck, in such a fall. Harry, animal-like, attempted to cling to the shape of the Other as he fell, and so broke the impact of his landing. On the floor, he let go of the Other and huddled away from the heavy shape, whimpering.

The Other looked down, and his round, yellow eyes focused on the stone Harry had clung to even through his fall. The Other reached down and grasped it, and Harry gave it up like a child releasing something he has been told many times not to handle. The Other made another, lower-toned, bubbling roar deep in his chest, examining the rock. Then he laid it carefully aside on a low table surface and turned back to stare down at Harry.

Harry cringed away from the alien stare and huddled into himself, as the blunt fingers reached down to feel some of the rags of a shirt that still clung about his shoulders.

The Other rumbled interrogatively at Harry. Harry hid his head. When he looked up again, the Other had moved over to a wall at the right of the alcove and was feeling about in some indentations there. He bubbled at the wall, and a second later Harry's voice sounded eerily in the room.

"... You are ... the one I ... made a beast ..."

Harry whimpered, hiding his head again.

"You can't ..." said Harry's voice, "... even speak now. Is ... that so ..."

Harry ventured to peek upwards out of his folded arms, but ducked his head again at the sight of the cold, yellow eyes staring down at him.

"... I thought ... you would be ... dead by now," said the disembodied voice of Harry, hanging in the air of the chamber. "... Amazing ... survival completely without ... equipment. Must keep you now ..." The eyes, yellow as topaz, considered

Harry, huddled abjectly on the floor, ". . . cage . . . collector's item . . ."

The alien revolved back to the indentations of the wall a little way from the alcove. The broad, fleshy back turned contemptuously on Harry, who stared up at it.

The pitiful expression of fear on Harry's face faded suddenly into a soundless snarl. Silently, he uncoiled, snatched up the rock the Other had so easily taken from him, and sprang with it onto the broad back.

As he caught and clung there, one arm wrapped around a thick neck, the stone striking down on the hairless skull, his silent snarl burst out at last into the sound of a scream of triumph.

The Other screamed too—a bubbling roar—as he clumsily turned, trying to reach around himself with his thick short arms and pluck Harry loose. His claws raked Harry's throat-encircling arm, and blood streamed from the arm; but it might have been so much stage make-up for the effect it had in loosening Harry's hold. Screaming, Harry continued to pound crushingly on the Other's skull. With a furious spasm, the alien tore Harry loose, and they both fell on the floor.

The Other was first up; and for a second he loomed like a giant over Harry, as Harry was scrambling to his own feet and retrieving the fallen rock. But instead of attacking, the Other flung away, lunging for the alcove and the control indentations there.

Harry reached the alcove entrance before him. The alien dodged away from the striking rock. Roaring and bubbling, he fled waddling from his human pursuer, trying to circle around the room and get back to the alcove. Half a head taller than Harry and twice Harry's weight, he was refusing personal battle and putting all his efforts into reaching the alcove with its rows of indented controls. Twice Harry headed him off; and then by sheer mass and desperation, the Other turned and burst past into the alcove, thick hands outstretched and grasping at its walls. Harry leaped in pursuit, landing and clinging to the broad, fleshy back.

The other stumbled under the added weight, and fell, face down. Triumphantly yelling, Harry rode the heavy body to the floor, striking at the hairless head . . . and striking . . . and striking . . .

VI

Sometime later, Harry came wearily to his senses and dropped a rock he no longer had the strength to lift. He blinked around himself like a man waking from a dream, becoming aware of a brilliantly lit room full of strange shapes—and of a small alcove, the walls of which were covered with rows of indentations, in which something large and dead lay with its head smashed into ruin. A deep, clawing thirst rose to take Harry by the throat, and he staggered to his feet.

He looked longingly up at the dark opening of the ventilator over his head; but he was too exhausted to jump up, cling to its edge and pull himself back into the ductwork, from which he could return to the stream outside the pyramid and to the flowing water there. He turned and stumbled from the chamber into unfamiliar rooms and corridors.

A brilliant light illuminated everything around him as he went. He sniffed and thought he scented, through the musky reek that filled the air about him, the clear odor of water. Gradually, the scent grew stronger and led him at last to a room where a bright stream leaped from a wall into a basin where it pooled brightly before draining away. He drank deeply and rested.

Finally, satiated, he turned away from the basin and came face-to-face with a wall that was all reflecting surface; and he stopped dead, staring at himself, like Adam before the Fall.

It was only then, with the upwelling of his returning humanness, that he realized his condition. And words spoken aloud for the first time in months broke harshly and rustily from his lips like the sounds of a machine unused for years.

"My God!" he said, croakingly. "I've got no clothes left!"

And he began to laugh. Cackling, cackling rasping more unnaturally even than his speech, his laughter lifted and echoed hideously through the silent, alien rooms. But it was laughter all the same—the one sound that distinguishes man from the animal.

He was six months after that learning to be a complete human being again and finding out how to control the pyramid. If it had not been for the highly sophisticated safety devices built into the alien machine, he would never have lived to complete that bit of self-education.

But finally he mastered the controls and got the pyramid into orbit, where he collected the rest of his official self and shifted back through the alternate universe to Earth.

He messaged ahead before he landed; and everybody who could be there was on hand to meet him as he landed the pyramid. Some of the hands that had slapped his back on leaving were raised to slap him again when at last he stepped forth among them.

But, not very surprisingly, when his gaunt figure in a spare coverall now too big for it, with shoulder-length hair and burning eyes, stepped into their midst, not one hand finished its gesture. No one in his right senses slaps an unchained wolf on the back and no one, after one look, wished to risk slapping the man who seemed to have taken the place of Harry.

Of course, he was still the same man they had sent out— of *course* he was. But at the same time he was also the man who had returned from a world numbered 1242 and from a duel to the death there with a representative of a race a hundred times more advanced than his own. And in the process he had been pared down to something very basic in his human blood and bone, something dating back to before the first crude wheel or chipped flint knife.

And what was that? Go down into the valley of the shades and demand your answer of a dead alien with his head crushed in, who once treated the utmost powers of modern human science as a man treats the annoyance of a buzzing mosquito.

Or, if that once-mighty traveler in spacegoing pyramids is disinclined to talk, turn and inquire of other ghosts you will find there—those of the aurochs, the great cave bear and the woolly mammoth.

They, too, can testify to the effectiveness of naked men.

THE CHEMICALLY PURE WARRIORS

Allen Kim Lang

I

From the head of the platoon Lieutenant Lee Hartford signaled Sergeant Felix, busy policing up stragglers at the rear, that he was taking over. Hartford tongued the volume setting of his bitcher to Low and softly singsonged to his three dozen troopers: *"Your girlfriend's just an hour away; There's a time to soldier and a time to play.* Pick it HUP, HUP, HUP! 'Toon, tain-HUT. HUP, twop, threep, furp; HUP, HUP; HUP, twop, threep, furp. Mondrian, pick up the cadence; you're marching like a man with a paper pelvis. *Swing 'em six to the front and three to the rear; When you sing to your Daddy, sing it loud and clear."* Hartford turned up the volume. *"Three weeks in the woods, eating squeeze-tube beans; We'd be better off in the Fleet Marines. Sound off!"*

"ONE, TWO," boomed the voice of the Terrible Third, sounding from the bitchers at the chests of thirty-six safety-suits. Dust slapped up from marching boots. A flock of scarlet blabrigars settled on the road ahead, chattering and watching like small boys.

"Sound hoff!"

"THREE, FOUR!" The road led uphill toward Stinkerville; they were some three miles from First Regiment Barracks. Three miles from now these troopers could shed their safety-

163

suits and helmets, shower off three weeks of sweat, drink a beer and leer at the short-skirted, taut-haltered girls of the Service Companies.

"Who are we?" Hartford chanted.

"COMPANY C," the troopers blatted back.

The blabrigars, fluttering up from the roadway, chanted too: "Who are we? Company See. Who, we? See, see. Company See Are Wee See See." These wild birds didn't memorize human speech as well as their captive cousins; they garbled their mockeries immediately. The flock settled into the sunflowers beside the road; and were joined by a pair of wild camelopards, chewing sunflower-leaf cud as they peered at the marching Axenites. Hartford looked about, but there were no Stinkers—Kansans—in sight. These natives didn't care to watch the occupying regiment stir up their homeland's dust. *"What platoon?"* Hartford called, his voice magnified by the bitcher till the whole column could hear him.

"THIRD PLATOON," the men bellowed back, singing against the percussion of their boots. "'Toon, click, click, click; 'toon, click, third platoon, click," mocked the blabrigars in ragged chorus, reflecting both the words and the marching feet.

"Best platoon?"

"THIRD PLATOON!" the men shouted. They'd turned up their bitchers to a volume the blabrigars couldn't match. Disgusted, the birds flapped their scarlet wings and flew off across the sunflower fields. "'Toon," one rear flier chanted, "'toon, 'toon, 'toon."

"Worst platoon?" Hartford asked.

"FIRST PLATOON!" That was for the benefit of Lieutenant Piacentelli, commanding the tail end of the Regiment, the platoon marching on either side of the lumbering Decontamination Vehicle, their safety-suit filters clogging with the dust.

"Sound off!" Hartford shouted.

"ONE, TWO!"

That'll rattle the windows in Stinkerville, Hartford thought. He pitched his descant louder and higher. *"Sound off!"*

"THREE, FOUR!"

"Run 'er on down!"

"ONE, TWO, THREE, FOUR; ONE, TWO, THREEP— FURP!" The men of the Terrible Third were grinning through the faceplates of their helmets, rejoicing in their reputation as the loudest bunch in the regiment, happy to help Hartford in waging his mock-feud with Lieutenant Piacentelli. They'd been classmates at the Axenite Academy; they'd been roommates in the Barracks until Pia's recent marriage to a Service Company officer.

Hartford lowered his bitcher to a confidential tone. "Square up, men; march tall; look rough and dirty. Show the Stinker girls what they're missing. HUP, HUP, HUP. Sling those rifles square. Mondrian, you march like you're wearing skis; HUP, twop, threep, furp!" Up and down the column came the commands of sergeants and platoon commanders, getting their troopers in parade trim for the march through Kansannamura: "Stinkerville." Somewhere up front a company was singing the anthem of the Axenite troopers, "Oh, Pioneers!" The chorus of twelve dozen men, their bitchers full up, filled the Kansan air and echoed from the walls ahead.

Stinkerville, all whitewashed, with flakes of mica glittering in the sunlight, sprawled across the road that led to the Barracks. The village wall, designed to keep wild camelopards from roaming the streets and to keep the tame beasts out of the sunflower fields, was some eight feet tall. Some Indigenous Hominid had heard the regiment's clatter and song, for the gates of Kansannamura were open, the brick streets were clear of Stinker commerce. The village seemed deserted. A few blabrigars perched on the tiled eaves of the rammed-earth houses, making echoic comments on the sounds of the troopers, singing fleeting snatches of "Oh, Pioneers!" A camelopard stretched its ridiculous, three-horned head at the end of its fathom of neck to peer, big-brown-eyed, at the caravan of fishbowl-headed men. Up at the head of the column the regiment's flags were unfurled and the regimental band was skirling the anthem; men were counting cadence as their boots clicked over the scrubbed bricks of Stinkerville's streets.

But no Kansan, Stinker, Indigenous Hominid, Gook or Native watched. No cowboy youngsters stared at the gunned-and-holstered men from another planet. No elders looked down their noses at the brash invaders. No mothers wiped their hands on their aprons as they thought of their sons, and the fleshly price they'd pay for freedom. No teenage girls, those patrons of parades, watched with lips half-open with apprehension and audacious thoughts about the hundreds of gift-wrapped young men marching past. This planet could have as well been named

Coventry as Kansas, Hartford thought. Out the far gate of Kansannamura marched Third Platoon, Company C, then First Platoon, flanking the Decontamination Vehicle. A villager came from the house nearest the gate and closed it. He did not look after the two columns of men winding up through the fields of sunflowers to the high plateau where they lived.

The sight of the Barracks gave the men's steps a new swing and spring. After three weeks of sleeping in safety-suits; of breathing, sweating, drinking, eating and excreting through germ-barrier valves and tubing, the prospect of stripping off the plastic battle dress was seductive. Inside those eight stories of windowless, doorless stone were gardens where the troopers could walk barefoot on the grass, pools whose water could splash their naked skin. In the Barracks were the three hundred Service Company women who made the big stone box home to their three thousand men.

The men of First Regiment massed on the parade ground. While they stood at ease, their plastic-sleeved rifles and packs growing heavier by the minute, their safety-suits staler, four of the five Service Companies marched out from the Syphon to join them. The women were suited in yellow plastic, giving rise to the gags about fool's gold. The four golden companies took up position at the center of the regiment.

Colonel Benjamin Nef, commander in chief, Kansas, CINCK, climbed to the reviewing stand in his command safety-suit of scarlet. Facing into the sun, the colonel had the polarizing shield dropped over his eyes, and seemed to be wearing a black bandage. His lower jaw beetled to give him a truculent look generally ratified by his actions. His hair glinted through the helmet like spun copper. Nef turned to his second-in-command, a lieutenant colonel in ordinary officer's blues, and murmured instructions. The light colonel saluted, turned the controls of his bitcher to Full Loud, and addressed the troopers assembled: "Regiment . . ."

Down the chain-of-command came the ripple of warning: "Battaaalion . . ."

"Commmpaneee . . ."

"'Toooon . . .'"

"Tain-HUT!" Fifteen hundred pairs of boots smacked together. The adjutant held up his clipboard and read precisely: "Attention to orders:

"One. Officer of the guard, Lieutenant Lee Hartford.

"Two. CINCK commends troopers involved in the just-completed three-week field exercise on not having had a single incident of compromise of sterility. Household, Maintenance and Security troopers are complimented on having maintained the integrity of the Barracks with a much-reduced force.

"Three. All male and female troopers are again cautioned that fraternization with Indigenous Hominids is an offense punishable by general court-martial, and that any unauthorized intercourse with the natives is prohibited."

There was of course a murmur of automatic laughter at this last bit of official double entendre. The idea of bedding down a Stinker wench was a favorite bit of pornographic fantasy. An airtight safety-suit, though fit with valves as functional as the drop seat in long johns, was no garment for romance. To undress, to appear in outdoor Kansas outside that head-to-foot sausage casing, appealed to none of the troopers. Healthy young men and women don't entertain the thought of painful suicide.

The reporting officer about-faced, saluted Colonel Nef, about-faced again. "Present . . ."

"Preezent . . ."

"Preeezent . . ."

"Preeeezent . . ."

"HAHMS!" Fifteen hundred Dardick-rifles, sheathed in plastic, slapped perpendicular. The blue-clad officers, armed with pistols, touched their index fingers to their helmet temples. The bandsmen's drums growled, the electronic horns sobbed against their mutes, and the flutes in lonely purity played the theme of "Oh, Pioneers!" For all his har-de-har-hardness, Hartford felt a sting in his eyes at this moment, as he did whenever the splendidly stage-managed ceremony of retreat was performed. After the anthem, much louder, the band played retreat. The colors crept down the flagstaff, into the reverent arms of a pair of Service Policemen.

"Oh-deph, HAHMS! By line-of-battalions, line-of-companies, line-of-platoons, line-of-squads, return to quarters and dismiss!" The light colonel made one last salute of CINCK, and the little ballet on the reviewing stand was over. The troopers were now free to go in to their showers, their latrines, their suppers, and their women.

"At ease," Hartford told the Terrible Third. "Rest. Smoke if you've got 'em."

The men chuckled dutifully at the oldest joke in the service.

An Axenite trooper, sealed in his germ-free safety-suit and helmet, is by definition a non-smoker outside his Barracks. It would be another hour they'd be outside, since the Third was next to the last of the fifty platoons to swim home through the Syphon. While the companies on the far left flank of the regiment were ballooning up and peeling off in columns-of-squads to enter the Barracks, Hartford went back to talk with Piacentelli, C.O. of First Platoon.

II

Getting inside the Barracks was a production. The safety-suits worn outside presumably bore on their outer surfaces all the dust-borne bugs native to Kansas. To carry these bacteria into the Barracks, to be inspired and ingested by Axenites—humans who'd never before had a bacterium inside their bodies—would wipe out the regiment. Axenites are chemically pure people. They have no immunological experience. Their gamma globulin is low, their intestinal walls are thin. They may be killed by a light salting of staphyllococci, a soupçon on strep, or just a pinch of B. subtilis, a buglet as innocuous to "normal" humans as the dust motes it inhabits.

The Syphon was the only entrance to the Barracks. It opened as the "Wet Gut," a ramp leading downward into liquid disinfectant which finally filled a tunnel, which ran the length of the Barracks. Each trooper, as he walked down into the disinfectant, grabbed the handholds at either side to pull himself along. Half-swimming through a turbulent portion that tugged at his suit with cavitations designed to loose the gummiest particle of bug-dirt, he came to a quieter section where he wormed along in silence, watching the man ahead of him, his stay in the antiseptic gauged to make the outside of his safety-suit as germ free as the inside.

The Wet Gut ended in an upslope. The troopers walked out, dripping, into a hallway returning in the direction from which they'd just swum. This upper arm of the Syphon was a hallway so brilliantly lighted that the trooper had to drop his polarizing shields over his eyes. The air here in the Hot Gut was spiced with ozone from the ultra-violet sources. As each man strode down the Hot Gut at a set pace, his suit was bathed in u-v light from lamps in the ceiling, floor and walls. Just as he was washed sufficiently in the Wet Gut to kill the sturdiest-shelled spore of anthrax, the most insistently cysted protozoan, in the Hot Gut he was laved in actinic radiation powerful enough to afford a one hundred per cent safety factor against his bringing viable bug-dirt into the Barracks. At the very end of the Syphon, so that his safety-suit wouldn't stink of disinfectant or crack from ozone-rot, the trooper was blasted from all sides by a needle shower of sterile water. Then he was home.

The platoon to the left of the Terrible Third had ballooned and was column-of-squadding toward the entrance to the Syphon. "At ease, men," Hartford said. "Increase suit pressure one pound. Open and check reserve air tanks. Close off filters." The men blimped a bit. Their suits sausaged out around their arms and legs. Should some trooper have a pinhole in his safety-suit, the positive pressure within would keep the deadly antiseptic solution from seeping in. "Okay, men. First squad off to the sheep-dip. Check the man ahead of you for bubbles. This is Save-Your-Buddy Week," Hartford said.

Fat-legged and stiff, the men of Third Platoon waddled through the doorway and down the ramp into the bug-juice. One by one they went under, tugging themselves along through the turbulent area, past that; then turning over in three planes so that the man behind them could spot bubbles coming from any part of their safety-suit. A leak, of course, meant decontamination. Decontamination meant an all-over shave, a load of antibiotics and quarantine. But it was better that one man should suffer this from time to time than that the Barracks should be sullied with a single bit of germ-laden dust.

The pale-green murk of the Wet Gut and the desert brightness of the Hot Gut were the gates of home, and welcome.

Hartford saw the Terrible Third off to their quarters, then got together with Piacentelli to go up to Officers' Country. It was good to unclam helmets and breathe the inside air, smelling faintly green from having swept across the gardens on Level Eight. Hartford shucked off his blue suit and draped it over a refreshing unit. The device buzzed into action, washing, drying and recharging the safety-suit with fresh filters and reserve air and water. The moment the refresher had grunted an okay to his safety-suit, Hartford carried it, clean and sweet, as the day it had left the Goodyear plant on Titan, to hang it up in his locker, ready for his next foray onto bug-dirt.

Piacentelli was already under a shower. "Come on, jaybird," he shouted. "Last one out buys the beers."

"No contest," Hartford said, setting the shower dial. "I'm gonna stay underwater for three weeks." He revolved blissfully beneath cold and angry needles.

Piacentelli, snowed in with suds and steam, yelled through the blasting water. "How'd you rate O.G. the night we get in?" he asked. "I thought you were Nasty Nef's fairhaired boy."

Hartford turned off his shower. "I got nothing better to do," he said. He stood on the drier for a minute. "I don't mind being officer of the guard, so long as I can eat supper off a plate instead of through a tube." He stepped into his shorts, pulled on sneakers and tugged on a tee-shirt that had stenciled over its shoulders the two half-inch gold stripes of his rank.

Pia dressed in a similar uniform. "It isn't the mess hall I miss," he said. "It's this. No number of ingenious engines, valves and relief tubes can still my nostalgia for the simple dignity of our Barracks latrines."

Junior Officers' Mess was set in what looked like a park, except that the bushes were tomato-plants and the trees grew apples. The tables were mostly full. "All the subalterns getting in a quick sundowner," Pia remarked, finding a two-place table yet untaken. A Service Company K.P. in the brief skirt-and-halter Class Bs the women wore informally in the Barracks came to take their order. "Big cold beer for me, honey," Pia said. "The other gentleman is tonight's O.G., so he'll have a black, black coffee."

Hartford stared after the girl. "You're right, Pia," he said. "No matter how comfy Goodyear makes those safety-suits, home is best."

"You bachelors are a threat to the Table of Organization," Piacentelli said. "You'd breed us right out of house and home if you had a chance."

"Damned right," Hartford said.

"You could find a girl," Piacentelli said.

"They all itch to get married," Hartford explained. "They come out to these germy planets like they used to go to Purdue. The man-woman ratio is in their favor. And biology. Pia, I've seen bears you wouldn't glim twice on Titan turn into love goddesses after six months here. I'll meet some Service Company corporal, say. She'll look to me like the prettiest li'l thing since Adam's costectomy, and I'll call in at the Orderly Room to have us assigned family quarters. Back at Home Base, she'll turn out to be something you scare kids quiet with. She'll talk all the time, leave lipstick on drinking glasses, or play bridge and talk about it. First thing you know, I'll be volunteering for another five years duty on bug-dirt, just for a chance to leave her behind."

"So pick up a local germ," Piacentelli suggested. "If they can't decontaminate you, they'll send you to Earth. Lots of women on Earth."

"I'd do it," Hartford said, "but I'm still more scared of microbes than lustful for a woman. Here's Dimples with our chow."

"Dimples?" Piacentelli asked as the girl came up with their tray.

"Watch her when she walks away," Hartford suggested.

"You must keep a carton of goat glands under your bunk, Lee," Piacentelli said. "Marriage isn't all bad. I've done pretty well with Paula."

Hartford nodded. Paula Piacentelli, a lieutenant in the Service Companies, was a pretty decent sort. "Where is she now?" he asked.

"She'll be on the Status Board tonight," Piacentelli said. "You'll be in the Board Room with her. Lee, I've got a favor to ask you. As O.G. you'll be in charge tonight."

"Paula will be in charge," Hartford said. "I'll be sleeping."

"If I go outside, though, it will need your okay as well as Paula's," Piacentelli said.

"Who's going outside with you?"

"That's the sticky bit," Piacentelli said. "I'd like to go outside alone."

"Want to run in the rain in your little bare skin?" Hartford asked. "Mix it up with a Stinker maiden? Paula wouldn't like that. Besides, you might get yourself jackrolled by some Indigenous Hominid who doesn't like Axenites running his planet."

"I want to work on my Kansan-Standard Dictionary," Piacentelli said.

"Bug-dirt," Hartford said. "Don't tell lies."

"All right, then," Piacentelli said. "I've got an idea that might lead to the most important discovery ever made on Kansas. Paula suggested it. I want to prove it."

"Tell Nasty Nef about your idea," Hartford said, signalling the waitress for a second cup of stay-awake. "Give CINCK something clever to report when the supply ship lands, and you'll have your silver stripes before I will. Wouldn't Paula love that, though? Captain Piacentelli. I'd have to salute first."

"Nasty Nef wouldn't consider our idea," Piacentelli said. "He wouldn't be happy to know that I've been studying the Kansan language, even. A common humanity between us Axenites and the Indigenous Hominids is a notion not welcome to the world of Colonel Nef. *Brother* Nef, I might say."

Hartford leaned against the table to press a fist against Piacentelli's propped elbow. "Don't say that, Pia," he whispered. "I'm not political; I'm not interested; I don't care whether the Brotherhood even exists."

"Yes, Virginia; there is a Brotherhood," Piacentelli said. "And our Nasty Nef is a Brother."

"He's a number of things," Hartford said. "He's our C.O.; he's CINCK; he's an SOB. But he's our boss, and 'Brotherhood' is a dangerous word." He sipped his coffee. "Tell you what, Pia. If you want to go out and talk Gook with the Gooks, I'll fix it for you to draw picket duty tonight. The man who's got picket has been married only a month, and spent three weeks of that in a safety-suit out in the woods. I'm sure he'll relinquish to you the pleasure of a night's romp as picket officer."

"Can you do it?"

"An O.G. can do anything, during those hours when his superior officers are asleep," Hartford said.

"You're a buddy," Piacentelli said. "I'll give you free tutoring in Kansan for the rest of our tour."

"*Do mo arigato gazaimashita,*" Hartford said. "Thanks to your mumbling the stuff in our room, I already talk like a Stinker." He stood up. "I'm going down to the Board Room. Pick your companion for picket, and come on down when you've dressed." Hartford bowed, Kansas-style. "*Shitsurei itashimasu ga . . .*" he said politely, and left to assume his duties as O.G.

III

As one of the seventy-six male lieutenants of the regiment, Hartford pulled O.G. about once every eleven weeks. His Terrible Third drew duty with him as guard platoon. All of them could expect to sleep through the night undisturbed, unless Nasty Nef held a dry run, falling them out for a Simulated Problem. Nef was tired tonight, though; the guard could sleep. Only the two men on picket and the handful of Service Company personnel on duty at the Status Board need stay awake tonight.

Awake or sleeping, the security of First Regiment would rest this night in the hands of Lee Hartford. It was he who bore the final responsibility for allowing no living thing to enter the Barracks except in a well-scrubbed safety-suit; for assuring that the air his sleeping comrades breathed was sterile and dustless; that the Syphon's poisonous bug-juice was of the proper pH and germicidity; and for checking that the whereabouts of every Axenite on Kansas was reflected on the Status Board. That these duties were complex was attested by the assignment of a Service Company officer to the Board, a woman who would watch the Board's bands of lights and meters every moment. Hartford could sleep; he was the Responsible Male. Mrs. Paula Piacentelli, 1/Lt. S.C. (Gnotobiotics Spec.), had to remain awake: she was the Knowledgeable Woman.

Hartford found Paula already at her work in the Board Room. Only a bit over five feet tall, Piacentelli's wife was concentrated woman of the most splendid sort. When Hartford had told her that Pia was taking the picket, she frowned. "I hope he doesn't plan anything foolish."

"Me? Foolish?" Piacentelli demanded from the elevator. He walked up, clammed shut his blue safety-suit, ready to hit bug-dirt. Under one arm he carried a package sheathed in opaque plastic. Behind him, in the gray safety-suit of an enlisted trooper, was a man Hartford recognized as Corporal Bond, machine gunner from Pia's platoon. "Lieutenant Gabriel Piacentelli reporting with one man, sir and ma'am," he said, saluting his wife and Hartford.

"At ease, Weenie-head," Hartford said. "With you and Bond on picket amidst the sunflowers, I won't sleep a wink all night." He turned to the corporal. "Did you sure-enough volunteer for this duty?" he asked.

"Yes, sir!" Bond said. "I voluntarily assumed the duty of absorbing a fifth of Lieutenant Piacentelli's Class VI Scotch. The lieutenant was kind enough to reciprocate by offering me this tour."

"He gave you Scotch?" Hartford turned to Piacentelli. "Gabe, for a jug of Scotch I'd have gone on picket with you myself. What's that you're taking outside with you? Lunch?"

"A microscope," Piacentelli said. "I'm doing a little research for Paula." His wife nodded. A gnotobiotics technician, responsible for maintaining the bacteriological security of the Barracks, she had business with microscopes.

"Want to give me the word on this romp of yours?" Hartford asked.

"Standard picket, Lee," Piacentelli said. "I'll learn a little Kansan, take care of Paula's project and tell you all about it when we get back."

"Let's see your weapons." Hartford inspected Bond's Dardick-rifle and Piacentelli's Dardick-pistol. Both weapons were loaded, clean and wrapped up for their trip through the Wet Gut in plastic sleeves. The trucks and heavy weapons stayed outside on bug-dirt. The lighter weapons and all ammunition came back inside the Barracks with the troopers who carried them. The weapons were detail-stripped on each re-entry, irradiated with u-v and fit with fresh sleeves. As had been discovered with the first axenic animals, in the 1930's, keeping a mammal germ-free is a formidable task. When that mammal is a human being and a soldier the job is double-tough.

"Check out a jeep," Hartford said. "Report each half hour. Don't shoot any Stinkers . . . sorry, I mean Indigenous Hominids. Try not to hit a camelopard with the jeep; we're low on replacement parts. In fact, be careful. Okay, Pia?"

"Done and done, Exalted One."

Hartford dropped his voice. "I'd feel easier in my mind if I knew what's so important as to require your desertion of our mutual womb tonight, Pia."

"Language study, you might say," Piacentelli replied.

"Ha! So desa ka?" Hartford replied. "That's so much bug-dirt, and you know it."

"Ha!" Piacentelli said. "See you at dawn. Take care of my wife, buddy."

"Aren't you going to kiss her good night?" Hartford asked.

Pia grinned through his clammed-shut helmet and clomped to the elevator with Bond. They were en route to the Hot Gut and the Wet Gut, the twisting hallway from the sterile First Regiment Barracks to the living night of Kansas.

Hartford turned.

Paula Piacentelli wore the short skirt, knee hose and short-

sleeved blouse of Pioneer green that was the Class B uniform
for females inside the Barracks. She looked, Hartford thought,
remarkably delectable; and he again congratulated his friend
on his luck in getting her. He returned his attention to the Status
Board, which Paula was conning. Two red lights flickered on
above the ground-floor diagram of the Barracks, indicating that
the two men of the picket had entered the Hot Gut. A moment
later these lights blinked off, and two lighted over the diagram
of the Wet Gut. Piacentelli and Bond were swimming now,
towing their weapons in ballooning plastic sleeves. Sterile, on
their way out into a filthy world, these two men were the outpost
that would protect through the night their hundreds of brothers
and sisters sleeping safe *in utero*. Freud, thou shouldst have
lived this hour! Hartford mused.

Piacentelli turned the ignition key of the jeep he'd chosen.
With the starting cough of the engine, one of the rank of TV
screens over the Status Board lighted. The camera eye was
looking out the rear view mirror of the jeep, and picked up
Pia's helmeted head and the shoulder of his companion. "We're
off to see the Wizard, the Wonderful Wizard of Oz!" Piacentelli
sang.

His wife spoke into the microphone before her. "Don't do
anything foolish, Lieutenant," she said. "And remember, all
transmissions are recorded and are audited, at random, by the
base commander."

"Transmission received, receiver contrite," Piacentelli reported back. "Okay, Paula-darling. From now on till Bond and
I swim home, we'll be as military as GI soap." He flicked the
TV monitor around to look out the windshield and started the
jeep down the road toward Stinkerville. The duty of the picket
was to chug around outside at random, hitting all the crossroads,
settlements and high spots of the countryside near the Barracks;
to interview late-riding Indigenous Hominids and inquire their
business being out; to conduct such searches of Stinker homes
and hideaways as might seem useful to the occupying Axenites;
and to remain at all times in contact with the officers on duty
at the Status Board.

As the picket got underway, Hartford went down to the
Terrible Third's area to check quickly through the two-man
apartments. Knock on the door; "As you were, troopers." A
brisk inspection of two safety-suits, gaping beside their owners'

bunks like firemen's boot-sheathed pants. The men were quiet.
Guard duty meant that any socializing with Service Company
troopers was impossible for a night, and militated against any
intake of alcoholic beverage. It was a bore, especially after
three dry and womanless weeks in the field. Hartford visited
his platoon sergeant last: "Sergeant Felix, could you have our
bunch standing on bug-dirt ten minutes after I blew the whistle?
Very well, then. Goodnight, Felix."

Having demonstrated to his troopers that he was suffering
the same strictures as they, Hartford went back to the O.G.
cubicle in the Board Room. He checked his own safety-suit,
his plastic-packaged Dardick-pistol, said good night to Paula
Piacentelli and lay down to begin his first night's sleep outside
a safety-suit in three weeks.

But sleep didn't come easily.

There was the murmur from the Board Room; Piacentelli's
half-hourly reports. "Nothing to report, Paula. I'm at Road
Junction (41-17). No I.H. activity. No excitement at all."

"Continue random patrol, Lieutenant."

"Yes, dear. I'm going to run down to Kansannamura (42-
19) for my next call-in."

"Carry on, Lieutenant."

Pia was in the best possible hands with Paula on duty,
Hartford mused. The Status Board was really a woman's job.
The girls of the Service Companies were the housekeepers of
the Barracks, the guardians of the regimental lares and penates.
Paula, for example, had as her primary duty gnotobiotic control:
the maintenance of the whole germ-free system of the Barracks,
from the Hot-&-Wet-Guts to safety-suit inspection and the up-
keep of the Decontamination Vehicles. Behind the women on
Board duty, however, was always at least one male, combat-
trained officer of the guard, ready (once awakened and briefed
by the female help) to take armed men into the field.

But meanwhile, Hartford wanted to sleep.

Half an hour passed, and at its end Pia made his report: "Picket
reporting. Paula, I'm going into the village. Corporal Bond
will remain with the jeep, and will keep the transmitter open
till I get back. Okay?"

"Be careful, Lieutenant," Paula Piacentelli said, combining
affection with military formality.

Hartford, deciding that sleep was impossible, got up and

cold-showered. Dressed in fresh Class B's, he walked out to join Paula at the Status Board. The TV screen showed Bond, the sheathed Dardick-rifle slung over his shoulder, pacing back and forth in front of the jeep, glancing from time to time toward the walls of Kansannamura, white in the light of the skyful of stars. He was nervous, evidently aware of the fact that Kansas was largely unexplored, her potential for midnight mayhem untested. Bond spoke across his shoulder. "The lieutenant has been gone for a quarter hour, ma'am," he said. "Do you want me to go in and ask him to come out?"

"Wait another quarter hour, Corporal," Paula said. She explained to Hartford, "What he's got to do may take a little time." They watched the screen. Bond climbed back into the jeep, where he sat with his rifle between his knees, sweeping his attention around him, at the village, at the road behind, at the sunflower fields, where the blossoms were bleached white and the leaves enameled black by starlight.

With Paula's agreement, Hartford pressed the microphone switch to talk with Bond. "Have you tried to tap Piacentelli on his suit-receiver, Corporal?"

"Yes, sir," Bond said. "First thing. No answer."

"Turn your bitcher full up, then," Hartford said. "Tell Lieutenant Piacentelli that the O.G. wants him out on the road within five minutes."

"Done and done, sir." Bond tongued the bitcher's controls to Full Loud and repeated the message. Echoes bounced back from the walls of Stinkerville and lost themselves in the tangle of sunflowers.

No one answered.

The village seemed as much asleep as it had been before Bond's bellow. The Kansans were never hasty to volunteer response to Axenites; they knew that troopers meant trouble.

"Piacentelli is busy at something," Hartford said, as much to reassure himself as Pia's wife. "I think I'll go out and have a look." He spoke to Bond: "Get out of the jeep, but stay close to it. Report any haps immediately. Watch for lights, listen for small-arms fire."

"Done and done, sir."

Hartford phoned Felix, his platoon sergeant. "Report to the Board Room to sub for me," he said. "Wake the platoon guide and tell him to stand ready to fall the guard out, but not to wake anyone else yet. This is probably a nothing, Felix; Lieutenant Piacentelli just went for a walk in Stinkerville."

The Command Light, top in the tier of all the hierarchy of red-yellow-green-white Status Board indicators, flashed alive.

"A nothing?" Nasty Nef's voice demanded. "What sort of talk is that, Lieutenant? If I've been properly interpreting the past five minutes' transmissions, we've got an Axenite officer stranded in the middle of a Stinker village. This, mister, is not a nothing. Call out the guard. Prepare to join me in a Stinkerville shakedown. Those Gooks got to learn they can't play fast-and-easy with Axenite troopers."

"Done and done, sir!" Hartford snapped. He toggled the phone to get Felix back. "Felix, fall the boys out beside the Syphon. We've got the Old Man hitting bug-dirt with us, so look sharp."

"The colonel's going out with us?" Felix asked.

"Yes. There must be more to this situation than meets the company-grade eye," Hartford said. "Diaper up our darlings and stand by in the Hot Gut, Felix."

"Done and done!"

Twenty seconds later a figure in Santa Claus red came clashing into the room. Hartford, half into his blue safety-suit, came to a clumsy attention. The newcomer, his helmet clammed shut all ready for contamination, bellowed,"Get with it, mister!"

"Yes, sir." Hartford fit himself into the suit, a sort of cockpit, a congeries of valves, gauges, counters and vetters. In a moment he'd sealed himself in the sterile suit, checked his air filters and air reserve. "The guard is assembled in the Hot Gut, sir, ready to take the field."

"Dam' well better be," Nef said. "Lead off, mister." He turned to Paula Piacentelli. "Send a Decontamination Vehicle after us, Lieutenant. No telling what those Stinker devils have cooked up with Piacentelli." Back to Hartford: "You're in command of the guard; I'll observe and offer suggestions."

"Tain-HUT!" Platoon Sergeant Felix saluted the scarlet-clad colonel and the blue-clad lieutenant as they stepped from the elevator into the electric atmosphere of the Hot Gut. The guard snapped to, their plastic-packaged Dardick-rifles at order arms.

"Take 'em out, Felix," Hartford said. "Two personnel carriers, a .50-caliber m.g.-mounted jeep fore and aft. You and the colonel take the rear jeep; I'll lead. Have the men unbag their weapons the instant we're outside. Any questions?"

"No, sir."

"Move out," Hartford said.

IV

The squads peeled off and double-timed down the Hot Gut. Man by man they dipped into the Wet Gut for their swim outside. They'd been drilled for speed in exiting. If the regiment were needed outside, the Syphon could become a literal bottleneck. As the last squad splashed into the antiseptic solution, Hartford turned to Colonel Nef. "Sir, I have a question," he said.

"Hurry it up, mister."

"Isn't this a bit extreme, sir? We're going out to take one man out of a primitive village where we're not even sure he's in trouble. And we're carrying enough firepower to blast into an armed city."

"I don't trust the Gooks," the colonel said. "Their bucolic way of life may be a fraud, designed to lull us into complacency. Tonight we may discover that they're plotting the overthrow of the garrison, using weapons and tactics they've kept secret. I hope such is the case, Lieutenant. It would give us adequate cause to wipe the Stinkers off Kansas and make this as clean a world as Titan."

"Sir . . ."

"Move, mister," Nef said. "Piacentelli has been in Stinkerville for fifty minutes. Let's get him out."

The four trucks roared down the plateau toward the Indigenous Hominid hamlet at its foot. When the first Axenite Pioneers landed on the planet, bacteria-free as all men in space had to be, they'd set up camp near the spot where First Regiment Barracks now stood. They saw the fields of sunflowers, grown for food and cloth, and heard the natives call the nearest village Kansannamura. From that time on, this world was Kansas.

There was no moonlight—Kansas has no moon—but the headlamps of the four vehicles were wasted against the bright ribbon of road, lighted as it was by the sheet of stars that melted together in a metallic ceiling over the night. The men sat with their rifles between their knees, the plastic sleeves stripped off. Each of these Dardick-rifles could fire a solid stream of death. Each round of ammunition was fitted with a matrix that served as chamber, cartridge and the first fraction-of-an-inch of barrel. A magazine of forty such rounds could be hosed through the rifle in half a second. The troopers sped downhill, through sunflower fields black and silver in the light of the stars.

The personnel carriers and the jeeps scuffed to a halt by the village gate, the men scattering like shrapnel, according to the book. Colonel Nef spoke to Hartford on the command-band. "Move in, Lieutenant. Bring out Piacentelli. Any Stinker resistance is to be treated as open rebellion."

"Yes, sir." Hartford spoke to his men: "First squad, lead scout, forward to the gate."

The scout, his plastic safety-suit and the glass of his helmet glinting highlights, scuttled to the gate. He kicked the gate open—Piacentelli had evidently left it ajar—and entered, rifle-first. "First squad, follow me in column. Open to line-of-skirmishers in the square. Second squad, follow in the same manner. Third squad, maintain your interval and stand ready."

Hartford ran, pistol in hand, through the open gate. It was like charging some Roman ruin unpeopled for three centuries, like a field exercise with boulders marking obstacles to be won. There was no sign of natives. Their shopboards hung bearing the picture-script the Kansans used, quiet as the marbles in a cemetery. Hartford directed first squad in a sweep through the alleys, searching for Piacentelli. Second squad clattered through the gate behind them, took up a skirmish line, and moved in to cover the square as first squad disappeared into the doorways and alleys of Stinkerville.

The village, except for its beasts, might have been deserted. These animals, camelopards used for riding and to carry burdens, woke and gazed serenely down at the interrupters of their vegetable dreams, blinking their liquid half-shuttered eyes. Boots clattered on cobblestones. The houses were unlighted. "Throw on your i-r," Hartford ordered. As they moved into the dark, narrow ways, the men beamed infra-red light from the projectors on their safety-suits, the bounced-back, invisible light being transduced to black-and-green chiaroscuro by passage through the stereatronic goggles dropped inside their helmets.

"Turn the Stinkers out, mister," Nef command-banded.

"Into the houses," Hartford signaled. Ahead, a boot slammed wood, and hinges burst. To the restless night sounds of the camelopards in their stalls, the click of military boots on brick, and the rustle of rifles against safety-suits was added the whispering of families rousing from their beds. Hand in hand from father to mother to elder brother, down the scale to the youngest, the Kansans stumbled out into their little courtyards. *"Ano hito wa dare desu ka?" "Abunai yo!" "Shikata ga nai . . ."*

"Any sign of Piacentelli yet?" Nef demanded.

"Not yet, sir," Hartford signaled.

"Feed a candle into every building, Lieutenant. We'll get these Gooks in the open and interrogate till we find our man."

"Done and done, sir," Hartford said, stepping out of the way of a little girl fleeing toward the village square with an even littler girl strapped on a packboard on her back. He passed on the order."Fire in ten seconds, nine, eight . . . now!" Each man of first squad tossed a Lake Erie Lightning Universal Gas Candle through the window nearest him. A little over a second later a dozen grenades spit out a cloud of smoke with a hiss like a bursting fire hose, and the outer air was filled with an eye-stinging gas. The Indigenous Hominids spilled out of their homes in all directions now, coughing, choking, children rubbing the smoke particles into their half-wakened eyes. Two camelopards, blinded like their masters, blundered into the square, tears streaming from their reproachful eyes, twelve feet above the pavement. Second squad's men danced clear of the beasts and hallooed them out the gate.

Somewhere back in an alley a first-squad trooper tapped his trigger, jetting steel against overhanging roof tiles. "Nail that shot, mister!" Nef demanded.

Hartford heard the squad leader: "It's Lieutenant Piacentelli, sir. He's here."

"Bring him out, man; bring him out!" Nef's excited voice triggered a new string of rifle bursts.

Hartford tongued his bitcher full volume: "Cease fire, you idiots! Piacentelli, head for the square."

"Stop it, for God's sake, stop it!" Piacentelli shouted, his unamplified voice coming from a smoke-filled alley. Hartford plunged into the dark smoke—a tear-gas grenade had set afire some of the sunflower-paper room dividers, and kindled with them a row of wooden houses—and shouted for Piacentelli.

A blabrigar, as blind in the smoke as the men, blundered against Hartford's helmet. *"Yuke! Yuke!"* the bird screamed, grabbing hold of the transceiver antenna that horned up from the helmet. Hartford grabbed the blabrigar and tossed it up above the melee. He heard it flying in circles, searching for its Stinker owners, chanting the last words they'd said to it: *"Yuke! Yuke! Yuke!"* — "Go!"

Everything was burning. Even through the safety-suit Hartford suffered from the heat. He retracted his i-r goggles, useless in all this smoke. Nef called. "I'm coming in, mister." Hartford acknowledged. Great. One more blind man wandering in the smoke was what he needed.

He tongued his bitcher loud and shouted, "Gabe! Come this way. Gabe! Gabe!" The heat was intolerable. He positive-pressured his suit, ballooning the fabric away from his skin. How hot, he wondered, would the rounds packed into the butt of his Dardick-pistol have to get before they exploded?

As though in answer, a snap of gunfire sounded from the fog ahead. Some meathead had spooked. There were more shots as other troopers fired at their fantasies. "Cease fire, damn it!" Nef shouted over the command-circuit. "If anyone was hurt by you idiots, I'll court-martial every man with smoke in his gun barrel." Hartford hurried on. Ahead of him in the alley he heard Colonel Nef's voice, uncharacteristically soft. "Hartford, join me. I've found Piacentelli." Ahead in the smoke was a pinkness: the scarlet-suited commander kneeling above a body on the bricks.

Here in the open of planetary air, available to all the microscopic beasts of Kansas, Piacentelli was wearing only Class B's, his sneakers, shorts and tee-shirt. The center of the shirt sopped blood from the bullethole that funneled into Axenite Lieutenant Piacentelli's chest.

Nef stood. "The Decontamination Vehicle should be standing by," he said. "Get Piacentelli outside. We may be able to save him." He sounded unhopeful.

Hartford draped his friend's body across his shoulder. The smoke was bad, but he'd memorized his course through it. The air sucked in through his filter was clean, but hot. His helmet steamed opaque. As he stumbled out, blind, but guided by the colonel's voice, two men came forward to take Piacentelli over to the Decontamination Vehicle parked by the village gate. In the cooler air Hartford's helmet cleared. A girl gnotobiotician from the Decontamination Squad pressed the pickup of her helmet's "ears" against Piacentelli's bloody chest.

She looked up. "He's dead, sir," she said.

Nef's voice boomed from his bitcher. "Burn the Stinker village!" he shouted. "These Gooks will pay for Piacentelli's death with their homes."

Hartford felt imminent danger of vomiting, bad business in a safety-suit. He fought it as he looked around. The column of smoke rising from the buildings already fired was sweeping around, carried by the morning wind that poured off the plateau. Everything within the walls of the rammed-earth houses would be incinerated. Kansannamura was destroyed. "Regroup by the vehicles," Hartford spoke to his troopers. He walked back to his jeep, the village flaming behind him.

The Decontamination Squad checked Hartford's safety-suit, and found it sound despite its roasting. Piacentelli they cocooned in plastic: he was contaminated and dangerous. As the five trucks rolled back toward the Barracks, they met families of Indigenous Hominids, smoke-stained, who retreated back into the sunflower fields as the troopers drew near them. The Stinkers seemed to have salvaged little from the flames beyond an occasional blabrigar, perched on an old man's shoulder, or now and then a camelopard, fitted with a saddle and carrying a blanket-wrapped bundle of clothing and cooking pots.

V

Hartford had to see Piacentelli's body placed in the Barracks morgue, where a necropsy would be performed by a safety-suited gnotobiotician. It was seldom that an Axenite was contaminated. Rarer yet was the death of a trooper who'd been exposed to bacteria. Information held in Pia's body might someday save lives.

Hartford, directing the sealing off of the morgue from the rest of the Barracks, was not comforted by these reflections. He unsuited, shaved and showered, and put on fresh Class B's to finish what remained of this O.G. tour. On his way back up to the Board Room he had to pass the morgue again. Colonel Nef, in the midst of a cluster of lesser ranks, was there. On a wheeled cart, covered by a sheet, was a second body.

Hartford stopped. "What happened, sir?" he demanded. "Who is it?"

Nef raised the corner of the sheet with a hand that seemed infinitely weary. The body was Paula Piacentelli. "Another accident," the colonel grunted.

A hydroponics corporal, S.C., spoke up. "She was relieved of duty as soon as she heard about her husband's death, sir. Someone should have stayed with her. She went up to Level Eight to be alone. There are only two of us on duty there through the night. She must have blundered off the walkway, blinded by her tears. However it happened, she caught hold of a lighting cable where the insulation was frayed, and was electrocuted the moment she touched the wet seeding bed. Colonel Nef found her there."

"I was going to console her on Gabriel Piacentelli's death," Nef said. "Leave the body here and clear out, all of you." No refrigeration was needed for Paula's corpse, of course. An uncontaminated Axenite was preserved by purity. The body might dry a bit, the integrity of the internal organs suffer somewhat from the corrosive effects of their own juices; but Paula's corpse would otherwise remain uncorrupted until taken outside and buried in bug-dirt. "Hartford," Nef said, "I'd like to have a talk with you."

"I'm still on O.G., sir," Hartford said.

"And I relieve you of that duty," Nef snapped. "Come up to my quarters."

Nasty Nef's sitting room had the only window in the Barracks, a skylight through which poured the brilliance of Kansas's pyrotechnic flood of stars. "Rest, Hartford. Sit down. Brandy?"

Hartford allowed that he could use some.

"What do you think of tonight's adventure, Lee?" Nef asked. "Don't look startled. I know the first name of every officer and noncom in the regiment."

"What happened, sir, was horrible," Hartford said.

"I understand your feelings," Nef said. "Two tragic accidents, killing your two closest friends the same night. I am certain that the loss of these comrades will fire your zeal for getting the Stinkers under control. Isn't that right, Lee?" Nef took a cigar from the humidor next his chair.

"With all respect, sir," Hartford said, placing his empty brandy glass on the table to his right, "I can hardly see how the events tonight were caused by the Indigenous Hominids."

"You must use the official name for the Gooks, mustn't you?" Nef mused. His voice turned harsh: "Someone stripped the safety-suit off Piacentelli, mister."

Hartford nodded, his face pale. The *A* of the Axenite's alphabet was *Apprehension,* As a germ-free—axenic, gnoto-biotic—human being, he is superior in most ways to ordinary men. He's usually larger and stronger. He never has dental caries, pimples, appendicitis, the common cold or certain cancers. No matter how much or how long he sweats, the Axenite doesn't stink; nor do his other excretions. On a contaminated world, however, the Axenite is a tender flower indeed. A baby's breath can be death to him, if that baby be a "normal" human; for no microbe is benign to the man without antibodies. To him a drop of rain may reek with pestilence, the scent of evening may be a lethal gas. "I can't understand their stripping Pia, sir," he said. "Why would they do such a terrible thing?"

"Because they're Stinkers!" Nef said. "Can you imagine what it must be like to be one of them? Every inch of your skin a-crawl with living filth, your guts packed with foulness, your whole frame a compromise with rottenness? Do you wonder that they'd delight to make us as unwholesome as they are themselves?" Colonel Nef lighted the cigar he'd been mulling. "Lee, do you think one Stinkerville destroyed is too high a price for them to pay for having murdered two Axenite troopers? For Piacentelli's wife is as much their victim as her husband."

Hartford shook his head. "I'm not sure, sir. What bothers me more than anything else is that it's my fault Pia went out last night. He asked me to arrange for him to replace the scheduled picket officer, and I did."

"Lee, why was Piacentelli so anxious to pull this extra duty?" Nef asked.

Hartford tried unobtrusively to squirm his chair out of the jet stream from Nef's cigar. "He told me he wanted to work on the language, sir," he said. "Pia really had such a project. He'd never had contact with anyone with a speech other than Standard before, and the problem of transducing one language into another fascinated him. The Kansans call their speech *Nihon-go.* Pia taught me to understand some of it."

"A waste of your time, Lee," Nef said. "You'll never have occasion to speak it. Be that as it may, unless Piacentelli was attempting to coax a course in Bedroom Kansan from a Stinker maiden, I can hardly understand why his lexigraphical labors should require him to unsuit himself. No, Piacentelli was deliberately murdered."

"I'm puzzled, sir," Hartford admitted. "When we tossed those smoke candles, I heard Pia shouting for us to stop it. Would he have done so if the Indigenous Hominids had him captive? Why did none of the natives lift a hand against us, though we were burning their homes? Why did Paula Piacentelli seem to know why Pia was going outside tonight? Why did he take a microscope with him? Why did Paula kill herself?"

"Don't noise that last 'why' around the Barracks, mister," Nef growled. "Officially, she died in tear-blinded grief, an accident." He smiled. "Whatever our reason for burning out Stinkerville, Lee, we got it done. The fact that those half-humans down the hill bred and sweat and poisoned the soil within half an hour's walk has been a stench in my nostrils ever since we got here. Now they're gone. I'm as sorry as you that the Piacentellis are dead. But the manner of their dying was such as to assure axenic mankind a new home."

"I'm not sure I understand you, sir."

Nef poured them each a second brandy. He raised his; Hartford of necessity followed suit. "To Brotherhood," the colonel said. He stared into Hartford's eyes. "To *the* Brotherhood," he amended.

Hartford was tired, confused and in awe of Nef's rank; otherwise he might have ventured protest. Nef sipped his drink. "I must emphasize, Lee, that what I say is my opinion only, not Axenite policy. You see my point."

"I do, sir," Hartford said.

"Forgive me, then, for prefacing my remarks with a bit of truism," Nef said. "In all history before gnotobiotic man was cut from his mother through cellophane, the human being was never pure organism. Before us, every man who ever lived was, in fact, one mammal plus the sum of millions of viruses, rickettsia, bacteria, fungi and molds. When the old philosophers asked, 'What is man?' the answer could only be: 'Foul smell and blood in a bag.' We're the first men beyond that, Lee. The first real men, True Men, members of the winner-species, *Homo gnotobioticus*.

"We must destroy the bridge that led to us. We must destroy the Stinkers. Not just these quasi-human natives here on Kansas, but the Stinkers on Earth, and on every other planet where bug-laden man has followed Axenite. What chance has *Homo sapiens* to match his sapiency against *Homo gnotobioticus*, when he is a bifurcate septic tank, a polyculture of a thousand kinds of living dirt?"

Hartford finished his brandy, wishing he were anywhere else than in Nasty Nef's quarters, tired, ill at ease and a little drunk from the two brandies. "What do you propose, sir?" he asked with Academy politeness.

"Aha!" Nef rejoiced, pouring them each another drink. "You justify my trust, Lee. You perceive that I speak not merely if-ly, philosophically, but as a man of action, leashed only by temporary practicality." He leaned back in his chair and regarded Hartford more as a sculptor might regard a recent product than a father a son, with uncritical approval. "Where were you born, Lee?"

"On Titan, sir."

"I thought so. You have the mark of natal excellence," Nef said. "You're a second or third-generation Axenite, then?"

"Third, sir," Hartford said.

"Splendid. Your grandparents were born from their mothers' wombs untimely ripp'd; your parents and yourself born normally, in germ-free ambience. How fortunate we are, you and I! Third-generation Axenites. Eff-two of a new race." Nef paused in his recital. "There is one fact that chafes us, though. We, perforce the Columbuses of tomorrow, explorers of the planets beyond even the stars we see here on the frontier, are held back by our Stinker cousins. They have the proper feeling, that only pure man might pioneer the alien worlds, for fear of destroying what he finds there. But who will inherit those planets when we've finished our explorations? Who will at the last till the fields of Kansas?"

"Colonists from Earth, sir," Hartford said. "From Eurus, Tinkle, Westside, Unashamed, T'ang, Williams's World and Hope. From all the planets normal man has colonized."

"Doesn't that annoy you, Lee?" Nef asked. "That our work's fruit is to be enjoyed by shiploads of Stinkers?"

"They're as human as we, sir," Hartford said. He smiled. "You might say they just haven't had our advantages."

"You're tender-minded, Lee," Nef said. "We garrison a hundred worlds on the Frontier, planets our Stinker masters mustn't visit yet, least Man contaminate some life-form yet unmet. We pioneer, clear planets as safe, and move on. For reward, we Axenites have three worlds of our own in the M'Bwene System, axenized for our use; we have the Academies on Luna and Titan, and a dome on Pluto. *It's not enough.* We are the new men, the next-comers to humanity. We must have worlds of our own. I, and the Brotherhood whose hand here I am, intend that Kansas shall be ours."

"What about the Stinkers?" Hartford asked. "What will happen to them if we decide to axenize Kansas?"

"Maybe they'll leave," Colonel Nef said, smiling in the manner that had won him the name "Nasty." "A few more punitive expeditions like tonight's—an incendiary grenade was thrown at Kansannamura, did you know that, Lee? I threw it— and we'll have no Stinkers underfoot. We soon will be able to mop and polish this world to our own high standards. We'll walk this lovely world without safety-suits and breathe unfiltered air. We'll enter into our birthright, Lee." Nef gazed at his cigar admiringly, though it had gone out. "So much for the moment, Brother Hartford," he said. "Perhaps we'd both do well to get some sleep."

Hartford jumped to attention and formally requested permission to withdraw. Nef nodded. Hartford about-faced and left the room.

VI

The things the colonel had told him hadn't fallen into place in his mind yet. Hartford was numb of thought.

Back in his own room in B.O.Q. the numbness cleared a bit. He poured himself a drink. Somehow, he thought, he'd become fairhaired boy to an Attila the Hun, an Alaric the Goth, a Hitler, a Haman; an Ashurbanipal I, a Rameses II. For Nef was equally with these a servant of Siva the Destroyer, with his plan to make Man pure.

His purification would involve the destruction of all nonaxenic men and women all the way from the Home World to the newest beachhead on the Frontier; the sterilization of a hundred worlds as culture media for the new race; and the planting on the newly axenized soil of colonies of *Homo gnotobioticus,* the feeder-on-hydroponic-greens, the inodorous, the thin-gutted, the strong-toothed Superman.

Nef's pogrom had begun with the raid on the village, Hartford mused, his arms behind his head as he lay on his bunk. Nef had decided that this green and pleasant world belonged to the silver men, the true men, the new men. Us, Hartford thought. Earth's Stinkers, ordinary humanity with its common cold and its caries, would follow the Kansan Indigenous Hominid, and the Great Auk, into history.

The double funeral of the Lieutenants Piacentelli was to be held at retreat, outside the Barracks. Hartford wondered a bit at the haste with which the two bodies were to be consigned to the earth of Kansas. Perhaps haste was necessary because of the micro-organisms with which poor Pia's corpse was necessarily contaminated.

Hartford grimaced. Contaminated humans must lead disgusting lives. They smelled of ferments, were bloated with bacterially elaborated gases, suffered rot in their very teeth. Their corpses—poor forefathers!—suffered corruption that would never touch an Axenite, whose unembalmed cadaver would last longer than the best-mummified Pharaoh.

Whatever mysterious errand it had been that had taken Piacentelli outside the Barracks, it had killed him. It was over.

Hartford marched the Terrible Third into position facing the graves, cut into the soil at the base of the hundred-foot flagpole. The entire regiment, less only the handful of men and women necessary to secure the Barracks, was on the Parade Ground. Colonel Nef, his scarlet safety-suit brilliant in the light of the setting sun, stood beside the graves, a finger of his right gauntlet inserted to mark his place in the black *Book of Honors and Ceremonies*.

The regiment stood at parade rest as a truck brought the bodies of two comrades through its ranks. As the improvised hearse halted and twelve blue-suited casket bearers stepped forward to lift the flag-draped boxes, Nef called the regiment to attention. The bearers slow-marched the caskets to the graves and placed them on the lowering devices.

Nef's words of funeral were few. He spoke of the dedication of the two Axenites being laid to rest and bitterly accused the Stinkers—this word seemed rude, in so formal a setting—of having murdered the young couple. He spoke of condign justice and of revenge.

This done, he called: "Escort, less firing party. Present HAHMS! Firing party, FIRE THREE VOLLEYS!"

The shots of the Dardick-rifles echoed down the plateau to the smoldering village below. The regimental bugler, standing between the heads of the graves, flicked on his instrument. As the last volley spat from the muzzles of the rifles, the bugler played taps.

Four men stepped forward to recover and fold the green silk Pioneer colors, and the caskets were lowered to corruption in alien earth. The banner crept down the flagstaff, and the funeral was over.

Bone-weary, Hartford went from the Syphon to the refresher room, where he checked his safety-suit and hung it.

Another officer was there, still in his blue safety-suit. Hartford wondered sleepily why he'd so long postponed unsuiting. Even the fellow's helmet was sealed. "Our first deaths on Kansas," Hartford remarked, wanting to coax the man into conversation and learn who he was. "I'd never realized till now that we're really soldiers, subject to violent death and formal burying." The man must be a replacement, come in on the supply ship a month ago, Hartford thought. Black hair, crewcut. Tanned. Must be from one of the M'Bwene Worlds, where an Axenite's naked skin can be exposed to unfiltered sunlight. "Both the Piacentellis were my friends," Hartford said, determined to coax speech from the stranger.

The man's bitcher boomed, evidently set on full volume. *"Mattaku shirazu,"* he said. "Excuse. Pia not teach entire use of Standard tongue."

Hartford's right hand tore through the plastic pellicle over his Dardick-pistol and brought the weapon to bear on the figure before him. "You're a Stinker!" he said. "Pia's safety-suit—that's the suit you're wearing."

"Tonshu," the Indigenous Hominid said, bowing his head. He indicated the empty holster at his side: he was unarmed. "I come *on taku,* here to your honored precincts, to speak of things done and of future things. You are Hartford?"

Hartford thought quickly. His responsibility was to the garrison. This stranger was above all else a possible source of contamination, a carrier of the micro-bugs that could kill every Axenite on Kansas. Shooting him would rupture the safety-suit he wore. As it was, his exterior surface was clean; he could have entered the Barracks only by marching in from retreat with the rest of the regiment, through the sterilizing Syphon. "I am Hartford. Lee Hartford."

"Pia said you are a good man," the stranger said, bowing. "What is your name?"

"Renkei. As you say, I take Pia's *uwa-zutsumi*, this smooth garment." Renkei indicated the safety-suit by slicking his hands over it. "I must enter here to talk with Hartford. To enter, I must have garment. Pia, my brother, is dead. I borrowed his garment. Can I, with you, stop the ugly thing that began last night in Kansannamura? *Kuwashiku wa zonzezu;* I do not know. I can but try."

What a perfect disguise a safety-suit made, Hartford thought. Besides, it was the only passport a man needed to enter the Barracks. He stared at the stranger. He looked no different to men Hartford had met before, Axenites whose grandparents had been born by aseptic Caesarian section in Nagoya or Canton, two of the great gnotobiotic centers of fifty years ago. Renkei was a Stinker, a Kansan, an Indigenous Hominid (ignominious name!); he was also, Hartford felt, a man.

"Tell me why you made the dangerous journey here, into the midst of your enemies," he said.

"The death of our friend Pia. The burning of Kansannamura. The war between my people and you who wear smooth garments," he said. "This is *aru-majiki koto.*"

"A thing that ought not to be," Hartford said, translating. He was glad for the practice he'd gotten with Pia, speaking the native tongue. "Sit down," he said. "You must explain, Renkei."

The refresher room, a hall filled with lockers and the machinery that automatically tested and refitted the safety-suits each time they returned to the Barracks, had a dozen entrances and exits. As Renkei, still completely sealed in Pia's safety-suit, sat on the bench beside Hartford, the doors all closed at once. They hissed as the pneumatic seals were set in their frames.

Contamination Alert! Someone, most likely the Service girl on watch at the Status Board, had discovered that there was one more person in the Barracks than could be accounted for. A crash-priority head count had been made. Each room and compartment had doubtless been eavesdropped through the built-in TV eyes and microphone ears.

One door at the far end of the hall burst open. A squad of safety-suited Service Police spilled in. At the point of their wedge was the scarlet uniform of Colonel Nef. Dardick-pistol in hand, he ran toward Renkei. "Don't shoot!" Hartford shouted, springing up.

"Get back, mister," the colonel yelled. He dropped to one knee and squeezed all twelve rounds into the seated figure to Hartford's right. Service Police swooped down to pull Hartford away from the shattered body of Renkei. The Lieutenant's tee-shirt was stained, however, by flecks of blood splashed up as the SPs' bullets chewed into the Kansan. Hartford was contaminated.

For the next hour, Hartford had no more to say about his disposition than an angry bullock being dipped and scrubbed against an epidemic of cattle ticks.

His purification consisted in a sudsing with antiseptic soaps, this administered by a team of three Service Company gnotobioticians who were completely indifferent to his modesty and who seemed determined to peel off the outer surface of his skin. The women, safety-suited against being themselves contaminated, shaved off all his hair and ostentatiously packaged up the shavings to be burned. They administered parenteral and enteric doses of broad-spectrum antibiotics. By the time the gnoto girls were finished, Hartford was as bald all over as a six-weeks foetus, as sore as though he'd been sandblasted, slightly feverish as a result of the injections and madder than hell.

Ignoring his demands to see Colonel Nef at once, the Service Company troopers helped him into his safety-suit. Hartford would have to live inside the suit for a week's quarantine, watched carefully to see whether a missed microbe would breed within him in spite of all the measures taken.

Hartford's company commander refused him permission to speak to the colonel. The lieutenant was to speak to no one concerning Renkei's invasion of the Barracks. He would remain safety-suited inside the Barracks or out, but would otherwise continue with his regular duties.

Hartford returned to the refresher room where the murder had taken place. Renkei's macerated body had been removed for burning. The room had been carefully decontaminated, to the extent of hosing it down with detergent steam and individually re-refreshing each safety-suit in the huge hall's rows of lockers.

There was nothing to be done against Nef's madness, Hartford thought. He sat on the bench where Renkei had sat. The ultimate breakdown in communication is silencing one side of the dialogue, he thought. That's why killing a man is the ultimate sin; it removes forever the hope of understanding him. It ends for all time the conversation by which brothers may touch one another's mind.

What crap to find in a soldier's thoughts, Hartford told himself. He was an Axenite trooper, a Pioneer, a pistol-packing officer of infantry, commander of the Terrible Third Platoon. He was an Axenite, dedicated by the immaculacy of his birth to the conquest of man's frontiers.

Hartford snapped his plastic-sheathed Dardick-pistol, death in a supermarket wrapper, from his belt and placed it on the shelf of his locker. He'd seen the village of Kansannamura burned. Pia had died across his shoulder. Paula lay buried, too. Renkei's life had been splashed out on a stream of bullets. Enough of death.

Hartford picked up a pack of field-ration squeeze-tubes and walked down the hallway toward the Syphon.

His leaving would show on the Status Board, of course, but that didn't matter anymore. He was deserting the regiment.

He walked through the valley of desert that was the Hot Gut, and down into the birth canal that was the Wet Gut, to emerge in the evening air of Kansas. The motor sergeant, stationed outside to guard the vehicles, saluted. "Going for a walk, sir?" he asked.

"If you'll lend me a jeep, I'll go for a ride," Hartford said. "I'd like to see how things look, down in the village."

"It's against regulations, but if you'll have the truck back by dark I can let it go, sir."

"Thank you, Sergeant." Hartford returned the salute and drove off downhill, toward Kansannamura.

What would happen to Hartford-the-deserter? he wondered. At best, he'd be booted out of the troopers and grounded on Titan, or Luna or one of the M'Bwene planets, to serve the rest of his life as a paper-pusher, the bureaucratic equivalent of an endless Kitchen Police. At worst, he'd be exiled to Earth.

That meant exposure to bacteria, a gradual contamination till he'd been exposed to the full dirtiness in which Earthlings daily lived, till he'd equipped himself with antibodies and a Stinker's immune response.

The Service Police would be after him soon. Once out of

sight of the Barracks, he turned his jeep off the road, onto one of the numberless paths used by camelopard riders on their trips between Stinker villages. He was headed upgrade, now, toward the mountains. On either side of the jeep were the fields of sunflowers, silent in the twilight calm. In a few moments the cool winds from the sea would flow into the land, stirring the billions of heart-shaped sunflower leaves into the whisper that filled the evening and early-morning hours of Kansas.

His heart filled with hope and hopelessness, feeling like a happy suicide, Hartford sang to himself as the sunflower heads and leaves tattooed against his windshield. "Pioneers! Oh, Pioneers," he sang, the anthem of the Axenites, the fellowship he was leaving forever:

> *Lo, the darting bowling orb!*
> *Lo, the brother orbs around, all the clustering suns and*
>   *planets,*
> *All the dazzling days, all the mystic nights with dreams,*
>   *Pioneers! Oh, Pioneers!*

The crunching of the jeep over the narrow track, the whipping of the plants against the vehicle and his singing all combined to drown out whatever noise it was the girl might have made. Hartford didn't see her till the jeep, rearing like a startled pony, climbing the flank of the camelopard the girl rode, tossed him into a tangle of green stalks and golden flowers.

VII

The riding camelopard bleated only a moment and was dead, its great neck broken by the jeep's charge. The girl, thrown clear, was up before Hartford.

A scarlet bird circled the scene of the wreck, the dead beast, the stalled jeep, the man and the woman sprawled by the side of the path. *"Miyo! Miyo! Miyo!"* cried the blabrigar: "See! See! See!"

Hartford rose and went to the girl, who was rubbing the shoulder she'd landed on. She stared, but didn't back away. *"Kinodoku semban,"* he said very carefully: a thousand-myriad pardons. His bitcher, unfortunately, was set on full volume;

his words of comfort blatted at the girl with parade-ground force. She put her hands over her ears.

The blabrigar above them, impressed by Hartford's stentorian voice, circled repeating *"Kinodoku semban"* over and over, till the girl called it down to rest quietly on her shoulder. The girl spoke to the bird, which stared at her lips with his head cocked to one side, an attentive student. She repeated four times the same message. The bird nodded, and repeated the phrase to her. *"Yuke!"* the girl said. The blabrigar spread its scarlet wings and flew up. It circled twice, then headed north, up into the mountains. Of the girl's message Hartford had understood only the native word for camelopard: *giraffu.* His Kansan was inadequate. He could understand it only if it was slowly spoken.

Hartford tongued his bitcher's controls to a conversational level. *"Kinodoku semban,"* he repeated, bowing.

The girl knelt beside the dead camelopard and stroked its head, over the central, vestigial horn. She looked up at Hartford with tears in her eyes. *"Tonshu,"* Hartford said: I bow my head.

"Anata we dare desu ka?" she asked.

"Lee Hartford," he replied.

The girl spoke slowly. "I am named Takeko." She knit her hands before her and bowed. "Forgive my bad actions," she said.

"The fault is entirely mine, Takeko," Hartford replied. He was sorry, of course, to have killed the girl's steed and to have subjected her to danger; he was very glad to have met her. Takeko wore what must have been the Kansan riding costume: short trousers and a jacket woven of floss from retted sunflower stalk, dyed a golden brown. Most curious, he thought, was her perfume; mild, flowerlike, slightly pungent. The smell of this lovely Stinker belied the trooper epithet.

Then it hit him.

The filters of a safety-suit remove, together with all the dust of the ambient air, all its character, including odor. The clean, characteristic smells of the Barracks, together with the bland spit-and-sweat odors of a long-worn safety-suit, were all an Axenite came in contact with.

If he was able to smell the outside world, it could only be because his gnotobiotic security was compromised.

Hartford inspected his safety-suit, peering where he could

and twisting and feeling the surfaces he couldn't see. Takeko laughed. She reached across his shoulder and lifted a flap of torn fabric, ripped loose when Hartford had flown from his jeep.

His panic would have been unmanly in a normal human; but Hartford all his life had been impressed with the horror of contamination. He ran blindly, though he knew that his deepened breathing was drawing the germ-laden air of Kansas deeper into his lungs. He ran through lanes of sunflowers, flailing his arms, into the darkness, away from the alien girl, away from the fear of going septic. He ran and stumbled and fell and ran again. All his life he'd been warned of the consequences of becoming infected with the bacteria against which he had no defenses. Now he was so infected.

When Hartford fell the last time it was for sheer lack of wind.

He opened his helmet and tossed it aside. Dead already, he could lose nothing by making himself comfortable for dying. He shivered. The chill of infection? No, the night was cool. He looked about him in the light of the sky of stars. The fields were below him, rustling in a million private conversations as the breeze filtered through them. It was a lovely place to die, here on the crest of a hill.

Hartford lay back and stared into the curtain of stars that rippled above him. Perhaps he wouldn't wake, he thought. With this thought he slept.

The sunlight stung his eyes. He sprang to his feet, then bent and groaned. Sore. He'd slept on naked soil, packed hard by the hillcrest winds. He stretched his hard-bedded muscles. For a dead man, he felt good. The alien bacteria and viruses within him were establishing beachheads, multiplying their platoons to companies, their companies to battalions. By the time they'd reached division strength, he thought, he'd be well aware of the invasion.

Meanwhile, breakfast.

He opened a package of field rations, squeeze-tube beans. He inserted the nozzle of the tube into his mouth and fed himself a dollop of the stuff. It felt strange to eat directly from the tube, not having inserted the adjutage into his helmet opening to be sterilized first. Being septic saved a lot of time.

He finished the squeeze-tube beans and was thirsty. Down

at the base of his hill was a little stream. Hartford thoughtfully peeled off his safety-suit. Dressed only in his shorts, shirtless, barefoot and tender, he made his way down to the water.

It was delicious.

Did bacteria impart that brisk taste? Hartford wondered. So far committed to contamination that nothing mattered, he shed his shorts and dived into the stream. It was chilly, delightful. He returned to shore and lay on the grass for the sun to toast him dry. He began to relax. . . . The girl giggled.

Hartford snatched up his shorts and pulled them on. It was Takeko. She was afoot, wearing the costume he'd last seen her with; but she had strapped on her back a leather wallet. A blabrigar sat on Takeko's shoulder. She spoke to it, repeating her message four times and listening to the bird repeat once. Then she shooed the scarlet bird away, to carry north the message that Hartford had been found.

"I laugh. Excuse me," she said. "But you funny." Takeko patted her head. Hartford understood. Shaved by the Decontamination Squad, he was bald and eyebrowless, entirely lacking in body hair. He smiled. *"Hai."*

"Your skin is like the hide of a *giraffu*," she said.

Hartford looked down at his freckled arm. True, the pattern of brown against pink was very like the reticulations of a camelopard. "Where did you learn to speak Standard, Takeko?"

"Pia-san talked to my cousin, and I listened," she said. "Kansannamura was my home. Pia often visited us." Hartford, who after Nasty Nef was the man most responsible for the burning of Takeko's village, was silent. "When your *jeepu-kuruma* hit my *giraffu*, I think you are Renkei," the Kansan girl said. "Renkei is my cousin. He go to see what can be done."

"Renkei is dead," Hartford told her.

"Iie!" Takeko pressed her hands against her face. "You strangers are quick to kill, to burn, to sweep away."

"I did not wish him harmed," Hartford said.

"You pink folk will not be happy until all our people are dead and under the ground," Takeko moaned. "You will not be pleased until you can march across our graves."

"That is not so."

"Pia-san said it," Takeko said. "He said that your Nef is a master of the Brotherhood, which wishes death to all people who do not wear glass heads."

"If that is true, I am no longer a part of it, Takeko-san," Hartford said. "I have left Nef and his Barracks. I am a dead man."

"You will come with me," Takeko said. "You will not be dead for many years, unless Nef and his Brotherhood kill you." She looked into the sky, where a red bird was circling. It hawked down to her shoulder and sat there, its head tilted to her. "Takeko," the girl said to the bird. With this key to unlock its message the blabrigar spilled its rote. Hartford recognized a word or two of the bird-o-gram, but not the full sense of the message.

Takeko reached into the pocket of her short trousers for a few zebra-striped sunflower seeds. The blabrigar picked these daintily from her hand, using its beak like a pair of precise tweezers, pinching up one seed at a time and cracking it. "There will soon come *giraffu* to take us to a further village," Takeko said. "You are to speak to our chief men there, to tell them what happened to Renkei, why he was killed in the Stone House."

"I may not live through this day," Hartford said. "It is not easy to explain. We wear the 'glass head' to keep out your air. It is deadly, *doku,* to us. Do you understand, Takeko?"

"You may be tired, having slept on the old bones of the hill," she said. "You may be hungry, having eaten only the squeezings of your metal sausages. But you are not hurt badly, nor are you old, Lee-san. Why should you die?"

"You cannot understand," Hartford said. He spoke more to himself than to the girl. "The medicine here is certainly primitive. You have no concept of the biological nature of disease. Tell me, Takeko-san, do you Kansans know anything of the very, very small . . ."

"Microscopic?" Takeko asked.

"Piacentelli did a splendid job of teaching you the Standard language," Hartford said. He looked up and down Takeko's trim, just post-adolescent figure in frank appraisal, jealously wondering whether Gabe could have achieved his remarkable pedagogical results by means of the pillow-book method of linguistic instruction so popular with soldiers of occupation in every time and climate. That thought, he rebuked himself, was unworthy of Pia's memory. In any case, his friend had conducted his researches wearing that guarantee of chastity, a safety-suit.

"We'll have to wait an hour or so until the *giraffu* come," Takeko said.

She unstrapped the wallet from her back and unpacked it on the grass at the edge of the little stream. The Kansan girl took out a coil of line, spun from the stalk of the sunflower, and a bronze hook. "We will feed the gentleman from the Stone House," she said. Hartford watched with amusement as she baited the hook with a bit of the bread from her knapsack, twirled the line about her head and dropped it into the center of the stream. "This place has many fish," she said. "We will not wait long before we eat."

It took Takeko only ten minutes to have three seven-inch fish, so plump and meaty looking that not even a xenologist would have wasted time studying them, lying on the grass.

Hartford demanded equal time with the fishline, and discovered to his gratification that the dough he pinched off the chapattis and molded to the hook took the fancy of Kansas fish as well as Takeko's offerings. With a sense of at last participating in the affairs of the universe, he decapitated and decaudated the six fish they ended with, and gutted them with a rich delight in the juicy messiness of the task.

Hartford and Takeko scissored the fillets in split twigs and roasted them, like aquatic weenies, over a fire built from the pithy stalks of dead sunflowers. The firepit, a saucer of scooped-out dirt, had buried beneath it half a dozen of the swollen roots of sunflowers, each wrapped in the cordiform, sharkskin-surfaced leaf of the parent plant to roast beneath the coals.

They seasoned their fish with *daikon*, a kind of horseradish; and their plates were the fresh-baked, flat, unleavened chapattis Takeko had brought in her pack. The tubers, eaten from a fresh leaf-plate, needed only butter. Takeko had this, too, churned of cameleopard-milk cream. Buds or flower heads of the sunflower were eaten with sunflower oil, like artichokes. "Your people have a good friend in the sunflower," Hartford remarked, wiping his lips.

"With the golden flower and the golden *giraffu*, with the *take*-grass and the good soil, we had a rich life here before you glass-headed men came," Takeko said. "Now we are treated in our own villages like rats to be driven out, in our fields as gnawing vermin. Why is your Brotherhood so angry with us, Lee-san, who live in only a few places on a wide world? Is there no law among the light-skinned people? We have lived here, on the world you call Kansas, for many generations. We were once of Earth, as were your grandfathers."

"All humans were once of Earth," Hartford said.

"If we are as much human as you," she said, "Why does your Nef call us *Hominids?* Is that a name to give a brother?"

"It is better than *Stinker,*" Hartford suggested.

"Hai! I tell you, Lee-san, why you must rename us. It is because men do not kill men until they give their brother-enemy a monstrous name. Why do you wish to kill us all?" she asked.

"I'm not a member of the Brotherhood," Hartford said. "I'm only a man who was born on Axenite. That means, until your beast and my jeep collided, tearing my safety-suit, I was an animal uncontaminated by microscopic life. These microscopic animals, Takeko, are deadly to an Axenite."

"You are not dead, though," Takeko suggested. *"Ne?"*

"I've been breathing contaminated air for twelve hours," Hartford said. "It's true. I cannot understand why I have no fever, no malaise, no symptoms of pneumonia."

Takeko giggled. "Forgive me," she said. *"Kinodoku sem-ban;* but you seem to be sorry to be alive." She was silent for a moment, listening. She pointed north. "My father will appear with our *giraffu* soon," she said. "I can hear them."

Takeko's father rode up a moment later, an unbent man of seventy. He sat astride his camelopard, a comic quadruped little better designed as a beast of burden than an ostrich, with as much dignity as though his steed were an Arabian stallion. His name, Takeko said, was Kiwa-san. The old man bowed from his saddle when his daughter introduced Hartford.

At Kiwa-san's command the two *giraffu* he'd brought along on lead-reins spread their legs to bring their down-sloping backs a scant four feet from the ground. The saddles, with dangling, bootlike gambadoes in place of ordinary stirrups, seemed inaccessible to Hartford. "Watch me," Takeko told him. She took a short run up behind her *giraffu* and, with a movement like a leapfrog hurdle, flipped herself up into the saddle.

Hartford stepped back, ran and leaped. He succeeded only in banging his shoes into the right sifle-joint of his mount and in flipping himself to the ground. In the interest of haste, grace was abandoned. Hartford monkey-crawled up a sturdy cane of bamboo growing nearby and, as Kiwa-san maneuvered his beast, stepped over into the saddle.

"I'd better take my safety-suit and helmet," he said. "If the troopers should find it, they could follow our trail."

"Hai!" Takeko said, agreeing. She leaped from her *giraffu,* packed the safety-suit and helmet onto the beast, and re-mounted. "We will now go to Yamamura," she said. Old Kiwa spoke, and she translated: "We must move quickly and with care," she said. "My father heard an *hikoki*—how do you say?" she asked, raising and lowering her hand.

"A veeto-platform," Hartford said. "I mustn't be seen, Tak-eko. Colonel Nef would use my presence as an excuse to kill any of your people around me."

The ride, though cautious, was indeed demanding. Hartford felt tendons stretch he didn't know he had. Muscles were bruised from his instep to his upper back, and the skin was chafed away from his inner thighs as though he'd been riding an unplaned plank. He understood, well before the journey to the mountain village was over, the importance of that lifetime ex-ercise, best begun by riding young, known to generations of horsemen as "stretching the crutch." He swore to himself that his future transportation, if he had a future through which to transport himself, would be by boots or wheeled vehicle.

The three of them were following no clear path. Kiwa led. Hartford noted that their course took them along the contours of streams, on the borders of fields, through contrasting back-ground that would make their presence less obvious from the air.

They were in a thicket of bamboo when the veeto-platform did appear.

The instant they heard its whistle, Kiwa spoke a sharp word. He and his daughter slipped from their mounts, loosed the brow-bands of their camelopards and unlocked their girths, tossed off the saddles and dangling gambadoes and gave the animals each a sharp slap on the rump that sent them crashing through the bamboo. They helped Hartford unsaddle and send his beast off in another direction, and lay down in the direction the late-morning sun dialed the shadows of the bamboo stems.

If the veeto-pilot saw the *giraffu* now, they were saddleless and innocent.

The downdraft of the veeto-platform puffed dust up from

the ground around them, and pressed down the leafy tops of the bamboo like a great hand stroking across the thicket. Hartford, aware of the way his bald head and pink face would stand out, dusted his hands with the soil and laced his dusty fingers over his scalp.

The platform passed almost directly over them, shooting fragments of dust and bamboo duff into every particle of clothing, into ears and eyes and nostrils, with the whirlwind of its passage.

VIII

It took them half an hour to recover their *giraffu* and saddle up again, but Hartford did not regret the delay.

Aboard the grotesque mount again, he groaned. To mask the misery of his unaccustomed pounding he paid scientific attention to the landscape, and the gait of the camelopards, the leather of the saddles, and the posture and person of Takeko—this last by far the most effective of his analgesic thoughts.

They rode on an ancient piedmont, among the foothills of a worn-down mountain range. The leather of their saddles and gambadoes was, by its pattern, obviously tanned camelopard hide. Hartford was certain that this pattern would by the end of their journey be an indelible part of his own hide. The *giraffu*, remarkably swift and easy-moving over the rugged, heavily grown terrain, ambled, moving both legs on the same side together. And Takeko was lovely.

Hartford decided to essay his Kansan. He practiced his question: "Is Yamamura far from here?" mentally, moving his lips, until he was sure he'd mastered the phrasing. Then he addressed Old Kiwa. *"Yamamura wa koko kara toi desu ka?"*

Kiwa smiled, and rattled off an answer much too brisk for Hartford to catch. He pointed ahead and up. "He says we must go through the pass, under the Great Buddha," Takeko explained. "We have only an hour to go."

"Arigato," Hartford said, suppressing a moan. Another hour!

The pass Kiwa had spoken of loomed ahead. It was quite narrow, and walled on either side by the almost perpendicular flanks of mountains, shoulder to shoulder. Kiwa went first, for the cleft could only be negotiated in single file. Takeko followed her father, and Hartford took up the rear. In the ravine it was dark. The camelopards, sensing their mangers up ahead, paced more quickly. Suddenly the canyon was light, the walls spreading further apart here.

Far up on Hartford's right, seated on a shelf left from some ancient avalanche, was a gigantic figure cast of a coppery metal, green now against the granite wall. "Who is that?" Hartford called to Takeko.

"It is our *Daibutsu*," Takeko said. "It is the *Amida Buddha*, the Lord of Boundless Light."

"Do you worship him?"

Takeko smiled and shook her head. "We worship not any man, but a Way," she said. *"Butsudo*—the Way of the Buddha. We are nearly to the village now, Lee-san."

"I thank the Lord Buddha for that," Hartford said, bowing from his saddle toward the great bronze image.

Yamamura nestled in a fold of the high mountains. The fields that supported the village, its population now doubled by the refugees from Kansannamura, were tucked here and there on narrow ledges, watered by bamboo flumes that stole water from the mountain streams. The crop of greatest importance was the ubiquitous sunflower, supplier of bread and soap ash, of cloth and bath oil, birdseed and writing paper. Bamboo grew in clefts and shelves too slight for cultivation. This was the wood for tools, the water pipe, the house wattles and, in its youth, the salad of the people, the only wood eaten in its native state. There were also carrots, beets and tiny plumtrees, and the horseradish, *daikon*. Yamamura was a lovely place, Hartford decided.

It was twenty hours from the moment of his contamination that Hartford dismounted. He moved into the house Kiwa invited him to with as much tenderness as though he'd been carefully bastinadoed and flayed. He was, nonetheless, free of febrile symptoms. He had breathed Kansan air, had eaten its fish and drunk its water; he'd spoken with a Kansan native and had lain with his face in Kansan dust. He was still as healthy as any Axenite, never before in the saddle, would be after a five-hour ride.

Kiwa's wife and Takeko's mother was a little woman named Toyomi-san, dressed in brightly patterned garments a good deal more formal than her daughter's jacket and shorts. Toyomi-san spoke no Standard, but she made quite clear to Hartford his welcome. She led him into a large, steam-filled room, where she indicated he was first to wash himself then soak, then dry and dress in the clean clothing she'd laid out for his use.

The soaking water was very hot, and very welcome. Hartford sat in the copper-bottomed tub, his muscles hard and sore, until he felt the very marrow of his bones had cooked. He stepped from the tub then and dried gently, easy on his chafed back and legs.

"The oil will help," Takeko said, slipping a screen shut behind her. She had bathed and brushed her black hair free of the bamboo-thicket dust, and wore now a brilliant silk *kimono* of the sort her mother was wearing.

Hartford held the towel at his waist.

"Excuse me," he said.

Takeko giggled. "Are you unique, Lee-san, that you must hide yourself? Lie down on the cot, and I will make you comfortable."

Wondering greatly at the folkways of Kansas, but determined to commit no gaffe that would imperil his relations with this girl, Hartford lay face down on the mat-covered cot. Takeko removed the *tenugi* towel with which he'd modestly draped himself and gently stroked sweet-scented sunflower-seed oil into his macerated skin. Using the radical border of her hands, which were remarkably strong, Takeko coaxed the muscles to relax with effleurage; and she further softened the clonic hardness with a kneading motion. "This is," she said, working her thumb knuckles up his spinal column as though telling the beads of his vertebrae, "one of the good things my ancestors brought from Earth."

"*Yoroshiku soro,*" Hartford grunted agreement. "It is good."

Half an hour later, his skin soothed with oil and his muscles suppled by Takeko's massage, Hartford joined the family for supper. The Kansans used paired sticks for eating. Hartford, who'd not yet been introduced to the skill of using these *o-hashi,* and who was too hungry to practice now, was given a metal spoon with which to eat.

When they'd finished their meal, several elder Kansans entered Kiwa-san's house. Each bowed to Hartford, who, bald-headed, his feet socked into unfamiliar *geta* and wearing mitten-toed stockings, bowed in return. The newcomers each spoke some Standard, but it was obvious that Takeko was the most fluent of them all. "Pia-san taught Renkei; Renkei taught me," the girl explained. "I was the second-best speaker. It would be better if Renkei were here."

"I regret his death more deeply than I can tell you," Hartford said. "Renkei and Pia my friend are both dead now. This is what Renkei told me: *aru-majiki koto*, a thing that ought not to be."

The Kansans, seated on the cushions about the room, nodded. "Do you know, Lee-san, the greatest law of life?" Takeko asked.

"You said, beside the stream where we fished that men do not kill men," Hartford answered. "But they do."

"It is an ideal we have more nearly than the glass-heads," one of the Kansan elders said. "In the past four days, Renkei has died, and Pia-san. In the years before you Latecomers came to build the Stone House and cut roads and practice making holes in paper at a distance, no man died here at the hand of another."

"We cannot teach the glass-heads our way when they walk about only with guns, when they live in the Stone House none of us can enter without dying, when they look at us with glass bowls over their faces and hate in their hearts," Takeko said.

"The hate is hardly needful," Hartford said. "But the helmets must remain if Axenites are to live on Kansas."

"Do you live?" Takeko asked quietly.

"I do," Hartford said. "It puzzles me."

"Does it not puzzle you that none of us harbors open sores, or coughs up phlegm, or dies of fever?" Kiwa asked, speaking through his daughter's intermediation.

"I had not thought of that," Hartford admitted. "I have never before lived so close to Stinkers." Embarrassed, he stopped short. "I'm sorry," he said. *"Shitsurei shimashita."*

"You meant us no discourtesy," Takeko said. "Think, Lee, of the word you used. Do we indeed stink?"

"No," Hartford said. "It's strange. I've been told all my life of the rot and fermentation within ordinary mammals, and of the evil smells elaborated by these processes. But you, and all of Kansas, stink no more than Axenites do. You have, as we, the mulberry odor of saliva, the wheat smell of thiamin, the faint musk oil of the hair. Even your camelopards smell sweet."

The girl laughed. "If you think all Kansas a place of sweet

perfumes, smell this, Lee-san," she said. She took a covered dish and opened it. "This is *takuwan*," she said. A smell strong as that of limburger cheese made itself known in the room. "It is pickled turnip, made in the old manner of our island forefathers on Earth."

"Whew!" Hartford said. "There is the true stinker of Kansas."

"Pia-san learned much from the bad-smelling *takuwan*," Takeko said. "His wife knew about the small stink-makers, these bacteria; she was a user of microscopes. She looked for them in the air of Kansas, and in our soil. Pia-san went even further. He took drops of our blood and other things to test."

"Tell our guest, Take-chan, what Pia found," Old Kiwa told his daughter.

"*Hai, Otosan.*" The girl turned to Hartford. "In our bodies there are no mischief-makers of the sort Earth people know. There are not even those juices Pia-san called 'footprints of the bugs.'"

"He must have meant you have no bacterial antibodies," Hartford said. "That explains the whole package," he went on, with growing excitement. "Why I'm alive without my safety-suit. What Piacentelli went outside to find. And, when he found it, why he unsuited himself, knowing this world as pure as Titan. You're Axenites, you Kansans! You're as germ-free as the troopers."

"The whole truth is less simple," said the lean old man who'd been introduced to Hartford as Yamata, the calligrapher.

"Does the rubble of your forest floors never turn to mould, then?" Hartford asked. "Do the bodies of your buried fathers lie uncorrupted in their graves?"

"Of course not," Takeko said. "If that happened, we would be buried ourselves in unmouldered leaves. The bodies of our ancestors would be stacked about us, unchanging, like logs for the charcoal burners. Our soil would die, and all men would die with it, if dead things did not crumble to make new soil."

"Show our friend the hero of our epic," the calligrapher told her.

"*Hai.*" Takeko stood and went to another room, going through the ritual of kneeling to slide the door screen, standing, kneeling, standing, with a grace that made the *kimono* she wore the loveliest of garments. She brought to the small table at the center of the room a heavy object wrapped in a yellow silk *tenugui*. Near this on the table she placed a small lamp, fueled with sunflower-seed oil. She lighted the lamp and uncovered the instrument she'd brought in.

It was the microscope Piacentelli had taken from the Barracks on his fatal expedition.

Takeko dipped a chopstick into a dish and placed it beneath the objective of the microscope. "We shall look at a spot of evil-smelling *takuwan* juice," she said. "There is light enough. Make it fit your eyes, Lee-san; and you will know the secret of Jodo, this world you call Kansas."

IX

Hartford knelt over the microscope in the yoga-posture called for by its being so near the floor and tried to adjust the instrument as he remembered having seen it done. He focused the coarse adjustment of the 'scope till he saw spots darting about the fluid Takeko had placed on the slide. He nailed the spots down with a gentle hand on the fine adjustment.

The juice of the pickled turnip was aswim with tiny bodies that looked like tadpoles. "What are they?" he asked, peering into the micro-world below him.

"Pia-san named them monads," said the carpenter, white-bearded Togo. "We all have them in our bodies. You have them now in yours. Our soil is alive with them. They chew the chaff of our fields into black loam; they turn to dust the flesh of our fathers. They cause turnips to become *takuwan*."

Hartford rocked back from the microscope to sit again on his heels. "You have no disease, no benign bacterial flora and of course no bacterial antibodies. Instead you have this whip-taled animalcule, this monad. Is this correct?"

"So Pia-san said," Takeko agreed. "He said that the monad is a jealous beast. It is a tiger among the pygmies, he said. No little nuisance-makers can exist on Kansas; the monad would eat them in a rage."

"The ultimate antibiotic," Hartford said. "A micro-organism that functions as a saprophyte, a soil former and a scavenger. Besides all this, it's a universal phagocyte, policing up the human environment inside and out, to keep it clean of any other microscopic organisms. The monad fills every niche in the micro-ecology of the planet."

"This is what Pia-san and his *okusama,* poor dead girl, discovered," Takeko said. "Renkei entered the Stone House to tell you that we do not stink, that we are not dangerous. Three people have died to tell this—and Nef still does not know."

"I think he may know it after all," Hartford said. "He knows about the monad, and fears it. This little bug means that every member of the human race can join his damned Brotherhood. A crew of monads in his gut would make every man on Stinker Earth a dignotobiote, germ-free except for his housekeeping protozoa."

"Until Pia-san told us," Yamata said, "we knew nothing except that we live longer than our ancestors had. We knew that we did not suffer from the strange tirednesses the books told of, ills caused by the little animals. We did not know that the smallest natives of this planet had made of us their fortresses."

"If I could only get past Nasty Nef to tell this to the Axenites," Hartford said.

"Ron yori shoko," Kiwa-san said. Takeko translated for her father. "He says, 'Proof is stronger than argument.'"

"Indeed," Hartford agreed. "But how do I prove to the troopers that the monad sweeps Kansas cleaner than their Barracks floors?"

"As Pia-san tried to," Takeko said. "He removed his glass-head and his silken suit. He breathed our air and ate our food. He wanted to prove that he could live, but he was killed before he could. Now you have made that proof. Your brothers of the Stone House must undress of their silken suits and come among us, Lee-san."

"That they will not," Hartford said. "They are certain they will die if they inhale a breath of Kansas air, chew a bite of Kansas food, drink your clear stream water. I was certain I would die when my safety-suit was torn: remember our meeting, Takeko-san? It will not be easy to persuade my brothers and sisters in the Barracks to forget their fears. We are so sure, we Axenites, that contamination will kill us that we'd rather dance with lightning and eat stones than walk this world unprotected and eat its fruits."

When Takeko had respoken these words to her father, the

old man said again: *"Ron yori shoko."* Proof is stronger than argument.

"Proof?" Hartford asked. "I am not proof enough to have a regiment of Axenites shed their safety-suits and declare the Kansans their brothers. It would take years of lab work before the first of them would walk suitless onto bug-dirt. We'd have to knock down the walls of the Barracks and burn two-thousand-odd safety-suits, before we'd have the Axenite troopers here trapped into being guinea pigs."

"Each trooper carries the Stone House with him when he walks our roads," the calligrapher remarked. "We have but to break through the silken suit he wears to make a trooper know the garment isn't needed here."

"He'd die of fright," Hartford said. "I very nearly did. Besides, each column of troopers, a squad of the regiment, goes out with a Decontamination Squad. If a man becomes septic through some sort of accident, he's hustled by a cleanup squad into a Decontamination Vehicle for his shower, shave and shots. I know the process well," he said, running his palm over his naked head.

"Ano ne," Kiwa said. "Will this decontamination-*kuruma* house two thousand men? Two hundred? Twenty?"

"It will hold two or three troopers at once," Hartford answered. "We have several of them, though."

"So . . . ka?" white-bearded Togo exclaimed. He leaned over to whisper into the ear of Takeko's father, who nodded and smiled.

Old Kiwa spoke, and Takeko interpreted. "We must surprise a group of troopers," he said. "We must cause all their silken suits to be torn, or all their glass heads shattered, at one time. It is so simple as that."

"Simple in all but the doing," said Yamata the calligrapher. He picked up a brush and sketched on the mat before him a line of trooper silhouettes, a platoon, marching single file. "How do we break into all those Stone Houses at once?" he asked.

Hartford's face was pale. "We could use grenades, perhaps," he said. "Or bombs. After all, these troopers we speak of are no more than my family, my village, my people. I may of course be expected to cooperate in their destruction."

Takeko reached over and took his hand, then dropped it. *"Ano ne!* You do not understand! We can no more injure your brothers than you can, Lee-san. We may not harm any living person. Forgive us. You misunderstand us. We are bound, Lee-sensei, by *Butsudo:* the Peaceful Path of the Lord Buddha." She bowed toward him, her hands clasped together, her head touching the *tatami*.

"It is my fault if I have misunderstood," Hartford said. The men were staring, Takeko's eyes were filled with tears, the room was silent. "I do not know you well. I did not know you do not kill."

"Let me tell you, then," Takeko said rising to sit beside him. "Our people, who once lived on islands in the greater sea of Earth, were folk mighty in battle. Their pride was named the Way of the Warrior, which is called *Bushido*. Their loveliest flower, the *sakura,* or cherry blossom, they made the symbol of the warrior, so highly did they hold his calling.

"After their villages had been crushed many times in war, our ancestors vowed forever to abandon *Bushido,* the warrior's path, and to place their feet in the path of the Lord Buddha, called *Butsudo*. This was many years ago, before any man had ventured into space, before our ancestors found this world you call Kansas. When they came here, they came in peace. And they named this place Jodo, which we still call it. It means the Pure Land, where men are just. And all justice is built on a single law. No man shall take man's life."

"I spoke of the Axenite Brotherhood," Hartford said. "These men are a group of our leaders—Colonel Nef is one; he invited me to join him—who have decided that Stinker humanity must go. They're dedicated men, prepared to extinguish all the rest of mankind, to sterilize Earth and reseed it as a gnotobiotopic Paradise. Nef has, I fear, already killed three people to this end.

"You who cannot kill will face an enemy trained to killing," he went on. "Your camelopard-mounted messengers will meet veeto-platforms with machine guns. Your peaceful words will be drowned out by the roar of Dardick-rifles. How can you hope to live if you will not kill?"

"If the choice were death or killing, Lee-san, we would gladly die," Takeko said. "We have a saying, *Muriga toreba dori ga hikkomu*. When might takes charge justice withdraws. We will not kill, and neither will we be defeated."

Yamata the calligrapher addressed Hartford. "How badly torn must a safety-suit be to make necessary the wearer's going into the purification cart?" he asked.

"Only so much as the point of a pin would make would be enough," Hartford said.

"We have to drive pins into several dozens of men's clothing at one time," Yamata said. He smiled. "So phrased, the mountain does not seem too tall to be climbed."

"It would be difficult to puncture the safety-suits without hurting the wearers," Hartford said. "Few armies are so solicitous."

"Butsudo forbids us to kill men," Takeko said. "It does not deny us the right, in pointing them to the path of knowledge, to jab them a bit." She smiled at Hartford.

"How do you propose to do this jabbing?" he asked. "I remind you all, if you need reminding, that our troopers travel with Dardick-rifles and machine guns, with rocket-mounted jeeps and veeto-platforms from which bombs can be dropped."

Kiwa spoke. "We are like a bear after honey," he said. "We are hungry, but do not wish to taste the stings of the guardians of the hive. We must surprise them."

Hartford, his knees stiff with kneeling, his backside sore from the camelopard saddle despite the expert massage, got up to pace the floor. "We need a needle-gun of some sort," he said.

"No gun," insisted white-bearded Togo.

"It need have only slight power," Hartford said. "It would throw its projectile only forcefully enough to penetrate the fabric of a safety-suit."

"It has been so many generations since we have been soldiers, we know nothing of weapons," Yamata-san said. He wet a fine brush with *sumi,* Chinese ink, and sketched rapidly. "I remember seeing pictures of *Bushi* carrying a sort of throwing-stocks with pointed ends in pockets on their backs, and flinging them like little spears with a kind of one-stringed lute."

Hartford stared at the calligrapher's drawing, then exclaimed, "Of course! A bow and arrow."

Takeko inspected the sketch. "The man who threw the stick is standing," she said. "Could we stand against troopers?"

"A man would have to stand exposed to shoot an arrow," Hartford admitted. "The Dardick-guns would mow us down before we'd punctured a single safety-suit." He paced up and down the room, the only trained warrior there, trying to devise his unkilling weapon.

"We have wine, Lee-san," Takeko said. "Please sit and drink."

Hartford, bemused with his problem, folded his legs onto his cushion and lowered himself gently. Takeko's mother appeared with tiny cups of hot wine, *sake*. Hartford bowed with the others and sipped. The stuff was good, rather like a dry sherry.

Takeko bowed to leave the room, returned, bowed and commenced playing a tune with the instrument she'd brought in. It was a flute made of bamboo, with a high-pitched, pure sound Hartford found quite pleasant. He frowned, though, after a moment. Takeko took the pipe from her lips. "You do not enjoy my playing?" she asked.

"What is that made of?" Hartford demanded. "Just bamboo, isn't it?"

"Hai, take," Takeko agreed. "It is my name. *Take*—bamboo. This is only a *shakuhachi*, for very simple music."

Hartford smiled and bowed toward Togo-san, the white-bearded carpenter. "Sir," he said, "if we may have your advice, I believe Takeko-chan has helped us find our weapon."

X

The meeting broke up to adjourn to Togo-san's workshop. There was bamboo there in plenty, and young men eager to help the ex-lieutenant of Axenites in testing his device. As the week wore on, young Kansans appeared from other villages, called by blabrigars and messengers on camelopard-back to join the army that was to make brothers and sisters of the troopers of First Regiment.

The blowgun Hartford finally established as his field model was some two yards long, made of bamboo bored through the joints and polished smooth within, of a caliber somewhat less than the diameter of a man's little finger. Though the bamboo tube was somewhat flexible, Togo-san and his apprentices were able to bind a front sight to the muzzle, allowing somewhat greater accuracy than could be obtained by pointing and hoping.

The dart was about the length of a man's hand. Its point was a sliver of bamboo, sharp as steel, entirely sharp enough to penetrate the tough material of a safety-suit if puffed from the blowgun with enough force.

All the craftsmen of the village became arms-makers. They drilled bamboo, polished the bore with abrasive-coated cord, fitted on the sights and tested their blowguns against the targets. Hundreds of darts were turned out for practice, and the most perfect were saved for the battlefield itself. The blowgunners began their drill, shooting from a prone position at targets as far as ten yards off, as great a range as amateurs could be expected to shoot with accuracy in the short time these had for practice.

To fire the blowgun, the dart was wrapped in a bit of silk of sunflower-stalk fluff, so that it would fit tightly into the tube. The puff that sent it on its way had to be sharp and hard. Achieving the proper slap of air took more practice even than aiming.

Hartford became every day a better horseman, or rather camelopardist. He in fact rejoiced in opportunities to leapfrog into his saddle, fit his feet and legs into the leather gambadoes, and go hailing off into the hills to recruit men and material. He carried with him the radio he'd salvaged from his safety-suit, and could from time to time pick up First Regiment transmissions. The bitcher from his suit was useful in training large numbers of recruits on the blowgun range, and would be used when the Kansan guerrillas took to the field against the troopers. He was picking up the language rapidly, now. He had to use Takeko's services as interpreter less and less. Her usefulness declined not a bit, though, as the girl became his first lieutenant in charge of details.

The band of expert puff-gunners was joined by a company of scouts. These men and women skulked the hills afoot or astride camelopards, spying out the programs of the regiment. Having no radio to maintain contact with Yamamura, each scout carried a pair of blabrigars, trained to report to a specific person in its home village when given a selected prompt-word.

Yamata-san, the calligrapher, became a cartographer. He drew in jet-black *sumi* ink the contours of the mountains, greened in the stands of bamboo, drew blue streams and broad brown fields of sunflowers, till at last the map that filled the largest room in Yamamura was almost as real as the Kansan soil it reflected. Walking across this map in his *tabi*-stockinged feet,

Hartford and the others of Kansas Intelligence would move toy troopers, made of wood like *kokeshi* dolls, into the positions where the blabrigars reported patrols to be.

The plan of battle of the Kansas forces was *yawarado*, the Gentle Way, also called *judo*. They would wait till the enemy made a move they could use, then they'd trip him up by redirecting his own strength.

The move they most wanted the troopers to make was into the ravine that led toward the village of Yamamura, the pass under the *Daibutsu*, the huge bronze Buddha set there by their ancestors. In that ravine, under the gaze of the Lord of Boundless Light, the Kansas forces would either prevail against the invader and make him their brother by darts and sweet reason, or they would all die in the attempt.

The camelopards were stabled, ready as the steeds of any march-patrolling cavalry troop. The dartsmen, and those of the women who'd shown skill in handling the blowgun, were trained and eager. The path through the pass had been memorized in infinite detail by every one of the guerrillas. The squad of sappers responsible for checkmating the troopers had prepared their levers, their blocks and skids. Nothing remained now but to coax the enemy into the battlefield of the Kansans' choosing.

"Take out what's left of the safety-suit," Hartford ordered one of his men. "Leave it here—" He stabbed a toe at the map they both stood on.

"Would it be well for me to leave beside the torn and broken suit signs of a fight?" asked the boy, Ito Jiro, son of Old Ito-san, the knife-maker. "If the troopers are angry, they will be careless."

"If only you believed in war, Jiro-chan, you'd make a fine warrior," Hartford grinned. "Do it your way, and hurry back."

Jiro placed the bait under the regiment's nose early in the day, and returned to Yamamura. It was midday when a blabrigar flew in from one of the scouts posted to watch First Regiment's reaction. The bird prated its message into the ear of its receiver. Troopers, a band of fifty-odd, were scouring the hills to the west, following the camelopard hoofprints left by Jiro. Aiding them in their search was the regiment's veeto-platform, skimming, hovering, pouncing to pick up clues. "They're on the scent," Hartford said. He turned again to Ito Jiro, fleetest of the camelopard riders. "Jiro-chan, lead them a chase that will bring them to the ravine no sooner than the Hour of the Dog. Be very cautious of the flying-thing; it can surprise you."

"Hai," Jiro said, bowing. "The Hour of the Dog they will call upon you near the *Daibutsu."* Ito-san the knife maker watched his son run toward the stables, the boy as excited as though he were going to a festival rather than to face alone half a company of full-armed Axenites. The blabrigars that would ride out with Jiro were trained to report to the father. It would be a long afternoon for the old man, Hartford thought.

There was much to do before the scarlet bird came winging in from Jiro's shoulder with the message that the trap was sprung. At the Hour of the Monkey, four hours before the troopers were to be in ambush, the first blabrigar flew in to report to Ito-san that the boy's mount was winded, the enemy was drawing nearer the ravine, and that Jiro was approaching the point of rendezvous where he would find a fresh camelo-pard. Hartford ordered out two youths to join Jiro there in his harassment of the foot soldiers from the regiment.

"It is time we take up our positions," he told his band of dartsmen. "Let us go in hope."

Kiwa-san, Takeko's father, stepped forward to pronounce a benediction upon the little company. "The Enlightened One, speaking at Rajagriha, spake, saying: 'Remember one thing, O beloved disciples, that hatred cannot be silenced by lies but by truth.'"

The irregulars, heads bowed, replied, *"Namu Amida Butsu."* Glory to the Amida Buddha! Hartford, though his training as an Axenite trooper had left him as untouched by religions as by microbes, joined the prayer, feeling that a degree of celestial interest in their stratagem would not be unwelcome.

The camelopardists vaulted into their saddles, adjusted their legs in the bootlike gambadoes, and slapped the reins to head their *giraffu* toward the ravine where the endgame would be played. Hartford rode at the head of the band, Takeko beside him. The others were dispersed at wide interval, a precaution against the veeto-platform's swooping over the horizon to surprise them en route. As they left Yamamura, the women and children of the village were leaving from the other side, together with the men too old to go out with the guerrillas. Yamamura was being abandoned until the outcome of battle made itself known.

The canyon that led up the mountain's groin had once been
the deep-cut bed of a stream. Collapse of overbeetling rock
had formed a vault over the stream, which was consequently
underground. Soil had filtered into the rocks, and bamboo had
taken root. In result the lower ravine was a green enfilade hardly
wider than a hallway, the walls on either side rising squarely
from its floor. Well within the pass, set into the left-hand wall
as one rode down from Yamamura, was a niche very like the
tokonoma, or honored alcove, of a Kansan home. In this alcove,
some fifty feet from the bottom of the pass, was set the great
bronze image of Buddha, the *Daibutsu* of Kansas.

Further down, below the *Daibutsu* niche, the canyon became
irregular. Along either side, some ten feet from the floor, were
ledges marking the fracture planes along which ancient ava-
lanches had calved. It was from these shelves that the Kansans
hoped to ambush the men from First Regiment. The narrowness
of the ravine, and the overhang of willow trees—these growing
in clefts of rock, fingering their roots down to the subterranean
stream—were enough, Hartford prayed, to prevent the veeto-
platform's pilot from spotting the Kansans lying in wait with
their blowguns.

Hartford disposed his troops on the shelves, checking to see
that each man had a good field of fire and adequate cover. He
glanced at the sun, the Kansan timepiece. It was between six
and eight in the evening, he judged, the Hour of the Cock.
He pressed his ear to the radio receiver. Short-range, the safety-
suit radio picked up only occasional orders from Axenite
officers and noncoms. Twice Hartford caught the name, "Lieutenant Felix." He smiled, feeling mixed emotions. Felix had
been his old platoon sergeant, and they would face each other
in an hour or so as enemies. Very likely the fifty troopers
chasing Ito Jiro and his fellows toward the canyon included
men of the Terrible Third Platoon, his old command. Hartford
checked to see his bitcher worked and waited the arrival of the
message-blabrigars with fresh news.

XI

The first bird arrived a few moments before the radio began
coming in clear.

"Sakura," Hartford said, this being the prompt-word to which the blabrigar was trained to reply.

"Fifty men, sir; fifty men, sir; on the way, sir; on the way sir," the bird chanted into Hartford's ear. He let the bird rest on his shoulder; it would have to fly back to the scout who'd sent it soon, to tell him to join the rest of them at the ambush point.

The sun was low in the sky. H-hour was near. The signals began coming closer together. "Saw one Stinker off your left flank, Miller. . . . Left flank guard reporting, sir. That Gook took off due east. Blabrigar on his shoulder. . . . Lieutenant Felix here. Anything on the right flank? . . . Nothing, sir. . . . Keep moving, Lieutenant." This last voice was the colonel's.

Hartford frowned. If Nasty Nef had come out in person, the game would have to be played fast and dirty.

Hartford set his bitcher low. *"Abunai yo!"* he said to his guerrillas, sprawled out all along the ledge like figurines on a mantelpiece. "Be cautious. Shoot your dart and get behind something. From now on, be silent. The enemy is near."

Takeko spoke: "You mean, Lee-chan, that our brothers draw near." The other Kansans smiled. Some saluted, a gesture they'd observed among the Axenites they'd been spying upon for the past few days.

The first of the scouts came galloping up the gullet of the canyon. Without a sound he signaled his watching comrades, invisible above him. He made a circle with his hand, pointing up. That meant the regiment's veeto-platform was scouting ahead of the approaching Axenites. The first man slapped his *giraffu* to hasten it up the pass, past the *Daibutsu.* Two other scouts, the foxes urging on the hounds, came shouting into the canyon. Neither of them was Ito Jiro. As his name signified, Jiro was the youngest son of Ito-san, the knife-maker. He was the darling of the family. Where was he? Hartford worried.

The radio, no longer masked by the rocks, was filled with information. Hartford heard the veeto-pilot reporting: "They're headed up the gulch past the big idol, sir," he said. "There's a village up there. That's where they're probably headed. What do you want me to do, sir?" The platform hovered over the canyon, unwilling to work its way into the jagged, bamboo-and-pine-prickly fissure.

"Keep in touch, Sky-Eye," Nef ordered. "We're coming right up."

"Felix here, sir," the lieutenant reported. "We've got one of the Gooks prisoner. He's just a kid. Doesn't seem to know a thing."

"Hold him till we get someone who talks Stinker," Nef said.

They got Jiro, Hartford thought. Damn.

The first of the troopers, an officer in the blue safety-suit, spearheaded the column. "Nothing in sight yet," Felix's voice reported. The officer signaled "Come on" with the sweep of his arm, and the first squad of Axenites, dispersed as skirmishers, formed themselves into a file to enter the canyon. The veeto-platform above kept the foliage pressed down with its jet of air, stirring dust that both improved concealment and threatened to trigger a sneeze from one of the ambushers.

Hartford peered cautiously over the edge of the shelf. He'd set his forces far enough back in the canyon that the entire Axenite column would be encased. "Sir, this is Felix," the radio said. "Do you agree, sir, that I should place one squad in reserve till the rest get through the gully?"

"Peel off one squad and stay with it, Felix," Nef said.

Felix's voice again: "Sir, it was our Lieutenant Hartford that the Gooks got. I'd like to go in early."

"Very well, Felix. Miller, hold your squad where it is. Disperse them well, and wait my order before bringing them into the ditch. Confirm."

"Done and done, sir," Miller snapped.

The first two dozen troopers were in the canyon now, half the Axenite force. Colonel Nef had shown the good sense to don an ordinary blue safety-suit; his scarlet command suit would have made him a splendid target. Another squad entered, their Dardick-rifles held at the ready. This would have to be quick, Hartford thought, or he'd lose his entire corps at their first volley. He raised his hand, a signal visible only to Takeko. She cupped her hands around her mouth and whistled the call of the nightingale, "Ho-o-kekyo . . . kekyo!"

Before the echoed notes had died, the darts had found their targets.

The radio was a clutter of undisciplined Damn's, cries of "I've been hit!" One trooper, quicker than the rest, caught sight of a Kansan. He raised his rifle and purred out a stream of Dardick-pellets. Yoritomo, apprentice to the paper-maker, tumbled over the lip of the ledge, his blowpipe falling with him like a jackstraw. There was a babble on the radio. Nef overrode all other circuits to command: "At ease! Rake the ledges with sustained fire."

The canyon was blasted with a confetti of metal and spalled rock as the troopers hosed the shelves with bullets.

The angle made aiming impossible. But by luck and the intensity of the barrage another man, the carpenter's son, had toppled to his death.

"Sky-Eye! Get your butt down here!" Nef bellowed. "Decontamination Squad! Bring the vehicle to the mouth of the canyon. We've got men septic." He tongued on his bitcher and bellowed at the troopers. "On the double, through the ditch."

"*Yuke!*" Hartford shouted to the men far up the wall, in the niche that held the *Daibutsu*. "Go!"

The sappers at the back of the giant bronze statue bent to their levers. The tons of metal scooted slowly forward, hit the fat-smeared edge of the shelf. As quietly as a man rocking forward in prayer, the *Daibutsu* dropped head-down into the ravine. It struck the bottom with the sound of a great gong, and rocked, unshattered, plugging the throat of the canyon, standing as a dam. The hands of the Enlightened One were held in the positions of Protection and of Giving. His face bore still a quiet smile. About the head of the image a fountain of water burst, squeezed up from the stream below. "*Namu Amida Butsu!*" Takeko said, cuddled against Hartford, staring down.

"Keep down," he said. He lifted his suit radio and flicked on the transmission switch. "This is Lee Hartford, late of the First Regiment," he announced. "The safety-suits of most of you have been breached. There is not room for more than three of you in the Decontamination Vehicle. You are not septic. I repeat: you have not been contaminated. Kansas is as safe for you as the Barracks, or Titan, or the M'Bwene planets, or in the cells at Luna. You do not need your safety-suits on Kansas."

"Find that man and gun the traitor down," Nef's voice demanded from the speaker on his suit.

"I am coming out unarmed," Hartford radioed.

"Fire the moment you see him," Nef said. One of the officers had his Dardick-piston drawn, his eyes traversing the canyon walls.

"No, sir!" Felix's voice snapped from his bitcher. "You can't shoot the man till he's had a chance to speak."

"Go to the rear at once, Private Felix," Nef bellowed.

Felix pointed his handgun toward Nef. "No, sir," he replied. "Hartford was my C.O., and an honest man. I'll hear him before I see him killed. Or by my life, sir, I'll kill you after him."

"This is treason," Nef said.

"Drop your pistol, sir, or I'll have to try to shoot it from your hand. Excuse me, sir," Felix said.

Nef's gun dropped.

"You all hear me?" Felix bitched. "Hear me out there, Miller?" There was a chorus of "Roger!" Felix went on: "I'm going to unclam my helmet, troopers. I'm going to take off my safety-suit. That's how much I trust Lee Hartford, troopers. The man who tries to stop Hartford better begin with me." Felix opened his helmet, removed it, and placed it on the rocks beside him. He went up to drink from the fountain that sparkled about the head of the *Daibutsu,* cupping his hands. "It's good water, men," he said. "Come on down, Hartford," he shouted through the clear night air.

Lee Hartford twisted over the edge of the shelf, held himself by his fingertips, and dropped. He stood before his old comrades in arms dressed as a country Kansan. His head bore only a stubble of hair, and a scarlet blabrigar came down to settle familiarly on his shoulder. "I caused your suits to be breached for good reason," he said, speaking into the bitcher he'd recovered from his safety-suit. "If any of you has a sore backside because of the darts my men sent at you, please accept my apologies." Two more Axenites removed their helmets, and stood grinning uncertainly at Hartford. "I have lived on Kansas for two weeks, living like a native. I've breathed Kansan air, eaten their wonderful food and even kissed one of their girls." There was a murmur of laughter. "I'm as healthy as ever I was inside the Barracks," Hartford said. "And I'm a good deal happier."

There was louder laughter among the Axenites, and more helmets opened. Hartford turned to look behind him. Takeko was hanging by her fingertips off the shelf, trying to work up the courage to drop. He went over to stand below her. "Fall to me, darling," he said. "Fall into my arms."

"I hear, *shujin,* and obey," Takeko squeaked, and dropped.

When Hartford released Takeko and turned to face the troopers, every helmet but Nef's was opened. Half a dozen of the men had already stripped to their Class B's. They had their faces tilted into the wind that was sweeping up the gullet of the canyon, smelling for the first time in their lives the scents of open nature, the spice of green life in the air. They were seeing the Kansas sky, a mosaic of stars, unfiltered by helmets. They were breathing air not humid with their own perspiration. Holding Takeko's hand in his, Hartford walked up to Felix. "You saved the day, old buddy," he said.

There was the cough of a tapped-off Dardick-round.

Felix fell. Colonel Nef, his pistol held at the hip, tilted it toward Hartford. He looked startled for a moment, then dropped the pistol. In his wrist were three blowgun darts. Clustered across his chest were half a dozen more. Hartford waved at the Kansans on the ledge. *"Arigato!"* he shouted, and told them to come down.

Two men had died in the engagement: Yoritomo the paper-maker and Sannosuke the carpenter's son. Felix's thighbone had been broken by Nef's shot; and Colonel Nef's right wrist would require attention. A medical officer had been sent for from the Barracks to set Felix's leg. The dead men were carried on litters up to the shelves and around the fallen *Daibutsu* to the village. Hartford splinted his friend's broken leg. "What now, Hartford?" Felix asked.

"I suggest that you all become guests in Yamamura."

"Done and done," Felix said.

Takeko came up to lay a bunch of flowers on his chest. "They smell sweet," she said. "Courage such as yours smells sweet in the nostrils of heaven."

"Thank you, ma'am," Felix said. He turned his head to follow the girl as she took a second handful of flowers to place it beside the fountain that jetted about the head-standing *Daibutsu*. "I can see where this will be a popular planet to do duty on, Lieutenant," he said. "What you discovered here will pretty well wipe out the Brotherhood."

"You're right," Hartford said. "The Brotherhood is doomed."

They watched as Takeko knelt before the inverted image. *"Namu Amida Butsu,"* she said. "All men are the same in the sight of Amida, the Lord of Boundless Light."

"Maybe I'm wrong, Lieutenant," Felix said. "Maybe the Brotherhood just got started."

RIGHT TO LIFE

Thomas A. Easton

Fred Ayala was a loser. So were his wife, his five kids, and several million other Americans. He hadn't had a job in over a year, for there were too many people and too little work, and every employer in the country preferred new bodies to giving raises.

But Fred was about to do something about his problems. He would give his kids some hope of getting off the welfare. He would open up their future, though it might be his last effort.

He tucked the cuffs of his green slacks deep into his heavy combat boots and tugged the laces tight. He eased the tension across his knees by pulling three inches of fabric from his boot tops. He stood, and the pants bloused exactly as they should.

Howe had given him a roll of red plastic tape. He handed it to his wife and watched her stretch it down one outer seam. "Be sure it's straight, Maria."

"It is. Turn." He turned to let her do the other leg. Her straight black hair, the clean pink line of the part, were just a few inches from his face. She smelled of soap and cooking. She owned no perfume.

Maria stood and stepped back. She looked appraisingly at the stripes that now ran down each leg. "They'll do. You want the tunic now, dear?"

He took it himself from the back of a rickety chair. The tunic was the one thing they hadn't been able to buy or steal. Maria had had to make it from cloth Howe had provided. It fitted better than the pants. He shrugged it into place and grinned. With his short hair and close-clipped mustache, and with his tanbark skin, he didn't look only like a soldier. He looked like a veteran.

"You look like you did when we got married."

"That was a lotta years ago." Three boys, two girls, and three miscarriages. Six arrests. "And too damn few paychecks."

"Good years, though. I wish this thing wasn't just cloth." Maria smoothed the tunic over his shoulders. The movement called his attention to how their life had broadened her. Naked, the stretch marks made her belly a washboard. Her breasts were already stretching. She was a palimpsest of ages, her fate an inevitable tradition. She had little notion that once, for a few brief decades, even poor women had been able to say "No!" to pregnancy.

Fred too wished the tunic were the flexible armor of the true military. Then, he thought, he might have some hope of real success. "We're expendable," he reminded her gently. "Where are the guns?"

"Under the couch." He moved as if to bend down for the weaponry, but she waved him back. "I'll get them. You don't want to muss those stripes."

She had to go to her knees to pull the heavy carton into sight. It bore the markings of a large downtown department store, and it had been delivered by one of that store's trucks. Maria's face, as she lifted the lid, was as expectant as if it held an impossible new coat.

She handed her husband the antique Uzi. He checked the magazine and slung it across one shoulder by the strap. She handed him a heavy belt with two holsters. She handed him the matching automatics, solid .45s, and a bandoleer. He strapped them on and accepted the grape-like cluster of grenades. One by one, he hooked them to his belt.

The carton was almost empty. Maria lifted out the long machete and stood. "Where does this go?" The answer wasn't obvious. Fred Ayala was already so festooned that there seemed no place for it to fit.

"Down my back. There's a catch on the bandoleer."

He stood stiffly while she fastened it into place. "I don't know why you have to have this. It won't do you any good."

"The outfit needs it, Maria. I wouldn't look right without it." He shrugged, and his load of metal clanged. "But it might be useful. You can never tell. Now, where's that placard?"

"By the door." As they left the room, he shook himself to settle his gear. The noise was less this time, but Maria added, "You shouldn't make so much noise. The kids might wake up."

"Okay, honey." He hesitated. "It wouldn't be fair to say good-bye."

"It would only stir them up."

"Yeah." He turned to face her. He cupped her chin with a gentle hand. "You'd better get that sign on me."

He stood still while she fitted his head between the sheets of cardboard and knotted the string ties around his waist. It was like a picket sign, one loudly printed announcement for his front, another for his back. Both read:

YENBO LEGION
Europe's
Fight for Fuel
STARRING
Philip Slayton
and
Ramona Trey

The accompanying photo might have been of Fred, except that it showed a black kepi on the star's head.

Fred's kepi still swung from the hook behind the front door. He took it down and fitted it carefully into place. The short neckcloth tickled his ears. "Well, that's it."

Maria tipped her face up to him. He cupped her chin again and kissed her. He did it thoroughly, and she responded eagerly. She might have wanted to keep him home this night.

As he closed the door behind him, he thought he heard her whisper, "Come back, darling."

"Damn it!" the delegate from Boston swore. "I'd hoped that Texas aggie wouldn't show."

"You knew he would, though." His wife stood by the hotel suite's single window. Her cornsilk hair caught a red gleam of neon from the city outside. Her purse sat on the bed behind her. "He was there when the Party was founded. He nominated our first President, William."

"And he seconded the next four. I know." William Notter ran bony fingers through thinning hair. "But he's the most meatheaded man here. Or woman, for that matter. He sees no need for change, Terry. It's all holy writ for him."

"Perhaps he's right." The woman turned to face him. She was three years older, and she was dressed conservatively, properly. But the heavy, blue cloth couldn't hide her body or dim the flash of her matching eyes. He ached for a moment, but there was no time. The big session was tonight, after three days of preliminaries, and he had to be on time. He was the leader of his faction, and if the Party was to stay in power much longer, they had to win.

"If he is, then we're all damned. The inflation hasn't stopped in thirty years, and unemployment hasn't gone below fifteen percent in ten. It's even getting worse." He gestured angrily. "We can't go on the way we have been."

"Ben Bowles won't compromise."

"Then we'll have to outvote him. I think we have enough of the delegates with us."

"He has a lot of friends, William. And some of them . . ." Terry crossed the room and laid a hand on her husband's shoulder. She didn't have to reach very far. She was nearly as tall as he. "And not everyone sees the crisis."

"I know." He sighed and put an arm around her waist. "But for twenty years we've been forbidding birth control. It's no wonder there are more high-school grads on the market now. They're fresh, they're cheap, and they're pushing older men out of work, when they can find jobs at all." His expression lightened when she kissed the line of his jaw. He rubbed his cheek with his free hand. The stubble wasn't long enough to deserve a second shave. He sought her eyes. "Nuts. I've got to run down there now, honey. Are you sure you don't want to sit in?"

She shook her head. "Still, I'm glad our two are in college."

"We'd have more than two if you didn't have that irregular period."

They both grinned at that. The rich and powerful had always

ignored their own laws. "Maybe I'll show up for your cousin's talk. About nine?"

Howe had assured him there would be no trouble as long as he remembered the placard. And she seemed to be right. The subway car was less than half full, but no one moved away from him, and the similarly equipped girl at the other end of the car had received only a glance when she took her seat beside an off-duty cop.

Fred Ayala had been on the train for only five minutes when a five-year-old boy tugged at his hand. He had been seated beside his mother when Fred had boarded, and his eyes had gone wide with wonder at the *soldier* so close. He was too young to read. "Hey, mister!" He tugged at Fred's hand again. "Hey! Are those things real?" He laid a hand on a grenade.

Fred gently pushed the small fingers aside. "Of course they are. Do you think a soldier carries toys?"

The boy's mother stifled a laugh. Fred grinned at her. "Have you seen the movie?"

"Not yet. We're all going on Saturday. Is it good?" Her dark eyes were still laughing at her son's eager curiosity.

"You bet. I'd give you some tickets, but I passed all mine out this afternoon." He shrugged apologetically.

"That's all right." She stood and caught her boy by the arm. The train was slowing for a stop. "At least you're working." As the doors opened, she waved and left. The boy struggled for a moment, but by the time they were out of sight, he was running ahead.

Fred turned from the door, still smiling. He raised an eyebrow at the girl down the car. Lisa was her name. He didn't know the rest of it, but she was serious, intent, and cool. She ignored him, just as she always did the men in their group. She gave all her attention to their plans.

So, he thought. Let her be. They would have to change trains soon, and then . . . He felt tight, apprehensive. He'd have to loosen up.

Perhaps he would feel better when he got there. They had all been waiting a long time for this night. Ever since they'd known it would be possible. Howe hadn't found it hard to recruit the few malcontents she needed. Fred felt a dim glow of pride that he had been chosen from the thousands in the city. Twenty years of being thrown in jail for possession of a rubber, of poverty and pain and frustration, had been too much. But Fred knew he was hardly the angriest of his fellows.

When he stepped aboard the new train, he was pleased to see three other Legionnaires already seated, though they weren't together. He and Lisa found places as far from each other and the rest as they could. Despite their costumes, they weren't supposed to seem together.

They stayed apart until their station loomed up on the line. Then all five arose and stood waiting by the doors. Uzis and grenades clashed together, but they didn't speak, not even when the doors slid open and they stepped onto the platform with twenty others. Every car had its handful of soldiers. For a moment, the subway looked like a troop train, but the advertising placards disarmed the few spectators, and there were no security men this far from the Party's meeting rooms.

Anna Howe, of course, was near the front of the train. She wasn't in uniform—she was too fat to be accepted as a sandwichman, even by a tugboat maker—but every eye sought her immediately. When she lounged toward the wall, the rest followed suit. They would prop up the walls until the rest had come. Two dozen were too few to storm the Secret Service.

Alone, none of them had drawn attention, but so many in one spot drew stares, and the stares doubled with their numbers when the next train pulled in. Still, *Yenbo Legion* was being shown at a theater a block away. If the sight was unprecedented, it was nevertheless comprehensible. Perhaps they were gathering to collect their day's pay, where they wouldn't have to sacrifice a piece of it to the turnstiles. Perhaps they were gathering to catch the show together. Sandwichmen did get free tickets.

At least, that was the impression they were supposed to give. Howe had counted on it, and Fred Ayala saw her grin when no one did anything but stare. No questions. No alarms. But she did seem relieved when the rest of her assault squad arrived. If she was three men short, it didn't matter. Sixty should be enough, and the three cowards might survive the night.

As soon as most of the bystanders had disappeared up the broken escalator, she bounced off the wall and started walking up the platform. Their intended exit led directly into the hotel's lower level.

Her sixty followed her.

• • •

From his place in the third of the thirty ranks of soft-bottomed folding chairs, William Notter had a good view of the podium. He could hear the clink of the glass when the speaker sipped his water. By craning his neck just a little, he could see the Secret Service men in the wings.

He had already had his say. "The right to life" had made a fine campaign slogan in the 1990s, but its consequences had been insidious. It had brought the Party into power, and it had let them ban abortion and birth control. However, in time it had stifled the economy. It had meant larger families and more unemployment, and taxes had had to rise to meet the welfare bill. The Party had been morally right, perhaps, but they had not met the country's needs.

The other delegates had received his reasoning coldly. For them, as for Ben Bowles, the moral right was the greater good, and nothing else mattered. He had got them nodding, though, when he spoke of the next elections. They could see the threat there.

They had been ready when he had turned the podium over to the California delegate. They had listened when he told them the Party would have to loosen up. Not that they would have to go whole hog and allow the evils of abortion again, but they should let the people plan their families, let them spend their money on themselves. Let them feel grateful to the progressive, humanitarian, beneficent Party. The Party that stood for everyone's right to a *good* life.

But now Ben Bowles was talking. He had let a dozen others precede him, but at last his impatience had got the better of him and he had asserted his seniority. "I don't care," he was saying. He waved a stray wisp of smoke away from his heavy face. "I don't care if we do go down to defeat in November. We will go down in glory, and we will not be the baby-murdering heathen the good Mr. Notter is asking us to become. We will not force the people to prevent the sacred union of seed and egg, to risk the wrath of a justly outraged God by murdering His handiwork." He was blustering, but not everyone would see it. His words had for too long been the Party line.

William Notter registered the sheen of metal fiber in the fabric of Bowles's suit coat. He noted the thickness of padding. He wondered why the man felt it necessary to wear armor in the bosom of his Party. Was he afraid someone would try to assassinate him? That was more his own style. Fascinated, Notter hardly felt the hand on his elbow. "Bill!" The hoarse whisper, though, did reach him. He turned his head.

"What is it, Rose?" His interrupter slipped into the seat beside him. She was the delegate from South Dakota, older, with the weather-beaten look still so necessary in the western states. Her gray hair was drawn back severely, but her smile was infectious.

"The President's here, Bill. He's waiting in the hall."

Of course, he thought. He'll want to hear the vote, and he's sure to know that just his being here will help it. It's too bad we banned the press. But secrecy was safe. Calling attention to yourself was not. They had proved that long ago.

"Then I'd better go get him," he said. "You tell Bowles his time's up." He rose and sidled past her.

He paused at the ballroom doors to straighten his tie and tuck his shirt in more firmly. When he pushed the doors open, he found his wife greeting his cousin with a kiss. The three of them had been friends for years, and she had, she said, once had trouble deciding between the two men. Though she had no regrets, she assured her husband.

The President's bodyguards shifted protectively as he entered the hallway, but his path cleared immediately. They knew him. "Hi, Jack." They both smiled at the old joke as they shook hands.

"How's it going in there, Bill? Did you get the idea across?"

"It's a pretty sure thing. Though Bowles is trying his damnedest to haul them back on the straight and narrow. Have a good trip?" Notter slipped his arm around his wife as he spoke.

"So-so. But the copter made it. Midway's a mess, you know?"

"O'Hare's worse, these days. Or so I'm told."

His cousin checked his watch. "What are we waiting for?"

Notter cocked his head toward the room behind him. "For Bowles to finish. Rosie's given him the word." As he spoke, the applause began to sound through the closed doors. "Ready?"

Two of the guards stood aside to watch the hall. The rest followed their master through the doors and into the crowded room. The noise died immediately as the President was recognized.

The Notters found seats together as Bowles stepped gravely down and the President approached the stage. He climbed the short staircase, faced his silent audience, and engulfed the microphone in one large hand. "Gentlemen," he said. "And ladies. I understand that you have all thoroughly discussed the most important plank in our platform. I trust you understand it."

His audience laughed politely. "Very well, then. As the titular head of our great Right-to-Life Party, I don't feel it would be amiss for me to conduct the voting on this issue. I will canvass you myself."

A few seemed disturbed at that. They had expected the Party's secretary to run the show. He was a traditionalist himself, and the other traditionalists felt they could count on him to interpret a voice vote correctly. The President, it seemed, was of another mind.

The results surprised no one. The score was 283 to 114, and the Party would change. The President said it when he closed the tally:

"The die is cast. We may not be as righteous as once we were, but we will continue to hold this nation's reins. We will continue to steer the nation's path as close to righteousness as is humanly possible. If we have had to loosen our grip on a principle, we may rest assured that our grasp of the right is still far, far firmer than that of the New Democrats. We know that they would return us all to the evil days of the mid-twentieth century. We . . ."

Anna Howe led her group into the nearly deserted underground tunnel. The stores that lined it were closed, and few people had any other reason to use it at this hour.

A wall clock said it was only 8:45. They had a quarter of a mile to go, and they had plenty of time to take their intended formation. Fred Ayala stepped up beside his leader. She seemed bulkier than usual, and he could feel the rigidity of cheap plastic armor beneath her jacket when he bumped her side.

"You know the way, Fred."

He nodded silently, suppressing a sudden wave of revulsion. He had rehearsed the route two weeks before. What had she rehearsed? They were supposed to be on a suicide mission, but she was plainly ready to survive if she could.

"Then take the point. We want to surprise them." She let herself slip back along the column, pausing regularly to encourage and promise, telling her people of the good they would do, reminding them of their roles. It wouldn't do for anyone simply to open fire. Their objective was more than mere random slaughter.

Fred squelched his thoughts and increased his pace. His weapons rang faintly together, in time with his step, but he could do nothing but pray they wouldn't give him away. Once he was a hundred feet ahead of the rest, he could slow down and be quiet once more. Until then, he could only pray.

There was no one in sight at the hotel door. Loosening his pistols in their holsters, he beckoned the others on. He unslung his Uzi, and then he thought of his machete. If he met anyone, that might really be better. Quieter. He used the sheath to prop the door open and advanced with the blade naked in his hand.

The hallway carpets muffled his tread. There was still no one in sight. He hesitated at the first intersection, waited for the others to reach him. He turned the corner. Still no one.

The stairs were where he'd found them before. He went up the three flights silently. The glass door to the second floor was ajar, and he could see a guard, his gun safely holstered, his back to the glass.

Fred Ayala slipped his arm between door and jamb. He slashed viciously, and the guard fell. The machete jammed in the broken skull.

Fred left it, and with it his last compunctions. He had not been sure he could really do it, for he had never killed before, not even in the army.

The next guard would surely not be alone. Machetes would be useless. He signed to the man behind him to remove the body and open the door.

They gathered on the landing and the stairs. Anna Howe cautioned them. "Just the pistols first," she whispered. "A few of you have silencers. Go first."

Five minutes later, Fred passed two more bodies. The shots had made no sound. No one had noticed, and now they stood just outside their target. As they doffed their placards, they could hear the sound of a speech. Anna seemed to listen. "Fine," she whispered. "Be sure you get him. Use the Uzis."

Fred glanced at the bodies by the wall. He felt only faint

surprise that they failed to disturb him. He wished he knew what was being said behind the ballroom doors. "Go on," Howe hissed. "Don't miss!"

He leaned on the room's ornate double doors. They all heard, ". . . to the evil ways of the mid-twentieth century. We . . ." A burst of gunfire rattled down the hall. He could wait no longer.

Fred leaped into the room. As Howe had instructed him, he let his Uzi chatter its message across the seated delegates and into the podium. The others poured past him, and their guns turned his chatter into thunder.

A Secret Service guard flung himself toward the President, but too late. The reinforced podium disintegrated in the storm. Body armor failed. Both men fell as other guards tried to return the fire. Fred saw a girl beside him go down, her back exploding from a dumdum. But all the guards, for all their training and dedication, were too slow, too frail.

The Party's delegates screamed and died as the intruders turned their fire upon them. Fred held back when he recognized the moderate leader, Notter, but others did not. Notter went down as an Uzi's slugs hammered his chest.

Silence fell. Anna Howe pushed through the rubble of toppled chairs and moaning wounded. She put her pistol to a young blonde's head, and then she kicked a slender body onto its back. Fred recognized Notter once more.

Anna's body blocked his view as she fired downward. "So much for him," came her words.

The occasional raps of pistols killing off the wounded punctuated the silence. Fred moved, seeking and finding his own bloody victims. Few of the bodies wore his uniform.

They had triumphed. The Party was now both headless and brainless. The New Democrats would have to win the election, and the people would regain control of their lives.

The sirens began screaming in the streets.

"Go now! Run!" As Anna Howe bellowed her final orders, they all turned, not quite stampeding for the open doors. Fred glanced behind him as he ran, and he stopped. Howe was stepping quickly toward the large room's only other door. Where was she going?

He turned and followed, eager to take a safer route if she knew one. He was only a step behind her when she stepped into the hall and bent. She had not heard him, her hearing dulled, perhaps, by all the recent thunder.

She was helping a burly man to his feet. Fred heard, "The money! Where's the other half of the money?"

"Drop your gun first," said the man. She did, and after he stepped on it, he turned and pointed down the hall. "In the first ladies' room, in a briefcase. It's all there."

Fred suddenly felt sick. He recognized the cultivatedly Texan accent of the one man they had railed against most of all.

There would, he knew, be another gun battle. There would be cops in the lower levels, on the street, in the subway. Maria might well wait for him in vain. But it would all be useless anyway. Bowles had found the way to land the presidency for himself and his vision of the Party, riding a wave of popular revulsion and sympathy he, himself, had stirred up.

Fred stiffened, determined. He knew he couldn't let it all fall through his hands. Not now. The armored suit coat may have saved Ben Bowles from stray shots, but the head was vulnerable, as was Howe's.

Gunfire echoed in the room behind him as he raised his Uzi. He felt the impacts of heavy slugs, but still he pulled his trigger even as he fell, and hoped the shots were destined to be true.

OR BATTLE'S SOUND

Harry Harrison

I

"Combatman Dom Priego, I shall kill you." Sergeant Toth shouted the words the length of the barracks compartment.

Dom, stretched out on his bunk and reading a book, raised startled eyes just as the Sergeant snapped his arm down, hurling a gleaming combat knife. Trained reflexes raised the book, and the knife thudded into it, penetrating the pages so that the point stopped a scant few inches from Dom's face.

"You stupid Hungarian ape!" he shouted. "Do you know what this book cost me? Do you know how old it is?"

"Do you know that you are still alive?" the Sergeant answered, a trace of a cold smile wrinkling the corners of his cat's eyes. He stalked down the gangway, like a predatory animal, and reached for the handle of the knife.

"No you don't," Dom said, snatching the book away. "You've done enough damage already." He put the book flat on the bunk and worked the knife carefully out of it—then threw it suddenly at the Sergeant's foot.

Sergeant Toth shifted his leg just enough so that the knife missed him and struck the plastic deck covering instead. "Temper, combatman," he said. "You should never lose your temper.

That way you make mistakes, get killed." He bent and plucked out the shining blade and held it balanced in his fingertips. As he straightened up, there was a rustle as the other men in the barracks compartment shifted weight, ready to move, all eyes on him. He laughed.

"Now you're expecting it, so it's too easy for you." He slid the knife back into his boot sheath.

"You're a sadistic bowb," Dom said, smoothing down the cut in the book's cover. "Getting a great pleasure out of frightening other people."

"Maybe," Sergeant Toth said, undisturbed. He sat on the bunk across the aisle. "And maybe that's what they call the right man in the right job. And it doesn't matter anyway. I train you, keep you alert, on the jump. This keeps you alive. You should thank me for being such a good sadist."

"You can't sell me with that argument, Sergeant. You're the sort of individual this man wrote about, right here in this book that you did your best to destroy..."

"Not me. You put it in front of the knife. Just like I keep telling you pinkies. Save yourself. That's what counts. Use any trick. You only got one life, make it a long one."

"Right in here..."

"Pictures of girls?"

"No, Sergeant, words. Great words by a man you never heard of, by the name of Wilde."

"Sure. Plugger. Wyld. fleet heavyweight champion."

"No, Oscar Fingal O'Flahertie Wills Wilde. No relation to your pug—I hope. He writes, 'As long as war is regarded as wicked, it will always have its fascination. When it is looked upon as vulgar, it will cease to be popular.'"

Sergeant Toth's eyes narrowed in thought. "He makes it sound simple. But it's not that way at all. There are other reasons for war."

"Such as what...?"

The Sergeant opened his mouth to answer, but his voice was drowned in the wave of sound from the scramble alert. The high-pitched hooting blared in every compartment of the spacer and had its instant response. Men moved. Fast.

The ship's crew raced to ther action stations. The men who had been asleep just an instant before were still blinking awake as they ran. They ran and stood, and before the alarm was through sounding the great spaceship was ready.

Not so the combatmen. Until ordered and dispatched, they were just cargo. They stood at the ready, a double row of silver-gray uniforms, down the center of the barracks compartment. Sergeant Toth was at the wall, his headset plugged into a phone extension there, listening attentively, nodding at an unheard voice. Every man's eyes were upon him as he spoke agreement, disconnected and turned slowly to face them. He savored the silent moment, then broke into the widest grin that any of them had ever seen on his normally expressionless face.

"This is it," the Sergeant said, and actually rubbed his hands together. "I can tell you now that the Edinburgers were expected and that our whole fleet is up in force. The scouts have detected them breaking out of jump space, and they should be here in about two hours. We're going out to meet them. This, you pinkie combat virgins, is it." A sound, like a low growl, rose from the assembled men, and the Sergeant's grin widened.

"That's the right spirit. Show some of it to the enemy." The grin vanished as quickly as it had come, and, cold-faced as always, he called the ranks to attention.

"Corporal Steres is in sick bay with the fever so we're one NCO short. When that alert sounded we went into combat condition. I may now make temporary field appointments. I do so. Combatman Priego, one pace forward." Dom snapped to attention and stepped out of rank.

"You're now in charge of the bomb squad. Do the right job and the CO will make it permanent. Corporal Priego, one step back and wait here. The rest of you to the ready room, double time—*march.*"

Sergeant Toth stepped aside as the combatmen hurried from the compartment. When the last one had gone he pointed his finger sharply at Dom.

"Just one word. You're as good as any man here. Better than most. You're smart. But you think too much about things that don't matter. Stop thinking and start fighting, or you'll never get back to that university. Bowb up, and if the Edinburgers don't get you I will. You come back as a corporal or you don't come back at all. Understood?"

"Understood." Dom's face was as coldly expressionless as the Sergeant's.

"I'm just as good a combatman as you are, Sergeant. I'll do my job."

"Then do it—now *jump*."

Because of the delay, Dom was the last man to be suited up. The others were already doing their pressure checks with the armorers while he was still closing his seals. He did not let it disturb him or make him try to move faster. With slow deliberation, he counted off the check list as he sealed and locked.

Once all the pressure checks were in the green, Dom gave the armorers the thumbs-up okay and walked to the air lock. While the door closed behind him and the lock was pumped out, he checked all the telltales in his helmet. Oxygen, full. Power pack, full charge. Radio, one and one. Then the last of the air was gone, and the inner door opened soundlessly in the vacuum. He entered the armory.

The lights here were dimmer—and soon they would be turned off completely. Dom went to the rack with his equipment and began to buckle on the smaller items. Like all of the others on the bomb squad, his suit was lightly armored and he carried only the most essential weapons. The drillger went on his left thigh, just below his fingers, and the gropener in its holster on the outside of his right leg; this was his favorite weapon. The intelligence reports had stated that some of the Edinburgers still used fabric pressure suits, so lightning prods—usually considered obsolete—had been issued. He slung his well to the rear, since the chance that he might need it was very slim. All of these murderous devices had been stored in the evacuated and insulated compartment for months so that their temperature approached absolute zero. They were free of lubrication and had been designed to operate at this temperature.

A helmet clicked against Dom's, and Wing spoke, his voice carried by conducting transparent ceramic.

"I'm ready for my bomb, Dom—do you want to sling it? And congratulations. Do I have to call you Corporal now?"

"Wait until we get back and it's official. I take Toth's word for absolutely nothing."

He slipped the first atomic bomb from the shelf, checked the telltales to see that they were all in the green, then slid it into the rack that was an integral part of Wing's suit. "All set, now we can sling mine."

They had just finished when a large man in bulky combat armor came up. Dom would have known him by his size even if he had not read HELMUTZ stenciled on the front of his suit.

"What is it, Helm?" he asked when their helmets touched.

"The Sergeant. He said I should report to you, that I'm lifting a bomb on this mission." There was an angry tone behind his words.

"Right. We'll fix you up with a back sling." The big man did not look happy, and Dom thought he knew why. "And don't worry about missing any of the fighting. There'll be enough for everyone."

"I'm a combatman . . ."

"We're all combatmen. All working for one thing—to deliver the bombs. That's your job now."

Helmutz did not act convinced and stood with stolid immobility while they rigged the harness and bomb onto the back of his suit. Before they were finished, their headphones crackled and a stir went through the company of suited men as a message came over the command frequency.

"Are you suited and armed? Are you ready for illumination adjustment?"

"Combatmen suited and armed." That was Sergeant Toth's voice.

"Bomb squad not ready," Dom said, and they hurried to make the last fastenings, aware that the rest were waiting for them.

"Bomb squad suited and armed."

"Lights."

II

As the command rang out, the bulkhead lights faded out until the darkness was broken only by the dim red lights in the ceiling above. Until their eyes became adjusted, it was almost impossible to see. Dom groped his way to one of the benches, found the oxygen hose with his fingers and plugged it into the side of his helmet; this would conserve his tank oxygen during the wait. Brisk music was being played over the command circuit now as part of morale sustaining. Here in the semidarkness, suited and armed, the waiting could soon become nerve-racking. Everything was done to alleviate the pressure. The music faded, and a voice replaced it.

"This is your executive officer speaking. I'm going to try

and keep you in the picture as to what is happening up here. The Edinburgers are attacking in fleet strength and, soon after they were sighted, their ambassador declared that a state of war exists. He asks that Earth surrender at once or risk the consequences. Well, you all know what the answer to that one was. The Edinburgers have invaded and conquered twelve settled planets already and incorporated them into their Greater Celtic Co-prosperity Sphere. Now they're getting greedy and going for the big one—Earth itself, the planet their ancestors left a hundred generations ago. In doing this . . . Just a moment, I have a battle report here . . . first contact with our scouts."

The officer stopped for a moment, then his voice picked up again.

"Fleet strength, but no larger than we expected and we will be able to handle them. But there is one difference in their tactics, and the combat computer is analyzing this now. They were the ones who originated the MT invasion technique, landing a number of cargo craft on a planet, all of them loaded with matter-transmitter screens. As you know, the invading forces attack through these screens direct from their planet to the one that is to be conquered. Well, they've changed their technique now. This entire fleet is protecting a *single* ship, a Kriger-class scout carrier. What this means . . . Hold on, here is the readout from the combat computer. *Only possibility single ship landing area increase MT screen breakthrough,* that's what it says. Which means that there is a good chance that this ship may be packing a *single* large MT screen, bigger than anything ever built before. If this is so—and they get the thing down to the surface—they can fly heavy bombers right through it, fire pre-aimed ICBMs, send through troop carriers, anything. If this happens the invasion will be successful."

Around him, in the red-lit darkness, Dom was aware of the other suited figures who stirred silently as they heard the words.

"If this happens." There was a ring of authority now in the executive officer's voice. "The Edinburgers have developed the only way to launch an interplanetary invasion. We have found the way to stop it. You combatmen are the answer. They have now put all their eggs in one basket—and you are going to take that basket to pieces. You can get through where attack ships or missiles could not. We're closing fast now, and you will be called to combat stations soon. So—go out there and do your job. The fate of Earth rides with you."

Melodramatic words, Dom thought, yet they were true. Everything, the ships, the concentration of fire power, all depended on them. The alert alarm cut through his thoughts, and he snapped to attention.

"Disconnect oxygen. Fall out when your name is called and proceed to the firing room in the order called. Toth . . ."

The names were spoken quickly, and the combatmen moved out. At the entrance to the firing room a suited man with a red-globed light checked the names on their chests against his roster to make sure they were in the correct order. Everything moved smoothly, easily, just like a drill, because the endless drills had been designed to train them for just this moment. The firing room was familiar, though they had never been there before, because their trainer had been an exact duplicate of it. The combatman ahead of Dom went to port, so he moved to starboard. The man preceding him was just climbing into a capsule, and Dom waited while the armorer helped him down into it and adjusted the armpit supports. Then it was his turn, and Dom slipped into the transparent plastic shell and settled against the seat as he seized the handgrips. The armorer pulled the supports hard up into his armpits, and he nodded when they seated right. A moment later, the man was gone, and he was alone in the semidarkness with the dim red glow shining on the top ring of the capsule that was just above his head. There was a sudden shudder, and he gripped hard, just as the capsule started forward.

As it moved, it tilted backwards until he was lying on his back, looking up through the metal rings that banded his plastic shell. His capsule was moved sideways, jerked to a stop, then moved again. Now the gun was visible, a half dozen capsules ahead of his, and he thought, as he always did during training, how like an ancient quick-firing cannon the gun was—a cannon that fired human beings. Every two seconds, the charging mechanism seized a capsule from one of the alternate feed belts, whipped it to the rear of the gun where it instantly vanished into the breech. Then another and another. The one ahead of Dom disappeared and he braced himself—and the mechanism suddenly and for no apparent reason halted.

There was a flicker of fear that something had gone wrong with the complex gun, before he realized that all of the first combatmen had been launched and that the computer was wait-

ing a determined period of time for them to prepare the way
for the bomb squad. His squad now, the men he would lead.

Waiting was harder than moving as he looked at the black
mouth of the breech. The computer would be ticking away the
seconds now, while at the same time tracking the target and
keeping the ship aimed to the correct trajectory. Once he was
in the gun, the magnetic field would seize the rings that banded
his capsule, and the linear accelerator of the gun would draw
him up the evacuated tube that penetrated the entire length of
the great ship from stern to bow. Faster and faster the magnetic
fields would pull him until he left the mouth of the gun at the
correct speed and on the correct trajectory to . . .

His capsule was whipped up in a tight arc and shoved into
the darkness. Even as he gripped tight on the handholds, the
pressure pads came up and hit him. He could not measure the
time—he could not see and he could not breathe as the brutal
acceleration pressed down on him. Hard, harder than anything
he had ever experienced in training; he had that one thought,
and then he was out of the gun.

In a single instant he went from acceleration to weightless-
ness, and he gripped hard so he would not float away from the
capsule. There was a puff of vapor from the unheard explosions;
he felt them through his feet, and the metal rings were blown
in half, and the upper portion of the capsule shattered and hurled
away. Now he was alone, weightless, holding to the grips that
were fastened to the rocket unit beneath his feet. He looked
about for the space battle that he knew was in progress and
felt a slight disappointment that there was so little to see.

Something burned far off to his right, and there was a wavering in the brilliant points of the stars as some dark object
occulted them and passed on. This was a battle of computers
and instruments at great distances. There was very little for the
unaided eye to see. The spaceships were black and swift and—
for the most part—thousands of miles away. They were firing
homing rockets and proximity shells, also just as swift and
invisible. He knew that space around him was filled with signal
jammers and false-signal generators, but none of this was visible. Even the target vessel toward which he was rushing was
invisible.

For all that his limited senses could tell, he was alone in
space, motionless, forgotten.

•   •   •

Something shuddered against the soles of his boots, and a jet of vapor shot out and vanished from the rocket unit. No, he was neither motionless nor forgotten. The combat computer was still tracking the target ship and had detected some minute variation from its predicted path. At the same time, the computer was following the progress of his trajectory, and it made the slight correction for this new data. Corrections must be going out at the same time to all the other combatmen in space, before and behind him. They were small and invisible—doubly invisible now that the metal rings had been shed. There was no more than an eighth of a pound of metal dispersed through the plastics and ceramics of a combatman's equipment. Radar could never pick them out from among all the interference. They should get through.

Jets blasted again, and Dom saw that the stars were turning above his head. Touchdown soon; the tiny radar in his rocket unit had detected a mass ahead and had directed that he be turned end for end. Once this was done he knew that the combat computer would cut free and turn control over to the tiny set-down computer that was part of his radar. His rockets blasted, strong now, punching the supports up against him, and he looked down past his feet at the growing dark shape that occulted the stars.

With a roar, loud in the silence, his headphones burst into life.

"Went, went—gone hungry. Went, went—gone hungry."

The silence grew again, but in it Dom no longer felt alone. The brief message had told him a lot.

Firstly, it was Sergeant Toth's voice; there was no mistaking that. Secondly, the mere act of breaking radio silence showed that they had engaged the enemy and that their presence was known. The code was a simple one that would be meaningless to anyone outside their company. Translated, it said that fighting was still going on but the advance squads were holding their own. They had captured the center section of the hull—always the best place to rendezvous since it was impossible to tell bow from stern in the darkness—and were holding it, awaiting the arrival of the bomb squad. The retrorockets flared hard and long, and the rocket unit crashed sharply into the black hull. Dom jumped free and rolled.

III

As he came out of the roll, he saw a suited figure looming above him, clearly outlined by the disk of the sun despite his black nonreflective armor. The top of the helmet was smooth. Even as he realized this, Dom was pulling the gropener from its holster.

A cloud of vapor sprang out, and the man vanished behind it. Dom was surprised, but he did not hesitate. Handguns, even recoilless ones like this that sent the burnt gas out to the sides, were a hazard in null-G space combat. Guns were not only difficult to aim but either had a recoil that would throw the user back out of position or the gas had to be vented sideways, when they would blind the user for vital moments. A fraction of a second was all a trained combatman needed.

As the gropener swung free, Dom thumbed the jet button lightly. The device was shaped like a short sword, but it had a vibrating saw blade where one sharpened edge should be, with small jets mounted opposite it in place of the outer edge. The jets drove the device forward, pulling him after it. As soon as it touched the other man's leg, he pushed the jets full on. As the vibrating ceramic blade speeded up, the force of the jets pressed it into the thin armor.

In less than a second, it had cut its way through and on into the flesh of the leg inside. Dom pressed the reverse jet to pull away as vapor gushed out, condensing to ice particles instantly, and his opponent writhed, clutched at his thigh—then went suddenly limp.

Dom's feet touched the hull, and the soles adhered. He realized that the entire action had taken place in the time it took him to straighten out from his roll and stand up....

Don't think, act. Training. As soon as his feet adhered, he crouched and turned, looking about him. A heavy power ax sliced by just above his head, towing its wielder after it.

Act, don't think. His new opponent was on his left side, away from the gropener, and was already reversing the direction of his ax. A man has two hands. The drillger on his left thigh! Even as he remembered it, he had it in his hand, drill on and hilt-jet flaring. The foot-long, diamond-hard drill spun fiercely—its rotation cancelled by the counter-revolving weight in the hilt—while the jet drove it forward.

It went into the Edinburger's midriff, scarcely slowing as it tore a hole in the armor and plunged inside. As his opponent folded, Dom thumbed the reverse jet to push the drillger out. The power ax, still with momentum from the last blast of its jet, tore free of the dying man's hand and vanished into space.

There were no other enemies in sight. Dom tilted forward on one toe so that the surface film on the boot sole was switched from adhesive to neutral, then he stepped forward slowly. Walking like this took practice, but he had had that. Ahead was a group of dark figures lying prone on the hull, and he took the precaution of raising his hand to touch the horn on the top of his helmet so there would be no mistakes. This identification had been agreed upon just a few days ago and the plastic spikes glued on. The Edinburgers all had smooth-topped helmets.

Dom dived forward between the scattered forms and slid, face down. Before his body could rebound from the hull, he switched on his belly-sticker, and the surface film there held him flat. Secure for the moment among his own men, he thumbed the side of his helmet to change frequencies. There was now a jumble of noise through most of the frequencies, messages—both theirs and the enemy's—jamming, the false messages being broadcast by recorder units to cover the real exchange of information. There was scarcely any traffic on the bomb-squad frequency, and he waited for a clear spot. His men would have heard Toth's message, so they knew where to gather. Now he could bring them to him.

"Quasar, quasar, quasar," he called, then counted carefully for ten seconds before he switched on the blue bulb on his shoulder. He stood as he did this, let it burn for a single second, then dropped back to the hull before he could draw any fire. His men would be looking for the light and would assemble on it. One by one they began to crawl out of the darkness. He counted them as they appeared. A combatman, without the bulge of a bomb on his back, ran up and dived and slid, so that his helmet touched Dom's.

"How many, Corporal?" Toth's voice asked.

"One still missing but . . ."

"No buts. We move now. Set your charge and blow as soon as you have cover."

He was gone before Dom could answer. But he was right. They could not afford to wait for one man and risk the entire operation. Unless they moved soon, they would be trapped and killed up here. Individual combats were still going on about the hull, but it would not be long before the Edinburgers realized these were just holding actions and that the main force of attackers was gathered in strength. The bomb squad went swiftly and skillfully to work laying the ring of shaped charges.

The rear guards must have been called in, because the heavy weapons opened fire suddenly on all sides. These were .30-calibre high-velocity recoilless machine guns. Before firing, the gunners had traversed the hull, aiming for a grazing fire that was as close to the surface as possible. The gun computer remembered this and now fired along the selected pattern, aiming automatically. This was needed because, as soon as the firing began, clouds of gas jetted out, obscuring everything. Sergeant Toth appeared out of the smoke and shouted as his helmet touched Dom's.

"Haven't you blown it yet?"

"Ready now, get back."

"Make it fast. They're all down or dead now out there. But they will throw something heavy into this smoke soon, now that they have us pinpointed."

The bomb squad drew back, fell flat, and Dom pressed the igniter. Flames and gas exploded high, while the hull hammered up at them. Through the smoke rushed up a solid column of air, clouding and freezing into tiny crystals as it hit the vacuum. The ship was breached now, and they would keep it that way, blowing open the sealed compartments and bulkheads to let out the atmosphere. Dom and the Sergeant wriggled through the smoke together, to the edge of the wide, gaping hole that had been blasted in the ship's skin.

"Hotside, hotside!" the Sergeant shouted, and dived through the opening.

Dom pushed a way through the rush of men who were following the Sergeant and assembled his squad. He was still one man short. A weapons man with his machine gun on his back hurried by and leapt into the hole, with his ammunition carriers

right behind him. The smoke cloud was growing because some
of the guns were still firing, acting as a rear guard. It was
getting hard to see the opening now. When Dom had estimated
that half of the men had gone through, he led his own squad
forward.

They pushed down into a darkened compartment, a store-
room of some kind, and saw a combatman at a hole about one
hundred yards from them. "I'm glad you're here," he said as
soon as Dom's helmet touched his. "We tried to the right first
but there's too much resistance. Just holding them there."

Dom led his men in a floating run, the fastest movement possible in a null-G situation. The corridor was empty for the
moment, dimly lit by the emergency bulbs. Holes had been
blasted in the walls at regular intervals, to open the sealed
compartments and empty them of air, as well as to destroy
wiring and piping. As they passed one of the ragged-edged
openings, spacesuited men erupted from it.

Dom dived under the thrust of a drillger, swinging his gropener out at the same time. It caught his attacker in the midriff,
just as the man's other hand came up. The Edinburger folded
and died, and a sharp pain lanced through Dom's leg. He looked
down at the nipoff that was fastened to his calf and was slowly
severing it.

The nipoff was an outmoded design for use against unarmored suits. It was killing him. The two curved blades were
locked around his leg, and the tiny, geared-down motor was
slowly closing them. Once started, the device could not be
stopped.

It could be destroyed. Even as he realized this, he swung
down his gropener and jammed it against the nipoff's handle.
The pain intensified at the sideways pressure, and he almost
blacked out. He attempted to ignore it. Vapor puffed out around
the blades, and he triggered the compression ring on his thigh
that sealed the leg from the rest of the suit. Then the gropener
cut through the casing. There was a burst of sparks, and the
motion of the closing of the blades stopped.

When Dom looked up, the brief battle was over and the
counterattackers were dead. The rear guard had caught up and
pushed over them. Helmutz must have accounted for more than
one of them himself. He held his power ax high, fingers just

touching the buttons in the haft so that the jets above the blade spurted alternately to swing the ax to and fro. There was blood on both blades.

IV

Dom switched on his radio; it was silent on all bands. The interior communication circuits of the ship were knocked out here, and the metal walls damped all radio signals.

"Report," he said. "How many did we lose?"

"You're hurt," Wing said, bending over him. "Want me to pull that thing off?"

"Leave it. The tips of the blades are almost touching, and you'd tear half my leg off. It's frozen in with the blood, and I can still get around. Lift me up."

The leg was getting numb now, with the blood supply cut off and the air replaced by vacuum. That was all for the best. He took the roll count.

"We've lost two men but we still have more than enough bombs for this job. Now let's move."

Sergeant Toth himself was waiting at the next corridor, where another hole had been blasted in the deck. He looked at Dom's leg but said nothing.

"How is it going?" Dom asked.

"Fair. We took some losses. We gave them more. Engineer says we are over the main hold now, so we are going straight down, pushing out men on each level to hold. Get going."

"And you?"

"I'll bring down the rear guard and pull the men from each level as we pass. You see that you have a way out for us when we all get down to you."

"You can count on that."

Dom floated out over the hole, then gave a strong kick with his good leg against the ceiling when he was lined up. He went down smoothly, and his squad followed. They passed one deck, two, then three. The openings had been nicely aligned for a straight drop. There was a flare of light and a burst of smoke ahead as another deck was blown through. Helmutz passed Dom, going faster, having pushed off harder with both legs.

He was a full deck ahead when he plunged through the next opening, and the burst of high-velocity machine-gun fire almost cut him in two. He folded in the middle, dead in the instant, the impact of the bullets driving him sideways and out of sight in the deck below.

Dom thumbed the jets on the gropener, and it pulled him aside before he followed the combatman.

"Bomb squad, disperse," he ordered. "Troops coming through." He switched to the combat frequency and looked up at the ragged column of men dropping down toward him.

"The deck below had been retaken. I am at the last occupied deck."

He waved his hand to indicate who was talking, and the stream of men began to jet their weapons and move on by him. "They're below me. The bullets came from this side." The combatmen pushed on without a word.

The metal flooring shook as another opening was blasted somewhere behind him. The continuous string of men moved by. A few seconds later a helmeted figure—with a horned helmet—appeared below and waved the all-clear. The drop continued.

On the bottom deck, the men were all jammed almost shoulder to shoulder, and more were arriving all the time.

"Bomb squad here, give me a report," Dom radioed. A combatman with a napboard slung at his waist pushed back out of the crowd.

"We reached the cargo hold—it's immense—but we're being pushed back. Just by weight of numbers. The Edinburgers are desperate. They are putting men through the MT screen in light pressure suits. Unarmored, almost unarmed. We kill them easily enough but they have pushed us out bodily. They're coming right from the invasion planet. Even when we kill them, the bodies block the way . . ."

"You the engineer?"

"Yes."

"Whereabouts in the hold is the MT screen?"

"It runs the length of the hold and is back against the far wall."

"Controls?"

"On the left side."

"Can you lead us over or around the hold so we can break in near the screen?"

The engineer took a single look at charts.

"Yes, around. Through the engine room. We can blast through close to the controls."

"Let's go then." Dom switched to combat frequency and waved his arm over his head. "All combatmen who can see me—this way. We're going to make a flank attack."

They moved down the long corridor as fast as they could, with the combatmen ranging out ahead of the bomb squad. There were sealed pressure doors at regular intervals, but these were bypassed by blasting through the bulkheads at the side. There was resistance and there were more dead as they advanced—dead from both sides. Then a group of men gathered ahead, and Dom floated up to the greatly depleted force of combatmen who had forced their way this far. A corporal touched his helmet to Dom's, pointing to a great sealed door at the corridor's end.

"The engine room is behind there. These walls are thick. Everyone off to one side, because we must use an octupled charge."

They dispersed, and the bulkheads heaved and buckled when the charge exploded. Dom, looking toward the corridor, saw a sheet of flame sear by, followed by a column of air that turned instantly to sparkling granules of ice. The engine room had still been pressurized.

There had been no warning, and most of the crewmen had not had their helmets sealed. They were violently and suddenly dead. The few survivors were killed quickly when they offered resistance with improvised weapons. Dom scarcely noticed this as he led his bomb squad after the engineer.

"That doorway is not on my charts," the engineer said, angrily, as though the spy who had stolen the information was at fault. "It must have been added after construction."

"Where does it go to?" Dom asked.

"The MT hold, no other place is possible."

Dom thought quickly. "I'm going to try and get to the MT controls without fighting. I need a volunteer to go with me. If we remove identification and wear Edinburger equipment we should be able to do it."

"I'll join you," the engineer said.

"No, you have a different job. I want a good combatman."

"Me," a man said, pushing through the others. "Pimenov, best in my squad. Ask anybody."

"Let's make this fast."

The disguise was simple. With the identifying spike knocked off their helmets and enemy equipment slung about them, they would pass any casual examination. A handful of grease obscured the names on their chests.

"Stay close behind and come fast when I knock the screen out," Dom told the others, then led the combatman through the door.

There was a narrow passageway between large tanks and another door at the far end. It was made of light metal but was blocked by a press of human bodies, spacesuited men who stirred and struggled but scarcely moved. The two combatmen pushed harder, and a sudden movement of the mob released the pressure; Dom fell forward, his helmet banging into that of the nearest man.

"What the devil you about?" the man said, twisting his head to look at Dom.

"More of them down there," Dom said, trying to roll his *r*'s the way the Edinburgers did.

"You're no one of us!" the man said and struggled to bring his weapon up.

Dom could not risk a fight here—yet the man had to be silenced. He was wearing a thin spacesuit. Dom could just reach the lightning prod, and he jerked it from its clip and jammed it against the Edinburger's side. The pair of needle-sharp spikes pierced suit and clothes and bit into his flesh, and when the hilt slammed against his body the circuit was closed. The handle of the lightning prod was filled with powerful capacitors that released their stored electricity in a single immense charge through the needles. The Edinburger writhed and died instantly.

They used his body to push a way into the crowd.

Dom had just enough sensation left in his injured leg to be aware when the clamped-on nipoff was twisted in his flesh by the men about them; he kept his thoughts from what it was doing to his leg.

V

Once the Edinburger soldiers were aware of the open door, they pulled it wide and fought their way through it. The combatmen would be waiting for them in the engine room. The sudden exodus relieved the pressure of the bodies for a moment, and Dom, with Pimenov struggling after him, pushed and worked his way toward the MT controls.

It was like trying to move in a dream. The dark hulk of the MT screen was no more than ten yards away, yet they couldn't seem to reach it. Soldiers sprang from the screen, pushing and crowding in, more and more, preventing any motion in that direction. The technicians stood at the controls, their helmet phones plugged into the board before them. Without gravity to push against, jammed into the crowd that floated at all levels in a fierce tangle of arms and legs, movement was almost impossible. Pimenov touched his helmet to Dom's.

"I'm going ahead to cut a path. Stay close behind me."

He broke contact before Dom could answer him, and let his power ax pull him forward into the press. Then he began to chop it back and forth in a short arc, almost hacking his way through the packed bodies. Men turned on him, but he did not stop, lashing out with his gropener as they tried to fight. Dom followed.

They were close to the MT controls before the combatman was buried under a crowd of stabbing, cursing Edinburgers. Pimenov had done his job, and he died doing it. Dom jetted his gropener and let it drag him forward until he slammed into the thick steel frame of the MT screen above the operators' heads. He slid the weapon along the frame, dragging himself headfirst through the press of suited bodies. There was a relatively clear space near the controls. He drifted down into it and let his drillger slide into the operator's back. The man writhed and died quickly. The other operator turned and took the weapon in his stomach. His face was just before Dom as his eyes widened and he screamed soundlessly with pain and fear. Dom could not escape the dead, horrified features as he struggled to drop the atomic bomb from his carrier. The murdered man stayed, pressed close against him all the time.

Now!

He cradled the bomb against his chest and, in a single swift motion, pulled out the arming pin, twisted the fuse to five seconds, and slammed down hard on the actuator. Then he reached up and switched the MT from *receive* to *send*.

The last soldiers erupted from the screen, and there was a growing gap behind them. Into this space and through the screen Dom threw the bomb.

After that, he kept the switch down and tried not to think about what was happening among the men of the invasion army who were waiting before the MT screen on that distant planet.

Then he had to hold this position until the combatmen arrived. He sheltered behind the operator's corpse and used his drillger against the few Edinburgers who were close enough to realize that something had gone wrong. This was easy enough to do because, although they were soldiers, they were men from the invasion regular army and knew nothing about null-G combat. Very soon after this, there was a great stir, and the closest ones were thrust aside. An angry combatman blasted through, sweeping his power ax toward Dom's neck. Dom dodged the blow and switched his radio to combat frequency.

"Hold that! I'm Corporal Priego, bomb squad. Get in front of me and keep anyone else from making the same mistake."

The man was one of those who had taken the engine room. He recognized Dom now and nodded, turning his back to him and pressing against him. More combatmen stormed up to form an iron shield around the controls. The engineer pushed through between them, and Dom helped him reset the frequency on the MT screen.

After this, the battle became a slaughter and soon ended.

"Sendout!" Dom radioed as soon as the setting was made, then instructed the screen to transmit. He heard the words repeated over and over as the combatmen repeated the withdrawal signal so that everyone could hear it. Safety lay on the other side of the screen, now that it was tuned to Tycho Barracks on the Moon.

It was the Edinburgers, living, dead and wounded, who were sent through first. They were pushed back against the screen to make room for the combatmen who were streaming into the hold. The ones at the ends of the screen simply bounced against the hard surface and recoiled; the receiving screen at Tycho was far smaller than this great invasion screen. They were pushed along until they fell through, and combatmen took up positions to mark the limits of operating screen.

Dom was aware of someone in front of him, and he had to blink away the red film that was trying to cover his eyes.

"Wing," he said, finally recognizing the man. "How many others of the bomb squad made it?"

"None I know off, Dom. Just me."

No, don't think about the dead! Only the living counted now.

"All right. Leave your bomb here and get on through. One is all we really need." He tripped the release and pulled the bomb from Wing's rack before giving him a push toward the screen.

Dom had the bomb clamped to the controls when Sergeant Toth slammed up beside him and touched helmets.

"Almost done."

"Done now," Dom said, setting the fuse and pulling out the arming pin.

"Then get moving. I'll take it from here."

"No you don't. My job." He had to shake his head to make the haze go away but it still remained at the corners of his vision.

Toth didn't argue. "What's the setting?" he asked

"Five and six. Five seconds after actuation the chemical bomb blows and knocks out the controls. One second later the atom bomb goes off."

"I'll stay around I think to watch the fun."

Time was acting strangely for Dom, speeding up and slowing down. Men were hurrying by, into the screen, first in a rush, then fewer and fewer. Toth was talking on the combat frequency, but Dom had switched the radio off because it hurt his head. The great chamber was empty now of all but the dead, with the automatic machine guns left firing at the entrances. One of them blew up as Toth touched helmets.

"They're all through. Let's go."

Dom had difficulty talking, so he nodded instead and hammered his fist down onto the actuator.

Men were coming toward them, but Toth had his arms around him, and full jets on his power ax were sliding them along the surface of the screen. And through.

When the brilliant lights of Tycho Barracks hit his eyes, Dom closed them, and this time the red haze came up, over him, all the way.

"How's the new leg?" Sergeant Toth asked. He slumped lazily in the chair beside the hospital bed.

"I can't feel a thing. Nerve channels blocked until it grows tight to the stump." Dom put aside the book he had been reading and wondered what Toth was doing here.

"I come around to see the wounded," the Sergeant said, answering the unasked question. "Two more besides you. Captain told me to."

"The Captain is as big a sadist as you are. Aren't we sick enough already?"

"Good joke." His expression did not change. "I'll tell the Captain. He'll like it. You going to buy out now?"

"Why not?" Dom wondered why the question made him angry. "I've had a combat mission, the medals, a good wound. More than enough points to get my discharge."

"Stay in. You're a good combatman when you stop thinking about it. There's not many of them. Make it a career."

"Like you, Sergeant? Make killing my life's work? Thank you, no. I intend to do something different, a little more constructive. Unlike you, I don't relish this whole dirty business, the killing, the outright plain murder. You like it." This sudden thought sent him sitting upright in the bed. "Maybe that's it. Wars, fighting, everything. It has nothing to do any more with territory rights or aggression or masculinity. I think that you people make wars because of the excitement of it, the thrill that nothing else can equal. You really *like* war."

Toth rose, stretched easily and turned to leave. He stopped at the door, frowning in thought.

"Maybe you're right, Corporal. I don't think about it much. Maybe I do like it." His face lifted in a cold tight smile. "But don't forget—*you like it too*."

Dom went back to his book, resentful of the intrusion. His literature professor had sent it, along with a flattering note. He had heard about Dom on the broadcasts, and the entire school was proud, and so on. A book of poems by Milton, really good stuff.

> *No war, or battle's sound*
> *Was heard the world around.*

Yes, great stuff. But it hadn't been true in Milton's day and it still wasn't true. Did mankind really like war? They *must* like it or it wouldn't have lasted so long. This was an awful, criminal thought.

He too? Nonsense. He fought well, but he had trained himself. It would not be true that he actually liked all of that.

Dom tried to read again, but the page kept blurring before his eyes.

HERO

Joe Haldeman

I

"Tonight we're going to show you eight silent ways to kill a man." The guy who said that was a sergeant who didn't look five years older than me. So if he'd ever killed a man in combat, silently or otherwise, he'd done it as an infant.

I already knew eighty ways to kill people, but most of them were pretty noisy. I sat up straight in my chair and assumed a look of polite attention and fell asleep with my eyes open. So did most everybody else. We'd learned that they never scheduled anything important for these after-chop classes.

The projector woke me up and I sat through a short tape showing the "eight silent ways." Some of the actors must have been brainwipes, since they were actually killed.

After the tape a girl in the front row raised her hand. The sergeant nodded at her and she rose to parade rest. Not bad looking, but kind of chunky about the neck and shoulders. Everybody gets that way after carrying a heavy pack around for a couple of months.

"Sir"—we had to call sergeants "sir" until graduation— "Most of those methods, really, they looked . . . kind of silly."

"For instance?"

"Like killing a man with a blow to the kidneys, from an entrenching tool. I mean, when would you *actually* have only an entrenching tool, and no gun or knife? And why not just

256

bash him over the head with it?"

"He might have a helmet on," he said reasonably.

"Besides, Taurans probably don't even *have* kidneys!"

He shrugged. "Probably they don't." This was 1997, and nobody had ever seen a Tauran; hadn't even found any pieces of Taurans bigger than a scorched chromosome. "But their body chemistry is similar to ours, and we have to assume they're similarly complex creatures. They *must* have weaknesses, vulnerable spots. You have to find out where they are.

"That's the important thing." He stabbed a finger at the screen. "Those eight convicts got caulked for your benefit because you've got to find out how to kill Taurans, and be able to do it whether you have a megawatt laser or an emery board."

She sat back down, not looking too convinced.

"Any more questions?" Nobody raised a hand.

"Okay Tench-hut!" We staggered upright and he looked at us expectantly.

"Fuck you, sir," came the familiar tired chorus.

"Louder!"

"FUCK YOU, SIR!" One of the army's less-inspired morale devices.

"That's better. Don't forget, pre-dawn maneuvers tomorrow. Chop at 0330, first formation, 0400. Anybody sacked after 0340 owes one stripe. Dismissed."

I zipped up my coverall and went across the snow to the lounge for a cup of soya and a joint. I'd always been able to get by on five or six hours of sleep, and this was the only time I could be by myself, out of the army for a while. Looked at the newsfax for a few minutes. Another ship got caulked, out by Aldebaran sector. That was four years ago. They were mounting a reprisal fleet, but it'll take four years more for them to get out there. By then, the Taurans would have every portal planet sewed up tight.

Back at the billet, everybody else was sacked and the main lights were out. The whole company'd been dragging ever since we got back from the two-week lunar training. I dumped my clothes in the locker, checked the roster and found out I was in bunk *31*. Goddammit, right under the heater.

I slipped through the curtain as quietly as possible so as not to wake up the person next to me. Couldn't see who it was, but I couldn't have cared less. I slipped under the blanket.

"You're late, Mandella," a voice yawned. It was Rogers.

"Sorry I woke you up," I whispered.

"'Sallright." She snuggled over and clasped me spoon-fashion. She was warm and reasonably soft.

I patted her hip in what I hoped was a brotherly fashion. "Night, Rogers."

"G'night, Stallion." She returned the gesture more pointedly.

Why do you always get the tired ones when you're ready and the randy ones when you're tired? I bowed to the inevitable.

II

"Awright, let's get some goddamn *back* inta that! Stringer team! Move it up—move your ass up!"

A warm front had come in about midnight and the snow had turned to sleet. The permaplast stringer weighed five hundred pounds and was a bitch to handle, even when it wasn't covered with ice. There were four of us, two at each end, carrying the plastic girder with frozen fingertips. Rogers was my partner.

"Steel!" the guy behind me yelled, meaning that he was losing his hold. It wasn't steel, but it was heavy enough to break your foot. Everybody let go and hopped away. It splashed slush and mud all over us.

"Goddammit, Petrov," Rogers said, "why didn't you go out for the Red Cross or something? This fucken thing's not that fucken heavy." Most of the girls were a little more circumspect in their speech. Rogers was a little butch.

"Awright, get a fucken *move* on, stringers—epoxy team! Dog 'em! Dog 'em!"

Our two epoxy people ran up, swinging their buckets. "Let's go, Mandella. I'm freezin' my balls off."

"Me, too," the girl said with more feeling than logic.

"One—two—heave!" We got the thing up again and staggered toward the bridge. It was about three-quarters completed. Looked as if the second platoon was going to beat us. I wouldn't give a damn, but the platoon that got their bridge built first got to fly home. Four miles of muck for the rest of us, and no rest before chop.

We got the stringer in place, dropped it with a clank, and fitted the static clamps that held it to the rise-beam. The female half of the epoxy team started slopping glue on it before we even had it secured. Her partner was waiting for the stringer on the other side. The floor team was waiting at the foot of the bridge, each one holding a piece of the light, stressed permaplast over his head like an umbrella. They were dry and clean. I wondered aloud what they had done to deserve it, and Rogers suggested a couple of colorful, but unlikely, possibilities.

We were going back to stand by the next stringer when the field first (name of Dougelstein, but we called him "Awright") blew a whistle and bellowed, "Awright, soldier boys and girls, ten minutes. Smoke 'em if you got 'em." He reached into his pocket and turned on the control that heated our coveralls.

Rogers and I sat down on our end of the stringer and I took out my weed box. I had lots of joints, but we were ordered not to smoke them until after night-chop. The only tobacco I had was a cigarro butt about three inches long. I lit it on the side of the box; it wasn't too bad after the first couple of puffs. Rogers took a puff, just to be sociable, but made a face and gave it back.

"Were you in school when you got drafted?" she asked.

"Yeah. Just got a degree in physics. Was going after a teacher's certificate."

She nodded soberly. "I was in biology . . ."

"Figures." I ducked a handful of slush. "How far?"

"Six years, bachelor's and technical." She slid her boot along the ground, turning up a ridge of mud and slush the consistency of freezing ice milk. "Why the fuck did this have to happen?"

I shrugged. It didn't call for an answer, least of all the answer that the UNEF kept giving us. Intellectual and physical elite of the planet, going out to guard humanity against the Tauran menace. Soyashit. It was all just a big experiment. See whether we could goad the Taurans into ground action.

Awright blew the whistle two minutes early, as expected, but Rogers and I and the other two stringers got to sit for a minute while the epoxy and floor teams finished covering our stringer. It got cold fast, sitting there with our suits turned off, but we remained inactive on principle.

There really wasn't any sense in having us train in the cold. Typical army half-logic. Sure, it was going to be cold where we were going, but not ice-cold or snow-cold. Almost by definition, a portal planet remained within a degree or two of absolute zero all the time—since collapsars don't shine—and the first chill you felt would mean that you were a dead man.

Twelve years before, when I was ten years old, they had discovered the collapsar jump. Just fling an object at a collapsar with sufficient speed, and out it pops in some other part of the galaxy. It didn't take long to figure out the formula that predicted where it would come out: it travels along the same "line" (actually an Einsteinian geodesic) it would have followed if the collapsar hadn't been in the way—until it reaches another collapsar field, whereupon it reappears, repelled with the same speed at which it approached the original collapsar. Travel time between the two collapsars . . . exactly zero.

It made a lot of work for mathematical physicists, who had to redefine simultaneity, then tear down general relativity and build it back up again. And it made the politicians very happy, because now they could send a shipload of colonists to Fomalhaut for less than it had once cost to put a brace of men on the moon. There were a lot of people the politicians would love to see on Fomalhaut, implementing a glorious adventure rather than stirring up trouble at home.

The ships were always accompanied by an automated probe that followed a couple of million miles behind. We knew about the portal planets, little bits of flotsam that whirled around the collapsars; the purpose of the drone was to come back and tell us in the event that a ship had smacked into a portal planet at .999 of the speed of light.

That particular catastrophe never happened, but one day a drone limped back alone. Its data were analyzed, and it turned out that the colonists' ship had been pursued by another vessel and destroyed. This happened near Aldebaran, in the constellation Taurus, but since "Aldebaranian" is a little hard to handle, they named the enemy "Tauran."

Colonizing vessels thenceforth went out protected by an armed guard. Often the armed guard went out alone, and finally the colonization group got shortened to UNEF, United Nations Exploratory Force. Emphasis on the "force."

Then some bright lad in the General Assembly decided that we ought to field an army of footsoldiers to guard the portal planets of the nearer collapsars. This led to the Elite Conscription Act of 1996 and the most elitely conscripted army in the history of warfare.

So here we were, fifty men and fifty women, with IQs over 150 and bodies of unusual health and strength, slogging elitely through the mud and slush of central Missouri, reflecting on

the usefulness of our skill in building bridges on worlds where
the only fluid is an occasional standing pool of liquid helium.

III

About a month later, we left for our final training exercise,
maneuvers on the planet Charon. Though nearing perihelion,
it was still more than twice as far from the sun as Pluto.

The troopship was a converted "cattlewagon" made to carry
two hundred colonists and assorted bushes and beasts. Don't
think it was roomy, though, just because there were half that
many of us. Most of the excess space was taken up with extra
reaction mass and ordnance.

The whole trip took three weeks, accelerating at two gees
halfway, decelerating the other half. Our top speed, as we
roared by the orbit of Pluto, was around one-twentieth of the
speed of light—not quite enough for relativity to rear its complicated head.

Three weeks of carrying around twice as much weight as
normal . . . it's no picnic. We did some cautious exercises three
times a day and remained horizontal as much as possible. Still,
we got several broken bones and serious dislocations. The men
had to wear special supporters to keep from littering the floor
with loose organs. It was almost impossible to sleep; nightmares
of choking and being crushed, rolling over periodically to prevent blood pooling and bedsores. One girl got so fatigued that
she almost slept through the experience of having a rib push
out into the open air.

I'd been in space several times before, so when we finally
stopped decelerating and went into free fall, it was nothing but
relief. But some people had never been out, except for our
training on the moon, and succumbed to the sudden vertigo
and disorientation. The rest off us cleaned up after them, floating through the quarters with sponges and inspirators to suck
up the globules of partly digested "Concentrate, High-protein,
Low-residue, Beef Flavor (Soya)."

We had a good view of Charon, coming down from orbit.
There wasn't much to see, though, It was just a dim, off-white
sphere with a few smudges on it. We landed about two hundred
meters from the base. A pressurized crawler came out and
mated with the ferry, so we didn't have to suit up. We clanked

and squeaked up to the main building, a featureless box of grayish plastic.

Inside, the walls were the same drab color. The rest of the company was sitting at desks, chattering away. There was a seat next to Freeland.

"Jeff—feeling better?" He still looked a little pale.

"If the gods had meant for man to survive in free fall, they would have given him a castiron glottis." He sighed heavily. "A little better. Dying for a smoke."

"Yeah."

"*You* seemed to take it all right. Went up in school, didn't you?"

"Senior thesis in vacuum welding, yeah. Three weeks in Earth orbit." I sat back and reached for my weed box for the thousandth time. It still wasn't there. The life-support unit didn't want to handle nicotine and THC.

"Training was bad enough," Jeff groused, "but *this* shit—"

"Tench-hut!" We stood up in a raggety-ass fashion, by twos and threes. The door opened and a full major came in. I stiffened a little. He was the highest-ranking officer I'd ever seen. He had a row of ribbons stitched into his coveralls, including a purple strip meaning he'd been wounded in combat, fighting in the old American army. Must have been that Indochina thing, but it had fizzled out before I was born. He didn't look that old.

"Sit, sit." He made a patting motion with his hand. Then he put his hands on his hips and scanned the company, a small smile on his face. "Welcome to Charon. You picked a lovely day to land; the temperature outside is a summery eight point one five degrees Absolute. We expect little change for the next two centuries or so." Some of them laughed halfheartedly.

"Best you enjoy the tropical climate here at Miami base; enjoy it while you can. We're on the center of sunside here, and most of your training will be on darkside. Over there, the temperature stays a chilly two point zero eight.

"You might as well regard all the training you got on Earth and the moon as just an elementary exercise, designed to give you a fair chance of surviving Charon. You'll have to go through your whole repertory here: tools, weapons, maneuvers. And you'll find that, at these temperatures, tools don't work the way they should; weapons don't want to fire. And people move v-e-r-y cautiously."

He studied the clipboard in his hand. "Right now, you have forty-nine women and forty-eight men. Two deaths on Earth, one psychiatric release. Having read an outline of your training program, I'm frankly surprised that so many of you pulled through.

"But you might as well know that I won't be displeased if as few as fifty of you, half, graduate from this final phase. And the only way not to graduate is to die. Here. The only way anybody gets back to Earth—including me—is after a combat tour.

"You will complete your training in one month. From here you go to Stargate collapsar, half a light away. You will stay at the settlement on Stargate 1, the largest portal planet, until replacements arrive. Hopefully, that will be no more than a month; another group is due here as soon as you leave.

"When you leave Stargate, you will go to some strategically important collapsar, set up a military base there, and fight the enemy, if attacked. Otherwise, you will maintain the base until further orders.

"The last two weeks of your training will consist on constructing exactly that kind of a base, on darkside. There you will be totally isolated from Miami base: no communication, no medical evacuation, no resupply. Sometime before the two weeks are up, your defense facilities will be evaluated in an attack by guided drones. They will be armed."

They had spent all that money on us just to kill us in training?

"All of the permanent personnel here on Charon are combat veterans. Thus, all of us are forty to fifty years of age. But I think we can keep up with you. Two of us will be with you at all times and will accompany you at least as far as Stargate. They are Captain Sherman Stott, your company commander, and Sergeant Octavio Cortez, your first sergeant. Gentlemen?"

Two men in the front row stood easily and turned to face us. Captain Stott was a little smaller than the major, but cut from the same mold: face hard and smooth as porcelain, cynical half-smile, a precise centimeter of beard framing a large chin, looking thirty at the most. He wore a large, gunpowder-type pistol on his hip.

Sergeant Cortez was another story, a horror story. His head was shaved and the wrong shape, flattened out on one side, where a large piece of skull had obviously been taken out. His face was very dark and seamed with wrinkles and scars. Half his left ear was missing, and his eyes were as expressive as buttons on a machine. He had a moustache-and-beard combination that looked like a skinny white caterpillar taking a lap around his mouth. On anybody else, his schoolboy smile might look pleasant, but he was about the ugliest, meanest-looking creature I'd ever seen. Still, if you didn't look at his head and considered the lower six feet or so, he could have posed as the "after" advertisement for a body-building spa. Neither Stott nor Cortez wore any ribbons. Cortez had a small pocket-laser suspended in a magnetic rig, sideways, under his left armpit. It had wooden grips that were worn smooth.

"Now, before I turn you over to the tender mercies of these two gentlemen, let me caution you again:

"Two months ago there was not a living soul on this planet, just some leftover equipment from an expedition of 1991. A working force of forty-five men struggled for a month to erect this base. Twenty-four of them, more than half, died in the construction of it. This is the most dangerous planet men have ever tried to live on, but the places you'll be going will be this bad and worse. Your cadre will try to keep you alive for the next month. Listen to them . . . and follow their example; all of them have survived here much longer than you'll have to. Captain?" The captain stood up as the major went out the door.

"Tench-*hut!*" The last syllable was like an explosion and we all jerked to our feet.

"Now I'm only gonna say this *once*, so you better listen," he growled. "We *are* in a combat situation here, and in a combat situation there is only *one* penalty for disobedience or insubordination." He jerked the pistol from his hip and held it by the barrel, like a club. "This is an army model 1911 automatic *pistol*, caliber .45, and it is a primitive but effective weapon. The sergeant and I are authorized to use our weapons to kill to enforce discipline. Don't make us do it, because we will. We *will.*" He put the pistol back. The holster snap made a loud crack in the dead quiet.

"Sergeant Cortez and I between us have killed more people than are sitting in this room. Both of us fought in Vietnam on the American side and both of us joined the United Nations International Guard more than ten years ago. I took a break in grade from major for the privilege of commanding this company, and First Sergeant Cortez took a break from sub-major, because we are both *combat* soldiers and this is the first *combat* situation since 1987.

"Keep in mind what I've said while the first sergeant instructs you more specifically in what your duties will be under this command. Take over, Sergeant." He turned on his heel and strode out of the room. The expression on his face hadn't changed one millimeter during the whole harangue.

The first sergeant moved like a heavy machine with lots of ball bearings. When the door hissed shut, he swiveled ponderously to face us and said, "At ease, siddown," in a surprisingly gently voice. He sat on a table in the front of the room. It creaked, but held.

"Now the captain talks scary and I look scary, but we both mean well. You'll be working pretty closely with me, so you better get used to this thing I've got hanging in front of my brain. You probably won't see the captain much, except on maneuvers."

He touched the flat part of his head. "And speaking of brains, I still have just about all of mine, in spite of Chinese efforts to the contrary. All of us old vets who mustered into UNEF had to pass the same criteria that got you drafted by the Elite Conscription Act. So I suspect all of you are smart and tough—but just keep in mind that the captain and I are smart and tough *and* experienced."

He flipped through the roster without really looking at it. "Now, as the captain said, there'll be only one kind of disciplinary action on maneuvers. Capital punishment. But normally *we* won't have to kill you for disobeying; Charon'll save us the trouble.

"Back in the billeting area, it'll be another story. We don't much care what you do inside. Grab-ass all day and fuck all night, makes no difference. . . . But once you suit up and go outside, you've gotta have discipline that would shame a Centurian. There will be situations where one stupid act could kill us all.

"Anyhow, the first thing we've gotta do is get you fitted to your fighting suits. The armorer's waiting at your billet; he'll take you one at a time. Let's go."

IV

"Now I know you got lectured back on Earth on what a fighting suit can do." The armorer was a small man, partially bald, with no insignia or rank on his coveralls. Sergeant Cortez had told us to call him "sir," since he was a lieutenant.

"But I'd like to reinforce a couple of points, maybe add some things your instructors Earthside weren't clear about or couldn't know. Your first sergeant was kind enough to consent to being my visual aid. Sergeant?"

Cortez slipped out of his coveralls and came up to the little raised platform where a fighting suit was standing, popped open like a man-shaped clam. He backed into it and slipped his arms into the rigid sleeves. There was a click and the thing swung shut with a sigh. It was bright green with CORTEZ stenciled in white letters on the helmet.

"Camouflage, Sergeant." The green faded to white, then dirty gray. "This is good camouflage for Charon and most of your portal planets," said Cortez, as if from a deep well. "But there are several other combinations available." The gray dappled and brightened to a combination of greens and browns: "Jungle." Then smoothed out to a hard light ochre: "Desert." Dark brown, darker, to a deep flat black: "Night or space."

"Very good, Sergeant. To my knowledge, this is the only feature of the suit that was perfected after your training. The control is around your left wrist and is admittedly awkward. But once you find the right combination, it's easy to lock in.

"Now, you didn't get much in-suit training Earthside. We didn't want you to get used to using the thing in a friendly environment. The fighting suit is the deadliest personal weapon ever built, and with no weapon is it easier for the user to kill himself through carelessness. Turn around, Sergeant.

"Case in point." He tapped a large square protuberance between the shoulders. "Exhaust fins. As you know, the suit tries to keep you at a comfortable temperature no matter what the weather's like outside. The material of the suit is as near to a perfect insulator as we could get, consistent with mechanical demands. Therefore, these fins get *hot*—especially hot, compared to darkside temperatures—as they bleed off the body's heat.

"All you have to do is lean up against a boulder of frozen gas; there's lots of it around. The gas will sublime off faster than it can escape from the fins; in escaping, it will push against the surrounding 'ice' and fracture it . . . and in about one-hundredth of a second, you have the equivalent of a hand grenade going off right below your neck. You'll never feel a thing.

"Variations on this theme have killed eleven people in the past two months. And they were just building a bunch of huts.

"I assume you know how easily the waldo capabilities can kill you or your companions. Anybody want to shake hands with the sergeant?" He paused, then stepped over and clasped his glove. "He's had lots of practice. Until *you* have, be extremely careful. You might scratch an itch and wind up breaking your back. Remember, semi-logarithmic response: two pounds' pressure exerts five pounds' force; three pounds' gives ten; four pounds', twenty-three; five pounds', forty-seven. Most of you can muster up a grip of well over a hundred pounds. Theoretically, you could rip a steel girder in two with that, amplified. Actually, you'd destroy the material of your gloves and, at least on Charon, die very quickly. It'd be a race between decompression and flash-freezing. You'd die no matter which won.

"The leg waldos are also dangerous, even though the amplification is less extreme. Until you're really skilled, don't try to run, or jump. You're likely to trip, and that means you're likely to die.

"Charon's gravity is three-fourths of Earth normal, so it's not too bad. But on a really small world, like Luna, you could take a running jump and not come down for twenty minutes, just keep sailing over the horizon. Maybe bash into a mountain at eighty meters per second. On a small asteroid, it'd be no trick at all to run up to escape velocity and be off on an informal tour of intergalactic space. It's a slow way to travel.

"Tomorrow morning, we'll start teaching you how to stay alive inside this infernal machine. The rest of the afternoon and evening, I'll call you one at a time to be fitted. That's all, Sergeant."

Cortez went to the door and turned the stopcock that let air into the airlock. A bank of infrared lamps went on to keep the air from freezing inside it. When the pressures were equalized, he shut the stopcock, unclamped the door and stepped in, clamping it shut behind him. A pump hummed for about a minute, evacuating the airlock; then he stepped out and sealed the outside door.

It was pretty much like the ones on Luna.

"First I want Private Omar Almizar. The rest of you can go find your bunks. I'll call you over the squawker."

"Alphabetical order, sir?"

"Yep. About ten minutes apiece. If your name begins with

Z, you might as well get sacked."

That was Rogers. She probably was thinking about getting sacked.

V

The sun was a hard white point directly overhead. It was a lot brighter than I had expected it to be; since we were eighty AUs out, it was only one-6400th as bright as it is on Earth. Still, it was putting out about as much light as a powerful streetlamp.

"This is considerably more light than you'll have on a portal planet." Captain Stott's voice crackled in our collective ear. "Be glad that you'll be able to watch your step."

We were lined up, single file, on the permaplast sidewalk that connected the billet and the supply hut. We'd practiced walking inside, all morning, and this wasn't any different except for the exotic scenery. Though the light was rather dim, you could see all the way to the horizon quite clearly, with no atmosphere in the way. A black cliff that looked too regular to be natural stretched from one horizon to the other, passing within a kilometer of us. The ground was obsidian-black, mottled with patches of white or bluish ice. Next to the supply hut was a small mountain of snow in a bin marked OXYGEN.

The suite was fairly comfortable, but it gave you the odd feeling of simultaneously being a marionette and a puppeteer. You apply the impulse to move your leg and the suit picks it up and magnifies it and moves your leg *for* you.

"Today we're only going to walk around the company area, and nobody will *leave* the company area." The captain wasn't wearing his .45—unless he carried it as a good luck charm, under his suit—but he had a laser-finger like the rest of us. And his was probably hooked up.

Keeping an interval of at least two meters between each person, we stepped off the permaplast and followed the captain over smooth rock. We walked carefully for about an hour, spiraling out, and finally stopped at the far edge of the perimeter.

"Now everybody pay close attention. I'm going out to that blue slab of ice"—it was a big one, about twenty meters away—"and show you something that you'd better know if you want to stay alive."

He walked out in a dozen confident steps. "First I have to heat up a rock—filters down." I squeezed the stud under my armpit and the filter slid into place over my image converter. The captain pointed his finger at a black rock the size of a basketball, and gave it a short burst. The glare rolled a long shadow of the captain over us and beyond. The rock shattered into a pile of hazy splinters.

"It doesn't take long for these to cool down." He stooped and picked up a piece. "This one is probably twenty or twenty-five degrees. Watch." He tossed the "warm" rock onto the ice slab. It skittered around in a crazy pattern and shot off the side. He tossed another one, and it did the same.

"As you know, you are not quite *perfectly* insulated. These rocks are about the temperature of the soles of your boots. If you try to stand on a slab of hydrogen, the same thing will happen to you. Except that the rock is *already* dead.

"The reason for this behavior is that the rock makes a slick interface with the ice—a little puddle of liquid hydrogen—and rides a few molecules above the liquid on a cushion of hydrogen vapor. This makes the rock or *you* a frictionless bearing as far as the ice is concerned, and you *can't* stand up without any friction under your boots.

"After you have lived in your suit for a month or so you *should* be able to survive falling down, but right *now* you just don't know enough. Watch."

The captain flexed and hopped up onto the slab. His feet shot out from under him and he twisted around in midair, landing on hands and knees. He slipped off and stood on the ground.

"The idea is to keep your exhaust fins from making contact with the frozen gas. Compared to the ice they are as hot as a blast furnace, and contact with any weight behind it will result in an explosion."

After that demonstration, we walked around for another hour or so and returned to the billet. Once through the airlock, we had to mill around for a while, letting the suits get up to something like room temperature. Somebody came up and touched helmets with me.

"William?" She had MCCOY stenciled above her faceplate.

"Hi, Sean. Anything special?"

"I just wondered if you had anyone to sleep with tonight."

That's right; I'd forgotten. There wasn't any sleeping roster here. Everybody chose his own partner. "Sure, I mean, uh, no

. . . no, I haven't asked anybody. Sure, if you want to . . ."

"Thanks, William. See you later." I watched her walk away and thought that if anybody could make a fighting suit look sexy, it'd be Sean. But even she couldn't.

Cortez decided we were warm enough and led us to the suit room, where we backed the things into place and hooked them up to the charging plates. (Each suit had a little chunk of plutonium that would power it for several years, but we were supposed to run on fuel cells as much as possible.) After a lot of shuffling around, everybody finally got plugged in and we were allowed to unsuit—ninety-seven naked chickens squirming out of bright green eggs. It was *cold*—the air, the floor and especially the suits—and we made a pretty disorderly exit toward the lockers.

I slipped on tunic, trousers and sandals and was still cold. I took my cup and joined the line for soya. Everybody was jumping up and down to keep warm.

"How c-cold, do you think, it is, M-Mandella?" That was McCoy.

"I don't, even want, to think, about it." I stopped jumping and rubbed myself as briskly as possible, while holding a cup in one hand. "At least as cold as Missouri was."

"Ung . . . wish they'd, get some, fucken, heat in, this place." It always affects the small women more than anybody else. McCoy was the littlest one in the company, a waspwaist doll barely five feet high.

"They've got the airco going. It can't be long now."

"I wish I, was a big, slab of, meat like, you."

I was glad she wasn't.

VI

We had our first casualty on the third day, learning how to dig holes.

With such large amounts of energy stored in a soldier's weapons, it wouldn't be practical for him to hack out a hole in the frozen ground with the conventional pick and shovel. Still, you can launch grenades all day and get nothing but shallow depressions—so the usual method is to bore a hole in the ground with the hand laser, drop a timed charge in after it's cooled down and, ideally, fill the hole with stuff. Of course, there's not much loose rock on Charon, unless you've already blown a hole nearby.

The only difficult thing about the procedure is in getting away. To be safe, we were told, you've got to either be behind something really solid, or be at least a hundred meters away. You've got about three minutes after setting the charge, but you can't just sprint away. Not safely, not on Charon.

The accident happened when we were making a really deep hole, the kind you want for a large underground bunker. For this, we had to blow a hole, then climb down to the bottom of the crater and repeat the procedure again and again until the hole was deep enough. Inside the crater we used charges with a five-minute delay, but it hardly seemed enough time—you really had to go it slow, picking your way up the crater's edge.

Just about everybody had blown a double hole; everybody but me and three others. I guess we were the only ones paying really close attention when Bovanovitch got into trouble. All of us were a good two hundred meters away. With my image converter tuned up to about forty power, I watched her disappear over the rim of the crater. After that, I could only listen in on her conversation with Cortez.

"I'm on the bottom, Sergeant." Normal radio procedure was suspended for maneuvers like this; nobody but the trainee and Cortez was allowed to broadcast.

"Okay, move to the center and clear out the rubble. Take your time. No rush until you pull the pin."

"Sure, Sergeant." We could hear small echoes of rocks clattering, sound conduction through her boots. She didn't say anything for several minutes.

"Found bottom." She sounded a little out of breath.

"Ice or rock?"

"Oh, it's rock, Sergeant. The greenish stuff."

"Use a low setting, then. One point two, dispersion four."

"God darn it, Sergeant, that'll take forever."

"Yeah, but that stuff's got hydrated crystals in it—heat it up too fast and you might make it fracture. And we'd just have to leave you there, girl. Dead and bloody."

"Okay, one point two dee four." The inside edge of the crater flickered red with reflected laser light.

"When you get about a half a meter deep, squeeze it up to dee two."

"Roger." It took her exactly seventeen minutes, three of them at dispersion two. I could imagine how tired her shooting arm was.

"Now rest for a few minutes. When the bottom of the hole stops glowing, arm the charge and drop it in. Then *walk* out, understand? You'll have plenty of time."

"I understand, Sergeant. Walk out." She sounded nervous. Well, you don't often have to tiptoe away from a twenty-microton tachyon bomb. We listened to her breathing for a few minutes.

"Here goes." Faint slithering sound, the bomb sliding down.

"Slow and easy now. You've got five minutes."

"Y-yeah. Five." Her footsteps started out slow and regular. Then, after she started climbing the side, the sounds were less regular, maybe a little frantic. And with four minutes to go—

"Shit!" A loud scraping noise, then clatters and bumps. "Shit—shit."

"What's wrong, Private?"

"Oh, shit." Silence. "Shit!"

"Private, you don't wanna get shot, you *tell me what's wrong!*"

"I . . . shit, I'm stuck. Fucken rockslide . . . shit. . . . DO SOMETHING! I can't move, shit I can't move, I, I—"

"Shut up! How deep?"

"Can't move my, shit, my fucken legs. HELP ME—"

"Then goddammit use your arms—push! You can move a ton with each hand." Three minutes.

She stopped cussing and started to mumble, in Russian, I guess, a low monotone. She was panting, and you could hear rocks tumbling away.

"I'm free." Two minutes.

"Go as fast as you can." Cortez's voice was flat, emotionless.

At ninety seconds she appeared, crawling over the rim. "Run, girl. . . . You better run." She ran five or six steps and fell, skidded a few meters and got back up, running; fell again, got up again—

It looked as though she was going pretty fast, but she had only covered about thirty meters when Cortez said, "All right, Bovanovitch, get down on your stomach and lie still." Ten seconds, but she didn't hear or she wanted to get just a little more distance, and she kept running, careless leaping strides, and at the high point of one leap there was a flash and a rumble, and something big hit her below the neck, and her headless body spun off end over end through space, trailing a red-black spiral of flash-frozen blood that settled gracefully to the ground, a path of crystal powder that nobody disturbed while we gathered rocks to cover the juiceless thing at the end of it.

That night Cortez didn't lecture us, didn't even show up for night-chop. We were all very polite to each other and nobody was afraid to talk about it.

I sacked with Rogers—everybody sacked with a good friend—but all she wanted to do was cry, and she cried so long and so hard that she got me doing it, too.

VII

"Fire team A—move out!" The twelve of us advanced in a ragged line toward the simulated bunker. It was about a kilometer away, across a carefully prepared obstacle course. We could move pretty fast, since all of the ice had been cleared from the field, but even with ten days' experience we weren't ready to do more than an easy jog.

I carried a grenade launcher loaded with tenth-microton practice grenades. Everybody had their laser-fingers set at point oh eight dee one, not much more than a flashlight. This was a *simulated* attack—the bunker and its robot defender cost too much to use once and be thrown away.

"Team B, follow. Team leaders, take over."

We approached a clump of boulders at about the halfway mark, and Potter, my team leader, said, "Stop and cover." We clustered behind the rocks and waited for team B.

Barely visible in their blackened suits, the dozen men and women whispered by us. As soon as they were clear, they jogged left, out of our line of sight.

"Fire!" Red circles of light danced a half-klick downrange, where the bunker was just visible. Five hundred meters was the limit for these practice grenades; but I might luck out, so I lined the launcher up on the image of the bunker, held it at a forty-five degree angle and popped off a salvo of three.

Return fire from the bunker started before my grenades even landed. Its automatic lasers were no more powerful than the ones we were using, but a direct hit would deactivate your image converter, leaving you blind. It was setting down a random field of fire, not even coming close to the boulders we were hiding behind.

Three magnesium-bright flashes blinked simultaneously about thirty meters short of the bunker. "Mandella! I thought you were supposed to be *good* with that thing."

"Damn it, Potter—it only throws half a klick. Once we get closer, I'll lay 'em right on top, every time."

"Sure you will." I didn't say anything. She wouldn't be team leader forever. Besides, she hadn't been such a bad girl before the power went to her head.

Since the grenadier is the assistant team leader, I was slaved into Potter's radio and could hear *B* team talk to her.

"Potter, this is Freeman. Losses?"

"Potter here—no, looks like they were concentrating on you."

"Yeah, we lost three. Right now we're in a depression about eighty, a hundred meters down from you. We can give cover whenever you're ready."

"Okay, start." Soft click: "*A* team, follow me." She slid out from behind the rock and turned on the faint pink beacon beneath her powerpack. I turned on mine and moved out to run alongside of her, and the rest of the team fanned out in a trailing wedge. Nobody fired while *A* team laid down a cover for us.

All I could hear was Potter's breathing and the soft *crunch-crunch* of my boots. Couldn't see much of anything, so I tongued the image converter up to a log-two intensification. That made the image kind of blurry but adequately bright. Looked like the bunker had *B* team pretty well pinned down; they were getting quite a roasting. All of their return fire was laser. They must have lost their grenadier.

"Potter, this is Mandella. Shouldn't we take some of the heat off *B* team?"

"Soon as I can find us good enough cover. Is that all right with you? Private?" She'd been promoted to corporal for the duration of the exercise.

We angled to the right and lay down behind a slab of rock. Most of the others found cover nearby, but a few had to hug the ground.

"Freeman, this is Potter."

"Potter, this is Smithy. Freeman's out; Samuels is out. We only have five men left. Give us some cover so we can get—"

"Roger, Smithy." *Click*. "Open up, *A* team. The *B*'s are really hurtin'."

I peeked out over the edge of the rock. My rangefinder said that the bunker was about three hundred fifty meters away, still pretty far. I aimed a smidgeon high and popped three, then down a couple of degrees, three more. The first ones overshot by about twenty meters; then the second salvo flared up directly in front of the bunker. I tried to hold on that angle and popped fifteen, the rest of the magazine, in the same direction.

I should have ducked down behind the rock to reload, but I wanted to see where the fifteen would land, so I kept my eyes on the bunker while I reached back to unclip another magazine—

When the laser hit my image converter, there was a red glare so intense it seemed to go right through my eyes and bounce off the back of my skull. It must have been only a few milliseconds before the converter overloaded and went blind, but the bright green afterimage hurt my eyes for several seconds.

Since I was offically "dead," my radio automatically cut off, and I had to remain where I was until the mock battle was over. With no sensory input besides the feel of my own skin (and it ached where the image converter had shone on it) and the ringing in my ears, it seemed like an awfully long time. Finally, a helmet clanked against mine.

"You okay, Mandella?" Potter's voice.

"Sorry, I died of boredom twenty minutes ago."

"Stand up and take my hand." I did so and we shuffled back to the billet. It must have taken over an hour. She didn't say anything more, all the way back—it's a pretty awkward way to communicate—but after we'd cycled through the airlock and warmed up, she helped me undo my suit. I got ready for a mild tongue-lashing, but when the suit popped open, before I could even get my eyes adjusted to the light, she grabbed me around the neck and planted a wet kiss on my mouth.

"Nice shooting, Mandella."

"Huh?"

"Didn't you see? Of course not. . . . The last salvo before you got hit—four direct hits. The bunker decided it was knocked out, and all we had to do was walk the rest of the way."

"Great." I scratched my face under the eyes, and some dry skin flaked off. She giggled.

"You should see yourself. You look like . . ."

"All personnel, report to the assembly area." That was the captain's voice. Bad news, usually.

She handed me a tunic and sandals. "Let's go." The assembly area—chop hall was just down the corridor. There was a row of roll-call buttons at the door; I pressed the one beside my name. Four of the names were covered with black tape. That was good, only four. We hadn't lost anybody during today's maneuvers.

The captain was sitting on the raised dais, which at least meant we didn't have to go through the tench-hut bullshit. The place filled up in less than a minute; a soft chime indicated the roll was complete.

Captain Stott didn't stand up. "You did *fairly* well today. Nobody killed, and I expected some to be. In that respect you exceeded my expectations but in *every* other respect you did a poor job.

"I am glad you're taking good care of yourselves, because each of you represents an investment of over a million dollars and one-fourth of a human life.

"But in this simulated battle against a *very* stupid robot enemy, thirty-seven of you managed to walk into laser fire and be killed in a *sim*ulated way, and since dead people require no food, *you* will require no food, for the next three days. Each person who was a casualty in this battle will be allowed only two liters of water and a vitamin ration each day."

We knew enough not to groan or anything, but there were some pretty disgusted looks, especially on the faces that had singed eyebrows and a pink rectangle of sunburn framing their eyes.

"Mandella."

"Sir?"

"You are far and away the worst-burned casualty. Was your image converter set on normal?"

Oh, shit. "No, sir. Log two."

"I see. Who was your team leader for the exercises?"

"Acting Corporal Potter, sir."

"Private Potter, did you order him to use image intensification?"

"Sir, I . . . I don't remember."

"You don't. Well, as a memory exercise you may join the dead people. Is that satisfactory?"

"Yes, sir."

"Good. Dead people get one last meal tonight and go on

no rations starting tomorrow. Are there any questions?" He must have been kidding. "All right. Dismissed."

I selected the meal that looked as if it had the most calories and took my tray over to sit by Potter.

"That was a quixotic damn thing to do. But thanks."

"Nothing. I've been wanting to lose a few pounds anyway." I couldn't see where she was carrying any extra.

"I know a good exercise," I said. She smiled without looking up from her tray. "Have anybody for tonight?"

"Kind of thought I'd ask Jeff. . . ."

"Better hurry, then. He's lusting after Maejima." Well, that was mostly true. Everybody did.

"I don't know. Maybe we ought to save our strength. That third day . . ."

"Come on." I scratched the back of her hand lightly with a fingernail. "We haven't sacked since Missouri. Maybe I've learned something new."

"Maybe you have." She tilted her head up at me in a sly way. "Okay."

Actually, she was the one with the new trick. The French corkscrew, she called it. She wouldn't tell me who taught it to her though. I'd like to shake his hand. Once I got my strength back.

VIII

The two weeks' training around Miami base eventually cost us eleven lives. Twelve, if you count Dahlquist. I guess having to spend the rest of your life on Charon with a hand and both legs missing is close enough to dying.

Foster was crushed in a landslide and Freeland had a suit malfunction that froze him solid before we could carry him inside. Most of the other deaders were people I didn't know all that well. But they all hurt. And they seemed to make us more scared rather than more cautious.

Now darkside. A flyer brought us over in groups of twenty and set us down beside a pile of building materials thoughtfully immersed in a pool of helium II.

We used grapples to haul the stuff out of the pool. It's not safe to go wading, since the stuff crawls all over you and it's hard to tell what's underneath; you could walk out onto a slab of hydrogen and be out of luck.

I'd suggested that we try to boil away the pool with our lasers, but ten minutes of concentrated fire didn't drop the helium level appreciably. It didn't boil, either; helium II is a "superfluid," so what evaporation there was had to take place evenly, all over the surface. No hot spots, so no bubbling.

We weren't supposed to use lights, to "avoid detection." There was plenty of starlight with your image converter cranked up to log three or four, but each stage of amplification meant some loss of detail. By log four the landscape looked like a crude monochrome painting, and you couldn't read the names on people's helmets unless they were right in front of you.

The landscape wasn't all that interesting, anyhow. There were half a dozen medium-sized meteor craters (all with exactly the same level of helium II in them) and the suggestion of some puny mountains just over the horizon. The uneven ground was the consistency of frozen spiderwebs; every time you put your foot down, you'd sink half an inch with a squeaking crunch. It could get on your nerves.

It took most of a day to pull all the stuff out of the pool. We took shifts napping, which you could do either standing up, sitting or lying on your stomach. I didn't do well in any of those positions, so I was anxious to get the bunker built and pressurized.

We couldn't build the thing underground—it'd just fill up with helium II—so the first thing to do was to build an insulating platform, a permaplast-vacuum sandwich three layers thick.

I was an acting corporal, with a crew of ten people. We were carrying the permaplast layers to the building site—two people can carry one easily—when one of "my" men slipped and fell on his back.

"Damn it, Singer, watch your step." We'd had a couple of deaders that way.

"Sorry, Corporal. I'm bushed. Just got my feet tangled up."

"Yeah, just watch it." He got back up all right, and he and his partner placed the sheet and went back to get another.

I kept my eye on Singer. In a few minutes he was practically staggering, not easy to do in that suit of cybernetic armor.

"Singer! After you set that plank, I want to see you."

"Okay." He labored through the task and mooched over.

"Let me check your readout." I opened the door on his chest to expose the medical monitor. His temperature was at two degrees high; blood pressure and heart rate both elevated. Not up to the red line, though.

"You sick or something?"

"Hell, Mandella, I feel okay, just tired. Since I fell I been a little dizzy."

I chinned the medic's combination. "Doc, this is Mandella. You wanna come over here for a minute?"

"Sure, where are you?" I waved and he walked over from poolside.

"What's the problem?" I showed him Singer's readout.

He knew what all the other little dials and things meant, so it took him a while. "As far as I can tell, Mandella . . . he's just hot."

"Hell, I coulda told you that," said Singer.

"Maybe you better have the armorer take a look at his suit." we had two people who'd taken a crash course in suit maintenance; they were our "armorers."

I chinned Sanchez and asked him to come over with his tool kit.

"Be a couple of minutes, Corporal. Carryin' a plank."

"Well, put it down and get over here." I was getting an uneasy feeling. Waiting for him, the medic and I looked over Singer's suit.

"Uh-oh," Doc Jones said. "Look at this." I went around to the back and looked where he was pointing. Two of the fins on the heat exchanger were bent out of shape.

"What's wrong?" Singer asked.

"You fell on your heat exchanger, right?"

"Sure, Corporal—that's it. It must not be working right."

"I don't think it's working at *all*," said Doc.

Sanchez came over with his diagnostic kit and we told him what had happened. He looked at the heat exchanger, then plugged a couple of jacks into it and got a digital readout from a little monitor in his kit. I didn't know what it was measuring, but it came out zero to eight decimal places.

Heard a soft click, Sanchez chinning my private frequency. "Corporal, this guy's a deader."

"What? Can't you fix the goddamn thing?"

"Maybe . . . maybe I could, if I could take it apart. But there's no way—"

"Hey! Sanchez?" Singer was talking on the general freak. "Find out what's wrong?" He was panting.

Click. "Keep your pants on, man, we're working on it." *Click.* "He won't last long enough for us to get the bunker pressurized. And I can't work on the heat exchanger from outside of the suit."

"You've got a spare suit, haven't you?"

"Two of 'em, the fit-anybody kind. But there's no place . . . say . . ."

"Right. Go get one of the suits warmed up." I chinned the general freak. "Listen, Singer, we've gotta get you out of that thing. Sanchez has a spare suit, but to make the switch, we're gonna have to build a house around you. Understand?"

"Huh-uh."

"Look, we'll make a box with you inside, and hook it up to the life-support unit. That way you can breathe while you make the switch."

"Soun's pretty compis . . . compil . . . cated t'me."

"Look, just come along—"

"I'll be all right, man, jus' lemme res'. . . ."

I grabbed his arm and led him to the building site. He was really weaving. Doc took his other arm, and between us, we kept him from falling over.

"Corporal Ho, this is Corporal Mandella." Ho was in charge of the life-support unit.

"Go away, Mandella. I'm busy."

"You're going to be busier." I outlined the problem to her. While her group hurried to adapt the LSU—for this purpose, it need only be an air hose and heater—I got my crew to bring around six slabs of permaplast, so we could build a big box around Singer and the extra suit. It would look like a huge coffin, a meter square and six meters long.

We set the suit down on the slab that would be the floor of the coffin. "Okay, Singer, let's go."

No answer.

"Singer!" He was just standing there. Doc Jones checked his readout.

"He's out, man, unconscious."

My mind raced. There might just be room for another person in the box. "Give me a hand here." I took Singer's shoulders and Doc took his feet, and we carefully laid him out at the feet of the empty suit.

Then I lay down myself, above the suit. "Okay, close 'er up."

"Look, Mandella, if anybody goes in there, it oughta be me."

"Fuck you, Doc. *My* job. My man." That sounded all wrong. William Mandella, boy hero.

They stood a slab up on edge—it had two openings for the LSU input and exhaust—and proceeded to weld it to the bottom plank with a narrow laser beam. On Earth, we'd just use glue, but here the only fluid was helium, which has lots of interesting properties, but is definitely not sticky.

After about ten minutes we were completely walled up. I could feel the LSU humming. I switched on my suit light—the first time since we landed on darkside—and the glare made purple blotches dance in front of my eyes.

"Mandella, this is Ho. Stay in your suit at least two or three minutes. We're putting hot air in, but it's coming back just this side of liquid." I watched the purple fade for a while.

"Okay, it's still cold, but you can make it." I popped my suit. It wouldn't open all the way, but I didn't have too much trouble getting out. The suit was still cold enough to take some skin off my fingers and butt as I wiggled out.

I had to crawl feet-first down the coffin to get to Singer. It got darker fast, moving away from my light. When I popped his suit a rush of hot stink hit me in the face. In the dim light his skin was dark red and splotchy. His breathing was very shallow and I could see his heart palpitating.

First I unhooked the relief tubes—an unpleasant business—then the biosensors; and then I had the problem of getting his arms out of their sleeves.

It's pretty easy to do for yourself. You twist this way and turn that way and the arm pops out. Doing it from the outside is a different matter: I had to twist his arm and then reach under and move the suit's arm to match—it takes muscle to move a suit around from the outside.

Once I had one arm out it was pretty easy; I just crawled forward, putting my feet on the suit's shoulders, and pulled on his free arm. He slid out of the suit like an oyster slipping out of its shell.

I popped the spare suit and, after a lot of pulling and pushing, managed to get his legs in. Hooked up the biosensors and the front relief tube. He'd have to do the other one himself; it's too complicated. For the nth time I was glad not to have been born female; they have to have two of those damned plumber's friends, instead of just one and a simple hose.

I left his arms out of the sleeves. The suit would be useless for any kind of work, anyhow; waldos have to be tailored to the individual.

His eyelids fluttered. "Man . . . della. Where . . . the fuck . . ."

I explained, slowly, and he seemed to get most of it. "Now I'm gonna close you up and go get into my suit. I'll have the crew cut the end off this thing and I'll haul you out. Got it?"

He nodded. Strange to see that—when you nod or shrug inside a suit, it doesn't communicate anything.

I crawled into my suit, hooked up the attachments and chinned the general freak. "Doc, I think he's gonna be okay. Get us out of here now."

"Will do." Ho's voice. The LSU hum was replaced by a chatter, then a throb. Evacuating the box to prevent an explosion.

One corner of the seam grew red, then white, and a bright crimson beam lanced through, not a foot away from my head. I scrunched back as far as I could. The beam slid up the seam and around three corners, back to where it started. The end of the box fell away slowly, trailing filaments of melted 'plast.

"Wait for the stuff to harden, Mandella."

"Sanchez, I'm not that stupid."

"Here you go." Somebody tossed a line to me. That *would* be smarter than dragging him out by myself. I threaded a long bit under his arms and tied it behind his neck. Then I scrambled out to help them pull, which was silly—they had a dozen people already lined up to haul.

Singer got out all right and was actually sitting up while Doc Jones checked his readout. People were asking me about it and congratulating me, when suddenly Ho said, "Look!" and pointed toward the horizon.

It was a black ship, coming in fast. I just had time to think it wasn't fair, they weren't supposed to attack until the last few days, and then the ship was right on top of us.

IX

We all flopped to the ground instinctively, but the ship didn't attack. It blasted braking rockets and dropped to land on skids. Then it skied around to come to a rest beside the building site.

Everybody had it figured out and was standing around sheepishly when the two suited figures stepped out of the ship.

A familiar voice crackled over the general freak. "Every *one* of you saw us coming in and not *one* of you responded with laser fire. It wouldn't have done any good but it would have indicated a certain amount of fighting spirit. You have a week or less before the real thing and since the sergeant and *I* will be here *I* will insist that you show a little more will to live. Acting Sergeant Potter."

"Here, sir."

"Get me a detail of twelve people to unload cargo. We brought a hundred small robot drones for *target* practice so that you might have at least a fighting chance when a live target comes over.

"Move *now*. We only have thirty minutes before the ship returns to Miami."

I checked, and it was actually more like forty minutes.

Having the captain and sergeant there didn't really make much difference. We were still on our own; they were just observing.

Once we got the floor down, it only took one day to complete the bunker. It was a gray oblong, featureless except for the airlock blister and four windows. On top was a swivel-mounted bevawatt laser. The operator—you couldn't call him a "gunner"—sat in a chair holding dead-man switches in both hands. The laser wouldn't fire as long as he was holding one of those switches. If he let go, it would automatically aim for any moving aerial object and fire at will. Primary detection and aiming was by means of a kilometer-high antenna mounted beside the bunker.

It was the only arrangement that could really be expected to work, with the horizon so close and human reflexes so slow. You couldn't have the thing fully automatic, because in theory, friendly ships might also approach.

The aiming computer could choose among up to twelve targets appearing simultaneously (firing at the largest ones first). And it would get all twelve in the space of half a second.

The installation was partly protected from enemy fire by an efficient ablative layer that covered everything except the human operator. But then, they *were* dead-man switches. One man above guarding eighty inside. The army's good at that kind of arithmetic.

Once the bunker was finished, half of us stayed inside at all times—feeling very much like targets—taking turns operating the laser, while the other half went on maneuvers.

About four klicks from the base was a large "lake" of frozen hydrogen; one of our most important maneuvers was to learn how to get around on the treacherous stuff.

It wasn't too difficult. You couldn't stand up on it, so you had to belly down and sled.

If you had somebody to push you from the edge, getting started was no problem. Otherwise, you had to scrabble with your hands and feet, pushing down as hard as was practical, until you started moving, in a series of little jumps. Once started, you'd keep going until you ran out of ice. You could steer a little bit by digging in, hand and foot, on the appropriate side, but you couldn't slow to a stop that way. So it was a good idea not to go too fast and wind up positioned in such a way that your helmet didn't absorb the shock of stopping.

We went through all the things we'd done on the Miami side: weapons practice, demolition, attack patterns. We also launched drones at irregular intervals, toward the bunker. Thus, ten or fifteen times a day, the operators got to demonstrate their skill in letting go of the handles as soon as the proximity light went on.

I had four hours of that, like everybody else. I was nervous until the first "attack," when I saw how little there was to it. The light went on, I let go, the gun aimed, and when the drone peeped over the horizon—*zzt!* Nice touch of color, the molten metal spraying through space. Otherwise not too exciting.

So none of us were worried about the upcoming "graduation exercise," thinking it would be just more of the same.

Miami base attacked on the thirteenth day with two simultaneous missiles streaking over opposite sides of the horizon at some forty kilometers per second. The laser vaporized the first one with no trouble, but the second got within eight klicks of the bunker before it was hit.

We were coming back from maneuvers, about a klick away from the bunker. I wouldn't have seen it happen if I hadn't been looking directly at the bunker the moment of the attack.

The second missile sent a shower of molten debris straight toward the bunker. Eleven pieces hit, and, as we later reconstructed it, this is what happened:

The first casualty was Maejima, so well-loved Maejima, inside the bunker, who was hit in the back and the head and died instantly. With the drop in pressure, the LSU went into high gear. Friedman was standing in front of the main airco outlet and was blown into the opposite wall hard enough to knock him unconscious; he died of decompression before the others could get him to his suit.

Everybody else managed to stagger through the gale and get into their suits, but Garcia's suit had been holed and didn't do him any good.

By the time we got there, they had turned off the LSU and were welding up the holes in the wall. One man was trying to scrape up the recognizable mess that had been Maejima. I could hear him sobbing and retching. They had already taken Garcia and Friedman outside for burial. The captain took over the repair detail from Potter. Sergeant Cortez led the sobbing man over to a corner and came back to work on cleaning up Maejima's remains, alone. He didn't order anybody to help and nobody volunteered.

X

As a graduation exercise, we were unceremoniously stuffed into a ship—*Earth's Hope,* the same one we rode to Charon—and bundled off to Stargate at a little more than one gee.

The trip seemed endless, about six months subjective time, and boring, but not as hard on the carcass as going to Charon had been. Captain Stott made us review our training orally, day by day, and we did exercises every day until we were worn to a collective frazzle.

Stargate 1 was like Charon's darkside, only more so. The base on Stargate 1 was smaller than Miami base—only a little bigger than the one we constructed on darkside—and we were due to lay over a week to help expand the facilities. The crew there was very glad to see us, especially the two females, who looked a little worn around the edges.

We all crowded into the small dining hall, where Submajor Williamson, the man in charge of Stargate 1, gave us some disconcerting news:

"Everybody get comfortable. Get off the tables, though, there's plenty of floor.

"I have some idea of what you just went through, training on Charon. I won't say it's all been wasted. But where you're headed, things will be quite different. Warmer."

He paused to let that soak in.

"Aleph Aurigae, the first collapsar ever detected, revolves around the normal star Epsilon Aurigae in a twenty-seven-year orbit. The enemy has a base of operations, not on a regular portal planet of Aleph, but on a planet in orbit around Epsilon. We don't know much about the planet, just that it goes around Epsilon once every 745 days, is about three-fourths the size of Earth, and has an albedo of 0.8, meaning it's probably covered with clouds. We can't say precisely how hot it will be, but judging from its distance from Epsilon, it's probably rather hotter than Earth. Of course, we don't know whether you'll be working . . . fighting on lightside or darkside, equator or poles. It's highly unlikely that the atmosphere will be breathable—at any rate, you'll stay inside your suits.

"Now you know exactly as much about where you're going as I do. Questions?"

"Sir," Stein drawled, "now we know where we're goin' . . . anybody know what we're goin' to do when we get there?"

Williamson shrugged. "That's up to your captain—and your sergeant, and the captain of *Earth's Hope*, and *Hope*'s logistic computer. We just don't have enough data yet to project a course of action for you. It may be a long and bloody battle; it may be just a case of walking in to pick up the pieces. Conceivably, the Taurans might want to make a peace offer,"—Cortez snorted—"in which case you would simply be part of our muscle, our bargaining power." He looked at Cortez mildly. "No one can say for sure."

The orgy that night was amusing, but it was like trying to sleep in the middle of a raucous beach party. The only area big enough to sleep all of us was the dining hall; they draped a few bedsheets here and there for privacy, then unleashed Stargate's eighteen sex-starved men on our women, compliant and promiscuous by military custom (and law), but desiring nothing so much as sleep on solid ground.

The eighteen men acted as if they were compelled to try as many permutations as possible, and their performance was impressive (in a strictly quantitative sense, that is). Those of us who were keeping count led a cheering section for some of the more gifted members. I think that's the right word.

The next morning—and every other morning we were on Stargate 1—we staggered out of bed and into our suits, to go outside and work on the "new wing." Eventually, Stargate would be tactical and logistic headquarters for the war, with thousands of permanent personnel, guarded by half a dozen heavy cruisers in *Hope*'s class. When we started, it was two shacks and twenty people; when we left, it was four shacks and twenty people. The work was hardly work at all, compared to darkside, since we had plenty of light and got sixteen hours inside for every eight hours' work. And no drone attack for a final exam.

When we shuttled back up to the *Hope*, nobody was too happy about leaving (though some of the more popular females declared it'd be good to get some rest). Stargate was the last easy, safe assignment we'd have before taking up arms against the Taurans. And as Williamson had pointed out the first day, there was no way of predicting what *that* would be like.

Most of us didn't feel too enthusiastic about making a collapsar jump, either. We'd been assured that we wouldn't even feel it happen, just free fall all the way.

I wasn't convinced. As a physics student, I'd had the usual courses in general relativity and theories of gravitation. We only had a little direct data at that time—Stargate was discovered when I was in grade school—but the mathematical model seemed clear enough.

The collapsar Stargate was a perfect sphere about three kilometers in radius. It was suspended forever in a state of gravitational collapse that should have meant its surface was dropping toward its center at nearly the speed of light. Relativity propped it up, at least gave it the illusion of being there... the way all reality becomes illusory and observer-oriented when you study general relativity. Or Buddhism. Or get drafted.

At any rate, there would be a theoretical point in spacetime when one end of our ship was just above the surface of the collapsar, and the other end was a kilometer away (in our frame of reference). In any sane universe, this would set up tidal stresses and tear the ship apart, and we would be just another million kilograms of degenerate matter on a theoretical surface, rushing headlong to nowhere for the rest of eternity or dropping to the center in the next trillionth of a second. You pays your money and you takes your frame of reference.

But they were right. We blasted away from Stargate 1, made a few course corrections and then just dropped, for about an hour.

Then a bell rang and we sank into our cushions under a steady two gravities of deceleration. We were in enemy territory.

XI

We'd been decelerating at two gravities for almost nine days when the battle began. Lying on our couches being miserable, all we felt were two soft bumps, missiles being released. Some eight hours later, the squawkbox crackled: "Attention, all crew. This is the captain." Quinsana, the pilot, was only a lieutenant, but was allowed to call himself captain aboard the vessel, where he outranked all of us, even Captain Stott. "You grunts in the cargo hold can listen, too.

"We just engaged the enemy with two fifty-bevaton tachyon missiles and have destroyed both the enemy vessel and another object which it had launched approximately three microseconds before.

"The enemy has been trying to overtake us for the past 179 hours, ship time. At the time of the engagement, the enemy was moving at a little over half the speed of light, relative to Aleph, and was only about thirty AUs from *Earth's Hope*. It was moving at .47c relative to us, and thus we would have been coincident in space-time"—rammed!—"in a little more than nine hours. The missiles were launched at 0719 ship's time, and destroyed the enemy at 1540, both tachyon bombs detonating within a thousand klicks of the enemy objects."

The two missiles were a type whose propulsion system was itself only a barely controlled tachyon bomb. They accelerated at a constant rate of one hundred gees, and were traveling at a relativistic speed by the time the nearby mass of the enemy ship detonated them.

"We expect no further interference from enemy vessels. Our velocity with respect to Aleph will be zero in another five hours; we will then begin to journey back. The return will take twenty-seven days." General moans and dejected cussing. Everybody knew all that already, of course; but we didn't care to be reminded of it.

So after another month of logy calisthenics and drill, at a constant two gravities, we got our first look at the planet we were going to attack. Invaders from outer space, yes sir.

It was a blinding white crescent waiting for us two AUs out from Epsilon. The captain had pinned down the location of the enemy base from fifty AUs out, and we had jockeyed in on a wide arc, keeping the bulk of the planet between them and us. That didn't mean we were sneaking up on them—quite the contrary; they launched three abortive attacks—but it put us in a stronger defensive position. Until we had to go to the surface, that is. Then only the ship and its Star Fleet crew would be reasonably safe.

Since the planet rotated rather slowly—once every ten and one-half days—a "stationary" orbit for the ship had to be 150,000 klicks out. This made the people in the ship feel quite secure, with 6,000 miles of rock and 90,000 miles of space between them and the enemy. But it meant a whole second's time lag in communication between us on the ground and the ship's battle computer. A person could get awful dead while that neutrino pulse crawled up and back.

Our vague orders were to attack the base and gain control, while damaging a minimum of enemy equipment. We were to take at least one enemy alive. We were under no circumstances to allow ourselves to be taken alive, however. And the decision wasn't up to us; one special pulse from the battle computer, and that speck of plutonium in your power plant would fiss with all of .01% efficiency, and you'd be nothing but rapidly expanding, very hot plasma.

They strapped us into six scoutships—one platoon of twelve people in each—and we blasted away from *Earth's Hope* at eight gees. Each scoutship was supposed to follow its own carefully random path to our rendezvous point, 108 klicks from the base. Fourteen drone ships were launched at the same time, to confound the enemy's antispacecraft system.

The landing went off almost perfectly. One ship suffered minor damage, a near miss boiling away some of the ablative material on one side of the hull, but it'd still be able to make it and return, keeping its speed down while in the atmosphere.

We zigged and zagged and wound up first ship at the rendezvous point. There was only one trouble. It was under four kilometers of water.

I could almost hear that machine, 90,000 miles away, grinding its mental gears, adding this new bit of data. We proceeded just as if we were landing on solid ground: braking rockets, falling, skids out, hit the water, skip, hit the water, skip, hit the water, sink.

It would have made sense to go ahead and land on the bottom—we were streamlined, after all, and water just another fluid—but the hull wasn't strong enough to hold up a four-kilometer column of water. Sergeant Cortez was in the scout-ship with us.

"Sarge, tell that computer to *do* something! We're gonna get—"

"Oh, shut up, Mandella. Trust in th' lord." "Lord" was definitely lower-case when Cortez said it.

There was a loud bubbly sigh, then another, and a slight increase in pressure on my back that meant the ship was rising. "Flotation bags?" Cortez didn't deign to answer, or didn't know.

That was it. We rose to within ten or fifteen meters of the surface and stopped, suspended there. Through the port I could see the surface above, shimmering like a mirror of hammered silver. I wondered what it would be like to be a fish and have a definite roof over your world.

I watched another ship splash in. It made a great cloud of bubbles and turbulence, then fell—slightly tail-first—for a short distance before large bags popped out under each delta wing. Then it bobbed up to about our level and stayed.

"This is Captain Stott. Now listen carefully. There is a beach some twenty-eight klicks from your present position, in the direction of the enemy. You will be proceeding to this beach by scoutship and from there will mount your assault on the Tauran position." That was *some* improvement; we'd only have to walk eighty klicks.

We deflated the bags, blasted to the surface and flew in a slow, spread-out formation to the beach. It took several minutes. As the ship scraped to a halt, I could hear pumps humming, making the cabin pressure equal to the air pressure outside. Before it had quite stopped moving, the escape slot beside my couch slid open. I rolled out onto the wing of the craft and jumped to the ground. Ten seconds to find cover—I sprinted across loose gravel to the "treeline," a twisty bramble of tall sparse bluish-green shrubs. I dove into the briar patch and turned to watch the ships leave. The drones that were left rose slowly to about a hundred meters, then took off in all directions with a bone-jarring roar. The real scoutships slid slowly back into the water. Maybe that was a good idea.

It wasn't a terribly attractive world but certainly would be easier to get around in than the cryogenic nightmare we were trained for. The sky was a uniform dull silver brightness that merged with the mist over the ocean so completely it was impossible to tell where water ended and air began. Small wavelets licked at the black gravel shore, much too slow and graceful in the three-quarters Earth-normal gravity. Even from fifty meters away, the rattle of billions of pebbles rolling with the tide was loud in my ears.

The air temperature was 79 degrees Centrigrade, not quite hot enough for the sea to boil, even though the air pressure was low compared to Earth's. Wisps of steam drifted quickly upward from the line where water met land. I wondered how long a man would survive exposed here without a suit. Would the heat or the low oxygen (partial pressure one-eighth Earth normal) kill him first? Or was there some deadly microorganism that would beat them both? . . .

"This is Cortez. Everybody come over and assemble on me." He was standing on the beach a little to the left of me, waving his hand in a circle over his head. I walked toward him through the shrubs. They were brittle, unsubstantial, seemed paradoxically dried-out in the steamy air. They wouldn't offer much in the way of cover.

"We'll be advancing on a heading .05 radians east of north. I want Platoon One to take point. Two and Three follow about twenty meters behind, to the left and right. Seven, command platoon, is in the middle, twenty meters behind Two and Three. Five and Six, bring up the rear, in a semicircular closed flank. Everybody straight?" Sure, we could do that "arrowhead" maneuver in our sleep. "Okay, let's move out."

I was in Platoon Seven, the "command group." Captain Stott put me there not because I was expected to give any commands, but because of my training in physics.

The command group was supposedly the safest place, buffered by six platoons: people were assigned to it because there was some tactical reason for them to survive at least a little longer than the rest. Cortez was there to give orders. Chavez was there to correct suit malfunctions. The senior medic, Doc Wilson (the only medic who actually had an M.D.) was there, and so was Theodopolis, the radio engineer, our link with the captain, who had elected to stay in orbit.

The rest of us were assigned to the command group by dint of special training or aptitude that wouldn't normally be considered of a "tactical" nature. Facing a totally unknown enemy, there was no way of telling what might prove important. Thus I was there because I was the closest the company had to a physicist. Rogers was biology. Tate was chemistry. Ho could crank out a perfect score on the Rhine extrasensory perception

test, every time. Bohrs was a polyglot, able to speak twenty-
one languages fluently, idiomatically. Petrov's talent was that
he had tested out to have not one molecule of xenophobia in
his psyche. Keating was a skilled acrobat. Debby Hollister—
"Lucky" Hollister—showed a remarkable aptitude for making
money, and also had a consistently high Rhine potential.

XII

When we first set out, we were using the "jungle" camouflage
combination on our suits. But what passed for jungle in these
anemic tropics was too sparse; we looked like a band of conspicuous harlequins trooping through the woods. Cortez had
us switch to black, but that was just as bad, as the light of
Epsilon came evenly from all parts of the sky, and there were
no shadows except ours. We finally settled on the dun-colored
desert camouflage.

The nature of the countryside changed slowly as we walked
north, away from the sea. The thorned stalks—I guess you
could call them trees—came in fewer numbers but were bigger
around and less brittle; at the base of each was a tangled mass
of vine with the same blue-green color, which spread out in a
flattened cone some ten meters in diameter. There was a delicate
green flower the size of a man's head near the top of each tree.

Grass began to appear some five klicks from the sea. It
seemed to respect the trees' "property rights," leaving a strip
of bare earth around each cone of vine. At the edge of such a
clearing, it would grow as timid blue-green stubble, then, moving away from the tree, would get thicker and taller until it
reached shoulder high in some places, where the separation
between two trees was unusually large. The grass was a lighter,
greener shade than the trees and vines. We changed the color
of our suits to the bright green we had used for maximum
visibility on Charon. Keeping to the thickest part of the grass,
we were fairly inconspicuous.

We covered over twenty klicks each day, buoyant after months
under two gees. Until the second day, the only form of animal
life we saw was a kind of black worm, finger-sized, with
hundreds of cilium legs like the bristles of a brush. Rogers said
that there obviously had to be some larger creature around, or
there would be no reason for the trees to have thorns. So we

were doubly on guard, expecting trouble both from the Taurans and the unidentified "large creature."

Potter's second platoon was on point; the general freak was reserved for her, since her platoon would likely be the first to spot any trouble.

"Sarge, this is Potter," we all heard. "Movement ahead."

"Get down, then!"

"We are. Don't think they see us."

"First platoon, go up to the right of point. Keep down. Fourth, get up to the left. Tell me when you get in position. Sixth platoon, stay back and guard the rear. Fifth and third, close with the command group."

Two dozen people whispered out of the grass to join us. Cortez must have heard from the fourth platoon.

"Good. How about you, first? . . . Okay, fine. How many are there?"

"Eight we can see." Potter's voice.

"Good. When I give the word, open fire. Shoot to kill."

"Sarge, . . . they're just animals."

"Potter—if you've known all this time what a Tauran looks like, you should've told us. Shoot to kill."

"But we need . . ."

"We need a prisoner, but we don't need to escort him forty klicks to his home base and keep an eye on him while we fight. Clear?"

"Yes. Sergeant."

"Okay. Seventh, all you brains and weirds, we're going up and watch. Fifth and third, come along to guard."

We crawled through the meter-high grass to where the second platoon had stretched out in a firing line.

"I don't see anything," Cortez said.

"Ahead and just to the left. Dark green."

They were only a shade darker than the grass. But after you saw the first one, you could see them all, moving slowly around some thirty meters ahead.

"Fire!" Cortez fired first; then twelve streaks of crimson leaped out and the grass wilted black, disappeared, and the creatures convulsed and died trying to scatter.

"Hold fire, hold it!" Cortez stood up. "We want to have something left—second platoon, follow me." He strode out toward the smoldering corpses, laser-finger pointed out front, obscene divining rod pulling him toward the carnage. . . . I felt my gorge rising and knew that all the lurid training tapes, all the horrible deaths in training accidents, hadn't prepared me for this sudden reality . . . that I had a magic wand that I could point at a life and make it a smoking piece of half-raw meat; I wasn't a soldier nor ever wanted to be one nor ever would want—

"Okay, seventh, come on up." While we were walking toward them, one of the creatures moved, a tiny shudder, and Cortez flicked the beam of his laser over it with an almost negligent gesture. It made a hand-deep gash across the creature's middle. It died, like the others, without emitting a sound.

They were not quite as tall as humans, but wider in girth. They were covered with dark green, almost black, fur—white curls where the laser had singed. They appeared to have three legs and an arm. The only ornament to their shaggy heads was a mouth, a wet black orifice filled with flat black teeth. They were thoroughly repulsive, but their worst feature was not a difference from human beings, but a similarity. . . . Whenever the laser had opened a body cavity, milk-white glistening veined globes and coils of organs spilled out, and their blood was dark clotting red.

"Rogers, take a look. Taurans or not?"

Rogers knelt by one of the disemboweled creatures and opened a flat plastic box, filled with glittering dissecting tools. She selected a scalpel. "One way we might be able to find out." Doc Wilson watched over her shoulder as she methodically slit the membrane covering several organs.

"Here." She held up a blackish fibrous mass between two fingers, a parody of daintiness through all that armor.

"So?"

"It's grass, Sergeant. If the Taurans can eat the grass and breathe the air, they certainly found a planet remarkably like their home." She tossed it away. "They're animals, Sergeant, just fucken animals."

"I don't know," Doc Wilson said. "Just because they walk around on all fours, threes maybe, and eat grass . . ."

"Well, let's check out the brain." She found one that had been hit in the head and scraped the superficial black char from the wound. "Look at that."

It was almost solid bone. She tugged and ruffled the hair all over the head of another one. "What the hell does it use for sensory organs? No eyes, or ears, or . . ." She stood up.

"Nothing in that fucken head but a mouth and ten centimeters of skull. To protect nothing, not a fucken thing."

"If I could shrug, I'd shrug," the doctor said. "It doesn't prove anything—a brain doesn't have to look like a mushy walnut and it doesn't have to be in the head. Maybe that skull isn't bone, maybe *that's* the brain, some crystal lattice . . ."

"Yeah, but the fucken stomach's in the right place, and if those aren't intestines I'll eat—"

"Look," Cortez said, "this is real interesting, but all we need to know is whether that thing's dangerous, then we've gotta move on; we don't have all—"

"They aren't dangerous," Rogers began. "They don't—"

"Medic! DOC!" Somebody back at the firing line was waving his arms. Doc sprinted back to him, the rest of us following.

"What's wrong?" He had reached back and unclipped his medical kit on the run.

"It's Ho. She's out."

Doc swung open the door on Ho's biomedical monitor. He didn't have to look far. "She's dead."

"Dead?" Cortez said. "What the hell—"

"Just a minute." Doc plugged a jack into the monitor and fiddled with some dials on his kit. "Everybody's biomed readout is stored for twelve hours. I'm running it backwards, should be able to—there!"

"What?"

"Four and a half minutes ago—must have been when you opened fire—Jesus!"

"Well?"

"Massive cerebral hemorrhage. No . . ." He watched the dials. "No . . . warning, no indications of anything out of the ordinary; blood pressure up, pulse up, but normal under the circumstances . . . nothing to . . . indicate—" He reached down and popped her suit. Her fine oriental features were distorted in a horrible grimace, both gums showing. Sticky fluid ran from under her collapsed eyelids, and a trickle of blood still dripped from each ear. Doc Wilson closed the suit back up.

"I've never seen anything like it. It's as if a bomb went off in her skull."

"Oh fuck," Rogers said, "she was Rhine-sensitive, wasn't she?"

"That's right." Cortez sounded thoughtful. "All right, everybody listen up. Platoon leaders, check your platoons and see if anybody's missing, or hurt. Anybody else in seventh?"

"I . . . I've got a splitting headache, Sarge," Lucky said.

Four others had bad headaches. One of them affirmed that

he was slightly Rhine-sensitive. The others didn't know.

"Cortez, I think it's obvious," Doc Wilson said, "that we should give these . . . monsters wide berth, especially shouldn't harm any more of them. Not with five people susceptible to whatever apparently killed Ho."

"Of course, God damn it, I don't need anybody to tell me that. We'd better get moving. I just filled the captain in on what happened; he agrees that we'd better get as far away from here as we can before we stop for the night.

"Let's get back in formation and continue on the same bearing. Fifth platoon, take over point; second, come back to the rear. Everybody else, same as before."

"What about Ho?" Lucky asked.

"She'll be taken care of. From the ship."

After we'd gone half a klick, there was a flash and rolling thunder. Where Ho had been came a wispy luminous mushroom cloud boiling up to disappear against the gray sky.

XIII

We stopped for the "night"—actually, the sun wouldn't set for another seventy hours—atop a slight rise some ten klicks from where we had killed the aliens. But they weren't aliens, I had to remind myself—*we* were.

Two platoons deployed in a ring around the rest of us, and we flopped down exhausted. Everybody was allowed four hours' sleep and had two hours' guard duty.

Potter came over and sat next to me. I chinned her frequency.

"Hi, Marygay."

"Oh, William," her voice over the radio was hoarse and cracking. "God, it's so horrible."

"It's over now—"

"I killed one of them, the first instant, I shot it right in the, in the . . ."

I put my hand on her knee. The contact made a plastic click and I jerked it back, visions of machines embracing, copulating. "Don't feel singled out, Marygay; whatever guilt there is, is . . . belongs evenly to all of us, . . . but a triple portion for Cor—"

"You privates quit jawin' and get some sleep. You both pull guard in two hours."

"Okay, Sarge." Her voice was so sad and tired I couldn't bear it. I felt if I could only touch her, I could drain off the sadness like ground wire draining current, but we were each trapped in our own plastic world—

"G'night, William."

"Night." It's almost impossible to get sexually excited inside a suit, with the relief tube and all the silver chloride sensors poking you, but somehow this was my body's response to the emotional impotence, maybe remembering more pleasant sleeps with Marygay, maybe feeling that in the midst of all this death, personal death could be soon, cranking up the procreative derrick for one last try . . . lovely thoughts like this. I fell asleep and dreamed that I was a machine, mimicking the functions of life, creaking and clanking my clumsy way through the world, people too polite to say anything but giggling behind my back, and the little man who sat inside my head pulling the levers and clutches and watching the dials, he was hopelessly mad and was storing up hurts for the day—

"Mandella—wake up, goddammit, your shift!"

I shuffled over to my place on the perimeter to watch for God knows what . . . but I was so weary I couldn't keep my eyes open. Finally I tongued a stimtab, knowing I'd pay for it later.

For over an hour I sat there, scanning my sector left, right, near, far, the scene never changing, not even a breath of wind to stir the grass.

Then suddenly the grass parted and one of the three-legged creatures was right in front of me. I raised my finger but didn't squeeze.

"Movement!"

"Movement!"

"Jesus Chri—there's one right—"

"HOLD YOUR FIRE! f' shit's sake don't shoot!"

"Movement."

"Movement." I looked left and right, and as far as I could see, every perimeter guard had one of the blind, dumb creatures standing right in front of him.

Maybe the drug I'd taken to stay awake made me more sensitive to whatever they did. My scalp crawled and I felt a formless *thing* in my mind, the feeling you get when somebody has said something and you didn't quite hear it, want to respond, but the opportunity to ask him to repeat it is gone.

The creature sat back on its haunches, leaning forward on

the one front leg. Big green bear with a withered arm. Its power threaded through my mind, spiderwebs, echo of night terrors, trying to communicate, trying to destroy me, I couldn't know.

"All right, everybody on the perimeter, fall back, slow. Don't make any quick gestures. . . . Anybody got a headache or anything?"

"Sergeant, this is Hollister." Lucky.

"They're trying to say something . . . I can almost . . . no, just . . ."

"All I can get is that they think we're, think we're . . . well, *funny*. They're not afraid."

"You mean the one in front of you isn't—"

"No, the feeling comes from all of them, they're all thinking the same thing. Don't ask me how I know, I just do."

"Maybe they thought it was funny, what they did to Ho."

"Maybe. I don't feel they're dangerous. Just curious about us."

"Sergeant, this is Bohrs."

"Yeah."

"The Taurans've been here at least a year—maybe they've learned how to communicate with these . . . overgrown teddy-bears. They might be spying on us, might be sending back—"

"I don't think they'd show themselves if that were the case," Lucky said. "They can obviously hide from us pretty well when they want to."

"Anyhow," Cortez said, "if they're spies, the damage has been done. Don't think it'd be smart to take any action against them. I know you'd all like to see 'em dead for what they did to Ho, so would I, but we'd better be careful."

I didn't want to see them dead, but I'd just as soon not have seen them in any condition. I was walking backwards slowly, toward the middle of camp. The creature didn't seem disposed to follow. Maybe he just knew we were surrounded. He was pulling up grass with his arm and munching.

"Okay, all of you platoon leaders, wake everybody up, get a roll count. Let me know if anybody's been hurt. Tell your people we're moving out in one minute."

I don't know what Cortez had expected, but of course the creatures followed right along. They didn't keep us surrounded; just had twenty or thirty following us all the time. Not the same ones, either. Individuals would saunter away, new ones would join the parade. It was pretty obvious *they* weren't going to tire out.

We were each allowed one stimtab. Without it, no one could have marched an hour. A second pill would have been welcome after the edge started to wear off, but the mathematics of the situation forbade it; we were still thirty klicks from the enemy base, fifteen hours' marching at the least. And though you could stay awake and energetic for a hundred hours on the tabs, aberrations of judgment and perception snowballed after the second one, until *in extremis* the most bizarre hallucinations would be taken at face value, and a person could fidget for hours deciding whether to have breakfast.

Under artificial stimulation, the company traveled with great energy for the first six hours, was slowing by the seventh, and ground to an exhausted halt after nine hours and nineteen kilometers. The teddybears had never lost sight of us and, according to Lucky, had never stopped "broadcasting." Cortez's decision was that we would stop for seven hours, each platoon taking one hour of perimeter guard. I was never so glad to have been in the seventh platoon, as we stood guard the last shift and thus were able to get six hours of uninterrupted sleep.

In the few moments I lay awake after finally lying down, the thought came to me that the next time I closed my eyes could well be the last. And partly because of the drug hangover, mostly because of the past day's horrors, I found that I really didn't give a shit.

XIV

Our first contact with the Taurans came during my shift.

The teddybears were still there when I woke up and replaced Doc Jones on guard. They'd gone back to their original formation, one in front of each guard position. The one who was waiting for me seemed a little larger than normal, but otherwise looked just like all the others. All the grass had been cropped where he was sitting, so he occasionally made forays to the left or right. But he always returned to sit right in front of me, you would say *staring* if he had had anything to stare with.

We had been facing each other for about fifteen minutes when Cortez's voice rumbled:

"Awright everybody, wake up and get hid!"

I followed instinct and flopped to the ground and rolled into a tall stand of grass.

"Enemy vessel overhead." His voice was almost laconic.

Strictly speaking, it wasn't really overhead, but rather passing somewhat east of us. It was moving slowly, maybe a hundred klicks per hour, and looked like a broomstick surrounded by a dirty soap bubble. The creature riding it was a little more human-looking than the teddybears, but still no prize. I cranked my image amplifier up to forty log two for a closer look.

He had two arms and two legs, but his waist was so small you could encompass it with both hands. Under the tiny waist was a large horseshoe-shaped pelvic structure nearly a meter wide, from which dangled two long skinny legs with no apparent knee joint. Above that waist his body swelled out again, to a chest no smaller than the huge pelvis. His arms looked surprisingly human, except that they were too long and undermuscled. There were too many fingers on his hands. Shoulderless, neckless. His head was a nightmarish growth that swelled like a goiter from his massive chest. Two eyes that looked like clusters of fish eggs, a bundle of tassles instead of a nose, and a rigidly open hole that might have been a mouth sitting low down where his adam's apple should have been. Evidently the soap bubble contained an amenable environment, as he was wearing absolutely nothing except his ridged hide, that looked like skin submerged too long in hot water, then dyed a pale orange. "He" had no external genitalia, but nothing that might hint of mammary glands. So we opted for the male pronoun by default.

Obviously, he either didn't see us or thought we were part of the herd of teddybears. He never looked back at us, but just continued in the same direction we were headed, .05 rad east of north.

"Might as well go back to sleep now, if you can sleep after looking at *that* thing. We move out at 0435." Forty minutes.

Because of the planet's opaque cloud cover, there had been no way to tell, from space, what the enemy base looked like or how big it was. We only knew its position, the same way we knew the position the scoutships were supposed to land on. So it too could easily have been underwater, or underground.

But some of the drones were reconnaissance ships as well as decoys: and in their mock attacks on the base, one managed to get close enough to take a picture. Captain Stott beamed down a diagram of the place to Cortez—the only one with a visor in his suit—when we were five klicks from the base's "radio" position. We stopped and he called all the platoon leaders in with the seventh platoon to confer. Two teddybears loped in, too. We tried to ignore them.

"Okay, the captain sent down some pictures of our objective. I'm going to draw a map; you platoon leaders copy." They took pads and styli out of their leg pockets, while Cortez unrolled a large plastic mat. He gave it a shake to randomize any residual charge, and turned on his stylus.

"Now, we're coming from this direction." He put an arrow at the bottom of the sheet. "First thing we'll hit is this row of huts, probably billets or bunkers, but who the hell knows. . . . Our initial objective is to destroy these buildings—the whole base is on a flat plain; there's no way we could really sneak by them."

"Potter here. Why can't we jump over them?"

"Yeah, we could do that, and wind up completely surrounded, cut to ribbons. We take the buildings.

"After we do that . . . all I can say is that we'll have to think on our feet. From the aerial reconnaissance, we can figure out the function of only a couple of buildings—and that stinks. We might wind up wasting a lot of time demolishing the equivalent of an enlisted-men's bar, ignoring a huge logistic computer because it looks like . . . a garbage dump or something."

"Mandella here," I said. "Isn't there a spaceport of some kind—seems to me we ought to . . ."

"I'll get to that, damn it. There's a ring of these huts all around the camp, so we've got to break through somewhere. This place'll be closest, less chance of giving away our position before we attack.

"There's nothing in the whole place that actually looks like a weapon. That doesn't mean anything, though; you could hide a bevawatt laser in each of those huts.

"Now, about five hundred meters from the huts, in the middle of the base, we'll come to this big flower-shaped structure." Cortez drew a large symmetrical shape that looked like the outline of a flower with seven petals. "What the hell this is, your guess is as good as mine. There's only one of them, though, so we don't damage it any more than we have to. Which means . . . we blast it to splinters if I think it's dangerous.

"Now, as far as your spaceport, Mandella, is concerned—there just isn't one. Nothing.

"That cruiser the *Hope* caulked had probably been left in

orbit, like ours has to be. If they have any equivalent of a scoutship, or drone missiles, they're either not kept here or they're well hidden."

"Bohrs here. Then what did they attack with, while we were coming down from orbit?"

"I wish we knew, Private.

"Obviously, we don't have any way of estimating their numbers, not directly. Recon pictures failed to show a single Tauran on the grounds of the base. Meaning nothing, because it *is* an alien environment. Indirectly, though . . . we count the number of broomsticks, those flying things.

"There are fifty-one huts, and each has at most one broomstick. Four don't have any parked outside, but we located three at various other parts of the base. Maybe this indicates that there are fifty-one Taurans, one of whom was outside the base when the picture was taken."

"Keating here. Or fifty-one officers."

"That's right—maybe fifty thousand infantrymen stacked in one of these buildings. No way to tell. Maybe ten Taurans, each with five broomsticks, to use according to his mood.

"We've got one thing in our favor, and that's communications. They evidently use a frequency modulation of megahertz electromagnetic radiation."

"Radio!"

"That's right, whoever you are. Identify yourself when you speak. So it's quite possible that they can't detect our phased-neutrino communications. Also, just prior to the attack, the *Hope* is going to deliver a nice dirty fission bomb; detonate it in the upper atmosphere right over the base. That'll restrict them to line-of-sight communications for some time; even those will be full of static."

"Why don't . . . Tate here . . . why don't they just drop the bomb right in their laps? Save us a lot of—"

"That doesn't even deserve an answer, Private. But the answer is, they might. And you better hope they don't. If they caulk the base, it'll be for the safety of the *Hope*. *After* we've attacked, and probably before we're far enough away for it to make much difference.

"We keep that from happening by doing a good job. We have to reduce the base to where it can no longer function; at the same time, leave as much intact as possible. And take one prisoner."

"Potter here. You mean, at least one prisoner."

"I mean what I say. One only. Potter . . . you're relieved of your platoon. Send Chavez up."

"All right, Sergeant." The relief in her voice was unmistakable.

Cortez continued with his map and instructions. There was one other building whose function was pretty obvious; it had a large steerable dish antenna on top. We were to destroy it as soon as the grenadiers got in range.

The attack plan was very loose. Our signal to begin would be the flash of the fission bomb. At the same time, several drones would converge on the base, so we could see what their antispacecraft defenses were. We would try to reduce the effectiveness of those defenses without destroying them completely.

Immediately after the bomb and the drones, the grenadiers would vaporize a line of seven huts. Everybody would break through the hole into the base . . . and what would happen after that was anybody's guess.

Ideally, we'd sweep from that end of the base to the other, destroying certain targets, caulking all but one Tauran. But that was unlikely to happen, as it depended on the Taurans' offering very little resistance.

On the other hand, if the Taurans showed obvious superiority from the beginning, Cortez would give the order to scatter. Everybody had a different compass bearing for retreat—we'd blossom out in all directions, the survivors to rendezvous in a valley some forty klicks east of the base. Then we'd see about a return engagement, after the *Hope* softened the base up a bit.

"One last thing," Cortez rasped. "Maybe some of you feel the way Potter evidently does, maybe some of your men feel that way . . . that we ought to go easy, not make this so much of a bloodbath. Mercy is a luxury, a weakness we can't afford to indulge in at this stage of the war. *All* we know about the enemy is that they have killed seven hundred and ninety-eight humans. They haven't shown any restraint in attacking our cruisers, and it'd be foolish to expect any this time, this first ground action.

"*They* are responsible for the lives of all of your comrades who died in training, and for Ho, and for all the others who are surely going to die today. I can't *understand* anybody who wants to spare them. But that doesn't make any difference. You have your orders and, what the hell, you might as well know, all of you have a post-hypnotic suggestion that I will trigger by a phrase, just before the battle. It will make your job easier."

"Sergeant . . ."

"Shut up. We're short on time; get back to your platoons and brief them. We move out in five minutes."

The platoon leaders returned to their men, leaving Cortez and ten of us—plus three teddybears, milling around, getting in the way.

XV

We took the last five klicks very carefully, sticking to the highest grass, running across occasional clearings. When we were five hundred meters from where the base was supposed to be, Cortez took the third platoon forward to scout, while the rest of us laid low.

Cortez's voice came over the general freak: "Looks pretty much like we expected. Advance in a file, crawling. When you get to the third platoon, follow your squad leader to the left or right."

We did that and wound up with a string of eighty-three people in a line roughly perpendicular to the direction of attack. We were pretty well hidden, except for the dozen or so teddy-bears that mooched along the line munching grass.

There was no sign of life inside the base. All of the buildings were windowless and a uniform shiny white. The huts that were our first objective were large featureless half-buried eggs some sixty meters apart. Cortez assigned one to each grenadier.

We were broken into three fire teams: team *A* consisted of Platoons Two, Four, and Six; team *B* was One, Three, and Five; the command platoon was team *C*.

"Less than a minute now—filters down!—when I say 'fire,' grenadiers, take out your targets. God help you if you miss."

There was a sound like a giant's belch, and a stream of five or six iridescent bubbles floated up from the flower-shaped building. They rose with increasing speed until they were al- most out of sight, then shot off to the south, over our heads. The ground was suddenly bright, and for the first time in a long time, I saw my shadow, a long one pointed north. The bomb had gone off prematurely. I just had time to think that it didn't make too much difference; it'd still make alphabet soup out of their communications—

"Drones!" A ship came screaming in just above tree level, and a bubble was in the air to meet it. When they contacted, the bubble popped and the drone exploded into a million tiny fragments. Another one came from the opposite side and suffered the same fate.

"FIRE!" Seven bright glares of 500-microton grenades and a sustained concussion that surely would have killed an unprotected man.

"Filters up." Gray haze of smoke and dust. Clods of dirt falling with a sound like heavy raindrops.

"Listen up:

> *"Scots, wha hae wi' Wallace bled;*
> *Scots, wham Bruce has aften led,*
> *Welcome to your gory bed,*
> *Or to victory!"*

I hardly heard him for trying to keep track of what was going on in my skull. I knew it was just post-hypnotic suggestion, even remembered the session in Missouri when they'd implanted it, but that didn't make it any less compelling. My mind reeled under the strong pseudo-memories: shaggy hulks that were Taurans (not at all what we now knew they looked like) boarding a colonists' vessel, eating babies while mothers watched in screaming terror (the colonists never took babies; they wouldn't stand the acceleration), then raping the women to death with huge veined purple members (ridiculous that they would feel desire for humans), holding the men down while they plucked flesh from their living bodies and gobbled it (as if they could assimilate the alien protein) . . . a hundred grisly details as sharply remembered as the events of a minute ago, ridiculously overdone and logically absurd. But while my conscious mind was rejecting the silliness, somewhere much deeper, down in that sleeping animal where we keep our real motives and morals, something was thirsting for alien blood, secure in the conviction that the noblest thing a man could do would be to die killing one of those horrible monsters. . . .

I knew it was all purest soyashit, and I hated the men who had taken such obscene liberties with my mind, but I could even *hear* my teeth grinding, feel my cheeks frozen in a spastic grin, bloodlust . . . A teddybear walked in front of me, looking dazed. I started to raise my laser-finger, but somebody beat me to it and the creature's head exploded in a cloud of gray splinters and blood.

Lucky groaned, half-whining, "Dirty . . . filthy fucken bastards." Lasers flared and crisscrossed, and all of the teddybears fell dead.

"Watch it, goddammit," Cortez screamed. *"Aim* those fucken things—they aren't toys!

"Team *A,* move out—into the craters to cover *B."*

Somebody was laughing and sobbing. "What the fuck is wrong with *you,* Petrov?" Strange to hear Cortez cussing.

I twisted around and saw Petrov, behind and to my left, lying in a shallow hole, digging frantically with both hands, crying and gurgling.

"Fuck," Cortez said. "Team *B!* Ten meters past the craters, get down in a line. Team *C*—into the craters with *A."*

I scrambled up and covered the hundred meters in twelve amplified strides. The craters were practically large enough to hide a scoutship, some ten meters in diameter. I jumped to the opposite side of the hole and landed next to a fellow named Chin. He didn't even look around when I landed, just kept scanning the base for signs of life.

"Team *A*—ten meters, past team *B,* down in line." Just as he finished, the building in front of us burped, and a salvo of the bubbles fanned out toward our lines. Most people saw it coming and got down, but Chin was just getting up to make his rush and stepped right into one.

It grazed the top of his helmet and disappeared with a faint pop. He took one step backwards and toppled over the edge of the crater, trailing an arc of blood and brains. Lifeless, spreadeagled, he slid halfway to the bottom, shoveling dirt into the perfectly symmetrical hole where the bubble had chewed indiscriminately through plastic, hair, skin, bone and brain.

"Everybody hold it. Platoon leaders, casualty report . . . check . . . check, check . . . check, check, check . . . check. We have three deaders. Wouldn't be *any* if you'd have kept low. So everybody grab dirt when you hear that thing go off. Team *A,* complete the rush."

They completed the maneuver without incident. "Okay. Team *C,* rush to where *B* . . . hold it! Down!"

Everybody was already hugging the ground. The bubbles slid by in a smooth arc about two meters off the ground. They went serenely over our heads and, except for one that made toothpicks out of a tree, disappeared in the distance.

"*B*, rush past *A* ten meters. *C*, take over *B*'s place. You *B* grenadiers, see if you can reach the Flower."

Two grenades tore up the ground thirty or forty meters from the structure. In a good imitation of panic, it started belching out a continuous stream of bubbles—still, none coming lower than two meters off the ground. We kept hunched down and continued to advance.

Suddenly, a seam appeared in the building and widened to the size of a large door. Taurans came swarming out.

"Grenadiers, hold your fire. *B* team, laser fire to the left and right—keep'm bunched up. *A* and *C*, rush down the center."

One Tauran died trying to run through a laser beam. The others stayed where they were.

In a suit, it's pretty awkward to run and keep your head down at the same time. You have to go from side to side, like a skater getting started; otherwise you'll be airborne. At least one person, somebody in *A* team, bounced too high and suffered the same fate as Chin.

I was feeling pretty fenced-in and trapped, with a wall of laser fire on each side and a low ceiling that meant death to touch. But in spite of myself, I felt happy, euphoric, finally getting the chance to kill some of those villainous baby-eaters. Knowing it was soyashit.

They weren't fighting back, except for the rather ineffective bubbles (obviously not designed as an antipersonnel weapon), and they didn't retreat back into the building, either. They milled around, about a hundred of them, and watched us get closer. A couple of grenades would caulk them all, but I guess Cortez was thinking about the prisoner.

"Okay, when I say 'go,' we're going to flank 'em. *B* team will hold fire. . . . Second and fourth platoons to the right, sixth and seventh to the left. *B* team will move forward in line to box them in.

"Go!" We peeled off to the left. As soon as the lasers stopped, the Taurans bolted, running in a group on a collision course with our flank.

"*A* team, down and fire! Don't shoot until you're sure of your aim—if you miss you might hit a friendly. And fer Chris' sake save me one!"

It was a horrifying sight, that herd of monsters bearing down on us. They were running in great leaps—the bubbles avoiding them—and they all looked like the one we saw earlier, riding the broomstick; naked except for an almost transparent sphere around their whole bodies, that moved along with them. The right flank started firing, picking off individuals in the rear of the pack.

Suddenly a laser flared through the Taurans from the other side, somebody missing his mark. There was a horrible scream, and I looked down the line to see someone—I think it was Perry—writhing on the ground, right hand over the smoldering stump of his left arm, seared off just below the elbow. Blood sprayed through his fingers, and the suit, its camouflage circuits scrambled, flickered black-white-jungle-desert-green-gray. I don't know how long I stared—long enough for the medic to run over and start giving aid—but when I looked up the Taurans were almost on top of me.

My first shot was wild and high, but it grazed the top of the leading Tauran's protective bubble. The bubble disappeared and the monster stumbled and fell to the ground, jerking spasmodically. Foam gushed out of his mouth-hole, first white, then streaked red. With one last jerk he became rigid and twisted backwards, almost to the shape of a horseshoe. His long scream, a high-pitched whistle, stopped just as his comrades trampled over him. I hated myself for smiling.

It was slaughter, even though our flank was outnumbered five to one. They kept coming without faltering, even when they had to climb over the drift of bodies and parts of bodies that piled up high, parallel to our flank. The ground between us was slick red with Tauran blood—all God's children got hemoglobin—and like the teddybears, their guts looked pretty much like guts to my untrained eye. My helmet reverberated with hysterical laughter while we slashed them to gory chunks, and I almost didn't hear Cortez:

"Hold your fire—I said HOLD IT, goddammit! *Catch* a couple of the bastards, they won't hurt you."

I stopped shooting and eventually so did everybody else. When the next Tauran jumped over the smoking pile of meat in front of me, I dove to try to tackle him around those spindly legs.

It was like hugging a big, slippery balloon. When I tried to drag him down, he popped out of my arms and kept running.

We managed to stop one of them by the simple expedient of piling half a dozen people on top of him. By that time the others had run through our line and were headed for the row of large cylindrical tanks that Cortez had said were probably for storage. A little door had opened in the base of each one.

"We've *got* our prisoner," Cortez shouted. *"Kill!"*

They were fifty meters away and running hard, difficult targets. Lasers slashed around them, bobbing high and low. One fell, sliced in two, but the others, about ten of them, kept going and were almost to the doors when the grenadiers started firing.

They were still loaded with 500-mike bombs, but a near miss wasn't enough—the concussion would just send them flying, unhurt in their bubbles.

"The buildings! Get the fucken buildings!" The grenadiers raised their aim and let fly, but the bombs only seemed to scorch the white outside of the structures until, by chance, one landed in a door. That split the building just as if it had a seam; the two halves popped away and a cloud of machinery flew into the air, accompanied by a huge pale flame that rolled up and disappeared in an instant. Then the others all concentrated on the doors, except for potshots at some of the Taurans, not so much to get them as to blow them away before they could get inside. They seemed awfully eager.

All this time, we were trying to get the Taurans with laser fire, while they weaved and bounced around trying to get into the structures. We moved in as close to them as we could without putting ourselves in danger from the grenade blasts, yet too far away for good aim.

Still, we were getting them one by one and managed to destroy four of the seven buildings. Then, when there were only two aliens left, a nearby grenade blast flung one of them to within a few meters of a door. He dove in and several grenadiers fired salvos after him, but they all fell short or detonated harmlessly on the side. Bombs were falling all around, making an awful racket, but the sound was suddenly drowned out by a great sigh, like a giant's intake of breath, and where the building had been was a thick cylindrical cloud of smoke, solid-looking, dwindling away into the stratosphere, straight as if laid down by a ruler. The other Tauran had been right at the base of the cylinder; I could see pieces of him flying. A second later, a shock wave hit us and I rolled helplessly, pin-wheeling, to smash into the pile of Tauran bodies and roll beyond.

I picked myself up and panicked for a second when I saw there was blood all over my suit—when I realized it was only alien blood, I relaxed but felt unclean.

"Catch the bastard! Catch him!" In the confusion, the Tauran had gotten free and was running for the grass. One platoon was chasing after him, losing ground, but then all of *B* team ran over and cut him off. I jogged over to join in the fun.

There were four people on top of him, and a ring around them of about fifty people, watching the struggle.

"Spread out, dammit! There might be a thousand more of them waiting to get us in one place." We dispersed, grumbling. By unspoken agreement we were all sure that there were no more live Taurans on the face of the planet.

Cortez was walking toward the prisoner while I backed away. Suddenly the four men collapsed in a pile on top of the creature. . . . Even from my distance I could see the foam spouting from his mouth-hole. His bubble had popped. Suicide.

"Damn!" Cortez was right there. "Get off that bastard." The four men got off and Cortez used his laser to slice the monster into a dozen quivering chunks. Heartwarming sight.

"That's all right, though, we'll find another one—everybody! Back in the arrowhead formation. Combat assault, on the Flower."

Well, we assaulted the Flower, which had evidently run out of ammunition (it was still belching, but no bubbles), and it was empty. We scurried up ramps and through corridors, fingers at the ready, like kids playing soldier. There was nobody home.

The same lack of response at the antenna installation, the "Salami," and twenty other major buildings, as well as the forty-four perimeter huts still intact. So we had "captured" dozens of buildings, mostly of incomprehensible purpose, but failed in our main mission, capturing a Tauran for the xenologists to experiment with. Oh well, they could have all the bits and pieces they'd ever want. That was something.

After we'd combed every last square centimeter of the base, a scoutship came in with the real exploration crew, the scientists. Cortez said, "All right, snap out of it," and the hypnotic compulsion fell away.

At first it was pretty grim. A lot of the people, like Lucky and Marygay, almost went crazy with the memories of bloody murder multiplied a hundred times. Cortez ordered everybody to take a sed-tab, two for the ones most upset. I took two without being specifically ordered to do so.

Because it *was* murder, unadorned butchery—once we had the antispacecraft weapon doped out, we hadn't been in any danger. The Taurans hadn't seemed to have any conception of person-to-person fighting. We had just herded them up and slaughtered them, the first encounter between mankind and another intelligent species. Maybe it was the second encounter, counting the teddybears. What might have happened if we had sat down and tried to communicate? But they got the same treatment.

I spent a long time after that telling myself over and over that it hadn't been *me* who so gleefully carved up those frightened, stampeding creatures. Back in the twentieth century, they had established to everybody's satisfaction that "I was just following orders" was an inadequate excuse for inhuman conduct . . . but what can you do when the orders come from deep down in that puppet master of the unconscious?

Worst of all was the feeling that perhaps my actions weren't all that inhuman. Ancestors only a few generations back would have done the same thing, even to their fellow men, without any hypnotic conditioning.

I was disgusted with the human race, disgusted with the army and horrified at the prospect of living with myself for another century or so. . . . Well, there was always brainwipe.

A ship with a lone Tauran survivor had escaped and had gotten away clean, the bulk of the planet shielding it from *Earth's Hope* while it dropped into Aleph's collapsar field. Escaped home, I guessed, wherever that was, to report what twenty men with hand-weapons could do to a hundred fleeing on foot, unarmed.

I suspected that the next time humans met Taurans in ground combat, we would be more evenly matched. And I was right.

AFTER THE WIZARDS
BECAME A POWER IN THE WORLD,
THEY DISCOVERED MANY THINGS...

"Thanks to the wizard of Drum," said the Brother, "we know where to find these boxes. The nearest is in the bottom of a green bottle in Prince Comedo's Castle Vaunting, in Estar. A monster protects the bottle from those who would acquire it. The box itself lies at the very bottom of the bottle and is Guarded."

"Guarded?"

"I don't know what is meant by that, and neither did the wizard of Drum. However, his Catalogue says it, emphatically, which means there's death waiting nearby."

"Charming," murmured Togura.

"What's that?" said the Brother.

"I said that would be a real challenge. Something I could get my teeth into."

"Yes—or something that could get its teeth into you!"

"Fiendishly clever...chockablock with magic, action, and probably the single cleverest use of magical devices I've come across in fantasy.... Cook maintains a mad stream of inventiveness; the fantastic people, places and things keep popping up without pause."
—*Isaac Asimov's Science Fiction Magazine* on this book and the Wizard War Chronicles

"Superior sword and sorcery...A stylish and horrific fantasy adventure awash with heroic derring-do and some of the most ingenious magic I've come across in many a moon."
—**Julian May, author of** *The Pliocene Exile* on *Wizard War*

ALSO BY HUGH COOK

WIZARD WAR CHRONICLES

Wizard War
The Hero's Return*

Published by
POPULAR LIBRARY   *forthcoming

THE QUESTING HERO

HUGH COOK

WIZARD WAR CHRONICLES II

Published in the United
Kingdom as part of *The
Wordsmiths and the Warguild*

POPULAR LIBRARY

An Imprint of Warner Books, Inc.

A Warner Communications Company

POPULAR LIBRARY EDITION

Copyright © 1987 by Hugh Cook
All rights reserved.

Published in the United Kingdom as part of
The Wordsmiths and the Warguild

Cover illustration by Don Maitz

Popular Library books are published by
Warner Books, Inc.
666 Fifth Avenue
New York, N.Y. 10103

 A Warner Communications Company

Printed in the United States of America

First Popular Library Printing: March, 1988

10 9 8 7 6 5 4 3 2 1

☆
CHAPTER
1

Sung was a land which was famous far and wide, simply because it was so often and so richly insulted. However, there was one visitor, more excitable than most, who developed a positive passion for criticising the place. Unfortunately, the pursuit of this hobby soon led him to take leave of the truth.

This unkind traveller once claimed that the king of Sung, the notable Skan Askander, was a derelict glutton with a monster for a son and a slug for a daughter. This was unkind to the daughter. While she was no great beauty, she was definitely not a slug. After all, slugs do not have arms and legs—and, besides, slugs do not grow to that size.

There was a grain of truth in the traveller's statement, in as much as the son was a regrettable young man. However, soon afterwards, the son was accidentally drowned when he made the mistake of falling into a swamp with his hands and feet tied together and a knife sticking out of his back.

This tragedy did not encourage the traveller to extend his sympathies to the family. Instead, he invented fresh accusations. This wayfarer, an ignorant tourist if ever there was one, claimed that the king had leprosy. This was false. The king merely had a well-developed case of boils.

The man with the evil mouth was guilty of a further malignant slander when he stated that King Skan Askander was a cannibal. This was untrue. While it must be admitted that the king once ate one of his wives, he did not do so intentionally; the whole disgraceful episode was the fault of the chef, who was a drunkard, and who was subsequently severely reprimanded.

Again, the traveller was in error when he claimed that the kingdom of Sung was badly governed. In fact, the kingdom was not governed at all. Indeed, even to imply that there was such a thing as the 'kingdom of Sung' was, to say the least, misleading.

The question of the governance, and, indeed, the very existence of the 'kingdom of Sung' is one that is worth pursuing in detail, before dealing with the traveller's other allegations.

It is true that there was a king, his name being Skan Askander, and that some of his ancestors had been absolute rulers of considerable power. It is also true that the king's chief swineherd, who doubled as royal cartographer, drew bold, confident maps proclaiming the borders of the realm. Furthermore, the king could pass laws, sign death warrants, issue currency, declare war or amuse himself by inventing new taxes. And what he could do, he did.

'We are a king who knows how to be king,' said the king.

And, certainly, anyone wishing to dispute his right to use the imperial 'we' would have had to contend with the fact that there was enough of him, in girth, bulk and substance, to provide the makings of four or five ordinary people, flesh, bones and all. He was an imposing figure; 'very imposing', one of his brides is alleged to have said, shortly before the accident in which she suffocated.

'We live in a palace,' said the king. 'Not in a tent like Khmar, the chief milkmaid of Tameran, or in a draughty pile of stones like Comedo of Estar.'

His remarks were, in due course, widely reported.

From Prince Comedo came the following tart rejoinder:

'Unlike yours, my floors are not made of milk-white marble. However, unlike yours, my floors are not knee-deep in pigshit.'

The Note from Comedo came promptly, for, pirates and sea monsters permitting, a few days by sea could take one from Estar to Sung. Receiving that Note, Skan Askander placed it by his commode, where it would be handy for future royal use.

Much later, and to his great surprise, he received a communication from the Lord Emperor Khmar, the undisputed master of most of the continent of Tameran. The fact that Sung had come to the attention of Khmar was, to say the least, ominous. Khmar had this to say:

'Your words have been reported. In due course, they will be remembered against you.'

The king of Sung, terrified, endured the sudden onset of an attack of diarrhoea which had nothing to do with the figs he had been eating. His latest bride, seeing his acute distress, made the most of her opportunity, and vigorously counselled him to commit suicide. Knowing Khmar's reputation, he was tempted—but finally, to her great disappointment, declined. Nevertheless, he lived in fear; he had no way of knowing that he was simply the victim of one of Khmar's little jokes.

In an effort to avert disaster, the king of Sung made the following law:

'Skan Askander, king of Sung, ruler of Ravlish East, emperor of the Lesser Teeth and of the Greater, rightful heir of Penvash and of Trest and of Estar, scourge of the Hauma Sea and lord of the Central Ocean, will and must and does with respect and piety thrice daily honour an image of the Lord Emperor Khmar, most noble and esteemed Overlord of All Lands and All Peoples for All Eternity.'

This law was obeyed, one of Khmar's far-flung coins serving as an image until a statue could be made.

Thus, thrice daily, Skan Askander bowed down to his idol, the graven image of the distant emperor of Tameran. Khmar, hearing this, sent him a present—a wine skin containing the death-blood of a traitor. The skin was many days in transit; the condition of the contents on arrival are better imagined than described. However, the king thanked Khmar for his gift, and sent him a side of bacon in return.

Skan Askander ordered the wine skin, bereft of contents, to be paraded in front of his household once a year, at a solemn ceremony at which all present were to take or affirm an oath of fealty to the distant emperor.

This was done.

So it is clear at least two of the king's laws were effective. Furthermore, obedient to his written commands, the sun rose in the east and set in the west; the moon waxed and waned; the tides rose and fell; the winds swept in from the open oceans and brought generous helpings of rain to his scrabble-rock kingdom.

Nevertheless, most of the laws passed by the king were widely flouted, or obeyed only by accident. He decreed that everyone should wash their clothes and their bodies at least once in every lunar month; scarcely one person in a thousand obeyed. He had more success with a law forbidding people to sleep by daylight, but no joy whatsoever with a ludicrous statue—he was drunk at the time he signed it into law—which endeavoured to compel people to obtain written permits from the state to authorise their births, deaths and marriages.

As for the king's wars, death warrants and taxes, these

were never fought, executed or raised; indeed, most of the king's putative subjects never heard of those wars, death warrants and taxes. In fact, many of them lived out their lives without hearing of the king.

For, if the unvarnished truth be told, the borders established with such exactitude by Skan Askander's part-time cartographer were, not to put too fine a point upon it, fatuous. In the continent of Argan, many leagues to the east of the king's palace and piggery, the lands of Trest and Estar had their own rulers, while Penvash was commanded by the Melski, green-skinned monsters who had defeated the king's ancestors in a disastrous war which had permanently undermined the credibilitty of the monarchy.

To the south, the islands of the Greater Teeth were under the sway of the Orfus pirates, those gentlemen occasionally known—but only to themselves—as the Honourable Associates of the Free Federation of High Sea Sailors. Skan Askander's claim to rule the Greater Teeth was spurious; even the fishermen and fisherwomen who inhabited the low-slung sandy islands of the Lesser Teeth defied him, for they lived independently, acknowledging no rulers whatsoever.

As for the eastern end of the Ravlish Lands, where the king had his home, most of it was effectively under the control of the barons who lorded it over huge country estates, or was supervised by self-governing towns which had persuaded the world to describe them as 'city states', though few had a population of more than two thousand talking heads.

To return to our unkind traveller, who so maligned the unfortunate land of Sung, it has now been demonstrated that there was no truth to his claim that the kingdom of Sung was badly governed. His statement was not just untrue but impossible, for, as there was in practice no such thing as 'the kingdom of Sung', the question of its governance did not arise.

The traveller, out of ignorance or malice, made another mistake when he claimed that the main amusements in the kingdom of Sung were scavenging gorse, drowning in peat bogs and playing at fumble in the smothering fog.

The non-existence of the kingdom in question has already been amply demonstrated, which in itself serves to prove the allegation false. Assuming that the traveller was speaking of that eastern part of the Ravish Lands commonly known as 'Sung' scarcely improves matters, for the statement would still be false both in its substance and its implications.

The traveller's accusation implies that Sung was a dull, foggy area dominated by gorse and peat bogs and inhabited by dull, provincial people at a loss for any reasonable form of entertainment.

Nothing could be further from the truth.

As a matter of fact, less than 7 per cent of the arable land was covered in gorse; in contrast, horse thistle, gripe and barbarian thorn accounted for 22 per cent between them, with another 12 per cent being dominated by snare, clox and blackberry. Overall, only 3 per cent of Sung was peat bog, a full 50 per cent being bleak-rock uplands, or trackless forests where ravening wolves would ravage the unwary, leaving the stripped skeletons to become bones of contention between bad-tempered porcupines and rabid foxes.

And to say that Sung was foggy! That was ridiculous. Foggy days were few and far between, there being only 10 days of fog a year, compared to 275 days of rain. Water is essential to life, so the inhabitants of Sung were particularly favoured and fortunate, for they were copiously supplied with this commodity, which was delivered free of charge or taxes.

Let it also be known that, contrary to the traveller's declaration, the amusements of the people were many. The principal pastimes were hunting, feuding, fighting and fornication. Drinking and gambling were also very popular. Certain hobbies, including fishing and rat-fighting, also had large followings, and, on occasion, the people found time for dancing, music and banqueting.

The inhabitants of Sung also had their own unique cultural heritage, the intricacies of which were seldom appreciated by outsiders; it included lively games such as 'Stone the Leper', and detailed religious rituals such as those laid down for strangling unwanted children and disposing of aged relatives.

Clearly, the unkind traveller whose comments have been the subject of this analysis did Sung a great wrong when he slandered it so unforgivably.

So who was he, and what were his motives?

The disgruntled tourist was none other than the renegade wizard of Drum, who lived on a high and barren island in the dangerous strait separating the continent of Argan from the Ravlish Lands. The wizard of Drum had passed through Sung frequently on his various peregrinations, and, for one reason or another, had never been very pleased with his reception.

Once, indeed, he almost became the victim of a game of 'Stone the Leper', which was unfortunate, as his incontinent reaction left fifty people dead and an entire village in smouldering ruins. It must be admitted, also, that the wizard of Drum was one of the victims of the Devaluation, which occurred shortly after he had been paid 5,268 punts for work he had done for the Wordsmiths and the Warguild. After that incident, he swore never again to have anything to do with Sung, or even to set foot in the place.

The Devaluation, which ruined many people, was the direct result of swine fever.

While the kingdom of Sung was at best a legal fiction, and the king of Sung little more than a handy butt for the jokes of most of his people, the currency issued by the king had for many years enjoyed great respect and stability.

King Skan Askander was passionately interested in pigs, which he bred on a large scale. The currency he issued was backed by pork, and consisted of elegant ceramic dials marked 'one rasher', 'five rashers' or 'fifty rashers', and of thin bronze disks which each declared that 'This Punt Will Be Redeemed By The Royal Exchequer For One Side Of Bacon'.

Then came the great swine fever epidemic of the year Askander 32. In the consequent and inevitable Devaluation, a punt became worth a single rasher of bacon, and the minor ceramic coins became worthless. Hence the wrath of the wizard of Drum, who, besides being rather partial to pork, had seven hungry dragons to feed.

While the wizard of Drum had nothing good to say of Sung, there was some good that could be said of it. There were no droughts and no deserts; the land was free from scorpions and crocodiles; nobody died of thirst and nobody of heatstroke; there were no forest fires, and there was virtually unlimited stone for building with.

Furthermore, despite the weakness of the king, the ferocity of the barons, the strictly parochial interest of the city states and the local penchant for feuding and fighting, the land was protected by a rough and ready form of law and order administered by the Warguild. The wizard of Drum once described the Warguild as a club for the promotion of amateur archery; while it is true that the Warguild held archery contests, with wine and women as the prizes, there was much more to it than that.

The Warguild was a league of the more aggressive barons who had made a mutual defence treaty to protect the realm. It had been formed thirty years previously, when the land had been plagued by bandits and warlords; having routed out those nuisances, the Warguild now occasionally exercised itself by undertaking mercenary forays, or by serving as guards with Galish convoys.

Many Galish convoys passed through Sung, as the main long-distance trading route, the Salt Road, ran through the land. Furthermore, convoys often wintered in Sung. The Galish found it attractive first and most importantly because the king was too weak to levy any residency taxes, and, second, because the local patois was a form of Galish, albeit much modified. Indeed, some generations previously, this land had been colonised by a number of Galish convoys at a time when war, plague and famine had made trading particularly difficult. The lifestyle of the inhabitants of Sung was now wildly different from that of the Galish traders, to put it mildly, but, when they spoke, they still found each other mutually intelligible.

If there had been any problems in mutual understanding, then the Wordsmiths, now busy perfecting their command of all known languages, could surely have translated. The Wordsmiths, an organisation slightly older than the Warguild, had formed their alliance shortly after the discovery of the odex, which, in the year Askander 35—three years after the Devaluation—was held in the Wordsmiths' stronghold in a city state in the mountains, a town known as Keep, which boasted a population of a full 5,000 souls.

Not far from Keep was the estate of Baron Chan Poulaan, who, on a certain night in the season of autumn, was keeping a close eye on his son Togura, who was dancing with the girl Day Suet. Now the Suets were a family from Keep, a powerful banking and trading family which actively supported the Wordsmiths. Baron Chan Poulaan, head of the Warguild, considered himself to be, in some respects, de facto ruler of Sung; he was suspicious of traders, bankers and of the Wordsmiths, and saw the family

Suet in particular as a potential rival for influence and power.

At this stage, it is worth noting that the palace of King Skan Askander lay close to the city state of Keep. The Suets were, therefore, in a good position to make a grab for any residual powers commanded by the royal family. It was said that one of the boys of the Suet family was bravely romancing the king's daughter, Slerma, who, at sweet sixteen, was alleged to weigh in at sixty bushels.

Baron Chan Poulaan had already determined that his son Togura would marry the king's daughter. He had come to a private agreement with Skan Askander, and had already informed Togura that he would soon be betrothed to Slerma.

Watching Togura and Day, Baron Poulaan noted how closely they held each other when the dance came to a clinch, and frowned.

CHAPTER
2

The banquet was in full swing. Buoyant with drink and excitement, Day and Togura danced to the skirl of the skavamareen. In the clinch, he brushed against her soft breasts, which flushed out against her light woollen chemise. Her sly little fingers dared his hard-fleshed buttocks, then stopped because:

'Your father's watching us.'

'I love you,' said Togura.

'No, really, he's watching us,' said Day. 'He doesn't look happy.'

'Kiss me. Kiss me quick!'

'Not here!'

As the music ended, she pulled away from him. He pursued her through the crowded hall. He chased her out through the main doors, and then, giggling, she allowed him to catch her.

They kissed.

Her mouth was warm and yielding. His embrace savoured the curves of her back and her buttocks. Moths danced around the doorway lanterns. The night was cool but he was hot, his lust shafting hard within his trews. He smelt her hair, her skin, her perfume.

He burped.

'Really!' said Day, breaking away.

She poked him in the belly, provoking another burp. She poked him again, teasing him with cunning jabs which he was helpless to resist. As he flinched, she giggled.

Then kissed him.

Seriously.

'Your father was watching us,' said Day, breaking the kiss. 'He wasn't happy at all.'

'He can shunk his cho and scavenge it,' said Togura, using the local gutter argot.

'Togura Poulaan!' said Day severely.

From inside the banqueting hall came a rowdy burst of laughter which rose above the general hubbub. What had so amused the banquet guests? Togura, knowing his people well, guessed that probably someone had been debagged, or that a helpless drunk had vomited over someone of high importance.

The laughter died down and the music started up again. A drone joined the wail of the skavamareen while a sklunk backthumped and a chanter whined.

'My lady,' said Togura, with a formal bow. 'Shall we dance?'

'Talatashee,' she said, assenting.

They danced the vigorous kola-ka-skee, kicking their heels and whirling on the changes, inventing partners for the passages known as romance and the flora—for the kola-ka-skee, of course, is for a foursome.

While they were dancing, an old man tottered into the lamplight. They danced on, until, disturbed by his silent scrutiny, they broke apart and turned to face him. He was a tattered vagrant with a ravaged face and a dirty grey beard.

'It is night,' said the old man in a thin, querulous voice.

'No,' said Day smartly. 'It's day.'

'Do you mean to make fun of me, little smut?' said the old man.

'Talatashee' said Day.

'Tala-shee? Now what's that, young lady? Yes or no?'

He was clearly a foreigner.

'Who are you, old man?' said Togura.

The old man leaning on his shepherd's crook, was about to answer when the music escalated to a stormburst crescendo. A thrum began to gallop, a kloo honked harshly, a krymbol crashed and scattered, a skittling nook began to campaign against the skavamareen and a plea whistle hooted.

'What,' said the old man, 'is that appalling noise?'

'Music,' said Day. 'Don't you like it?'

The old man sniffed.

'The miscreants perpetrating that dismal cacophony should be fed to the dragon pits,' he said.

Togura could not figure him out. His manner was bold, and had, indeed, a hint of lordliness about it. Yet he was clearly a tramp of one kind or another. He was wearing a roughwork patchwork skirt, which finished above his knees, and a battered short-cut weather cloak of the type favoured by fishermen. His boots were coming apart at the toes, exposing his feet.

'What are you doing on my father's estate, old man?' said Togura.

'Child, I had the misfortune to be shipwrecked here,' replied the ancient.

'Shipwrecked!' said Togura.

Day giggled.

'Don't laugh, gamos,' said the old man, naming Day with the Galish word for a female horse, which was unpardonably vulgar.

'Why you—'

'No, Tog,' said Day, holding him back.

'Did you hear what he called you?' said Togura, burning with anger.

'She heard me, boy,' said the old man, in his stilted, strangely accented Galish, so unlike the smooth-flowing local patios. 'How about some hospitality for a shipwrecked mariner now?'

'If you find yourself afloat, then hard liquor's to answer, not the sea,' said Togura. 'In case you didn't notice before you started drinking yourself silly, you're up in the mountains, not down by the coast.'

'I know that,' said the old man steadily. 'Now have a little pity on poor old Pitilkin and show him a bed for the night. I've sailed from Chi' ash-lan, and that's a hearty journey my boy. Chi' ash-lan to Quartermain, that's a fair old step.'

'You're not in Quartermain,' said Togura. 'You're in Sung.'

'Ah!' said the old man, eyes bright with revelation. 'That explains everything. The barbarities inflicted on the human ear in the name of music. The provincial manners of the local peasants. The—'

'Are you calling me—'

'Tog,' said Day. 'Don't argue, you're only encouraging him. He's a poor harmless old man. Why not have the servants show him to a garrow for the night? Alternatively—'

At that moment a rowdy party came barrelling out of the banquet hall—seven or eight reeling drunks laughing and jostling as they staggered out into the fresh night air. Amongst them was Cromarty, Togura's hefty half-brother, who was three years his senior.

'Why, hey!' said Cromarty. 'It's Spunk Togura and little girl Day. Hitting the eiderdown tonight, chids? Getting

in some of the old kerna tamerna?' His cronies guffawed
and ribbed each other. Then Cromarty saw the stranger.
'This is new, boys, hey hey? What ho! I say, grandad, past
your bedtime, isn't it? Shall we put him to bed, boys? Hey
what?'

'You can help me fix my ship if you would,' said the
ancient mariner. 'If not, I'll do it by daylight once I've
slept.'

'A ship, hey. A ship? Boys, this we have to see. Snaffle
the lantern, Lanks. Nids, you salvage the other.' On Cromarty's orders, the two lanterns guarding the banqueting
hall's entrance were snaffled and salvaged. 'Come along,
grandad,' said Cromarty. 'Show us your ship. Coming for a
sail, Day? Come along now!'

Cromarty's bounders seized her.

'Let her go!' said Togura.

He waded into them, flailing wildly, but he was grossly
outnumbered. The scungers grabbed him, and he was frog-
marched into the night. As they swaggered along with lanterns swinging wildly, the drunks roared out the Kanover
drinking song.

'Where now, grandad?' said Cromarty.

'This way,' said the ancient mariner. 'This way!'

Gaining a small knoll, the drunks dropped Togura face-
first into the long rough grass. This, of course, was dew-
damp, and appeared to contain more than the usual quota
of gorse.

'What ho!' said Cromarty. 'The ship, hey?'

Getting to his feet, Togura saw, by lantern-light, a clutter
of sticks which looked like a gargantuan parody of a crow's
nest. Cromarty hefted one of the heavier sticks.

'Careful with that, boy,' said he old man sharply. 'That's
the rudder.'

'Rudder, hey? Then this is the jakes, suppose, suppose.'

And Cromarty hauling out his penis, began to piss on the sticks. The old man swiped at his buttocks with his shepherd's crook. Cromarty, startled, lost control of his shlong, and pissed all over his pants.

'You klech!' shouted Cromarty, tucking away his shmuck. 'You ornskwun vig of a hellock!'

And he gave the old man a push, sending him reeling back into one of the drunks, who dropped the lantern he was holding. It smashed, leaving them with a single light.

'That's enough, Cromarty!' said Togura. 'You're disgracing the estate!'

'Why so,' said Cromarty softly. 'Our little Spunk Togura is riding the angers, hey? All up and on about the precious estate. It's my estate, little boy! I'm the one who inherits.'

'Then behave yourself until you do,' said Togura manfully. 'Now pack your rabble out of here. Go!'

'Not so swell, my hearty,' said Cromarty, unshipping a knife. 'Not so swell.'

Togura was unarmed. He grabbed for a stick, but one of Cromarty's scungers stepped on it.

'Cut him good, Crom!' said one.

'I will,' said Cromarty, his face turning ugly. 'Oh, certain, certain. It's ribbons for little Togura!'

'No fighting, children,' said the old man, trying to intervene. 'Pitilkin doesn't like fighting.'

'Stand aside, grandad,' said Cromarty, giving him a hearty push.

'Kill him, Crom!' yelled an eager admirer.

'I will,' said Cromarty. 'For sure.'

And he moved in on the attack. He slashed at Togura, who leapt backwards. Cromarty advanced. He was good with a blade. Even when drunk, he was good.

'Stop this!' screamed Day.

She tried to intervene, but was restrained. Cromarty's mobsters had their blood up. They were shouting:

'Into him, Crom!'

'Scallop him!'

'Finish him!'

Suddenly the old man swung his shepherd's crook. The stout wooden shaft smashed Cromarty's wrist. Quick as a flash, the old man demolished the surviving lantern. There were shouts, roars and cries of pain in the darkness. Togura hit the dirt and stayed down. Someone trampled over him, fleeing for shelter. He heard the vicious whistle of the old man's stick slicing through the air.

Then it was all over. Cromarty and his friends had fled. They could be heard swearing in the darkness; then, as their cries diminished in the distance, Togura became aware that music was still playing in the banquet hall. While he was in danger of getting sliced and diced, his father's guests had been amusing themselves all unawares of the drama taking place out in the night.

'Tog!' called Day, loudly, almost directly overhead.

'Here,' said Togura, feeling for her in the darkness as he tried to get to his feet.

His blundering hand slid straight up her dress to the warmest part of her flesh. She screamed. He jerked his hand away as if it had been burnt.

'Tog,' said Day uncertainly. 'Was that you?'

'Me,' admitted Togura, blushing in the darkness.

'What the feck and fuckle did you think it was, girl?' said the ancient mariner. 'An octopus? Come on, children, pull yourselves together.'

They did not answer, for they were now embracing.

'Tog, oh Tog,' said Day, holding him close and tight. 'I was so worried. Are you all right?'

'Fine,' said Togura. 'If only I had a blade! I would've cut him from spleen to kidney. I would've—'.

'Leave your heroics till later,' said he old man sharply. 'If we can't work on the boat tonight, I want to get to sleep. Where's my bed for the night?'

'You've got a nerve!' said Togura, who bitterly resented the fact that it was this querulous old madman who had just saved his life or his beauty, or maybe both.

'Come on,' said Day. 'Don't be nasty. I'm sure we can find him a place to stay for the night.'

'Oh, all right then,' said Togura. 'Let's go.'

They went back to the banquet hall, where they met Quail the rouster. He was bearing a lighted candle, which he was trying to shield with his hand. As they drew near, he recognised them.

'Master Togura!' said Quail. 'Have you seen the doorway lanterns by any chance?'

'Why, has someone lifted them?' said Togura.

'Yes. Some of your young friends, perhaps? That little sod Cromarty was on the muck tonight.'

'Is that so?' said Togura. 'Well, a couple of lanterns isn't the end of the world. Tell me, man Quail, can you bed down this gentleman for the night?'

Quail peered at their ancient mariner.

'Are you sure we want to house this individual, Master Togura?'

'Pitilkin sleeps quietly,' said the old man, his voice quavering. 'No trouble, no trouble.'

'Just for the night,' said Togura.

'It won't do any harm,' said Day.

'Well . . . just for the night then,' said Quail, doubtfully. 'There's probably a spare garrow at the backstop, if the incest twins haven't bedded themselves down for the night. Otherwise, I'm afraid, it'll be the stable.'

'Thanks,' said Togura, turning to go.

'Oh, and Master Togura—if you see Cromarty and his spry young brags, ask them about the lanterns, will you?'

'We will,' said Day. 'Thanks for everything.'

Togura took her hand, and they walked off into the night together. His hopes were high, but they were soon to be disappointed: he did not lose his virginity that night.

CHAPTER 3

'I don't suppose you know how your brother damaged his wrist,' said Baron Chan Poulaan.

'I don't keep track of his business,' said his son Togura.

The baron harrumphed, but did not press the point.

The two were riding side by side. They were on a road, or what passed for a road in those parts, which led to the city state of Keep. The baron was riding a brindled mare and his son was riding a donkey. Following on behind, riding Kloggles the Mule—and it took a brave man or a foolish man to venture that—was Prick, the baron's venerable secretary.

'The fog seems to be closing in,' said Togura, looking around.

'I'd noticed that,' said his father.

'Perhaps we should stop till it clears.'

'We might be here all day,' said his father. 'We'll go on.'

And they did.

Visibility swiftly became zero. The road abruptly became peat bog. After floundering around in the mist for a while, they staggered out of the bog, hauling their animals along with them, only to find themselves waist-deep in flourishing gorse. The baron cursed and struck out with his sword, accidently clouting Prick with the flat of the blade.

Fortunately, it then began to rain, causing the fog to dissipate swiftly. Unfortunately, they found themselves on a small gorse-covered island surrounded by peat bog.

'There's the road!' said Togura, pointing to an indeterminate ribbon of mud and stones lying some distance from the island.

'Your powers of observation astound me,' said the baron grimly, leading the way back into the bog.

Kloggles the Mule was most reluctant to leave their little island, but, after a savage battle with no holds barred, they forced him back through the bog to the road. By this time, they were mud from ankle to shoulder. Fortunately, the rain was rapidly becoming a solid downpour, suggesting that they might be able to strip off their dirty clothes, take a shower in the rain then change into clean clothes. Unfortunately, they had no clean clothes to change into.

'I think,' said Togura, 'That perhaps this is not the best of days on which to go and visit the king.'

'You are young, my son,' said his father, 'But not entirely devoid of wisdom. Come, let us make for home.'

And they retreated back down the road, which was rapidly becoming a quagmire.

The next day, in fine clear weather, they set out again. The road was muddy, but they reached the outskirts of Keep in good order. It was then that they encountered what appeared to be a free-floating monster.

In some places, this apparition might have been taken for a ghost, a hallucination or a trick of the light, but this was Sung, and they knew the intruder for what it was—an ilps.

The ilps was very large.

It had seventy-nine teeth, shared between two mouths of generous dimensions.

Five of the teeth were poisoned.

It stank of rotten oranges.

Its fingertips smoked with blue light.

'Who are you?' said Baron Chan Poulaan, speaking roughly.

'Ska,' said the ilps.

'Where do you come from?'

'Ska. Nanesh stel.'

It was fading rapidly.

'Where were you born?'

One of its mouths collapsed.

The baron assaulted the ilps with harsh, insistent questions. Disintegrating under the attack, it started to retreat. But he followed, urging his horse forward, asking one question after another. Finally, battered to death by his verbal assault, it broke apart into a dozen rainbows, which scattered into discordant chords of music.

Nothing remained but the smell of rotten oranges.

'That was a large one,' said Prick.

'They get larger all the time,' said the baron. 'And more numerous. Unless someone brings the Wordsmiths to heel, we'll have a regular disaster on our hands.'

The Wordsmiths claimed that their precious odex held all the knowledge of all the ancient long-lost civilisations which had existed before the Days of Wrath. They claimed to be learning how to control and manipulate the odex, but all they had produced so far was a string of distorted monsters.

Baron Poulaan could reasonably claim to be the most powerful man in Sung, but that meant little; as yet, he lacked the power to challenge the Wordsmiths, for his fellow barons were not yet convinced that the odex was a bad thing.

Brooding about the ilps, the odex and the Wordsmiths, the baron led the way into Keep, passing between mountainous slag heaps. They passed a few houses then a mine shaft. A fire was burning by the shaft, helping to draw stale air up from the depths and keep the miners alive. A creaking bucket lift was bringing up gemstock ore from the veins which ran far underground.

'Dismount,' said Baron Poulaan.

They went by foot thereafter, leading their mounts through the tilted, canting streets. After five generations of mining, which had hollowed out a considerable portion of the rock beneath the town, the whole urban area was very slowly subsiding. Hence the odd angles of the streets, which were buckling and twisting, and the nightmarish angles of the shops and houses.

After a slow and dangerous journey, they reached the far side of Keep and set off for the palace of King Skan Askander, scourge of the Hauma Sea and lord of the Central Ocean. They had gone through the town rather than around it because Baldskull Mountain lay on one side and Dead Man's Drop on the other.

Once out of town, they mounted up again, but soon had to climb down to lead their animals past a massive subsidence in the road, which was only slowly being filled in with slag.

'That's new since I was here last,' said Baron Poulaan. 'And that was scarcely a month ago.'

One day, he expected to come this way and find that the entire town of Keep had fallen into a hole. He would not be unhappy when it did. After all, his estate never saw a single flog or splorin's worth of the town's mining profits. He had no love for the earthgrubbing miners, or for the merchants who fattened on the profits of the trade in opal, topaz, jade, japonica, russsellite, kolzaw, fuze, buff, celestine and carnelian which the miners recovered from the gemstock.

'My lord!' said Prick, pointing. 'Ahead! The palace!'

'I saw it some time ago,' said the baron.

Togura, who had never been this way before, looked for the building of white marble which so many people had spoken of, but could not see it for the fences, sheds, huts and granubles of the surrounding piggeries.

Shortly afterwards, they were shown into the presence of the king, who invited them to dine with him.

'We will be having swedes, rutabaga and the kidneys of several pigs,' he said.

'We will be honoured,' said Baron Poulaan.

'And, dear baron,' said King Skan Askander, 'my darling daughter will be dining with us, so your son will have a chance to meet his future bride.'

Togura nerved himself for this ordeal. But he was confident that it could not be as bad as people had led him to believe. After all, Slerma was only sixteen years old; there was scarcely time for her to have grown to the monstrous size which she was alleged to have attained. She was probably just a little fat and sludgy. Well, he could endure that —he thought. It would mean that he would one day inherit the palace and the piggery, which would be a valuable asset once it had fully recovered from the effects of the swine fever which had caused the Devaluation.

If Slerma was no great beauty, she would doubtless welcome the attentions of a real man like himself. She would at least be a real woman, hot and wet in the right places. She would complete his sentimental education and initiate him into manhood.

They were shown into the dining room. The king seated himself on a couch, which creaked ominously beneath his weight. Then he snapped his fingers, and a young woman entered. Togura's face fell. This was Slerma? She was worse than he had expected. She was more than plump: she was positively bloated.

'My wife,' said the king.

And the young woman bowed to them.

Togura was relieved.

'Where is Slerma, dear?' said the king.

'She's just coming now, my lord,' said his wife.

'Ah, there you are!' said the king. 'Hello, Slerma. Meet our new guests.'

As he was speaking, a vast and slovenly giantess was in the process of forcing her way into the room. She was huge. She was gross. She was impossible. Togura wanted to scream and run, but found himself paralysed by fear.

'Is this it?' she said in a thick, slurred voice, eyeing him with disapproval.

'Yes, my dear,' said the king happily.

'There's not much to it,' said Slerma, laying one prodigious paw on Togura's shoulder.

She squeezed. He felt as if he was being crunched by a vast nut cracker. Then, just before she did permanent damage to flesh and bone, she released the pressure.

'There's no meat on it,' she complained. 'I want Guta.'

'No!' said her father sharply. 'You cannot marry the baker's boy. I forbid it.'

'He's a real man,' said Slerma. 'Not like this—this thing. Do you speak, thing?'

'I am articulate, intelligent and proud of it,' said Togura, finding his voice at last.

'What does articulate mean?' said Slerma.

'It means,' said the king, 'that all his working parts are in good order.'

'They'd better be in good order, thing,' said Slerma, addressing Togura. 'I'm a girl with big appetites. Remember that! Once we're married, you'd better be faithful, too. Or I'll kill you.'

'Now dear,' said her father mildly. 'Don't frighten him. He's a good little boy. I'm sure he'll behave himself.'

'Far too little!' said Slerma. 'Not like Guta.'

'I'm sure you can fatten him up,' said the king. 'In fact, now is a good a time as any to start.'

He clapped his hands, and their meal was brought in. There were two or three plates apiece for Togura, the baron and Prick, a number of heavy platters for the king and his wife, and a large trough for Slerma.

Togura found his appetite had failed him.

'Eat!' ordered Slerma, filling the room with the ominous rumble of her thick, slurred voice. 'Eat! Food is good for you!'

And she set an example, gouging out huge handfuls of swede, rutabaga and kidney, slapping them into her mouth then swallowing, apparently without chewing. Togura tried to see if her teeth were missing, but failed. It was impossible even to tell whether her vast, wallowing face had a jawbone. Seasick folds of flesh swayed, buckled and lurched as she ate. Technically, some of that flesh must have belonged to her cheeks and some to her chin, but such distinctions vanished in the awesome slurry of fat which constituted her face.

'You're not eating!' she bellowed.

She seized Togura and plastered his face with kidney. Some went up his nose, some squeezed its way into his mouth and some fell into his lap.

'Eat!' she yelled, hurting his ears.

She gave him a shake. If she used any more force, she was going to dislocate bones. Togura tried to wriggle free, but it was impossible.

'Eat, thing!' hissed Slerma, spraying him with spittle.

To his dismay, he began to weep, crying with hot tears of agony and shame. Slerma gave him another shake then tossed him to one side.

'Your son insults us,' said King Skan Askander, his voice going very cold.

'Togura!' shouted Baron Poulaan. 'Pull yourself together!'

His son got to his knees.

'I hate you!' he said, clenching his fists. He sniffed.

Then he took another look at Slerma, and suddenly vomited.

Then he fled.

★

CHAPTER
4

Towards the end of the day, Baron Chan Poulaan finally managed to locate his son Togura, who had taken refuge in the Murken Hotel. This building, the victim of a subsidence, looked just about ready to fall over. Outside, huge timbers shored up the walls. Inside, the place was a maze of props and cross-struts. As the baron entered, the building was alive with hammering; it had taken an alarming lurch sideways that afternoon, and emergency reinforcements were now being put into place.

The proprietor, a foul-smelling hunchbacked dwarf with a huge goitre, directed the baron to Togura's room.

'Take me there,' said the baron.

The dwarf flattened his nose against the back of his hand, which, in those parts, was an emphatic gesture of refusal.

'I don't venture upstairs,' said the dwarf.

The baron saw the wisdom of that as soon as he started up the rickety stairs, which creaked and groaned beneath his feet, imploring him for mercy. Reaching Togura's door, he hammered against it with both fists. A slow dust of powdered dry rot began to sift down from the beams above; alarmed, the baron stopped hammering.

'Togura!' he yelled. 'I know you're in there.'

Silence from within.

The baron threw his shoulder against the door. The floor shook, the stairs creaked alarmingly, but the door held.

'Come out, boy,' shouted the baron.

From within, a muffled voice responded:

'Go away!'

'Open the door, so we can talk.'

Silence replied.

'Come on, open the door!'

There was a pause, then confused sounds from within. Then the door was opened a crack. The baron, with a roar, threw his weight against it. A crossbeam overhead ruptured, showering him with sawdust. But the door still refused to admit him.

'What have you done to the door?' demanded the baron.

Togura replied, but the baron, sneezing vigorously because of the sawdust in his nose, failed to hear.

'What was that?' he said.

'You heard me,' said Togura.

'I suppose you've wedged the door with a baulk of timber.'

'That's what I said.'

'You're not going to cry again, are you?' sneered the baron, hearing the distress in his son's voice.

'Go away,' said Togura.

'I will not go away,' said his father. 'You will open the door, quit this place and come home with me. Then, once we've had a little talk together, we'll go back to the palace. To see Slerma.'

'No!' howled Togura. 'No, no, not that. I'd rather die.'

'Stop being melodramatic,' said the baron impatiently. 'I can't see what you're making all this fuss about. When all's said and done, she's a healthy young girl with a moderately wealthy father.'

'She's obscene.'

'Many men like their women a little plump. After all, you've got to have something to hold onto once you get in the saddle.'

'A little plump! Paps, that woman's a horse, a cow and a whale all rolled into one. She's—"

'Don't call me paps,' snapped the baron, who hated hearing that kind of tiny-tot talk from his son. 'It's time to grow up, Togura. Be a man. You're not going to kill yourself, so you'll just have to live with the life you've got.'

'Yes, I want to live. That man-eater would kill me. I—'

'Stop that! Togura, face facts. You're not going to inherit. Cromarty gets the estate. If you marry, you get the king's title and his property once he dies. He's an old man, he can't last much longer.'

'Neither will I if I—'

'Enough! Listen! Soon, Togura, this wretched town of Keep is going to fall into the ground or slide into Dead Man's Drop. The king's property will be more valuable than ever then. Anyone wanting to mine the gemstock will have to—'.

'I won't sell myself for money,' shouted Togura. 'I want to marry a woman, not a walking slime pit.'

'You don't have much option,' said the baron.

'If I have to, I'll go down to the coast and sell myself to the first slaver passing through. I'd rather—'

'This nonsense has gone far enough,' said the baron, cutting him off. 'Open this door properly and come out. We're going home. Now!'

'No.'

'No?'

'No!'

'No!!??'

'No!!!!'

'By the sperm of my ancestors,' raged the baron, using the most fearsome oath he knew. 'You'll come out of there right now or suffer the immediate and unlimited consequences. No son of mine is going to defy his father like that.'

'Push off, paps,' said Togura, all defiance.

The baron then assaulted the door vigorously. A chunk of rotten wood fell from the ceiling, and one of the risers of the stairway split open, but the door itself was solid, and held. Finally, cursing and muttering, spitting sawdust and swearing ferociously, the baron retreated downstairs. He took rooms for himself and for Prick, paying the ground floor premium; they would spend the night there, and deal with Togura in the morning.

Togura, alone and lonely in his room, barred the door then cried himself to sleep. The bed on which he slept was a huge, solid and incredibly ancient affair made of stout timbers standing waist-high off the floor; as he slept, he was a small crumpled island of misery in an ocean of dirty linen. Bed bugs, oblivious of his emotional agony, feasted merrily on his helpless flesh.

Sleeping, Togura dreamt that he was in a castle which was under siege. Invaders were attacking the main gate with a battering ram. The sullen thud and thump of the assault began to undermine his composure. The ram charged again, hitting the door with a crash so loud that it woke him up.

Togura, starting from sleep and blinking at darkness, stared in the direction of the door. Someone was demolishing it. With a final crash, the door splintered and gave way. A faintly aromatic smell of ancient timbers percolated through the room. Outside, on the stairway, some large animal was breathing heavily with a kind of wet, guttural wheezing.

'Paps?' said Togura uncertainly.

'Prepare yourself, little man,' said the animal, in a thick slurred voice.

'Slerma!' screamed Togura.

The animal outside made strenuous efforts to enter, but failed. The doorway was too small.

'Slerma,' said Togura, in a shaky voice. 'I'll do anything you say. Just don't hurt me, that's all. I love you.'

He was answered by a scream of rage.

'Love? Love! Little man, I'll kill you! Guta will kill you. How dare you make love to his Slerma?'

Too late, Togura realised his fatal mistake.

'No, Guta!' cried Togura. 'I didn't mean it. I don't want Slerma. I don't want anything to do with her.'

'Liar! You were seen. Their serving girl told me. You were seen. Embracing! Deep in her charms, her arms enfolding you. She fed you with her own magnificent hand.'

'Guta, I really don't want her. She's appalling. She's hideous. She's a mess of flab and sausage meat. She makes me sick, she—'

'You insult my darling. My true love. My fondest dream. The one and only real woman in the world. Animal! I'm going to kill you!'

The building shook, timbers groaned, the roof strained, and Guta forced himself into Togura's room. As darkness crashed toward him, roaring, Togura rolled out of bed and took cover underneath the bed. Guta, finding the bed in the night, hoisted himself aboard and began to trample it with his knees. He roared out incomprehensible obscenities as he sought for his victim.

Frustrated at finding nothing, Guta tore the sheets apart. Then he grabbed hold of the mattress and ripped it open, spilling mouldy old straw and bracken into the night, together with bedbugs, lice, dead spiders and a virile colony of the kind of red ants that bite. Then he began to jump on the bed.

Just before the bed splintered and gave way, Togura rolled out from underneath and sprinted for the doorway. He tripped, fell, recovered himself, barked his shins against something, cracked his head against a low-lying beam, then gained safety. At least for the moment. Where now? Up, down? Togura ascended, pounding up the stairs, thinking the fearsome young troll behind him would not dare to attempt the increasingly fragile heights of the Murken Hotel.

He was wrong.

Hauling himself back out through the doorway, Guta started up the stairs after Togura. He began to gain on him. Togura strove for extra speed. But Guta was fast and ferocious. He grabbed hold of Togura's foot. Togura screamed. The stairs collapsed. Guta roared. Screaming and roaring, the two plunged downward to their doom. Guta landed first, smashing his head open and breaking his back, which killed him. Togura landed on top of the corpse of his recently deceased rival. A shower of rotten wood rained down on the two of them.

Togura became aware of doors opening. There was a muttering of voices in the darkness. Then the proprietor came on the scene. The hunchbacked dwarf was bearing a candle, an evil-smelling stump of black wax which burnt with a greenish-blue light, filling the air with smoke and shadows. The dwarf was doing his best to restrain a huge rat which he had on a short leash. It was the size of a mastiff, had blood-red eyes and razor-sharp teeth, and was slavering as it strained against the leash, which was attached to a collar ringed with spikes of sharpened metal.

The dwarf surveyed the damage.

Then he kicked Guta in the head.

'Leave,' said the dwarf.

The dwarf knew that Guta was a valuable catch. The city state of Pera Pesh, a fishing town of some one thousand people down by the coast, had put a price on his head. He was wanted, dead or alive, for a variety of crimes including grave robbing, necrophilia, the theft of a small whale and the destruction of a small stone bridge which he had incautiously walked across. The reward would more than compensate for the cost of repairs.

'I'm going right now,' said Togura, with what fraction of his voice he had so far been able to recover.

'Togura,' said a loud voice from one of the darkened doorways. 'You come here this instant.'

It was his father, the formidable baron.

Togura got to his feet, and fled.

☆
CHAPTER
5

Togura found refuge in a fire watcher's hut by a mine shaft. It gave him at least a modicum of shelter against the cold autumn weather. Exhausted, he slept. He woke, once, to find something gnawing at his boots. He kicked it away. Hissing and spluttering it retreated; after that, he found it hard to get back to sleep again.

At dawn, a fire watcher arrived, a big, gruff man with a red beard and bloodshot eyes, and big dirty boots, one of which had marked Togura's backside by the time he made his escape. Outside, a light drizzle was falling. Miners, with pick axes and shovels slung over their shoulders, were trooping to the climbing shafts.

Shivering, Togura wandered off, wonderering what to do now. He had already considered turning to Day Suet for help, and had rejected the notion; he was too proud to beg, and, in any case, doubted that her family would welcome him if he came as a beggar.

The streets of Keep were dangerous, as always, for housewives were going through the morning routine of emptying chamber pots out of the window. Ducking and dodging, Togura escaped with no more than a few stray licks of splatter. His zigzag course through the drunken streets brought him to the very brink of Dead Man's Drop.

Togura stood on the Edge, looking out at the dim grey horizon now soured by stormclouds. The ground dropped away sheer to the pinnacles of the Claws which would receive his body if he jumped, fell or was pushed. Between the Claws and the enclosing horizon lay the leagues of the Famines, a regular wasteland of scoured rock and eroding hillsides speckled with colonies of gorse, clox, snare and barbarian thorn. Down in the hollows there was the occasional glint of lake or slough.

Far below Togura's feet, some nimble birds darted through the dull-weather sky. They, at least, had homes to go to, and regular occupations to follow.

Overcome by a sudden access of self-pity, Togura considered throwing himself over, but decided against it. The pleasures of self-pity were, for the moment, far too sweet. Besides, he still had some money left. It would be foolish to suicide before spending all his cash.

Turning away from Dead Man's Drop, Togura walked down the street. He had only just departed when the piece of stone had had been standing on fell away, almost soundlessly, and toppled into the gulf. Hearing the faint sound the stone made when it slipped away, Togura turned. But, seeing nothing, shrugged, and went on his way.

Two streets from Dead Man's Drop, Togura bought some roasted chestnuts from a street vendor, a crippled hag with a festering rupia despoiling the skin beneath her left eye. She tried to cheat him. They argued. He swore. She cursed him. They parted on bad terms, he with her chestnuts and she with his money, both convinced that they had got the worst of the bargain; rounding a corner, he kicked at a cat with ringworm, swore again, then stopped to eat.

As he ate, he began to feel better.

As Togura savoured his chestnuts, he watched two raff-taff street dogs fighting. Then a man came hurrying down the road; after him came a hunting harridan dressed in harn, who screamed abuse at him.

Togura thought to himself:

—Now what was all that about?

He was accosted by a rough, burly swordsman of middle years, who spoke to him in a strangely accented Galish:

'Which way to the king's palace, boy?'

'Who is it who wants to know?' said Togura.

'Barak the Battleman, hired killer and trained assassin,' said the swordsman.

That was a lie. The stranger was, in fact, Guest Gulkan, sometimes known as the Emperor In Exile. He was the son of Onosh Gulkan, the Witchlord; he had been wandering the world for years now, travelling to places as far distant as Dalar ken Halvar and Chi' ash-lan. He lied about his name because there was a price on his head in many parts and places.

'The palace lies that way,' said Togura, pointing firmly, and hoping that he was right; at the moment, he was more than a little disorientated.

'Thank you, lad,' said the stranger, and strode away with an easy, rolling gait.

Togura watched him go, struck, momentarily, with horror. The king was angry with him! The king had hired an assassin! He was going to be hunted and tortured and killed!

Then Togura realised he was being ridiculous. There was no way the king could have got hold of an assassin so soon, even supposing that he had been made that angry; the stranger's appearance in this place was probably just idle coincidence.

Togura's analysis was correct.

Realising that the stranger was no danger to him, Togura

was taken by the wild notion of following him and questioning him. Perhaps the swordmaster-assassin could use a road companion to carry his burdens and light his fires, to cook his food and to haggle for provisions in the marketplace. There was no harm in trying.

Enthusiastic about this idea, Togura set off in pursuit of the swift-striding man-killer, but lost him in a tangle of narrow streets crowded, suddenly and without warning, by a flock of sheep which were being driven through the town. He contemplated pursuing his quarry to the palace, but the thought of going anywhere near Slerma made him decide against it.

So it was that Togura Poulaan came within an ace of becoming the road companion of Guest Gulkan. The fact that he failed probably saved his life, for the Emperor In Exile was on a dangerous quest which would in time decide the fate of powers, kingdoms and empires; there was horror behind him and peril ahead, and the life expectancy of anyone travelling with him would probably have been short.

The last of the sheep went by. Togura idly squished a knobbly dropping with his foot, chewed on another chestnut, and wondered what do do now.

As he was wondering, a small procession went by. It consisted of about twenty people dressed in mourning who were carrying amidst them a bier on which there reclined a man who was both very old and very sick. Togura, as a native of the district, knew enough to guess that the old man was going to be fed to the odex. He had never yet seen this process; as his meal had nourished his curiosity along with his other organs, he fell in behind the procession.

By and by, they came to the stronghold of the Wordsmiths. The original building, made of stone, had collapsed five years previously; the Wordsmiths had rebuilt in wood. The main gate in the stockade was open, but a grey-robed wordmaster halted the procession before they could enter. After a low-voiced argument, the leader of the procession signed his people to one side, and they sat down to wait.

Was it too early in the day? Or was the odex not hungry yet? Or was there an argument how much the people should pay to dispose of their sick old man? Togura did not know, and was not rude enough to ask. While waiting to see what would happen, he loitered beside an abandoned mine shaft, kicking occasional stones into the darkness, which fell straight and sheer to a pool of water far below.

From inside the stronghold of the Wordsmiths there came sounds of confusion. There was some banging and crashing and shouting, then three wordmasters sprinted through the open gate, running for their lives.

'Curiouser and curiouser,' said Togura.

Then there issued forth a monster, which came striding out of the gate on five or six of its seven or eight legs. It was not terribly imposing, as monsters go; it was scarcely twice the girth of a bull, and barely twice the height of a man; its grappling claws were hardly the size of a pair of shears.

Nevertheless, people screamed and ran.

Togura, amused, wondered why people were making so much fuss about the manifestations of an ilps. As it bent over the sick old man, he sauntered forward. The creature lifted its head and regarded him. Its skull was bald bone like that of a vulture. Its eyes were as green as gangrene, and its breath was fetid. Its skin was covered with warts and fents. The warts were a mixture of pink and grey; a few seemed to be purulent, while stark yellow pus oozed from the fents.

'Who are you?' said Togura, his voice loud and strong.

The creature blinked.

'Where do you come from?' he insisted.

It took no notice.

'I demand your nature!'

Losing interest in Togura, the creature bent down over the old man once more. And something terrible happened. As Togura screamed and screamed, the creature raised its head, slushed a mouthful of flesh and spat out a bone. Blood ran down its chin.

'Who?' screamed Togura. 'When? What?'

But the creature remained undamaged by his questions. Belatedly, he realised it was not an ilps at all. It was a genuine monster. As it forked, scrabbled and glutted, spraying the area with blood and offal, he turned and ran.

The creature roared and followed.

Blindly, Togura fled. The ground opened up in front of him. In a moment of sickening horror, he realised he had fallen into the mine shaft. He gasped for air as he fell. Then he went barrelling into the water, which went riveting up his nose. Stunned to find himself still alive, Togura struggled for the surface and looked around. In all directions were rock walls, dimly lit by wavering, splintered reflections of half-light from the water.

To his relief, he saw there was a ladder fastened to the side of the shaft. He swum across to it, took hold, and hauled himself out of the water. He had climbed to three times his own height when the wood, many years rotten, gave way, and sent him plummeting back into the sump.

'Help!' cried Togura, floundering.

He looked up and saw, far overhead, someone looking down at him.

'Help!' he cried. 'Help! For the love of Mothra, help me!'

Someone began to climb down. Too late, he realised it was not someone but something. The monster was coming to get him. Suddenly, it slipped, scrabbled then fell. He cowered against the side of the shaft. The monster shattered the water beside him. As it heaved up out of the depths, he took his only chance, and leapt onto its back.

Shoving his hands into two of the larger fents which disgraced the creature's hide, Togura hung on for dear life. The creature snapped and thrashed and shook and bucked. He thought it was urgently trying to get at him, but in fact it was urgently trying to save itself from drowning.

Finally, the monster got claw-hold on the flanks of the shaft and began to climb, slowly and painfully. Once it slipped, and almost went crashing back to disaster. But it struggled on, gaining, at last, the daylight. Togura, still back-riding, looked round and saw a small crowd watching from a distance.

A man advanced, bearing a meat cleaver.

As the man drew near, the monster attacked with a lurch and a slither. Its intended victim dropped his cleaver and fled. Exhausted, the monster collapsed. Togura, in danger of sliding off, shifted his weight. A mistake! Remembering his presence, the monster rolled over suddenly, almost crushing him. He fell off, leapt away from the grappling claw, ducked under the monster's scooping jaw and fell, almost on top of the meat cleaver.

Snatching the weapon by the handle, Togura slashed the next claw which tried for him. He lopped it off. The monster screamed and tried to scoop him with its jaw. He weaved and evaded, then hacked. His blade chopped into the monster's neck. In a frenzy, he slashed, stabbed, gouged and underthrust, fighting in a beserker fury. He never noticed when the monster died. Then, finally, one wild swipe took its head off entirely, and he realised it must be dead. Or, if not dead, then pretty sick.

Panting, sweating, swaying, Togura halted. He became

aware of distant cheering, and realised it was for him. He felt dizzy and very distant.

A wordmaster advanced and clapped him on the shoulder.

'That was very well done, young man.'

'Thank you,' said Togura, good manners providing him with something to say.

'Come with me,' said the wordmaster.

'I must clean my blade,' said Togura, dimly remembering that it was something heroes were said to say after battle.

He tried wiping the bloodstained blade against the monster's flank, but succeeded only in getting it stained with yellow pus. He tried again, and failed. He was shaking. He was rapidly becoming tearful.

Realising the meat cleaver was causing his young charge some distress, the wordmaster wisely removed it from Togura's grasp and threw it to one side. Then he led Togura into the Wordsmiths' stronghold. As they walked along together, Togura tottering, and leaning on the older man for support, the crowd cheered once more.

'Who was that who just went in?' asked Baron Chan Poulaan, arriving on the scene.

'A young man. He killed the monster.'

'What kind of young man?' asked the baron, on the off chance. 'Do you know his name?'

'Oh yes, sir,' said a young milkmaid, who was more knowledgeable than her years might have suggested. 'He's Barak the Battleman.'

'And who might he be?'

'A visitor, sire,' said a woodcutter from Down Slopes. "Assassin and swordfighter, they say. Escaped gladiator from the murk pits of Chi' ash-lan, if you ask me.'

And he pulled down one eyelid in a very suggestive gesture.

'Oh,' said the baron, losing interest.

He turned away, and set off for the Suets. He would challenge them, and find out where they had hidden his son. If the Suets failed to yield up Togura, then there might be feuding about this.

CHAPTER
6

Within the Wordsmiths' organisation the ranks, from lowest to highest, were:

1. servitor;
2. scribe;
3. translator;
4. wordmaster;
5. governor.

Brother Troop was a wordmaster. As befitted his rank, he wore a multicolored harlequin robe and felt slippers. He was a short, bouncing, jovial man with a ready smile which showed him to be both pleased with himself and pleased with the world. He wore much of his worldly wealth beneath his skin, but Togura, after his recent encounter with Slerma, could not bring himself to describe the Brother as fat.

'So you're the hero,' said Brother Troop, rubbing his hands together.

'I suppose I am,' said Togura, with some surprise.

He had been given a change of clothes and the chance to cleanse himself of monster muck, but he was still a little disorientated.

'Ahaha!' said Brotherr Troop, not quite laughing and not quite not. 'You suppose you are. Of course you are! The vigour of the very young. Amazing, isn't it?' And he touched his nose. 'Youth is a wonderful thing.'

'You're not so old yourself,' said Togura.

'Perhaps not, but I was never as wild as you. I was born sensible. And more's the pity! A great handicap, I think. All power to the brave and reckless, eh? Hey? Ahaha! Come, I'll show you around.'

'Well, really I'd—'

'Later, later,' said Brother Troop, giving him no chance to say that he'd really like a little to eat, a little to drink and a lot to sleep. Instead, the good Brother swept him away on a whirlwind tour which took him through kitchens—too quickly alas—sleeping quarters, lecture rooms, study rooms, dungeons and cloisters, and then to the main court-yard of the Wordsmiths' stronghold.

'Here's where it all happens,' said Brother Troop. 'And that, my son, is the odex.'

'That?'

'Believe me. You stand in the Presence.'

The odex was a thin grey disk; Togura could just have spanned its diameter with his outstretched arms. Seen side-on, it appeared to disappear entirely. Seen from an angle, it acted as a mirror, reflecting the surroundings.

'Stand in front of it,' said Brother Troop.

Togura moved round in front of the odex, which hung in the air, standing knee-high off the ground without any ap-parent means of support. As he came directly in front of it, the mirror surface broke up into discordant cascades of col-our and light. These shimmered, swirled, stretched, con-tracted and pulsed.

'Is it angry?' said Togura warily.

At his words, a puff of red mist broke loose from the surface of the odex. It twirled lazily in the air.

'Who knows?' said Brother Troop.

At his question, the red mist broke apart with a sound like a breaking harp string; a dozen bubbles of bright light frolicked out of the odex and began chasing each other through the air. Similar manifestations and dispersions continued as the two spoke together.

'Where do these things come from?' said Togura.

'From the odex, of course. You can see that for yourself.'

'Is it dreaming?' asked Togura.

'No,' said Brother Troop, uncertainly; it had never occurred to him that the odex might dream. 'We don't think it dreams. We don't really think it's alive. After years of study, we've come to think that it's like a knife. It means neither good nor ill. If it cuts, that's due to our clumsiness. We don't think it dreams—or gets angry.'

'But it sent you the monster,' said Togura. 'Why did it do that?'

'It does nothing on its own,' said Brother Troop. 'Left to its own devices, it just sits there meditating. We speak. We summon. We call things out from its infinite resources.'

'Then how did you summon the monster?' said Togura.

'By accident.'

'Could you summon another?'

'Only by another accident. You see—'

A tangle of spiderweb came floating out of the odex. Brother Troop knocked it aside with a casual sweep of his hand. It grabbed hold of him, battened onto his flesh and began to feed. It hurt. His senses demolished by pain, Brother Troop fell to the ground, flailing at the invader. Togura helped him destroy it. They succeeded, but there was a violent red rash on the wordmaster's hand where the web had been feeding.

'Look!' said Brother Troop.

Overhead floated on ilps. It was a large one, mostly teeth, horns and trailing tentacles. It had just escaped from the odex.

'Who are you?' shouted Brother Troop.

But the ilps was nimble. It floated fast and high, soaring up and over the roof and out of sight.

'Let's go inside,' said Brother Troop. 'We've endured the Presence quite enough for one day.'

At his words, there was a roar. Both of them jumped. But, fortunately, the odex had not generated another monster. Just the roar of a monster.

Inside, Togura asked a question:

'Why does questioning destroy an ilps?'

'Because every ilps is anomalous,' said Brother Troop. 'They don't belong in our world. We don't think they belong anywhere. They're birthed at random by the odex every time we excite it. Make the anomalous question its own nature, and it destroys itself.'

'How do we excite the odex?'

'By the use of words, young man. You should have guessed that much from what you've seen today.'

'Then what words do what?'

'Different words do different things. That's for certain. But our real problem is that the same words also do different things every time they're used.'

'Hmmm.'

'Very much hmmm! Marry a woman who doesn't speak your language, and you'll be chatting away merrily in less than a year. Our conversations with the odex began in my father's day. We still don't know how to say hello.'

'At this rate, you never will,' said Togura. 'So why bother?'

'Because of the treasure, my boy. The treasure!'

Brother Troop took him to the treasury so he could see. A day's conversation with the odex would usually produce at least one real, solid, genuine piece of treasure.

By the time they reached the treasury, Togura was eagerly expecting to see miracles. He was bitterly disappointed at the motley assortment of oddments which was actually on view.

'This is it?' he said.

'Won with great pain, my boy,' said Brother Troop. 'Won with great pain.'

There were two lightweight diamond-shaped objects with holes in them—possibly buttons, and possibly not. There was a disk of thin metal stamped with concentric circles; it had jagged edges, and was rusting. There was a pale, slightly translucent object, very thin and sharp, about the length of a finger, which Togura was almost certain was a fishbone.

Next there was a curious square box, blue in colour, which was riddled with holes. Togura was about to explore the holes with his fingers when Brother Troop slapped his hand down.

'No, my boy, don't do that. Brother Dorban lost a finger to that little box.'

Togura stared into the holes and saw a wavering, everchanging light inside. The box was humming.

'I'll tell you one thing for certain,' he said. 'You'll never find out what this is for.'

'Ah, my boy,' beamed Brother Troop. 'We know already. It's an insect trap. It lures them and kill them—or, at least, they go inside and they're never seen again. Fleas, flies, cockroaches—it doesn't discriminate. Leave your clothes by the box overnight, and they'll be free of lice by daybreak.'

There were more things. A pile of old rags. A curious

stone globe which appeared to be filled with stars. Some objects made of lead which might have been said to imitate the shape of knucklebones. A length of strong, translucent green cord which appeared to be made all of one seamless piece; it was slippery, and difficult to knot. A stone adze, bearing cryptic markings in red paint. A friable, lumpy grey object which Togura was far too polite to identify as a rather old and shabby dog turd.

'All this comes from the odex?'

'Yes,' said Brother Troop nodding. 'And other things, too dangerous to keep. Today's monster was a case in point. Come, I'll show you the reading room.'

They went to the reading room where there was a single very old and ancient book. Its cover, and its individual pages, were coated with a hard, transparent substance; thus protected, they did not seem to suffer decay.

'This is the Book of Odex,' said Brother Troop. 'It was discovered together with the odex itself in the Old City in the Valley of Forgotten Dreams, in Penvash.'

'There's no such thing as the Old City,' said Togura. 'That's just a tale to frighten children with.'

The Brother shook his head.

'No. There really is a city. Men went there seeking wealth. Many died. Even before they got to the city, one was turned into a monster after a flower swallowed him; they killed him after he killed five.'

Togura nodded politely, though he scarcely believed a word of it, and the Brother continued.

'Of those who went, three returned alive. One was my father. They gained three things in the Old City: the Book, the odex, and their nightmares. Open the Book.'

Togura did so. The patterns within, splattered across the pages as if at random, made a bewildering maze of angles, corners and stunted lines.

'Can you read, boy?'

'A little. But not this.'

'That's scarcely surprising. It's written in two languages. Part is written in the Voice of Jade and Gold, which the scholars of former times used both before and after the Days of Wrath. A travelling wizard was able to translate it for my father. Thus he learnt that the odex was used in former times to store both knowledge and objects. There is vast wealth inside the odex, boy.'

'But you can't get it out.'

'Not unless we gain the index.'

'The index?'

'We summon things forth from the odex by talking to it. The ancients of former times used the index instead. The Book tells us that the index speaks in the Universal Language, whatever that might be. For want of an index, we've been trying to make our own Universal Language. That's why we've been gathering together all the world's languages, trying to make them one.'

'And does that promise you success?' asked Togura, unable to conceal his doubts.

'Nothing gives us any guarantee of success,' said Brother Troop. 'But! Knowledge! Wealth! Power! It's worth striving for, boy, it's worth striving for.'

'You said the Book was written in two languages.'

'That's right, my son. One's the Voice of Jade and Gold, which I've spoken of already. The other's the Cold Tongue, which even the wizards can't read. Back before the Devaluation, we paid the wizard of Drum to make the attempt, to see if he could succeed where others had failed. He couldn't. But he told us where we could find an index.'

'He did?'

'He did. After consulting his Catalogues, he told us where we could find a number of them. After the wizards became a power in the world, they discovered many things left over from the Days of Wrath; they didn't understand most of them, but kept them nevertheless, for thousands and thousands of years.'

'So where—'

'I'm coming to that, boy. Give me time, give me time. Over the years, the wizards acquired a number of small, flat boxes, each marked with the sign of a hand and a heart. They could never find out how to open them, or what was inside. Now, thanks to the Book of the Odex, we know. Each contains an index. Each will open on a Word. That Word is Sholabarakosh.'

'Shola—?'

'Later, boy. You'll have plenty of time to memorise it before we send you seeking.'

The Brother's words gave Togura something of a shock. They gave him a hint of what was in store for him. He thought of protesting, but held his tongue. As the old saying goes, it's best to hear out the bargain before you break it.

'Thanks to the wizard of Drum,' said the Brother. 'We know where to find these boxes. The nearest is in the bottom of a green bottle in Prince Comedo's Castle Vaunting, in Estar. A monster protects the bottle from those who would acquire it. The box itself lies at the very bottom of the bottle, and is Guarded.'

'Guarded?'

'I don't know what is meant by that, and neither did the wizard of Drum. However, his Catalogue says it, emphatically, which means there's death waiting nearby.'

'Charming,' murmured Togura.

'What's that?' said the Brother.

'I said, that would be a real challenge. Something I could get my teeth into.'

'Yes—or something which could get its teeth into you. Anyway, to continue. There's also a box in the Secret Store in Tormstarj Castle in the Ironband Mountains. That's south of Estar, as you know.'

'Yes,' said Togura, who didn't, but didn't like to say.

'There may possibly be a third box in the Castle of Controlling Power. There is definitely one in the possession of the Silver Emperor in Dalar ken Halvar. But that, of course, is a step and a way.'

'Yes,' said Togura, from habit.

'Galsh Ebrek may hold another box.'

'Who?'

'It is not a who, it's a where. It's the High City in Yestron. You know where Yestron is, of course.'

'Yes,' said Togura. 'It's west of here.'

'No! East! Beyond Argan. Beyond Ashmoles. Beyond Quilth. The west has nothing of interest, not to us. Unless there's a box in Chi' ash-lan, which is problematical. You know where Chi' ash-lan is, I hope.'

'Yes,' said Togura, who had a vague inkling.

He feared he had disappointed Brother Troop already, and that he would shortly have to disappoint the wordmaster again. For he suspected that he was about to be offered a job fit for a hero, and he had no intention whatsoever of accepting. He would rather stay alive.

'Well, boy,' said Brother Troop, beaming. 'I expect you know by now precisely what we want of you.'

'Yes,' said Togura. 'You want me to go to Estar to get the bottle which holds the box which holds the index.'

'Excellent!' said Brother Troop, slapping him on the back. 'I thought you'd accept. Let's celebrate with some bread and wine, hey?'

'Tai-ho!' said Togura, using a local idiom which meant something similar to 'whoa!', 'wait' or 'stop'.

'What is it?' said Brother Troop. 'You're not going to decline the honour of questing for the index, are you?'

Togura hesitated. He meant to say 'yes', but did not

want to leave without indulging in the bread and wine he
had been offered. With a swiftly-developing survivor's
cunning, he equivocated:

'The question of payment arises.'

'Payment? But, my boy—the glory! Isn't that enough?
No? If not . . . no, this is neither the time nor the place.
Come, let us eat and drink. The dinner table, my lad, is the
civilised place for prolonged discussion.'

Togura was gratified by the success of his stratagem.
Over their meal, he rewarded Brother Troop for his hospitality by showing an eager interest in the odex, the index
and related matters.

Precisely what markings identified the box which held
the index? Brother Troop sketched the heart and the hand
for him.

What was that Word which opened the box? Brother
Troop gave him he Word once more, and he memorised it:
Sholabarakosh.

What did the index itself look like?

'Ahaha,' said Brother Troop. 'An astute question, truly.
When you open the box, you'll know. Remember, it speaks
the Universal Language.'

'Whatever that is.'

'Yes,' said Brother Troop, with an unfamiliar hint of
sadness and defeat in his voice. 'Whatever that is.' Then,
brightening: 'Ah, the chicken! They've brought us the
chicken. Beautiful. Come on, eat, eat. You're not full already, are you?'

'No,' said Togura, who was, but thought it wise to stock
up a little. He started on a chicken wing. 'What,' he said,
'happened to everyone else who went questing for the
odex?'

'An interesting question.'

'Interesting indeed, as the chicken said to the chopper.

Come on, I'll know the truth sooner or later. It might as
well be now.'

'Then young man, since you insist, I must tell you that
the truth is that we don't know. Five have been sent so far.
None have returned.'

'Hmmm,' said Togura, thinking.

He was trying to calculate how many more meals he
could get out of the Wordsmiths before they forced him to
make a decision and commit himself.

'I see the quest takes your fancy, hey?' said Brother
Troop. 'Your young blood boils with hot excitement. Horizons call you! Oh, you'll be a hit with the girls when you
come back, young man. Every damsel loves a hero.'

'Give me a day to think it over,' said Togura.

And, after some further discussion, the good Brother
did.

However, Togura did not get the chance to spend that
day in rest, reflection and decision making. Events were
moving swiftly now; unbeknownst to him, he was well and
truly embroiled in the world's turmoil. As he would soon
find out.

CHAPTER
7

Disturbed by the manifestation of the monster which had escaped from the odex, the City Council of Keep met in an emergency session at noon that very same day, and passed a Resolution Regarding Care And Confinement Appertaining To Monsters. Subsection 5(c) of Schedule 9 of Annex 5 attached to the Resolution stated that:

Any organisation which does or can or may or might buy breed produce summon forth unearth uncover tempt call attract or otherwise obtain any demon fiend bog-crawler crocodile griffin dragon death-lizzard creature of the Swarms or related being or any similar or unsimilar scarth jinn brute beast or monster MUST protect the public security of obtaining the services of a suitably qualified and experienced hero sword-master death-dealer dragon-killer or similar.

Aware that the manifestation of the monster had excited a certain groundswell of public disfavour, the Wordsmiths sought to comply. They offered Togura the job on a temporary basis, while he decided whether he would quest for the index. He accepted, fully aware that only one real monster had emerged from the odex in more than three decades of operation.

The Wordsmiths then announced that they had recruited the young monster-slaughterer Togura Poulaan, who had proved himself by killing a monster for them earlier in the day, in full view of the public. This announcement was met with derision by the citizenry, who were by now fully aware that the monster had been killed by Barak the Battleman, assassin and swordfighter, previously a gladiator in the murk pits of Chi'ash-lan.

'How many people in Keep know you to your face?' asked Brother Troop.

'A couple of dozen,' said Togura.

'Two dozen people can scarcely overturn the world's belief. From now on, till further notice, you're Barak the Battleman.'

'Agreed,' said Togura.

Armed with his new name, he stood taller and felt stronger; he began to walk with something of a swagger. The Wordsmiths equipped him with a sword, a stabbing knife and a helmet, and made an announcement correcting the name of their resident hero.

Togura, remembering his encounter earlier in the day with the swordmaster-assassin who had prior claim to the name of Barak the Battleman, wondered with some trepidation what would happen if that rough, burly swordsman of middle years heard that his name had been usurped.

The swordsman did hear.

And he shrugged, for it was nothing to him. He should have changed his name leagues ago in any case. That evening, as he set off east, his business with King Skan Askander completed, he decided that henceforth he would call himself Genu Vay Chanay. He would identify himself as a free-lance executioner.

Genu Vay Chanay gave no further thought to Keep or to its people or to the theft of his last roadname; he had plenty of things to worry about without troubling himself over trivialities like the use and abuse of his former name.

That very same evening, an invitation arrived at the Wordsmiths' stronghold for the Governor and the new monster-slaughterer to attend a Banquet of Celebration to be given by the Family Suet that very night. This gave Togura an attack of stage fright.

As Brother Troop was attempting to calm his nerves, the calm of the night was interrupted by a roar from the odex, followed by he manifestation of a dragon's head. Unfortunately, the head was very much alive. But, fortunately, it was not attached to any body, and consequently was soon dead.

'It's yours, boy,' said Brother Troop. 'Proof positive to all the world of your ability.'

'I can't claim it,' said Togura blushing. 'I cannot tell a lie.'

That in itself was a lie, or at least an exaggeration; he could easily tell a small lie, and often had and did, but he was unable to tell a lie on such an exaggerated scale.

'You needn't say anything about it at all,' said Brother Troop. 'We'll have it carried to the Banquet of Celebration. If anyone asks about it, then murmur politely and say it's beneath your dignity to discuss such trifles.'

'That's excellent advice,' said Togura, struck by the brilliance of this idea. 'It's very kind of you.'

'Not at all,' said Brother Troop, dismissing his thanks with a wave of his hand. 'It's us I'm thinking of. We have to have the confidence of the community we live amongst. You're a valuable asset to us, boy. Do us proud.'

So it was that Togura went to the Banquet of Celebration

in triumph, together with the dragon's head, which took pride of place at the dinner, occupying a table all to itself.

Togura was rather miffed when he discovered that the banquet was not to celebrate his own success at monster killing. It was, instead, to celebrate the engagement of young Roly Suet to the king's daughter, Slerma, and to announce the launch of a new coinage in bronze, gold and silver. The coinage would bear the head of King Skan Askander but would be backed by the assets of the Family Suet.

However, Togura's ego was boosted by the fuss the young and beautiful Day Suet made of her hero. She was a little puzzled about his new name. He explained the misunderstanding which had forced it upon him. And, as he brought proof positive of his abilities in the form of the dragon's head, she could not doubt his courage.

'You're a real man,' she said, breathing admiration.

'I'm growing up,' Togura conceded.

'Your father was round here earlier today, real man,' she said. 'He was talking of spanking you.'

'I doubt that he'll get the chance,' said Togura, really cool and collected.

'Yes,' said Day Suet. 'But it would be interesting to watch one real man spank another.'

'Minx!' said Togura, swatting her.

She evaded him, and laughed.

And, before very long, she had persuaded him to laugh with her.

They ate.

They drank.

They danced.

The musicians, robust and virile men, laboured and belaboured their instruments, pumping, hammering, stretching, scraping and churning, till their faces went beetroot-red and the sweat poured down to their beards and their broad moustaches.

As Togura danced with Day, he dared, and she dared with him. Her breasts were soft. Her lips were hot and eager. Her eyes spoke just a little more than she would voice. His confidence grew. When he suggested they leave, she never asked him where. She led him to her room. As if in a trance, he stripped her to her skin. Her body, smooth and glabrous, glimmered in the light of a single candle. She closed with him, and gave him a drunken kiss. She smelt of sweat and musk, of perfume and spices, of hard liquor and youthful desire.

He undressed.

Standing before her, naked, he realised that now was the moment. Now he was really going to become a man. A real man. Initiated into the mysteries of the flesh. His desire was hard, urgent, swelling. He touched her thigh, lightly, finding it warm as new bread. Overwhelmed by her heat and aroma, he felt an irresistible imminence taking control of his flesh. Horror-struck, he tried to restrain himself.

He failed.

His male organ began to pump.

At the last possible moment, Togura clapped a hand to his cock, which pumped hot jism over his palm. That saved him from splattering Day from bosom to thigh with his semen. But the disaster was still absolute, unmitigated and irretrievable.

'Oh no!' he cried, in agony.

'What is it?' said Day.

Then, realising precisely what it was, she began to laugh. Blithe spirit that she was, she could not take this technical hitch seriously. She was puzzled when Togura began to ram himself into his clothes.

'Tog,' she said. 'No. Don't go. Tog, it's nothing. Talk to me, Tog. Tog. Wait!'

But, when she clutched at him, he broke free and fled, still fastening his garments. He was so embarrassed he could not endure her presence. He wanted to die. Or bury himself in a hole for half a thousand years.

He escaped to the autumn air and stalked through the streets, furious. Raging. Hating himself and the world and his own rebellious flesh. He had failed absolutely and miserably at a man's most important test. He was worse than nothing. He was disgraced. He would never be able to look Day in the face again. She knew!

When his half-brother Cromarty had accused him of being a day-dreaming masturbator, that had been bad enough. But he had been able to deny it with a straight face, even though it was true. After all, masturbation was furtively acknowledged or hinted at by many. But to fail with a woman!

Togura remembered Cromarty boasting about Toff the milkmaid:

'She was hot, boys. Hot, drunk and flat on her back. So I stuck it in to the hilt. Rammed it in. She loved it. She begged for more. I gave it.'

Everyone had their stories. Even Togura had his stories, though his were not true. (Could Cromarty's be untrue? He'd like to think so, but it was difficult. Cromarty was so brash, so arrogant, so confident.)

Brooding on his disaster, Togura grimly resolved that tonight would be the night, no matter what. He could never face Day again, but he would find a way. He would lose his virginity by morning, or die in the attempt.

Thus resolved, he bent his footsteps toward the tower-house of Melladona, one of the town's five whores, and rumoured to be the cheapest. She was awake and working;

she had only lately discharged her last customer. He struck a bargain and paid.

He thought himself confident.

But when he actually saw her rancid flesh, her flaccid thighs, the fat veins snaking up her legs, the stale bruises and the odd blotched marks on her breasts, and the crinkling scar running from her neck to her navel, his courage failed. In her cold and narrow room, his worm disgraced him by shrinking to a cringing stump of flesh scarcely the size of his thumb.

He asked for his money back.

Melladona laughed, then, realising he was serious, attacked him. After he escaped into the street, she cursed him from her window. Trying to recover something from the debacle, he eased his ego by shouting a few well-chosen insults. Melladona responded promptly by emptying her chamber pot over his head.

Togura eventually washed himself off in someone's rain water barrel, then, sadder but not necessarily wiser, mooched through the night to the Wordsmiths' Stronghold. The gate was open, and someone, dressed in a winter-weight coat and swaddled in a blanket, was sitting by the gate waiting for him.

'Togura Poulaan!' said Day Suet severely, standing up as he approached. 'So there you are at last. Well? Aren't you grateful to see me? Don't you realise you're lucky to see me at all? Running off into the night like that! Stupid fellow! Most girls would have given you away forever.'

'Day,' said Togura, not knowing what to say.

She had come for him. She was his. This must be true love! But, all the same, she was a source of mortification to him. She knew! Standing in the light of the gatelamp, he hesitated.

'Don't just stand there, stupid!' said Day, impatiently. 'Kiss me!'

Togura gathered her into his arms, and they kissed.

'Now take me inside,' said Day, 'And get me something to eat. It's cold out here, and I'm hungry.'

'I don't know if the brothers would approve,' said Togura.

Day kicked him in the shins, hard.

'I'm running out of patience, Togura Poulaan. You've used up most of your chances. You don't have many left.'

'My lady,' said Togura, the formality of romance coming to his rescue.

He took her hand in his and kissed it, gracefully. Then he led her inside. Unable to resist the opportunity to show off a little, he took her to the central courtyard to show her the odex. By night it was, when they stood in front of it, an amazement of brilliant colours, far brighter than the night lamps arrayed around the courtyard.

While they were standing watching, two figures dressed in black jumped down from the roof above and landed in the courtyard. Day squealed. The intruders drew swords. They were masked with darkness: only their eyes showed.

'We seek Togura Poulaan,' said one, speaking a foreign variety of Galish rather than the local patois.

'The swordmaster-assassin otherwise known as Barak the Battleman,' said the other.

'Here I am,' said Togura—and instantly wished he had held his tongue.

'Joke with us again and you're dead,' said one of the intruders, grabbing Day Suet by the throat. 'The girl dies, too. Now tell us where we find our quarry. We know he's here! The whole town knows. We know him to his face, so try no substitutes. We know the head required in Chi'ash-lan.'

Togura stood rooted to the spot, paralysed with terror.

He had no weapons. Face to face with this twin death, what could he have done with weapons anyway?

'Tog,' gasped Day. 'He's hurting me!'

'Silence girl!' snarled the man holding her, looking around. For the first time he looked directly into the odex, and so, for the first time, he saw its ever-changing maze of kaleidoscopic colours. 'What,' he said, slightly startled, 'Is that?'

Day did not answer, but Togura found voice enough to say:

'A kind of Door.'

'You can go through it?'

'In a manner of speaking,' said Togura.

At that moment, they were interrupted by sounds of argument beyond the courtyard. Then in came the Baron Chan Poulaan with a squad of bowmen and spearmen. Two wordmasters were clinging to the baron, trying to restrain him.

'This place is forbidden by dark,' cried one.

But the baron advanced remorselessly.

'I'll have my son tonight,' he said. 'Or know the reason why. Ah, Togura! There you are! Come, boy. Heel!'

'Stay where you are,' hissed one of the men in black.

'Who are your funny friends?' said the baron, advancing, with his men behind him. 'Drawn swords, I see. Do we have a problem here?'

So speaking, the baron drew his own sword. He was by no means a master of the weapon, but he was strong, aggressive and enthusiastic. In Sung, he was regarded as fearsome.

The man holding Day in a throttle edged closer to the odex. His companion gave Togura a shove which sent him sprawling to the ground, then menaced the baron and his men.

'Back, rabble!' he said, speaking now in a loud, hard voice.

Baron Chan Poulaan was amused.

'There's at least seven of us and only two of you,' said the baron, reasonably. 'Throw down your weapons and surrender.'

'I,' said the man confronting him, 'am a ninth-grade adept of the Zenjingu fighting cult. I can kill all of you without thinking. Your very existence here is at your peril.'

'Your grammar suffers under stress,' said the baron, dryly.

'Out, vermin! Do you not know the dread doom which walks in the midnight black of Zenjingu fighters?'

'No,' said the baron, frankly.

He was essentially a provincial man who led a narrow and provincial life; he knew nothing whatsoever of the Zenjingu fighters, whose very name was terror in the lands around Chi'ash-lan.

'You have outlived your life,' snarled the Zenjingu fighter, raising his sword.

The baron snapped his fingers. An archer standing behind him unleashed an arrow. The Zenjingu fighter lurched, dropped his sword, threw up his arms, then waddled round in circles, gasping as he clutched at the arrow, which had pierced his throat.

'Thus we do in the highlands,' said the baron, striding forward with an easy gait.

As the Zenjingu fighter tottered, the baron hacked into the unruly fellow's head. On the third blow, the man dropped dead at his feet. Whistling tunelessly, the baron turned his attention to the remaining trespasser.

'Get back!' shouted the survivor. 'Get back, or I kill the girl.'

'The life of a female Suet is nothing to me,' said Baron

Chan Poulaan, who saw no harm in telling the truth. 'Go ahead. Make my day.'

'No!' screamed Togura, launching himself at the Zen-jingu fighter.

The fighter threw Day Suet into the odex, which had been described to him as a Door. Then jumped in after her. Both were briefly visible, then gone, disintegrating—with a jangle of music—into a storm of colours. An ilps, popping out of the odex, celebrated the occasion with hearty laughter.

'So much for that,' said the baron crisply, wiping his sword then sheathing it. 'Come along, Togura, we're going home. What is it, boy? Not crying, are we? Now now, don't be a baby.'

'I loved her,' said Togura wretchedly.

'I'm sure you did,' said the baron, unsympathetically. 'We all suffer these fevers in our youth. Stop snivelling, boy!'

'You killed her!' screamed Togura.

'She's gone into the odex,' said the baron. 'I've heard the Wordsmiths say that it stores whatever's fed into it. If that's so, then get them to unstore it. Or do it yourself. Or if it can't be done, forget about it. Suets copulate like ferrets. There's plenty more where that came from. Come come, there's no use crying over spilt milk.'

When Togura continued crying, the baron slapped him briskly. Togura clenched his fist and smashed him. His father fell unconscious at his feet, poleaxed. There was a murmur amongst the bowmen and spearmen.

'Take him,' said Togura, in a thick wet ugly voice. 'Him and his sword. Take him, and get him out of here!'

The men obeyed.

The two wordmasters who had tried to prevent Baron Chan Poulaan from entering their stronghold muttered to each other. Togura Poulaan, now of the Wordsmiths, had made war on the head of the Warguild: no good would come of this.

They had more to mutter about shortly, for Togura, bloodlust in his heart, began to attack the odex.

CHAPTER
8

The night was cold, but Togura Poulaan was hot, feverish, burning. Armed with a sword which had recently graced the hand of a Zenjingu fighter, he was attacking the odex, hacking and slashing at its soft, yielding surface. It bled colour and music. As he fought, he became lost in a cloud of jangling rainbows, in a delusion of humming auras, in sprays of pealing orange and rumbling red, in veils of hissing mist and belching steam.

Finally, he stopped. He was panting harshly. His legs were shaking. Blisters had puffed up hard and ripe on the palms of his hands where the hard labour of battle had taken its toll on his innocence; he had never used a sword before, except in the occasional desultory half-hearted sparring match. The odex reformed and repaired itself, effortlessly, making itself perfect once more. The last free-floating colour died with a chord of music.

Togura hawked, and spat, and swore.

As he swore, an ilps jacked itself out of the odex and hoisted itself to the sky, smacking its bulbous lips, which were seven in number.

'Who are you?' cried Brother Troop, who had been standing to one side watching Togura's performance.

The ilps wavered.

'Where do you come from? Who owns you?'

Half of the ilps collapsed with a brief stench like twinge of silage; the rest escaped.

And Togura, having recovered his breath, began to attack the odex with his voice. Once started, he did not stop. Seeking the words which would recover Day Suet, he poured out the language of love, hate and obscenity, of eating and drinking, of battle and war, of farming and forestry; he cried out the names of birds, trees, mountains, rivers, seas, lakes, weapons, cities, people, pets, insects, stars and uncouth diseases; he called upon gods known and unknown, upon the powers of earth and sky, air and water, fire and stone.

Anything that served his purpose was pressed into use. He bawled out snatches of drinking songs and musical bawdry; he sung half-remembered phrases of love songs and madrigals, inventing his own words when memory failed him. And then, yielding to despair and fury, he poured out meaningless word-strings, shouting, demanding, pleading, screaming, commanding. As he excited it, the odex threw forth random assemblages with multiple heads, voices, smells, legs, arms, teeth, tentacles, manes, pseudopods, carapaces, eyes, ears, tongues and tails. As each ilps escaped, it drifted away, giggling, chuckling, snoring, roaring, swelling, pulsating, gleaming and shining, until the night sky above the stronghold of the Wordsmiths was cluttered with a positive fantasia of shapes and forms.

Sometimes, as Togura's words accidentally hit upon some transient code of retrieval, the odex sent real things out from its storehouse. Once it spat fire. Once it ejected a tiny corn-coloured disk which swelled in a couple of

breaths to a huge wheel of hay the height of a man and
girth of a bullock. Once a shower of coins blasted their
way into the air, stinging and burning where they hit, for
they were red-hot.

As the night wore on, an ever-changing audience
watched Togura's frantic performance. Servitors, scribes,
translators, wordmasters and even the governor himself
joined the gathering crowd. Togura, scarcely aware of their
presence, shouted, cursed, stormed, raged and pleaded, as
if immune to all embarrassment.

Alerted by the plague of ilpses above the Wordsmiths'
stronghold, the citizens of Keep began to wake; it would
have been hard for them to sleep, as all the dogs were
howling and barking, for an ilps has the peculiar property
of being very disturbing to dogs. Muttering imprecations,
many hauled themselves out of bed and went to investigate. Picking their way through the night, wary of mineshafts and mad dogs, citizens began to gather outside the
stronghold, a conclave of lanterns and speculations. Some
infiltrated the stronghold to become astonished witnesses to
an unprecedented scene.

They saw Togura, harsh and hoarse and sweating, berat-
ing the odex, threatening it and lashing it with the iron-
edged fury of his tongue. As his non-stop attack continued,
the odex no longer manifested one object or apparition for
each of his assaults, but spat them out in twos or threes,
and then a dozen at a time. More and more of its produc-
tions were real things rather than randomly formed ilpses.

A little red snake, folded like a concertina, jumped out
of the odex and hopped around on the ground, rupturing
itself with a string of explosions. Then Togura was
drenched and almost swept away by an onslaught of water,
foam and spray in which a horde of fresh and saltwater fish
kicked, thrashed and jumbled—pike, snapper, bream,
bluefin, dogfish, cod, carp, smelts, dabs, haddock, lam-

preys, flounder, trout, salmon, catfish, whitebait, gurnet,
mullet, groper, flying fish, mau mau, rays, eels, gudgeon
and perch, all mixed in a slurry with sea slugs, sea urchins,
crayfish, lobsters, gaplax, whelks and seaweed. While he
was still thrashing round in the water, screaming and
yelching and screeching and yelping, he was hit by a blast
of vegetable scrapings.

Then a child fell bawling at his feet.

A newborn child, swaddled in a kind of soft white sheet.

A woman darted out of Togura's audience, snatched up
the child and carried it off. As if a spell had been broken,
people started to scrabble for the valuables ejected by the
odex, and soon the central courtyard was filled with a turmoil of bodies and voices pushing, shoving, complaining,
shouting, scratching, wrestling, pinching, pulling, Fish
were torn apart or trampled underfoot or eaten raw on the
spot before they could be snatched away. The courtyard, lit
by the unearthly phosphorescent glow of more than a thousand ilpses, became a seething, pullulating mass of mud,
bodies, greed, avarice, jealousy and outright violence.

Oblivious to the anarchy all around, Togura, sword in
hand, continued to fight the odex. Now, excited not just by
his voice by the raging, screaming, shrieking crowd, it
spat, pumped and ejected, spraying the crowd with parts of
dead animals and mangled bits of human bodies, with
lumps of gold and chunks of silver, with mine tailings by
the bucket-load, with peaches, leeks and baby hedgehogs
and then—

A monster!

Lurching out of the odex it came, a fearsome beast with
scales of jacinth and claws like knives, with three snake-
like heads on long and weaving necks. Togura swung with
his sword and chopped off one of his heads. Fleeing from
his death-bright blade, it ran straight into the clutches of a
rabble of housewives, who swamped it, strangled it, tore it

apart and crammed its separate pieces into their bargain bags.

The ilpses were now popping out from the odex in a never-ending stream. Togura, filthy, bloodstained, stinking, reeking, was shaken by a fit of riotous madness, and laughed. His laugh provoked an onslaught of birds which battered into the night sky. Some struck out for the darkness while others went looning around in the light of the ilpses, or fluttered here and there and everywhere, bewildered, shocked and disorientated. The air was a daze of feathers, a cacophony of screams, cries, chirrups and distress calls. Togura was lost in the swirling maelstrom of sparrows, thrushes, fan tails, gulls, gannets, petrels, budgerigars, huias, yodel birds, cockatoos and laughing owls, moreporks and dancing fins, ravens, jackdaws, crows, keas, sparrow hawks, skypes, mynahs, skylarks, starlings, strutting breckons, hens, wood pidgeons, nymphet skarks, muttonbirds and dark lartles.

The feather-storm cleared.

An egg fell out of the odex, bounced, and rolled to one side; it was hard-boiled. A penguin, very far from home, hobbled away as best it could. Togura cried in a hoarse, cracked voice:

'Give me Day Suet!'

A horde of ilpses stormed out of the odex. As he ducked and covered his head, the noise of the crowd of looters rose to a fresh peak. The odex responded with cheeses, showering one and all with a stream of weird, bizarre and alien concoctions—green mould and yellow stink, cheddar and kray, cantal, marolles, olivet, port-salut, livarot, limbourg, skwayjeg, soo, parmesan, brie, gournay, roquefort, troyes, romantours, brazlets and mont d'ors.

The air filled with screams of delight as the housewives packed into the cheeses.

Togura, hit, thumped, battered, plastered and knocked

almost senseless by cheeses, fell to his knees and crawled away through the sour, dank, fetid reek of cheese. Soon the odex was buried in cheese, which pulsed, twitched and billowed, forcing itself ever-upward.

Forced upward till he was level with the guttering, Togura hauled himself onto the roof and crawled upward to the roof-ridge. There, exhausted, he slumped down, collapsing under a sky now elbow to elbow with giggling ilpses. Eventually, he roused himself and looked downward.

The night was fading. It was growing light. The cheeses were no longer piling themselves up to the sky; the courtyard full of cheese began to empty rapidly thanks to a bucket brigade of citizens. It seemed that everyone in Keep who was not crippled or bed ridden, and several who were, had gathered in the stronghold or on its roof or in the surrounding streets or on the surrounding roofs. As the cheese-level fell, survivors were hauled out of the wreckage, choking and gasping or shocked and silent.

Suddenly cries of rage, fear and horror rose to Togura's ears. He saw that a tide of red was rising fiercely, swamping cheeses and people. The hot reek of blood rose to his nostrils.

Soon torrents of blood were pouring out of the courtyard, which was a swirling red maelstom. The blood swept out into the streets, drowning down into the mineshafts, flooding the cellars, racketing knee-deep through the alleyways, piling up at the squeezes and pinches, then shooting away into the gulf of air beyond the brink of Dead Man's Drop. The slow, the lame and the unwary were carried away down the streets, swept into mineshafts or, thrashing and screaming, tossed over Dead Man's Drop.

The blood-letting subsided, until finally the odex itself could be seen, standing in the courtyard. It was still pumping blood at a steady rate; a stream ankle-deep ran from the courtyard.

From the odex there then emerged a steady stream of clanking cantankerous machines and cute little stag fawns with ear tags of blue or green or gold. The stag fawns wandered out into the streets, picking their way through the blood and rubble and the litter of corpses with their delicate bloodstained feet. The machines, some taking to the air, others lumbering along the ground, began to fight each other.

As the machines fought, the air filled with the sullen cough of projectile weapons, the sibilant hiss of energy beams, the hollow, booming thud of contact explosions, the thud of collisions and the high-pitched intolerable scream of despairing steel.

A light wind got up, sending the ilpses drifting away. The battle between the machines continued. Many of them sought refuge underground. The others followed, and the continuation of a very ancient war proceeded underfoot. The ground shook with muffled explosions.

The flow of blood diminished to a trickle. The last few stag fawns jumped out of the odex. The last thing to come forth was a female human dressed in silk. She slithered out of the odex and landed on her backside in the mud and muck.

'Day!' screamed Togura, with the very last of his voice.

Heedless of the danger, he raced down the roof and leapt into the courtyard. He landed, fell, and went sprawling into the soft, reeking squilg of blood and mud and water and bird droppings. As he hauled himself out of the ooze, the human female regarded him with distaste. She was, he saw, most definitely not Day Suet; she was taller, older and wore diamonds. Despite her muck-stained backside, she carried herself with all the hauteur of an empress.

'Help me,' said Togura, shambling through the mud toward her.

She took a tiny oddment from about her person and pointed it at him. The air sizzled. His limbs disco-ordinated and dropped him down in the filth. Slowly, cautiously, he raised his head, blinked, and peered at the woman. She asked him a question in a very foreign language.

'I don't understand,' said Togura, in a voice made of dry straw, sand, wood-shavings and iron filings.

The woman looked around, taking stock of the situation. She wrinkled her nose with distaste at the shambles around her. She had nothing but contempt for everything she saw. Picking up her skirts, she began to pick her way toward the nearest exit.

'Wait!' screeched Togura, wallowing through the filth on knees and elbows. 'You have to help us. Don't go!'

The woman turned, sneered, aimed her weapon again and fired, this time giving him a blast which knocked him unconscious for a day and a night. Then she turned on her heel and left, and was never seen again in Keep.

CHAPTER
9

The servitor lanced one last blister. Clear fluid eased out, forming a painless tear which the servitor wiped away with a fleece-white dabbing cloth. Togura flexed his hand, which felt stiff and sore.

'Another time, bandage your hands before you fight,' said the servitor, a rough-bearded man with a strange accent. 'Until such time as your hands are battle-hardened.'

'Where did you learn that?' said Togura.

'In another place, another time.'

'Tell me about it.'

'Not today. No—don't get up. Rest. I'll be back soon with something good.'

'What?'

'Wait and see.'

The servitor departed. Togura lay back in bed, staring at the cobwebs sprawled across the timbers overhead, and listening to the fury of the autumn storm which raged without. The wilderness weather was scattering the ilpses far and wide across the land, or blowing them out to sea; it was killing or dispersing the mobs of birds; it was grounding most of those quarrelsome machines which had not yet run out of fuel. The war weather was dealing with the pests and enemies unleashed by the odex, bringing a kind of peace back to the city state of Keep.

The servitor returned, bearing a two-handled drinking jug filled with something hot and sweltering.

'Drink,' he said.

Togura did so. Warmth paunched in his belly and invaded his veins. His senses slurred. The colours of the darkened timbers overhead began to drift.

'Drink,' said the servitor, encouraging him.

Togura drank his fill. Though he was lying in bed, he felt that he was floating. He tried to ask a question. On the third attempt, he managed to curl his tongue round the words.

'What is it?'

'Quaffle,' said the servitor.

'And what's that?'

'A mixture of all good things. Alcohol, opium, hemlock, dark nightshade, the red-capped mushroom and the blue, a foreign herb called ginseng and a little oil of hashish. And honey, of course.'

'I could learn to like it.'

'You could learn too well,' said the servitor, with a laugh. 'But it's good for the sickness. Sleep now.'

And, at his command, Togura drifted off into silk-bosomed drug dreams which suckled him with nectar and fed him on honey-basted melody cats.

He woke, later, in darkness. The rain and the wind were still at work beyond the walls. He was alone, without the company of so much as a candle. Lying there in the darkness, he remembered Day Suet, in spring, cradling a tiny bird in her little hands, and laughing when it stained her fingers with a tiny bit of lime. Hot tears blistered his eyes.

He wept.

Later, in the darkness, he found the two-handled drinking jug. What was left in the bottom was cold to the touch. It sidled down his throat, cold as a snake, then transmuted itself to living fire. Sweating from the heat of that fire, and reeling from weariness, he allowed his bones to compose themselves once more for sleep.

When he woke, it was morning.

The servitor brought him mutton chops, swedes, rutabaga and water-cress. He ate, ravenously. For lunch, there was leek soup, venison and the brains of a pig, with a side-helping of fried snails and pickled slugs. He devoured everything. In the evening, there was a slab of bread loaded down with beefsteak and a gill of milk, with blackbird pie to follow. He polished off the lot.

'Why am I so hungry?' said Togura.

'Good health makes you so,' said the servitor.

For days, as Togura recovered from the effects of the unknown weapon which the strange woman from the odex had used to knock him unconscious, the cold rains of autumn lashed the town, washing away dead fish, drowned rats and the smells of blood and cheese. While Togura ate and slept, while the days shortened and the rains pounded down, the townspeople counted the cost of their orgiastic session with the odex, and argued as to whether it was a blessing or a disaster.

'Of course it was a disaster, no question about it!' said Shock the Cobbleman, who had broken both legs on the Night.

But not everyone was quick to agree.

On the debit side, at least thirty-four people had been killed, fifty houses flooded, seventeen other properties damaged or demolished, and incredible devastation wrought underground by war machines fighting to death in the mines. Through autumn and winter, the miners would be able to retrieve little gemstock; they would be too busy repairing and shoring up mineshafts.

On the credit side, three of the fighting machines, burrowing deep into the rock, had finally burst out into the daylight at the very bottom of Dead Man's Drop. Water was now cascading out of their escape tunnels. The problem of flooding in the mines, which had worsened as the miners delved deeper over the years, was now easing. This unexpected solution to the drainage problem meant that the total amount of gemstock available in the long term had greatly increased.

Bankers at banquet, gleaming with perspiration, toasted Togura Poulaan—also known as Barak the Battleman—with goblets of diluted ambrosia or strong mulled wine. The Gonderbrine mine, the largest in Keep, which had been threatening to default on its loans because assets underground had proved to be also underwater, had now negotiated a very satisfactory repayments schedule.

'To chaos,' went one of the more drunken toasts. 'To havoc.'

That was daring, but another toast capped it:

'To the unexpected.'

Now that, for a banker, was truly extraordinary.

While bankers celebrated, and while miners, though grumbling, admitted that they ultimately stood to benefit, a few dour, incorrigible pessimists argued that drainage would hasten subsidence, leading to a swifter collapse of the town. They were ignored.

Meanwhile, also on the credit side was the personal wealth so many had garnered. Many houses in Keep were now glutted with venison, and also with cheesestock, the name the people invented for the unholy mish-mash of half a hundred different cheeses which had resulted from the excessive generosity of the odex.

Others had gained birdmeat, fishmeat, gold, silver or

interesting articles of metalwork. And many of those who had gained nothing had, nevertheless, abandoned themselves shamelessly on the Night; aware that they had fought and scrabbled and kicked and clawed, squabbling over the loot like so many carrion eaters, they were, for the most part, too ashamed to speak out and criticise the Wordsmiths, the odex or Togura Poulaan. Collective benefits and collective guilt served to nullify the chance of retribution.

Togura scarcely thought of the damage to the town and its people, but was deeply worried about the probable reaction of the Wordsmiths.

'Will I be punished?' he said.

'No, boy,' said the servitor. 'They're quite pleased with you, if anything.'

Indeed, within the ranks of the Wordsmiths there was general agreement that the Night had been a good thing. For more than three decades they had explored the odex in a slow, cautious, deferential fashion, learning little of its practical use. Now, in one wild, rampaging Night, Togura Poulaan had taught them something very important about its use.

Brother Troop, the new Governor—the old one had died from an allergic reaction to an unfamiliar type of cheese—codified their new knowledge in Brother Troop's First Law of odex:-

The volume, variety and reality of production by the odex increases in proportion to the length of unbroken linguistic stimulation and the variety of linguistic excitement employed for that stimulation.

In order words, a long shouting match with the odex, with plenty of people shouting, would lead to a great many things being produced, lots of those things being real objects instead of ilpses.

Brother Troop, pleased to be wearing the Governor's pink felt jacket and fur-lined codpiece, had his First Law Of Odex inscribed on a piece of the finest timber available. He ordered it to be done in letters of fire, by which he meant red paint; what he actually received was a fine example of poker-work, but he decided that his words looked splendid even when rendered in charcoal.

Now that he was head of his little empire, Brother Troop set about a little empire building. Even though the Wordsmiths were having little success with the Universal Language they were trying to develop, there was still the possibility of recovering great wealth from the odex. However, as Keep might not take kindly to further frenetic experiments being conducted within city limits, a new location was in order.

Brother Troop sent scouts out into the surrounding countryside to search for a high, well-drained place where they could build a new stronghold, well away from inhabited places. A suitable spot was soon found on the estate of Baron Chan Poulaan, who objected violently to Brother Troop's proposal.

'My estate,' said the baron, 'is not uninhabited. Even if it was, I would not permit vermin to spawn and fester upon my freeholding. I demand the return of my son, the disbanding of the Wordsmiths and the destruction of the odex.'

Brother Troop thus became aware that his order now had an enemy. He decided that the baron was upset at the fame and acclaim his son had won by killing a monster, slaying a dragon and so on and so forth. That was true, but there was more to it than that.

Baron Chan Poulaan was worried about the forthcoming marriage between the king's daughter, Slerma, and the valiant Roly Suet. King Skan Asklander, on his own, was harmless, but the Suets were a wily breed—cunning, scheming and devious. And rich. And numerous.

The Suets had already taken the matter of the currency in hand, and now the baron's spies brought him unconfirmed rumours of plans for a praetorian guard, a police force, a small army of infantry, a poll tax, a mining tax, a road toll and a bridge toll, and, in addition to this, a special estate tax to be levied on barons.

It seemed that the wealth, power and energies of Keep were about to be harnessed and directed, undoubtedly with the idea of establishing a true kingdom which would end the privileges and freedoms of the barons. For his part, Baron Chan Poulaan was coming to see the Wordsmiths as part of an alliance of his enemies; he was sending horse-back messengers across Sung, summoning a meeting of the Warguild.

This could mean civil war.

As Brother Troop refused to yield up Togura, Baron Chan Poulaan finally sent Cromarty to Keep to bring the errant lad to home and to heel. Cromarty, admitted to the Wordsmiths' stronghold, found Togura matching swords with a rough-bearded servitor. As Cromarty had arrived with no more than a boot-blade to his name, and with no bully boys to back him up, he had to attempt diplomacy; his wretched efforts in this direction excited laughter from the servitor and open contempt from Togura; Cromarty, to his shame, had to go home empty-handed.

Togura was training with the sword because he was pre-paring to go questing. His mission: to venture to Castle Vaunting in Estar, and there, hopefully with the permission of Prince Comedo, to contend against the monster guarding the green bottle, retrieve that bottle, recover the index, re-turn to Sung, find out how to use the index, and rescue his true love from the clutches of the odex.

A jovial Suet had already told him that the loss of a daughter was of no account; there were plenty more in stock, and, if he wanted, he could marry one tomorrow.

'I have to save her,' said Togura. 'It's a matter of honour.'

It was a matter of many things. It would be one in the eye for his father, if he could rescue Day Suet from the odex. It would raise his status in Keep, confirming him as a hero. It would make him rich, because he had negotiated an agreement with Brother Troop which would guarantee him one per cent of the wealth generated by the odex. It would prove that he was a real man. It would make him famous. And, apart from all that, he was in love with Day. He thought.

So he trained with the sword, and received good advice from all quarters. The more he learnt, the easier his mission seemed to be. The chance of getting killed came to seem comfortably remote; he could not understand how other people had failed, and suspected that they were misfits who had not really gone questing, but had sneaked off into the never-never to start their lives afresh elsewhere.

After all, Estar was fairly close. Galish convoys went there all the time. Prince Comedo of Estar was, according to his reputation, not the nicest of men, but a promise of a percentage of the gains from the odex should sweeten his temper enough to bring him to let Togura have a crack at the monster guarding the green bottle.

The monster itself, he learnt, was a kind of disk-shaped slug known as a lopsloss; he could not imagine an overgrown slug giving him much trouble. He was startled when told that he would actually have to go inside the green bottle to get at the box holding the index; he doubted that this would be possible until the magic of bottle-rings was explained to him, at which point it came to seem easy.

In fact, he thought the whole thing was going to be a

doddle. When he heard that Brother Troop was laying on an escort to take him to Estar, it seemed easier than ever. There was not a cloud on his horizon. Until he received his invitation to Slerma's wedding.

Then he panicked.

☆

CHAPTER 10

In the end, Togura Poulaan accepted the invitation to attend Slerma's wedding. As resident hero, he hardly had a choice. By declining, he would have offended both the Suets and the royal family, which would in turn have earned him the disapproval of the Wordsmiths.

Because of the wedding, Togura's departure for Estar would be delayed by two days. He was not entirely unhappy with this. Though he had only been with the Wordsmiths for a short time, he felt at home in the Wordsmiths' stronghold; though his mission no longer seemed suicidal, he was not exactly enthusiastic about setting out.

For the wedding, Togura dressed in new breeches, new boots, a stout jerkin and a padded jacket; he wore a sword at his side and flaunted a feather in his cap.

'Etiquette does not permit swords at weddings,' said Brother Troop.

'For ordinary people, no,' said Togura. 'But certain things are expected of a hero.'

'You may be right my son, you may be right,' said Brother Troop, and let him go dressed as he pleased.

The wedding was scheduled to take place in the morning in the Suets' Grand Hall, a building which Togura had never visited before. Arriving early in bright autumn sunshine—a good omen, surely, as it had been unbroken rain for days previously—he found this immense wooden building almost empty except for workmen who were finishing off reinforcements to a section of the floor, and Suet women who were responsible for catering.

Togura walked through the building, strutting a little in his fine new clothes, and admiring all the good things to eat which had been provided in such profusion. Among other things, there were marvellous cakes created in the image of the new coinage.

The building echoed with bright, happy voices. Louder, ominously hollow echoes came from underfoot as people walked this way and that across the wooden floor. Togura walked across one spot where queasy floorboards sagged beneath his weight; he cleared the area quickly, then tapped the floor with his heel and toe, listening to the echoes.

'There's a mine shaft underneath us,' said a well-fleshed well-dressed elderly man.

'It must be a big one,' said Togura.

'One of the biggest. It was Shaft Suet, the richest gemstock sounding in all of Keep. It gave the family its start in life. By the time Shaft Suet was exhausted, the family was rich. Anyway, enough history. You're Barak the Battleman, aren't you?'

'I am. And you?'

'Name's Raznak the Golsh. I'm a Suet by birth and by breeding.'

They idled there for a while, talking of nothing in particular—weddings, cakes, music, the weather. But Togura sensed that Raznak the Golsh had a proposition for him. He was not wrong. Soon Raznak began to speak his mind:

'I hear you're soon to set off on your quest.'

'Very soon. Tomorrow, in fact.'

'What a pity. At the moment, we've got an opening which would just suit a fierce young warrior like yourself. We need a commander for the fighting force we're forming.'

'Honesty compels me to tell you that I'm not the fighter I'm cracked up to be,' said Togura. 'Besides, I'm too young. Few men would follow me.'

'We can use your reputation,' said Raznak. 'You'd grow into the job. We've got people who can help you find your feet. You'd be a regular sword-slaughterer in a few short years.'

'I'm not the type,' said Togura, who had heard the rumours of civil war, and wanted nothing to do with it. 'I'll never have the fighting prowess.'

'Don't run yourself down. I was lucky enough to see you kill the monster which you rode up out of the mine pit. You've got what it takes, young man.'

'That was a fluke."

'Perhaps. But your reputation's solid. So I'm making you an offer. Join us. Sung will soon be a proper kingdom. Soon enough, we'll be the royal family. Skan Askander won't live forever.'

And Raznak winked.

'I've got my duty to Day,' said Togura.

'You've been offered a daughter Suet before,' said Raznak. 'The offer still stands. It wasn't your fault that the little girl met her unfortunate end. Don't go throwing away your life on an impossible quest. I met some of those who went questing and were never seen again. Strong men. Brave men. Not a fool amongst them. They were strong, determined, capable. But they vanished, one and all.'

'All five of them.'

'Five! The Wordsmiths told you that? There's been fifty men go questing, if there's been one.'

This revelation shook Togura.

'Tell me you'll join us,' said Raznak the Golsh.

'I'll think about it,' said Togura.

'You do that, young man. You do that.'

And he most certainly did, pondering his options while the hall filled with guests. Fifty heroes, all missing in action! Could it be true? If it was, then Raznak's offer certainly had its temptations. So who could he trust? Who could he believe?

His troubled mind worried away at the problem until his cogitations were interrupted by the announcement of the arrival of Roly Suet. The young groom, fatter than most people but thin for a Suet, was dressed like a peacock. He looked calm—too calm. His eyes had a glazed, fixed expression. Togura suspected he had been drugged.

'Enter the sacrifice,' muttered a voice.

'The things people do for power!' said another.

Shortly after, the hum of conversation in the hall fell away to an absolute silence as Slerma entered. She was led into the hall and then seated by guides and helpers who made sure she kept strictly to the reinforced sections. At the sight of her, one tender young lady blanched and fainted. Two old ladies, a spinster and a relict, began to titter, and then, unable to help themselves, broke into frank and horrified laughter.

Slerma did not appear to hear. She stared around her, letting her eyes ooze slowly over the vast mounds of food which were on display.

'Slerma will eat well,' she said. 'This is good.'

Two female Suets with fixed smiles draped a veil over her countenance, but Slerma mauled it away from her face. She had gone to a lot of trouble with her appearance, and did not want her efforts to go to waste.

Slerma's make-up represented a unique experiment in abstract art. Stains of green and red were smeared across the flanks of her face, creating washes of gently undulating colour which swelled and contracted as she chewed her cud. She had applied mascara; dabs and dobs of black were scattered above her eyebrows, looking like the distant heads of soldiers peering over the brow of extensive earthworks.

Togura felt it rude to stare, yet could not help himself. He was not alone. Slerma was as huge as he had remembered—if anything, worse. A buxom girl could have been made from the flesh of each of her forearms, and a respectable whore from each of her thighs; her belly could have given birth to a regular conclave of washerwomen. Her fingers, as fat as sausages, looked deceptively soft and helpless; remembering the true strength of her bone-crushing hands, Togura shuddered. To think that he had almost been married to this!

Watched by a disbelieving audience, the wedding ceremony was conducted.

'If any man alleges prior claim to possession of this woman, let him speak now or for ever afterwards remain silent,' said the marriage celebrant, looking around sternly. No claims being forthcoming, he announced: 'I find, rule and declare that there are no prior claims on this woman.'

'What woman?' cried a wit.

Who was promptly suppressed, strenuously.

At the conclusion of the wedding ceremony, Slerma embraced Roly Suet, engulfing him in her arms. She held him close. She had decided to be very loving today. After a while, Roly began to make violent, animated movements with his arms and legs. It appeared he was suffocating. This was highly embarrassing! Senior Suets stood by, one openly wringing his hands, while people pushed and shoved to get a good view, standing on tiptoe and craning their necks. Gladiatorial sports were unknown in Sung, so they had never seen anything like it.

Finally, Slerma released her prey. He slid down to the ground and lay at her feet, limp but still breathing. Taking him by the hair, she hauled him onto her lap, where he lay like a rag doll, his face plastered with red and green and black; he had been kissed.

Someone cheered. Infected by an outbreak of mob hysteria, the others took up his theme; the hall rocked and resounded with applause. Slerma beamed. She was a success. She was glorious. She was beautiful. She was loved. Her happiness would have been complete if her father had been here to see her triumph, but unfortunately he was laid up with gout.

Determined music began; the cheering died away, and was replaced by a babble of talk, gossip and speculation. The festivities were underway.

As a skavamareen wailed along in the wake of a galloping thrum, Togura encountered a girl named Zona, who made it appear that she met him almost by accident.

'Are you a Suet?' he said.

'Yes. How did you guess?'

'What else would they send to seduce me?'

'The cheek of the animal!' she said.

'A kiss would be a good way to start,' said Togura.

She blushed, and Togura knew his suspicions were correct. The Suets had sent one of their expendable females to romance him. He was flattered.

'Dance with me,' he said.

She yielded, so soon they were dancing the Dalataplash, kicking their heels and punching the air, whooping at the warscream and shouting at the hoot, then embracing each other in the couple and the grind. She laughed a lot. She might have been sent, but she was willing. He was young, handsome and a hero, and a baron's son besides, heir to the estate if he killed his half-brother Cromarty. There was good meat on her bones; he knew himself lucky.

They danced then ate, danced then drank, then danced
again. Togura cast occasional glances in the direction of
young Roly Suet, who seemed to be making a remarkable
recovery from his traumatic experience with Slerma. The
royal couple were not dancing: Slerma was still eating,
with Roly at her side feeding her choice morsels from a
bucket.

'Would you marry me?' said Togura to Zona.

'Would I if what?'

'If I asked.'

'Ask.'

'That's no answer.'

'Still, it's the answer deserved. Are you a hero or aren't
you?'

'I'll think about it,' said Togura. 'Come, the music's
wasting. Let's dance.'

And dance they did. She was smooth, lithe, clean-
limbed and lively. He wanted her. She was his answer to
the urgency of the flesh. She was part of a contract for a
fabulous future. In the face of such offers, what wisdom in
questing? Fifty men missing, most probably dead? Where
was the temptation in that?

It was many generations since Togura's ancestors had
been sharp-bargaining Galish merchants, but, nevertheless,
a trader's caution was still part of his heritage; he disliked
unnecessary danger on principle, being entirely lacking in
the kind of hang-devil recklessness which welcomes impossible odds.

But Day!

How could he forget about Day?

How could he just write her off like that?

He tried to bring her face to mind, but failed. He could
not remember what she looked like! He tried, in a dutiful
way, to fabricate feelings of regret and remorse, but failed.

'Kiss me,' said Zona.

And he could hardly decline.

As they danced, the music grew louder. An old-fashioned canterkade beat out a rhythm in direct opposition to a newfangled clay. A sklunk back-thumped, a chanter whined, a snot-pipe shrilled, then massed plea whistles hooted and honked, joining the screaming high pinions in a caterwauling fanfarade.

'So what's it to be?' said Zona, as the last of the music jogged down to nothing. 'Where will you sleep tonight and tomorrow? By some bone-rotting mountainside bog? Or elsewhere, far warmer?'

'Give me time to think,' said Togura, with a laugh of joy and triumph which he was unable to suppress.

Already he knew his answer. It was no contest. The people of Sung—even the young men—were essentially too sane and sober to make good questing heroes. They seemed wild enough, with their feuding and fighting, but such localised sports are essentially civilised in that they never take you more than a couple of days from your own warm bed and a hot-bread kitchen.

Though the Wordsmiths did not know it yet, Togura had just cancelled his quest for the index.

'Let's find a seat,' said Zona.

'Let's,' said Togura, coughing.

'It's rather smoky,' said Zona, waving a hand in front of her face.

'Rather,' said Togura, looking round to see who was smoking the acrid pipe.

He blinked. His eyes were stinging. People were starting to shout. Somebody screamed. Suddenly Togura realised there were clouds of smoke curling and coiling overhead. People were panicking, rushing for the exits. Togura drew his sword, then looked at it in astonishment. Why had he done that? He sheathed it hastily, before Zona noticed. Zona?

'Zona!' shouted Togura.

His voice was lost in the uproar. She was gone. She had fled. Somewhere, a loud voice boomed, roaring:

'Fire! Fire! Fire!'

Togura jumped on a table.

'Don't push!' he bawled. 'People will get crushed!'

But he was ignored. He coughed; the air was harsh with smoke. Looking round, he saw a disturbance. He saw part of a wall breaking down, admitting bright sunlight and a wedge of—masked men!

'We're under attack!' shouted Togura.

But nobody heard him.

He jumped down from the table and waded toward the attackers. With Suets and their guests crushing each other to death in the jam-packed exits, he figured that the break in the wall offered him his best chance of escape from a building now definitely burning.

He drew his sword again, and this time did not feel stupid for doing so.

☆

CHAPTER
11

Togura, dizzy with smoke, fear and excitement, hung back as the masked men attacked. His drawn sword was strictly for self-defence. He saw them close in on Roly Suet, who fought as best he could, crowning one with a food bucket and kicking another in the privates. They overwhelmed him and carried him off.

'Give me back my man!' said a vast, slurred, grubbing voice.

It was Slerma. She was not pleased.

A man slashed at her with his sword. She threw up a forearm to defend herself. By rights, sword versus arm should lead to instant amputation. But the blade scarcely managed to cut deep enough into her blubber to reach the bone. Next moment she had seized the miscreant by neck and by ankles, and was tearing him apart. As Togura blinked, gaped and boggled, the man ruptured and split, spilling—.

Togura closed his eyes, feeling sick.

By now, others had realised what was going on. Suets and guests, arming themselves with tables, chairs, carving knives and roasting spits, gave battle. Those with no weapons flailed at the attackers with jackets, coats, cloaks and capes, seeking to entangle their swords or beat them down so they could close for a stranglehold. Roly's kidnappers were cut off from their escape route. Two sat on Roly, holding him down, while the others fought in the burning building.

Slerma, thinking the battle was going against her side, went to the rescue.

'No!' screamed Togura, seeing her bulking off the reinforced section of the floor.

But he was not heard or was not understood or was ignored. Slerma rumbled ahead, spitting and growling, ready to defend her true love with her life, ready to kill, crush, mutilate and mangle. Some of the masked intruders fled howling at her approach. Slerma advanced in triumph.

Then floorboards broke beneath her, precipitating her into the abandoned mine shaft below. The invaders raised a cheer, and began to prevail. Then a squad of musicians joined the affray, their instruments becoming weapons of war. As battle raged, huge bubbling roars came from underground. Slerma was still alive, and most indignant about her predicament. Two Suets, overwhelming an invader, tossed him into Slerma's pit. Shortly his pitiful screams maimed the air, then came a slubbering groan, and then—from him, at least—silence. The din of battle masked the sounds of feeding.

Togura, sword in hand, skirted round the outskirts of the brawl, making for the daylight. But a masked fighting man stepped forward to confront him.

"Who is it who dares to trifle with Barak the Battleman?' shouted Togura.

'Me!'

And the masked man tore away his disguise. It was Cromarty, claymore in hand.

'Crom!' cried Togura.

'None other,' said Cromarty, grinning with open delight. 'And what have we here? Why, why it's little Tog-Tog. Gather round, boys. Now it's really party time!'

But there were no boys free to gather round.

'You're on your own this time,' said Togura.

'That's all right,' said Cromarty evenly. 'I'll manage.'

And, turning ferocious without further ado, he attacked. Their war-blades clashed. Togura sliced Cromarty's thigh. Cromarty nicked his nose. Blooded, they broke apart, coughing and panting, their eyes stung with tears as smoke whirled about them. They began to circle, posing fiercely and talking tough.

'Come closer,' said Togura, 'and I'll slice you from pox to piles.'

'Not so hasty, salami minor, or you'll be eating your arsehole for breakfast.'

'Talk's cheap, you son of a slut.'

'A slut? Look who's talking. I raped your mother on the night she died.'

'Shut your filth and swallow it.'

'Believe me, Tog-Tog. She loved it. She asked for more and more and more. She licked my—'

'Liar!'

A burning beam crashed down between them. A smaller timber fell, striking Cromarty, knocking him to the ground with a glancing blow. As the building broke up, the fight was breaking up. People were running for their lives. Togura started to scream a threat at Cromarty, but broke out into a fit of coughing instead. His half-brother was lost in the swirling smoke. Togura sheathed his blade. A man came blundering his way, blinded by blood streaming from a cut on his forehead. It was Roly Suet.

'This way!' shouted Togura, grabbing him.

Roly tried to fight him.

'It's me, stupid! Barak the Battleman, rescuing you!'

Togura hustled him out into the street. Smoke reeled up into the sky. Roly, coughing, tried to wipe the blood from his eyes. The street was filled with skirmishing fighters, rearing horses, screaming children and indignant citizens of all descriptions.

'Togura!' yelled a black-masked fighter standing at bay some distance up the street. 'Give us the boy!'

Togura knew that voice. It was his father. As Baron Chan Poulaan cut away the sundry Suets opposing him, Togura fought to control a frightened horse. He mounted up. The animal almost threw him, but he got control. He helped Roly up behind him. Cromarty came stumbling out of the building, still armed with his claymore.

'Cut him down, Crom!' roared the baron, wounded now, but still fighting his way toward them.

Half-blinded by smoke, Cromarty glanced round then attacked. Togura kicked him away, getting slashed on the calf in the process. He saw a gap in the scrabbling fight, and rode for it, with Roly hanging on for dear life. Behind him, the Suet's Grand Hall collapsed with a prolonged crash, sending burning debris sprawling across the street.

The baron was separated from his sons by a pile of burning wreckage. Gathering his wits, Cromarty ordered the nearest half dozen warriors to join him in pursuit. Seizing what horses they could, they did.

Togura rode for hell and high clappers, taking the road to the palace. When they came to the outskirts of the piggeries, he reined in the horse, thinking them safe.

Then he looked round and saw the pursuit closing in behind.

'You should have stayed in the town!' yelled Roly. 'We would have lost them in the side streets.'

'Thanks for the good advice,' snapped Togura. 'It's brilliantly timed.'

He was tempted to push Roly off into the mud and the slother, but resisted the temptation. Roly was what Cromarty wanted. Togura was not going to let him have it that easily. Togura kicked the horse in the flanks, and they rode past palace and piggeries. The road, such as it was, soon plunged downward. They hastened down recklessly, making one of the fastest descents ever of that particular piece of track, which was known as the Slippery Skaddle. The pursuit followed remorselessly.

'Where are we going now?' cried Roly, as they started down a track between bogland and gorse.

'Ahead, unless you've got any better ideas,' said Togura.

He knew they were now on the Fen Route, a raggle-tag half-road picking its way across some of the worst country in all of Sung. The horse was close to failing, but before it could collapse they came to Skob Crossing, a festering marsh crossed by a disintegrating one-step bridgeway.

'Dismount,' snapped Togura, getting down.

When Roly hesitated, Togura gave him a push. As the Suet scrabbled up out of the muck, Togura, half-running, ventured the creaking bridgeway, which was green with moss and soggy with wetrot.

'Don't leave me!' cried the plaintive Suet.

Togura paused long enough to shout 'Follow!', then was off again. The Suet scuttled over the bridgeway behind him. Skidding, slipping and sliding, they panted down a rutted track. Behind them they could hear Cromarty and his mobsters baying at high hunt.

The track grew narrower, and became overgrown. They

sprinted through nettles, yelping. Blackberry clawed at
them. They shoved aside vines, hoping none were poison
ivy. The gaunt trees overhead, their leaves a clatter of autumn, were drenched with draggle-moss, blighted by
canker and pockled with fungus. Roly, glistening with
sweat, was failing fast.

'I can't—keep—up,' he gasped.

'I'd guessed that much,' said Togura. 'Down! Take
cover! I'll lead them off.'

And he shoved the Suet into a thicket of clox, kicking
his backside when he hesitated. Then Togura ran on, holding his side, for he was getting the stitch. He blinked as
sweat scabbed into his eyes, stinging fiercely. He could
feel his strength failing. Behind him, the enemy cheered.
They had him in sight now.

Togura slowed almost to a walk as he padded up the
knoll ahead. On the far side was a narrow ribbon of
swamp, just too wide to jump over. Togura sprinted
down, tore a rotten pole tree from its foundations and
swiftly probed the water, failing to find its depth. It was
green with swamp grass; to the casual eye it could have
been any depth from ankle onwards. Quickly, Togura
nipped round the flank of the swamp, then used his
snapped-off pole tree to thrust and stir, confusing the
surface of the swamp so it looked as if he had sprinted
straight through it.

Cromarty and his bounders came panting over the
knoll. They saw Togura on the far side of the swamp,
apparently untangling himself from some barbarian thorn.

'Have him, boys!' screamed Cromarty.

Whooooping and hallooing, they charged down the slope
and into the swamp, plunging in up to their noses. All
except two. Who began to skirt the swamp as Togura
turned and fled.

'You klech!' shouted Cromarty. 'You gan-sucking jid of

veek-nuckling ornskwun hellock! Come back here, you gamos-eating son of a toad-mother. Scalp him, boys! Cut his oysters and shaft him!'

Togura, labouring up another rise, stumbled. There were rocks underfoot. He picked up a large one, turned, and hurled it at his nearest pursuer. His victim flung out his hands. Snatching up one stone after another, Togura pelted them both. Battered, bruised and bleeding, they made a hasty retreat. Togura had no breath with which to celebrate his triumph.

Down below, the victims of his swamp-trap were extricating themselves from their predicament with some difficulty; the swamp did not have a quicksand bottom, but it was certainly soft. Togura managed a slight smile. Which vanished the next instant as reinforcements came over the knoll on the far side of the swamp-strip. They pointed, shouted, then joined the pursuit.

Togura turned and ran.

But he did not go far.

He ran a hundred paces, hit another rocky stretch which would show no footprints, leapt sideways, went down into a boggy wallow, crawled into a thicket of stilt trees, then hugged the ground and lay still. He waited. He did not have to wait for long. The pursuit panted past. As soon as he thought they were gone, Togura shuffled deeper into the stilt trees. Then, thinking himself out of sight of the track, he rose to a crouch and began to run, nipping from tree to tree, casting frequent looks backward.

He came to a stretch of swamp and plunged in heedlessly, going in up to his neck. He waded across, hauled himself up on the far side, and was off again. For a while he sometimes heard faint, distant shouts and cries, but after a while even these died away. He blundered on, losing track of place and time. Then, finally, he heard the far-off baying of hounds. It terrified him. Dogs! They were using dogs! He went crashing through the undergrowth, till he found a narrow, wending, slovenly stream snaking its way through sedge and mud.

Togura waded down his stream, determined to kill his scent so the dogs would be unable to follow. Unfortunately, he broke enough twigs, grasses and creepers for even the clumsiest tracker to follow, and splattered mud on vegetation that escaped his trampling feet. Fortunately, the dogs were not looking for him: they were seeking a member of the pursuit team, who, realising Togura had left the road, had ventured to search for him in the wilderness, and had become hopelessly lost. Unfortunately, Togura himself, by the time he stopped, was also hopelessly lost.

At first, Togura did not realise his predicament. What he did realise was that his dog-bewildering highway was full of leeches. He left hastily, and counted his assailants. There were seventeen of them, nine of them having battened onto his flesh where his calf had been slashed by Cromarty's sword. He had no fire with which he could burn off the leeches; he decided it was best to leave them to bloat themselves with blood, after which they would drop away of their own accord.

Still concerned about the dogs, he set off across country at the best pace he could manage. The predominant vegetation here was sickle trees, tall, thin and stringy, their shafts of autumn foliage closely clustered, soaring up into the sky above. As he went on, he became half-aware that the going was getting easier; the ground was getting firmer.

Then the sickle trees began to give way to some kind of vegetation he was unfamiliar with: tall, thick, scabrous grey trees set far apart, their foliage so dense that virtually nothing grew beneath them. These trees were covered with long, cruel, jagged hooks, barbs, spikes and claws; their leaves, when Togura was incautious to touch a few, snagged at him with myriads of tiny teeth. He decided they deserved the name claw trees.

Realising he was in a very strange neck of the woods, Togura stopped, and went no further. He decided it was time to orientate himself. He looked around for a landmark, but the thick-foliaged claw trees and the high, spindly sickle trees cut him down to hundred-pace horizons in all directions. He could see bits and pieces of the sky, which was now a diffuse, misty grey; the good weather which had graced the start of the day had failed. He could not climb the claw trees because they would cut him to pieces; the sickle trees, while harmless, would never support his weight. Without landmarks or sunlight, he could not judge his location or the time of day.

He sat down to think things over, and stood up immediately. The dead dried leaves of the claw trees, which littered the ground underfoot, retained their teeth even after they had littered down from their parental branches. Leaning against a couple of convenient sickle trees, Togura took stock of his situation.

He was lost.

He was tired.

He was hungry.

His clothes were damp and caked with mud.

He had no food, excepting half a dozen persistent leeches, which did not really count.

He had one sword, which by rights should now be cleaned, but which was not going to be because he couldn't be fagged.

He had no water.

He had a painful sword-cut on his nose; though only a tiny little piece of his nose appeared to be actually missing, this was not calculated to improve his beauty.

He had a more serious wound in his calf, which was not disabling—no tendons had been severed, and he did not think it was deep—but which was filthy with muck and mud and was now throbbing painfully.

The day was not getting any younger.

So what should he do?

He first tried to retrace his steps, but found himself rapidly getting lost amidst a featureless expanse of sickle trees. He managed to get back to the claw tree forest, then reconsidered his position. Whatever the dangers, he had no doubt that a return to Keep was his best option. But his chances of getting anywhere by blundering about the wilderness at random were slim.

The ground on which the claw tree forest grew appeared to be sloping steadily uphill. He decided to follow the rising incline, hoping to come to a prominence which would give him an all-round view, or, failing that, at least a prehensile tree capable of supporting his weight.

Togura set off, walking slowly, for he was weary; he limped, as his wounded leg was very sore. Remembering Cromarty floundering in the swamp-trap, he managed a slight smile. All in all, he could be proud of himself. He had kept his head in the burning building. He had matched Cromarty, blade against blade. Riding out of Keep, he should by rights have been able to shake off the pursuit; it was just bad luck that the enemy had managed to follow him through the streets and out of the town. Even then, hunted and outnumbered, he had scored a resounding success with his minor tractics. But that didn't alter the fact that he was lost.

Gradually, his little glow of self-satisfaction faded; he plodded onward, getting slower and slower. The day aged; the light faded; a little rain began to drizzle down through the trees. Eventually, he realised it was evening, and would soon be night.

The smart thing to do now would be to climb a tree, to be safe from wolves. Or find a cave, and barricade it. Or at least cut branches to make a lean-to shelter in which he could bivouac. Then eat, scavenging worms, snails, slugs and fungus. A country boy born and bred, he knew what he had to do. But the landscape was singularly unhelpful. He was surrounded by unclimbable claw trees; there was now no undergrowth at all, the ground below the trees being littered with sharp-toothed leaves; there were no helpful rocks or hollows; to the best of his recollection, he had not seen or heard any bird or insect since entering the claw tree forest, nor had he sighted any fungus, edible or otherwise.

He was in a cold, dead, evil place, barren of life and bare of water; the rain sifting down through the creaking, rheumatic branches was strong enough to chill and dampen him, yet insufficient to give him any hope of assuaging his thirst; a cold wind soughed through the leaves overhead, promising a bitter night.

Togura came to a decision.

What he had was nothing, but it was all he was going to get, so he had better make the most of it. Drawing his sword, he scraped away the leaves, clearing a space where he could lay his body down. Then it occurred to him that he could dig a shallow grave in which he could lie down out of the wind. Better still, he could dig a foxhole in which he could sleep with his knees drawn up to his chest to conserve warmth.

Eagerly, Togura set to work, but found the ground hard and unyielding, seamed and knotted with tangles of tough, fibrous roots. It was hopeless.

He ended up spending the night huddled on the bare ground, sleeping in snatches; whenever he fell asleep, he soon shivered himself awake again. By the time morning came, as unfriendly as a hangover, he was feverish. His wounded leg was almost too painful for him to walk on. The lymph node in his groin was swollen, hard and painful; he suspected that if he had been able to clean his wound and examine it, he would have discovered an angry red line running up his leg, denoting blood poisoning.

He had no food: even the last of his leeches had left him.

'On your feet, Togura Poulaan,' he said.

Rising, he sought for support, and tried to take hold of the branch of a claw tree. A mistake—and one that he immediately regretted.

☆
CHAPTER
12

'Zaan,' said the sun.

The ice-white light ran through his blood in splinters.

It was fading.

'Clouds,' he said.

A frog answered him. He spoke. It answered again. His teeth hurt. Then came the rain, drenching away the last of the sunlight. The skirling wind fladdered and scooped, outpacing his eyesight; it came in rents and buffets, sending the shimmy-shimmy leaves stappering and plattering from down to around. Some dead at his feet. He kicked them from ventral to dorsal.

'Tog,' he said.

Asking for someone.

He couldn't remember who.

His legs went balder-shalder-tok through the rain perhaps autumn or winter. His third leg was a gnarled unyielding strake padded with moss and wort where it jammed home to his armpit. The music of a flute cut closer than a knife; hard, high, unyielding, it lacerated his heart. He felt his pulse-beats bleeding through his body. The wind blew furnace hot; he shivered, his teeth tok-tok chin-cha-chattering.

'Hello,' he said.

A frog answered.

'Go away, frog.'

And then, again, hoping against hallucination:

'Hello?'

They didn't seem to notice him. Instead, they kept to their dance, tracing formalities between the green of green boughs and the red of red blood. He waved in their direction with what had once been a hand but which was now a club, a poisoned mass of striving darkness. The ground was rhythmic underfoot. A swathe of wind took him from behind and flattened him to an undug grave.

'Once I had a sword,' he said, or thought he said. 'But I lost it. Perhaps.'

She answered him in the cadence of birdsong, feeding him something which was honey and yet not honey.

'That is good,' he said.

'Sleep,' she said, or thought she said.

Then she was feeding him again, then hurting his hand; he tried to protest, but she fed him with even, placid spoonfuls which slurred and slubbered on his tongue. Her hands were diligent, the blankets very warm. Yet so uncomfortable.

His troubling fingers plucked bits of moss and lichen from the blankets. Dry. Tasteless. He spat them out. It occurred to him that perhaps he was not in a bed at all, but swallowed by some hole in the forest, chewing on moss and dreaming strange dreams while he eased his way toward death.

The rocks above looked solid, sullen, certain.

A cave, then.

The shiftless wind came shifting in through a cold square hole in the cave. Beyond lay a high harsh light which might have been daylight. Things clawed at the hole, scratching, scraping, grasping, gaping. They wanted him.

Frightened, he called for help.

She came to him. Her voice was half birds and half water. Or was it rainbow? Her eyes, dark. Her hands, slender. She fed him soup; he tried to hold the spoon, but found himself clumsy as a baby. She did not laugh.

The next time she came, she was shorter, heavier, and just a little bit sour. Her eyes had changed from dark to grey, her hair from black to fair. The blankets were still scratching him. He complained about them. This time, she said nothing.

Attempting diligence, he tried to remember her face, but it shifted with uncanny agility. As in a nightmare, he tried to stabilise his memories, only to have them prove incompetent each time she entered. Finally he thought:

—Different women tend me.

And knew his thought for truth.

He was healing.

He began to take stock of his situation.

The room was small. Square. Dark. One door. The door led through shadows to a coffin-lid dungeon of darkness. One window. From the bed, he could see the bare branches of a tree, grasping and clutching at the thriftless wind.

What was the room made of? Stone. Vast slovenly blocks of stone. No mortar. Above him a single grey tombstone stretched from wall to wall. He thought of himself as a tiny huddle of flesh and sensation hunched up inside a dull, grey, senseless prison of dour mass, monotonous weight, inertia, and habitual oppression.

'I'm hungry,' he said.

She entered, matching none of his memories. By the windowlight, he saw she was dressed in bulky, padded clothes of woven bark. Tufts of moss and lichen peeked out between the warp and weft; perhaps, beneath that padding, she was as slender as a tree in sunlight. Or perhaps not. It occurred to him that, in any case, not all trees were slender. Not even in sunlight.

She did not frown or smile; though courteous, she was grave, restraining in her dealings with him.

She brought food.

He ate gruel, pap and watered bread.

It was all he could manage.

The bread was very strange. It was heavy and loamy, tasting sometimes of honey and sometimes of fish. Was it made from grain? Or from some kind of pasted root? Eating, he scented swamp. The bread was not to blame. The wind coming in through the window was bringing him the smells of marsh, bog and slough.

When she came again, he ate the soup without help; he could sit up by himself. His blankets were the same woven bark as her clothes, padded with the same mosses and lichens. He resented their million million insect-creeping legs, claws and feelers.

'Wool makes better blankets,' he said.

She answered him with words which were half music, half ripening fruit. Which was strange, for it was the wrong season for ripening fruit. Unless he was mistaken, it was winter. So thinking, he spun down in a dizzy spiral, fainting.

When he woke, it was night.

The shutters had not been fastened properly; they creaked, groaned and laboured in the knock-kneed wind.

'Shutters,' he said, complaining.

And nothing answered no-one.

His head was light yet his limbs were death-heavy. His knees-joints were made of curdling milk. Hands alien. His throat was dry; he was thirsty. Perspiring, he reached the shutters; he could not remember getting out of bed. He found a cord which secured the shutters, tying one to the other. He pulled it free. The shutters swung apart.

He saw bright moonlight, broken buildings, and the titubant shadows of trees reeling in the violent, gusting wind. Banners of turbulent cloud streamed across the moon; when the clouds cleared, the moonlight showed him the dull, low-slung outline of a heavyweight wall which caught the moonlight in its open crescent. Set in the middle of that crescent, like a stump about to be reaped by a sickle, was a vast stone beehive, many times the height of a man. It had no windows, and only one door. Sullen fire glowed within.

—Where am I?

Leaves, thin scampering prey, fled before the wind. Others followed close behind, cruel scuttling predators which kept close to the ground as they moved on the kill. Then all the leaves were suddenly flung upward in turbulent spirals as the buffeting wind switched and turned.

The change in the wind brought Togura a whiff of something foul. It was not swamp or mud or wet water. It was the rot and decay of the flesh. It was a putrid, evil smell of degenerating nightmares, of soft fat becoming fungus, or bones riddled with worms, of eyeballs subsiding into dark pools of purulent liquid.

Togura was almost certain that the smell was coming from the beehive.

The wind changed. And the fire which he could see within the beehive was suddenly obscured, as if someone was walking down a passageway, blocking the view to the centre. Suddenly, terrified, Togura knew that he must not be caught here at the window, watching, witnessing.

He closed the shutters and secured the cords which held them against the wind. Returning to bed, he found himself unable to sleep. Yet when he opened his eyes again, it was morning. Feeding on soup and the meat of a small freshwater turtle, he comforted himself with the thought that the wall, the beehive and the sudden stench must all have been part of a nightmare.

But when his recovering health allowed him to totter around at liberty, he found the window's daylight view the same as its night-time aspect. He had not been dreaming. Sometimes, indeed, the shifts of the wind brought him hints of something foul, and always he identified those hints with the beehive.

He did not know whether he was a guest, a slave or a prisoner, but when he was well enough to walk along a stone shaft as blind as darkness and make the turns which took him to the outer world, they put him to work.

It was most certainly winter now. His old clothes had disappeared, together with his leather boots; he wore clogs, and clothes of woven bark stuffed with mosses and lichens, and a great big ear-comforting flap-hat consisting, as far as he could tell, of several birds' nests held in a net of woven bark. His skin broke out into strange red rashes, which itched. But he endured.

They put him to work at first on the simplest of tasks. A woman took him to a fire which was burning outside a building inhabited by females. He had already once tried to enter that building, and had been prevented.

She pointed at the fire.

'Koo'-l'na-ve'e'esha,' she said, giving different musical values to each of her fleeting syllables, so that this, the simplest of her communications, became an intricate telestic pronouncement.

'What?' said Togura.

'Ko'laaskaa-n'esha-esa. Cha?'

'Ko?' he queried, trying to get her to repeat the phrase.

Impatiently, she slapped her elbow. He had seen these people use this gesture before. Sometimes it seemed to be employed as a form of negation, but in some people it seemed to be simply a kind of nervous tic. She showed him a cut-down hollowed-out gourd which was lined with clay. She took a stick and scraped red-hot coals into it. Shoved it into his hands.

'Ondolakon'n-puru-sodarasonsee. Cha?'

'Cha,' he said, experimentally.

She slapped his face.

'Why did you do that?' he said, sharp tears pricking his eyes.

She made no answer, but went into the females' building which was forbidden to him, returning shortly with a long stick which had a hook at one end. She spoke sharply, then set off. He followed, holding the clay-lined gourd, breathing in the heat which ascended from the coals.

Their clogs clicked down a broad, deserted street flanked by dull, squat, pyramidal buildings, The street ended abruptly in swamp. They crossed a series of rickety bridges between swamp trees and swamp islands. Here and there, occasional bits of masonry obtruded from the chilly waters—a single column, or a bit of wall, or a stairway to nowhere. He blew on the coals to keep them alive. They glowed hot and red, relishing the life fed to them by his breath. He was glad that at least something in this cold, desolate universe appreciated his existence.

In the grey waters, he caught sight of their reflections. Dressed in their gross, bulking clothes of bark and moss and lichen, crowned with their swollen, shrouded head-gear, they looked like strange, deformed insects. The bridges ended. They had reached a place half swamp, half city. Huge, decayed buildings hulked up out of the grey waters. Paths and roads walked variously above and below water. The buildings were drenched in winter-withered vines; he saw that the dead vegetation was poison ivy.

'Lora-ko-lara-sss-daz'n'n'boro,' she said, kicking together a few fragments of stick.

He guessed her purpose, and helped build a fire. They lit

it with one of the hot coals from the gourd. Then, using the hooked stick, she raked down some dead poison ivy. When it was heaped on the ground, she set it alight. She passed him the stick. He did the same, keeping well clear of the ivy, for he knew better than to handle it, for all that it was dead.

'Shor-nash-n'esha-esha-ala'n-cha,' she said.

Then clicked her tongue and walked away, heading back the way they had come. When he followed, she turned on him, screaming. She gave him a push. He retreated. She kicked the stick. He picked it up and began to pull down poison ivy. She clicked her tongue once more, slapped her elbow, then left him.

He worked all day. In the evening, another woman came and led him back to the settlement. There was a meal waiting, of sorts; it was prepared by women, it was served by women, and he ate amongst the women,

This, for a time, was the pattern of his days. He was woken at first light and served a solitary breakfast. Then he was led along the bridges to his place of work. He was never trusted to go alone. The person who took him would wait until he had a fire going and had started on the poison ivy, and would then depart. He once returned of his own accord, and was severely beaten; after that, he knew that he was not supposed to go home until he was fetched.

He worked, all day, alone, eating a communal meal with the women in the evening.

And sleeping alone.

He was bored and lonely.

And hungry.

And puzzled.

He saw old men, who held themselves apart from the rest of the community; there seemed to be about thirty of them, living in the massive stone beehive. But where were the old women? And where were all the people of middle years? Some of the young women were pregnant, but where were their husbands?

For the most part, work appeared to be done by children of both sexes, who began to toil away from the earliest age, and by young women. Togura saw a few young men; he guessed their number at half a dozen in a community of perhaps three hundred people. The young men were always silent and withdrawn; they seemed to be sleep-walking. As far as he could tell, they never spoke.

In the evenings, the women talked at Togura readily, but he could never make sense of anything they said. He found it impossible to learn their names; they, for their part, seemed to think that he was concealing his own identity. He named himself first as Togura and then as Togura Poulaan; they memorised that with no trouble at all, but never seemed satisfied with it. His own attempts to come to grips with their half-sung names were disastrous; his efforts provoked frowns, shock, pain, dismay or open contempt. Nobody laughed. These people did not seem to know what laughter was.

Togura came to suspect that these people changed their names according to the time of day, or swapped and traded their names between each other, or identified themselves with one form of a name yet expected to be addressed in an entirely different fashion. He was baffled, frustrated by his failure to unravel the tantalising mystery of their liquid, ever-singing language.

Not that he had all that much time for philological research. For many days, that evening meal was his one link with the rest of humanity; for the rest of the time, he was as solitary as a hermit, enduring the long cold nights spent in his small stone cell, or working alone in his own quadrant of the city.

As the days grew shorter and colder, and the weather grew worse and worse, he did less and less work. Sometimes he spent all day huddled by a tapering fire lit in a mute stone room in the mute stone ruins, listening to a storm howling outside and watching for cracks in the sky.

The numb days of isolation, one much the same as the next, seemed to run together to become one single, endless day. Exiled from all effective community, he began to hallucinate. The stones mumbled to him. His ears sang with high, distant voices. He watched the sky twist into yellow flame then bleed with purple. Trees stirred and shifted at the periphery of his field of vision, though he was never able to actually catch them in the act of walking.

The days hardened to ice. The storms died away, giving him brittle, frosty mornings of absolute silence. He worked hard on those days, for it became a pleasure to see the swift, passionate flames leaping to the sky, to hear the wing-beating roar of the burning as incendiary passions consumed his tangled ivy, and to warm himself by that energy treasured up from the long-gone sun.

Yet, though he worked to the best of his ability, he did not get all that terribly much done. The food was meagre now. He realised that he was very weak. He had boils and chilblains; his gums bled. He feared scurvy.

Once, in a thaw, he inspected his reflection in the waters of the swamp, and did not recognise what he saw. Was this Togura Poulaan, this thing with long hair, dull sunken eyes, a notched nose and vast birds' nest excrescences? How could these thin legs, these cold aching hands, these clog-clad feet, belong to the son of the strong, powerful and well-fleshed Baron Poulaan, that brave, stout-hearted fighting man who commanded all the Warguild?

'I am Togura Poulaan,' he said.

But his words carried no conviction. He was no longer certain of his own identity. Who was he then? And what? He was something cold and hungry which lived in a cold, unsmiling place where the people spoke like birds and wind and water. He examined the livid purple scar where the wound on his leg had healed. He tried to remember Cromarty's steel cutting home, but could not focus on his memories. His recollections of people and places seemed blurred, dim, unreal.

Perhaps he had always lived here amidst these ruins in the swamp. Perhaps the whole world without and beyond was nothing more than an idle half-formed fantasy he had conjured into being to give himself some solace in his misery. He tried to dismiss the thought, believing himself, apart from anything else, to be incapable of inventing the language he used to think in, which was certainly not the tongue of the community he now endured.

Nevertheless, his hold on his own identity grew steadily weaker and weaker until, on a day which was suddenly warm, and which startled him with the sight of fresh green growth, he saw one of the old men was wearing his jacket.

'Hey grandad!' cried Togura, without thinking. 'What are you doing with my jacket?'

And he approached the ancient. Who looked at him with a gaze of such implacable contempt and disdain that Togura, frightened, retreated.

That evening, Togura became aware of a number of old men regarding him from a distance. He had the impression that they were discussing him. And now, frightened, he could no longer suppress his knowledge of the full gravity of his situation. He was trapped in an alien city ruled—he was sure of it now—by a coven of evil old men who exercised sufficient terror and power to keep every man, woman and child from ever smiling or laughing.

He could only guess at the cause of the noticeable dearth of young men of his own age. He knew nothing of what happened inside the beehive where the old men held court; any conclusions he came to regarding the nameless abominations practised within must be pure speculation. He could not say who impregnated the young women of the community. He could not say for sure why no women survived their youth.

Yet, while all his knowledge was based on guesswork and speculation, lacking any hard evidence, and lacking all possibility of conclusive proof, he was, nevertheless, certain of one thing—if he wanted to live to be much older, then he had to escape.

That spring, he dedicated himself to the pursuit of life and liberty. His life, and his liberty.

It proved very difficult.

He did not know where he was, and he did not know how he had come to be there. Possibly he had walked in over the hills; alternatively, he might have been salvaged from the wilderness and carried here while his mind was still blurred with fever. His memories of his wanderings were vague and fragmentary; some, indeed, were frankly hallucinatory.

His memories could not help him escape, so what he needed to do was to explore. This, unfortunately, was easier said than done.

Now that spring was here, and the poison ivy was spreading its brisk fresh green over the buildings he had cleared during the winter, he was taken off his incendiary detail and made to turn his hand to many different kinds of work. He worked all through the day with the women, who instructed him by example.

In the swamps of the half-sunken city, which was ringed round by steep, forest-covered hills, he drew water, cleared fish traps and used a dull, stone-bladed axe to fell lean, stringy swamp-trees for firewood. He helped make tools, grinding away at bits of the city stone with powdered grit. He worked on the fragile punts used for getting around the swamps. He helped repair bridges, and was taught how to weave ropes and cordage from human hair.

When he found a little free time in the evenings, he never managed to go far. Whichever direction he took led him to despairing bogs and quicksands, swamps deeper than drowning, or dry ground hopelessly infested with poison ivy and barbarian thorn.

In the end, he decided that the only way to escape would be to steal a punt and set out by water.

He made his plans accordingly.

CHAPTER
13

Spring performed its ritual poetry. Flowers budded and bloomed. Eggs hatched in hidden nests. Togura Poulaan in the manner of the young, lusted hopelessly after a certain set of thighs; rebuffed and forced to retreat—at knifepoint —he celebrated the allure of that flesh by secret acts of onanism in musty corners of the darkness.

He was very lonely.

Once, Togura caught a duck-billed fledgeling with webbed feet. It had been running on the loose, skittering through the undergrowth with an urgent peep-peep-peep. Once in his hands, it struggled at first, then lay still. He stroked its yellow-brown plumage. He wished that he could keep it to be his friend, but he did not know what he could feed it on. Besides, other people would probably think of it as food, and act accordingly.

He kissed the little bird, and then released it. The earnest little creature ran off, once more going peep-peep-peep; he watched it until it was out of sight, hoping it knew where it was going. For days afterwards, he wondered just what had become of it.

The flowers aged, curled into senescence, withered and died. The birds, growing to maturity, left their nests. The swamps hummed with a delirium of insects. Togura Poulaan cut a wisdom tooth, which made a slow painful passage through the gum. He invented fantasies in which he saved Day Suet from the odex, and lived with her in splendour. With great care, he designed her undressing and conjured her in heat.

As day followed day, his fantasies became more and more elaborate, dulling the reality of the world he lived in. He still thought that he was diligently planning his escape, but in fact he was doing nothing of the sort. Stealing away in the evenings, after work, he would make tentative little forays into the wilderness, but would always retreat when he got muddy, or when some insect stung him, or when he found the way barred by open water or poison ivy, or by impenetrable screed-growths of swamp-plants reminiscent of bulrushes but much taller.

Thwarted by the swamps, he concentrated on the preliminaries necessary for escape. He would need a store of food. He explored as many of the city's buildings as he could, finding spiderweb passages and darkened stairs which led him to the silent chambers within, and, sometimes, to the roof tops. He found places where he could cache food, but there was never any food to cache; on the rare occasions when he had a surplus, he ate it regardless, finding himself unwilling to leave good food in the dark, where scavenging rats might claim it.

Escape then, was no more than a hobby which complemented his idle fantasies. Settling into the routines of his working days, he had become slow, idle, lethargic, complacent. His diet, which was poor, undermined his ambitions; he had no conspirators to support and encourage his hopes of escape; he was not entirely certain that the outside world existed to escape to. It would have taken a real shock to his system to overcome his inertia and finally force him to decamp.

At the height of summer, he got such a shock when the community tortured a child to death.

Togura Poulaan was so appalled that he refused to believe what he was seeing. Because he did not believe it was happening, he watched from start to finish. It took from dawn to dusk; it was a regular holiday. Belief finally came to him in a dream. He woke from nightmares, screaming, and knew that he had to flee. Immediately.

In fact, it was three days before he departed. He left at twilight, stealing a punt and poling it away through the swamps. He had no certain idea of where he was going. He had hoped to be helped by the moon, which should have been almost full, but he had no such luck. The stars were soon bedimmed by clouds; by the time moonrise was due, the clouds had ceiled the sky. The night was warm, but black.

He went on through a darkness that was alive with singing insects. Progress became difficult; the punt was slowed, delayed and then halted by a shoal of water lilies. He was not surprised to find that he was lost. Maybe it would have been better to run away in the daytime. But, somehow, he doubted that he would have had the nerve to slip away in broad daylight.

He curled up as best he could on the bottom of the punt and tried to sleep. He was not very successful. Inquisitive insects tasted him, and, finding his flesh acceptable, they spread the word. Something bumped into the punt from underneath, spent some time gnawing at it, then, disheartened, left. An animal went flipperty-flopperty through the blacked-out swamps with a blood-curdling chuckling scream.

Togura several times considered punting on, but, knowing that he would only succeed in getting himself more lost than he was, he stayed put. Dreams claimed him briefly, then nightmares woke him; he found it was early morning.

Sunlight slouched through the swamp. A dawdling insect lumbered through the air amidst nearby osiers, lulling him with his dull, lethargic drone. Though it was still the cool of the early morning, his limbs were heavy with a siesta-sun weariness. He wanted to lie down and sleep. Now that it was daylight, he thought he would sleep quite well.

Resisting temptation, Togura poled his way through the waters, habitat of eel and ewt. Slowly, he negotiated the hazards of the swamp. Occasionally, bubbles stirring on the surface hinted at the direction of a current which might lead him to an outlet from the swamp. He followed one hint after another, only to find that the current dispersed and disappeared, or that the way ahead was an impossible acreage of sedge, or a morass of oozing mud where his punting pole could not find the bottom.

Often the punt ran aground on a slop, a stinking mudflat riddled with wormholes. Then he had to back it off and try some other avenue. He wished—though there was no use in wishing—that he had tried to escape in spring, when the water level would have been higher. He was now more tired than ever. He passed a low-hanging tree, the largest he had seen in the swamp; he was sorely tempted to make camp, and let one of its ergonomically-designed branches nurse him to sleep.

He forced himself onward, driving the punt over a splodge-shaped fresh-water nettle-fish. The day was now alive with the steady hum and blur of insects. The sun had ascended to the heights. High, willowy swamp-trees arched overhead; sunlight, warm and heavy, settled down through a fantasia of branches and foliage. Little scraps of blue sky were mixed into that dense green soup of bough and leaf. In the wake of the punt, which left scarcely a ripple on the waters, tipsy reflections wavered momentarily, then composed themselves. It was now a long time since Togura had seen any hint of a current.

He blinked against the heavy lull of the sun. He tried to convince himself that he was a hunted fugitive, running for his life. But it was impossible. Everything was slow, heavy, lazy. The leisurely rhythms of punting refused to support his claims to urgency.

As he eased the punt down hidden channels between overhanging trees, he slapped away an overhanging branch. Irritated, it retreated: it was a snake. He felt no sense of alarm. Everything was too lazy to consider hurting him. Violence was impossible.

He halted, for water weed and water lilies barred the way ahead. He could go no further. The gnarled voices of frogs, in concord with the droning insects, were persuading him toward sleep. Then, excited, he saw signs of a current in the water. Looking closer, he saw it was a rat swimming, nosing its way between intolerably bright sun-dapple reflections. The waters congealed behind it.

A gaudy dragonfly, child of the sun's pleroma, hovered above the humid waters. As Togura watched, a free-floating rainbow cascaded away from its colours. He blinked, and the hallucination was gone. He decided he had better rest, at least for a few moments. There were trees around him and branches overhead; he was well concealed. A little sleep would do no harm. He curled up in the bottom of the punt, heedless of its discomforts, and was soon lost in slumber.

Togura slept, dreaming of Day Suet asleep in a bed of turquoise, jacinth and ligure. She woke, a sultry melon-light glimmering in her eyes. Giff-gaff, said an insect, eating her nose. He tested her jymolds. She was hot. He was swollen. A sheep pushed him to one side. He plucked mint and ate it, gnawing the sheep. He watched his mother, now

perissodactyl, walk across the water lilies. I raped her, said
Cromarty. Not so, said Togura; you're just saying that because this is a dream. He closed with Cromarty. His swelling spat. Hot. As birdsong sang.

Togura woke and heard the birdsong. There was something wrong with it. True birdsong should not be like that.
He was hearing people talking. They were hunting him.
Hunting me, said Togura. His words took flight, becoming
shovels of goldleaf; with relief, he realised he was still
dreaming. Sleep on, said Togura to Togura. He did, but his
dream soon became a nightmare.

Togura Poulaan dreamt of the gaping mouth of a child,
which sweated blood. He heard the heavyweight thud of a
waterlogged club. White bone splintered through ruptured
skin. A woman pulled out a tooth, licked the bloody
stump, then swallowed it. The sun licked down, licking his
face, stripping away the skin as it did so.

Then something shaded out the sun.

Togura woke for real, and opened his eyes.

In the trees above him, something lurched and giggled.
And moved. Sunlight stabbed downwards. He flinched,
blinked, and shaded his eyes. He saw bright eyes staring
down at him. He leapt to his feet, almost strangling himself. Clawing at his throat, he fell back to the floor of the
punt. Someone had looped a noose round his throat as he
slept.

They attacked him then, swarming down out of the
trees. It was the young women who had hunted him and
found him. They beat him, punched him, pinched him,
scratched him. The punt, of course, got swamped in the
process. They ducked him, forced him underwater and
held him there until he almost drowned.

He cried out, his words gashing the air with incoherent
fear. The noose was still round his neck. As he floundered

in the water, the other end of it was passed up to someone in the trees, who held it while the punt was bailed out.

Then they started off for the city.

Some of the women waded through the swamp on long, high stilts, which he had never seen before. Others rode in punts. Togura was dragged the whole distance behind one of the punts. As his clothes caught on underwater obstacles, the bark was slowly torn to pieces; he left a trail of waterlogged moss and lichen behind him. He had already lost his clogs. By the end of their journey, he was cold, muddy, exhausted and entirely naked.

They imprisoned him in a wickerwork cage hung in a half-submerged hall on the outskirts of the inhabited area of the city. They left him there overnight, without food or water. In his misery, he thought that they were going to starve him to death, so he was most relieved when a woman came early in the morning, opened as hatch which was too small for him to escape through, and passed him a gourd filled with potable water, and a wooden bowl filled with a steaming pot-pourri of turtle meat, snake meat, bird meat, boiled vegetables, steamed herbs and caterpillars.

She watched while he ate the lot, then she took back the bowl, gestured for him to drink, took back the gourd, and then, to his surprise, slipped him a tiny ornamental knife. She slashed a finger across the side of her neck in a swift, emphatic gesture. He understood. She was counselling him to commit suicide. That was what the knife was for.

She left.

He contemplated the knife, which was scarcely the length of his little finger. The diminutive handle was of nacreous mother-of-pearl; the blade, catching a gleam of light in that gloomy place, was of a kind of steel which was brittle yet would take a keen edge.

'I will not die,' said Togura, slowly.

He refused to kill himself. There were so many things he

had to do! He heard voices; people were coming into the hall. He had to hide the knife. But how? He had no clothes and no clogs. The blade was razor sharp—he could hardly secrete it in a body orifice. Deciding swiftly, he knotted it into his thick, straggling hair, which had not been cut for more than half a year.

He barely had time to finish the job before his handlers were upon him. They took him from the cage and soon brought him before the stone beehive. Out in the open air, the old men of the community were sitting in state on ornately carved benches which must have been brought out especially for the occasion.

Togura, naked, stood facing the old men. He was aware that the rest of the community, perhaps three hundred people in all, was gathered behind him, keeping at a cautious distance. He was cold. The sun, withdrawing from the scene, consoled itself with its celsitude. Togura coughed. He wondered if he was coming down with a chill. He coughed again. The old men glared at him;

'I can't help coughing,' he mumbled.

Someone screamed at him.

He tried to hold himself rigid, as if that would suppress his coughing. His fingers made small, meaningles, involuntary movements. The old men sat like statues, saying nothing. There was not a sound from the crowd gathered behind him. He felt unearthly, unreal. Dizzy. The light staggered. He swayed. Then the light ebbed away entirely, and he fainted.

When Togura came to, he found himself lying in a crumpled heap on the ground. One of his elbows was hurting badly, but, rising to a half-sitting position, he found the joint was still functional. A long and entirely unintelligible speech was in progress. It was being given by a wart-faced little man, an undershapen gnomish figure who clapped his

hands repeatedly to emphasize the points he was making.
Somewhere, a drum was beating.

Togura, sitting up properly, tried to work out what was
going on. He nursed his elbow, which made it a little more
comfortable, which in turn made him realise just how
much of the rest of his body was sore and aching. He felt a
little bit feverish. The dwarf, an old, old man whom Togura had never seen before, continued his speech, assault-
ing the air with his high, harsh, glittering voice. On and on
he went, evidently tireless, incapable of being bored by his
own words. In the background, the monotonous thung-
thung-thung of the drum continued relentlessly.

'Shabana loy, zerd-nek,' muttered Togura, thus giving
voice to the worst obscenities available to him in his native
patois.

A scream menaced him. He doubted that anyone had
understood what he had just said—if they had, they would
have torn him to pieces—but they were giving clear warning that they were not prepared to tolerate any noise from
him at all.

'Well up yours,' said Togura, hauling himself to his feet.
'You can't push me about forever,' he said. His voice, half
anger, half anguish, rose to a shout. 'I am Togura Poulaan!' His voice hurt his throat. The rusty sound it made
was so strange that it almost frightened him to silence. But
he kept going. 'You hear me? I! I am Togura Poulaan. I! I
am the son of Baron Chan Poulaan! I! I! I!'

The dwarf, enraged, screamed at him. Togura continued
regardless.

'You have brought me here without my consent. You
hold me here now against my will. I demand—I demand!
—to be returned to my own home immediately. Failing
that—'

He was taken from behind by two strong women. As the
dwarf capered, dancing out his anger, gesticulating wildly

as he shrieked and shrilled in his high-pitched voice, Togura was marched toward the beehive. He struggled all the way.

When they reached the doorway, Togura's resistance intensified. The two women responded by lifting him off the ground and ramming his head into the stone roof. Stunned, with thick blood trickling down from a cut on his scalp, he stopped fighting. He made himself a limp deadweight, pinning his hopes on passive resistance. It was useless. They womanhandled him down the hallway without any trouble at all. His feet, bumping over the stone floor, were getting hurt. He had just decided it would be better to co-operate when, without any warning, they let him go. He fell face first to the stone floor.

He was in a hot, close room which stank of rot, filth, slime and decay. A roaring fire was cackling-clakling in the centre of the room. The old men came crowding into the room; the women, as if dismissed, departed. A door was thrown open on the far side of the room. A strange door, for it was small and circular. Half a dozen of the old men grabbed burning brands from the fire and menaced Togura. Warily, he eased himself round the room, forced toward the circular door by the threatening flames. The old men shouted to each other in high, excited voices. Their eyes gleamed with unhallowed joy.

Togura knew there was something terrible beyond the circular door. It was the source of the stench which filled the room. Reaching the door, he glanced inside. He saw a circular room with a stone ledge running round the wall and—

With a shout, the old men came hustling forward, jabbing at him with their burning brands. Togura leapt through the door and almost went hurtling into the pit which lay beyond. He scrabbled for balance on the narrow stone ledge, slipped, saved himself, was jabbed by a burning brand, crawled along the stone ledge circling the room, then, when out of reach of the old men, stopped to take stock of his situation.

Some of the old men came crowding in through the circular door to watch. One or two of them threw their burning brands into the pit; something in the pit creaked or groaned with a noise half owl, half pig. Togura looked down.

On looking down, Togura saw a stinking confusion of rubbish crowding the pit below. The reek was appalling; it stormed his senses and laid siege to his sanity, slapping his naked body in hot, wet, putrid waves, cramming his nostrils with its intolerable unclean insinuations, clambering into his lungs and making him want to vomit. He screamed at the smell, but it did not go away.

The old men bellowed and cheered. Another threw his burning brand into the pit, stirring up more noise down there. Quite apart from the burning brands, the pit was lit, toward the bottom, by its own clear, harsh, unwavering light; despite the illumination, Togura could not make much sense of its jumbled contents.

Togura looked around, examining the massive stone-block walls, which had been built without mortar. The circular walls rose sheer toward the sky. Peering upwards, he saw that the room was open to the sky. If he had to, he should be able to climb the wall, if these old men would go away and leave him in peace.

As Togura was so thinking, he looked down again, and saw what seemed to be a snake. It was in amongst the rubbish. It was weaving slowly. But it was too hard and bright to be a snake. And too long. It seemed to be some kind of tentacle. And it seemed to be made of metal. A metal tentacle?

Yes.

Having made sense of that detail, he slowly began to

make sense of the others. And began to realise just what he was looking at. Down in the pit, those dark-stained filthy bubbling things, crusted with scabs and writhing with degenerating fluids . . . they were not random assemblages of rubbish. They were bodies. Human bodies. Gleaming, convoluted metal penetrated their flesh. The metal hummed softly.

As Togura watched, one of the slowly weaving metal tentacles kissed a body and tasted it. The body flinched. Somewhere in the degenerating mass, an eye closed. Then opened.

'They're still alive!' screamed Togura.

Hearing his scream, the old men began to laugh. They cackled with unconcealed glee, jeering at him and at their victims, who endured a slow, agonised death of endless torment, decaying while still alive.

Then they left, scrambling out through the circular door. They closed it behind them. Togura crept along the stone ledge, reached the door, and hammered against its unyielding timbers, crying for mercy.

It did not good.

Nobody answered.

Nobody came.

He was on his own.

Shuddering, he yielded to urgent necessity, and voided his bowels, adding marginally to the stench which pervaded the room. He moved to a cleaner spot and sat down to think. One last drop of blood fell from his bleeding scalp to the stones, which were scalloped and sculpted in a most peculiar way.

What now? He decided he should think, and rest, then try to escape. Rest! It was easy to say, but almost impossible to do. His body was trembling uncontrollably. He could not keep himself from looking down into the pit. Remembering how he had almost fallen into it on first entering the

room, he could not keep himself from imagining his own
body already pierced to a scream and beyond by hard metal
shafting into his armpit, his omphalos, his . . . his . . .

Overcome by his fear, by the stench, by the pitiless horror, he vomited. And felt better, as if he had purged his
body of some kind of poison. He felt calmer. He could
deliberate, analyse and plan. He wished he knew how all
those people had got into the pit. Had they been thrown in?
Or had they chosen to consign themselves to the pit rather
than die of thirst and hunger. And, quite apart from all
that, how had the pit come into existence in the first place?

Looking down into the pit with a cold, clinical eye, Togura decided it must be an ancient device for torture and
punishment dating back to the ages before the Days of
Wrath. As he studied it, one steel tentacle slowly reared
upward and started questing in his direction. It searched
toward him, slowly but surely. It knew he was here! And it
wanted him!

He could not break the door down. The walls were solid,
as far as he knew. There was only one way out: straight up
to the open sky. But that was too easy. Too obvious. Peering upward, he caught a glimpse of something sharp. There
were blades or knives embedded in the walls. That, then,
was part of the torment: to see a way of escape, to climb
with a growing sense of triumph, and then to be slashed,
gouged and mutilated by the waiting blades, and finally to
fall screaming to the waiting pit.

The metal tentacle drew nearer. He edged away. It tasted
the blood which had spilt to the stone, then, with a convul-
sive thrust, it skewered its way into the rock, seeking the
source of the blood. Finding nothing, it withdrew, leaving
a fresh scar in the stone. It started hunting again. Out of the
corner of his eye, Togura saw another tentacle rising from
the pit.

They were hunting him, and him alone. If only there had

been someone else! Some other source of hot blood! If the tentacles had been forced to hunt two people simultaneously, he might have had at least the shadow of a chance. But there was nobody else. No other source of blood. Just him.

Blood! That was it! The answer! As the tentacle swerved toward him, Togura skipped sideways and tore away the knife which was knotted in his hair. It came free, together with a hunk of hair. He slashed his arm.

A bright pulse of arterial blood pumped from Togura's wound. He let it splatter across the wall, directing it deep into the cracks between the mortar-free blocks of stone. Slowly, he walked along the wall, wounding the architecture with his blood. Then, feeling light-headed, he crushed the bleeding down to nothing with the heel of his hand.

By now, a dozen tentacles were in pursuit of him. They savaged their way into the cracks between the masonry, striving for the source of the blood. Huge blocks of stone shifted, grated and cracked. A trickle of rubber went clobber-sklabber-klop as it rattled down into the pit.

Then one massive block of solid rock, attacked by half a dozen tentacles at once, splintered, burst and collapsed. The whole wall shifted. It began to fall. With a roar, an avalanche of stone pounded down into the pit. Steel screamed in agony. A fine yellow spray hissed from ruptured tubing. The light from the pit blinked, wavered, then abruptly died.

Togura, trembling, realised he was still alive. A block of stone nudged him, hinting. He scampered away, gaining a position on the rubble-slide. The bit of wall he had been crouching by promptly collapsed; if he had stayed where he was, he would have been killed.

The air was heavy with rock-dust. Togura coughed, then coughed again, then spat. He could hear confused shouting. High, over-excited voices squalled in fear and panic.

Something came questing up out of the rubble.

A metal tentacle!

Togura went scampering up the new-born scree slope, and found himself in the room with the fire burning in the centre. A lot of rock had spilt into the room, crushing some of the old men; he could hear someone moaning under the rubble. All the survivors had fled, but for one—the speechmaking dwarf, who, incoherent with rage, grappled with him.

Togura smashed him.

Then picked him up and threw him in the fire.

The dwarf writhed and screamed, his agony rising to a frenzy as the brisk flames licked away his skin. Togura picked up chunks of rock and hurled them at his victim shouting with unholy joy. Then, as the dwarf subsided, unconscious or dead, Togura snatched up a burning brand and strode down the corridor to the outer world.

Outside, to his astonishment, he found a revolution in progress. The sight of the old men panicking out of the wrecked beehive, many of them cut, bruised and bleeding, had been enough to trigger off an uprising. The balance of power had changed more swiftly than the weather.

Togura, who had no experience of revolutionary politics, was amazed at the transformation of the people. He knew them only as sullen but reliable servants of the ruling regime. Now they had gone berserk. Before his very eyes, the young women who had so diligently hunted him down in the swamps were mobbing the old men to death. Children of both sexes, giving vent to high, hysterical, manic laughter, were helping with the slaughter. The community's handful of young men, no longer sleep walking, had crippled one greybeard and were now kicking him to pulp.

'This is excessive,' said Togura. 'This is insane.'

He was rapidly becoming experienced in the more bloodthirsty aspects of revolution. Despite hunger, fatigue, shock and terror, his mind was still acute enough to realise that there might be a lot to be said for the idea of getting out of town—and fast. The crowd would soon run out of old men to murder, but their bloodlust would still be running high and hot, and there was no telling what they might do then.

Togura padded through a mixture of blood and brains to the nearest doorway, which led to female quarters he had never entered. They were empty, as everyone had joined the slaughter. He bound up his self-inflicted wound with a bit of bark and some cordage, found a set of clothes and clogs and dressed himself, then exited the building through a door on the far side, well away from the administration of revolutionary justice.

As the screams of hate and agony faded away behind him, he walked click-clock through deserted streets to the swamp. There he stole a punt and poled away.

As Togura poled through the swamp, his wound started bleeding again, despite his attempt to bandage it. He tore away his makeshift dressing, salvaged some spiderweb from some swamp vegetation, and used that on the wound. It stopped the bleeding. When he halted toward evening, he felt very weak, perhaps as a consequence of losing so much blood. But he knew he would live.

CHAPTER
14

It took Togura three days to get out of the swamp. He never once relaxed during those whole three days. He would sleep, but only lightly, waking for any unusual sound. Finally, he found himself on a stream, which became a creek, which he followed down to the sea.

By the sea was a tiny hamlet housing thirty-two fisherfolk. When they saw him approaching in his clothes of moss and bark and lichen, wearing his birds' nest headgear, they fled screaming; perhaps they were not entirely unaware of the abominations practised until so recently in the swamps of the hinterland.

Togura looted their houses shamelessly, dressing himself in sealskin clothes, and loading what food he could carry into baskets of woven flax. Then he left, hurrying off before they could gather their courage and come back to kill him.

He had not been able to steal any proper shoes, but the clogs he wore were hateful to him, contaminated as they were with bad dreams and claustrophobic memories. Two days along the coast, he tossed them into the sea. They bobbed up and down in the waves; he imagined he heard them over the thunder of the surf, walking the waters with a steady tromp-chop-tromp; he watched until they were out of sight, floating away, perhaps, to the smudged, hazy distances where the horizon was burdened with cloud, or by an island, or by, perhaps, the coast of the continent of Argan.

Then he marched on, barefoot.

☆

CHAPTER
15

In his early childhood, Togura Poulaan had once visited the coast in the company of his parents. They must have gone there on business connected with the Warguild, for the baron would seldom stir from his estate for any other reason. Or perhaps that had been the year of the plague, and they had fled to the coast for their health. That was long, long ago, back in the days before his mother had gone mad and died, back in the days before his little brother Stoat had died of rabies.

From that visit of long ago, Togura had dim, distant memories of a quayside clatter and of a hot, clamorous harbour where boats like broken insects sculled to the leering hulks floating in a stifling calm. On that hot, hot summer's day, the harbour had been filled with simmering sewage; he had spent an entire afternoon on the quayside, stoning helpless turds to death.

That was how he remembered the coast.

Here, however there were no close-shouldering houses loud with voices and barking dogs; there were no cobblestone streets reeking of fish nets and onions; there were no vendors offering cockles, whelks and whitebait for sale; there was no putrefying mass of enclosed harbour waters, quiescent as a jellyfish.

Instead, there were open shores of rock and sand; there were cliffs, headlands, inlets and bays; there were creeks, streams, and rifts of coastal marshland alive with herons, shags and nameless stilt-legged birds; there were sheltered dells, fragrant with herbs, lumberous with bees, swamped with heat in the noonday summer sun; there were rolling hillsides and uprearing cliffs, a mix of stunted trees, wild roses and impoverished coastal grasslands; there were wide, wild vistas, bare of habitation, where even the slightest summer breeze hinted at the possibility of summer storm.

And there was the wide-shouldering sea, booming in from the far-flung horizons. The sea! The sea, the ultimate cuspidor, here running clean and empty, bare leagues of weather-water where the white-whip winds scoured away to the distance. Togura was fascinated, watching blue rolling upon green upon grey as the lumbering billows swayed switch-back onto the shore to break—break!—with a coruscating roar of turbulent thunder, a roar swiftly dissolving to a clattering rush of baubling light shimmering over pebble, sand and rock, ending with a final hiss, that hiss itself annunciating the start of the sea suck which would haul back all in an incoherent jumble of rock-sliding shale and snake-sliding light.

The sound of the sea was always with him as he tramped along the coast for day upon day. At nights, sometimes he slept in caves high above the sealskin rocks, or laid himself down beneath a fallen log, or rested beneath the open sky on a patch of pebbly sand on a scrubbly beach nestled between high-pitched headlands.

He was almost alarmed to find himself free.

For the time being, his march along the coast provided

him with necessities which liberated him from the problems of free will. Dealing with the demands of the march,
and the day-to-day difficulties of survival, he did not have
to trouble his head about the probable political situation in
Keep, or about where he stood in the conflict between his
father and the Suets, or about what, if anything, he should
do about the quest he had promised to undertake for the
Wordsmiths.

He was at peace.

His peace was interrupted when he sighted a tower on a
promontory in the distance. He approached with circum-
spection, and, drawing near, he laid himself down in the
sea-heather while he puzzled out his next move. The tower
was of white stone which dazzled in the sealight. It appeared to be octagonal. Concluding that it was deserted,
Togura approached, and walked round the tower.

Each side was pierced by a single doorway. As there
were no doors to bar the way, he entered. Inside, the stone
floor was bare but for a few broken snail shales; there were
no windows, but it was bright with doorlight and skylight.

Togura looked up—and up—and up—and saw above
him an octagon of day. The building had no roof. He was
reminded of another place which had had no roof. Remembering the torture pit inside the stone beehive, he imagined
that he smelt an intolerable stench of decay. Half-singing
voices yakkered and laughed. A tentacle clutched for him.

He staggered outside, fleeing from the tower, screaming
as he ran. Then, panting, he stopped. He shuddered, and
looked back. The tower rose, high, white and graceful,
gleaming in the bright, clean light. He could see through
one door and out through another. It was an open place
which could imprison nothing. He shook his head at his
own foolishness.

Then, to give himself time to recover completely, he sat
himself down on a convenient rock, breathed slowly and

deeply, and watched the thick brown slubbery kelp rising and falling in the sea surge. Waves came billowing in, drenching over the rocks, flinging spray to the sky. When the waves withdrew, bright fish scales of sunlight glittered on the rocks; pebbles, momentarily gemstones, gleamed with smooth satisfaction. Out across the ocean, two gulls tangled in the sky, contending for possession of a fish.

'This is a good place,' said Togura.

Calmed, he returned to the tower, and laid his cheek against the dry skin of its whitework masonry. The rock underfoot was warm, but the tower was cool.

'Forgive me,' he said.

Then he entered its hospitality. With eight open doorways and no roof, it hardly offered him much shelter against bad weather, but he was minded to stay. It had frightened him at first, but he was starting to realise that for a long time a great many inconsequential things might alarm him.

'I will be happy here,' he said, coming to a decision.

And, with his flight along the coast at an end, he explored the promontory and the hinterland beyond, singing makeshift little songs to himself, peculiar melodies which he invented on the spur of the moment, thinking himself very musical.

Deep in the hinterland, amidst thickets of conifers loud with clicketing insects, he found a dry, deep cave half-concealed by tumbledown rocks. It was not very dark, for flaws in the roof admitted shafts of daylight. They would also admit rain, in season, and the cave would be draughty. Nevertheless, someone had once lived here for many years, carving a stone sleeping platform out of one side of the cave. On a stone shelf, there were half a dozen stone jars, in which were the blackened husks of some food now many years dead.

'I will stay here,' said Togura.

He lived there for many days. He made snares to catch
rabbits and birds and traps to catch fish. The sea gave him
the rotting wreck of a whale; it was foul beyond eating, but
he salvaged bones which he later sharpened against rock.
He made a stabbing spear, a bow, and arrows without
fletching. He plaited the intestines of animals to make
cordage. He ate seaweeds, frogs and butterflies, raw fish,
raw meats, wild mushrooms, limpets gathered from the
rocks, snails, grassland grubs and incautious beetles.

He repeatedly tried to make fire, rubbing sticks together,
trying to build a fire drill, and, finally, trying to conjure
wood to flame by force of will alone. Although he failed,
he was not unhappy. He cut fish and flesh to thin strips and
dried it in the summer sun, arranging black rocks in a sheltered spot to form a suntrap. When he got bored, he found
a cliff which was difficult but not quite suicidal, and
climbed it, or swam in the surf, coming out shuddering
from the cold of the summer sea.

But he was not often bored, for he had so many things to
do. There were things which properly belong to childhood,
yet he did them shamelessly, for there was no-one to dis-
parage his play. He investigated the close-coiling shells of
the sea, the articulation of the claws of the crab, the quill-
pen feathers of the gull. He built a sand castle, and thought
it an original invention. He sorted sand from pebbles and
sifted it through his hands, letting it drift down to make
patterns on flat black rocks.

As the days went by, he had fewer nightmares.

Sometimes, he saw sails in the distance, but he had no
desire to join their journeys.

'Time is my journey,' he said.

And, having said it, wondered if he would become a
philosophical hermit living out his days amidst wind and
rocks.

A day later, he was sunbathing when something shadowed out the sun. Opening his eyes, he saw a stranger standing over him. A man. Black hat, black beard, black cloak. Weapons? A dagger. Black strides, black boots, black bootlaces. A weatherbeaten face.

'Hello,' said the stranger, in a barbarous accent.

'Greetings,' said Togura.

Then closed his eyes, to make the hallucination go away. When he opened his eyes again, the hallucination was still waiting patiently.

'Are you real?' said Togura.

He meant the words to mean what they meant in his native patois: do you truly exist? But the stranger interpreted them to mean what they meant in mainstream Galish, which was, literally, 'Is your presence sincere?', and implied 'Do you really wish to make a bargain?'

'Boy, I've said nothing of trade,' said the stranger.

'Neither have I,' said Togura.

'Where is your keeper, boy?'

'What do you mean by that?' said Togura, speaking slowly, and with some difficulty; he had fallen out of the habit of language.

'Have you no keeper then?'

'What would I need a keeper for? Do you think I'm simple or something?'

'If you're not simple, then how else do you explain yourself?'

'I don't explain myself at all to nameless earth-walkers,' said Togura. 'Name yourself.'

'My name is Jotun,' said the stranger, meaning 'dwarf'.

'That's a strange name for a fellow of your height,' said Togura, for the man was the same size as he was.

'Truth to tell, I guard my name amidst strangers. But whatever you are or aren't, you look honest enough to me. So I'll give you my true name, which is Soy Doja. I'm a healer by trade; I'm on this coast to look for the plant they call Moonbeam. Very rare. Do you know it?'

'No,' said Togura, who had never heard of it. He felt it was now time to name himself, but, since the other had lied about his name—and was, incidentally, still lying—Togura decided not to trust him with the truth. 'I'm Parax Gemenis myself,' said Togura. 'I'm a fisherman from many leagues along the coast. There's a feud in my village which threatens my life, which is why I'm here.'

After telling each other a great many more elaborate lies, and exchanging a considerable amount of deliberate and accidental misinformation, they did a little trading. Togura sold the traveller some sun-dried fish, accepting in payment a small coin which bore the head of Skan Askander.

The traveller stayed the night in Togura's cave. He had a tinder box, so they had a fire; when the traveller moved on the next day, Togura kept the fire burning. He would need it in the winter.

Now that he had fire, he should have been happier still, but he was not. He was restless all day. Brooding. That evening, he sat by the fire, turning the coin over in his fingers. Part of the new coinage minted by the Suets, it brought back memories of the wedding feast in Keep. Of the cakes baked in the shape of coins. And of Slerma, who must surely be dead by now.

Overwhelmed by homesickness, he remembered, with an intolerable sense of longing, the pleasures of his former life. Drinking, jokes and conversation. Real shoes. Horses which would carry you over the league-roads and eat out of your hand. Hot meals cooked by women. Women themselves, their eyes alive with temptation, their breasts hot and swollen beneath their clothes, their reception waiting. Real blankets. The welcome of friends. Lying in bed in the morning, dozing. Spending days being utterly idle. Eating real bread. Shutting out the wind at night. Cock fighting.

Togura knew what he had to do. He had to return home. He would be reconciled with his father. He would beg his father's forgiveness, and would become a true brother to Cromarty. They would live together happily ever after.

Enthused, animated and excited, he could hardly sleep. He rose at first light, tied his bow, spears and arrows into a bundle he could carry over one shoulder, ate the little bit of dried food he had left after dealing with the traveller, knotted the traveller's coin in a bit of bark then knotted the bark to his wrist, and was ready to go.

'Goodbye cave,' he said. 'Goodbye rocks. Goodbye tower.'

He spent some time sentimentalising in this manner, then turned his back on the place and trudged along the coast, heading in the direction his itinerant stranger had come from.

He was making for D'Waith.

☆

CHAPTER
16

The weather broke up; Togura Poulaan travelled through storm, wind and rain, enduring the worst which summer could bring. Once, the night caught him out in the open; he huddled in the lee of the largest rock he could find, and shivered there, sleepless, until dawn. Once he slept in a sea cave, and was washed out of it by the high tide. The next evening, harried over a hill by an electrical storm, he was close to despair when he surmounted the summit and saw, on a clifftop at the bottom of the hill, a ruinous cottage near an ancient horned cairn.

Togura went bounding down the hill and went burrowing in through the door of the cottage. It was cold inside, with rain dripping through rotting thatch, the wind blowing in through windows now without shutters, and turbulence playing piffero in the chimney. Nevertheless, it was a vast improvement on the world outside, where thunder exploded across the sky, and forked lightening—hot as molten silver and as bright as sunrise—stabbed down through the slashing rain to the laundering sea.

'Hello house,' said Togura.

'Hello, Togura Poulaan,' said the house—not by means of voice, for it had none, but by embracing him with a load of rotten thatch.

'Pleased to make your acquaintance,' said Togura, brushing thatch from his hair, neck, eyes, and ears; he sneezed, expelling it from his nose.

Gronnammadammadamyata,' said the thunder, shattering the sky with a blast which shook the cottage, or what was left of it.

'That too,' said Togura, vaguely, not sure what he meant by his own words; he was exhausted, and very close to collapse.

But, in a way, happy. For the cottage helped prove the existence of the world he remembered, which was the world he belonged to. He was approaching civilisation; soon he would be back in the society of men—and women, too—and his disfellowship would be at an end.

He moved to the driest spot he could find, and very shortly was asleep. And dreaming. Outside, as the thunder slowly blundered away into the distance, and the rain eased, the last of the light subsided to the sea, and was gone. Swift-moving clouds rucked across a sky of absolute darkness. At the foot of the cliff, sullen waves heaped themselves against the rocks of the Ravlish Lands, pounding home with a beat too deep, heavy and protracted for any drum to match it. Togura, accustomed to that sound, did not notice it; the surf did not figure in his dreams.

Instead, Togura Poulaan dreamt of Day Suet. Her breasts winked at him lewdly through holes cut in the dolman which fell weeping to her feet; her eyes and her lips were smiling. She stretched out her arms to him, but he found himself floating in a meditative sea, watching the underwater world. A fish went by, hideously maimed, crabbing through the sea with blood and clear fluids scuppering out of old, old, ulcerated wounds in its flanks.

'Kill it for pity,' said Day.

'We can negotiate,' said Togura.

Then woke, and wondered what he had meant by that. Then, alarmed, wondered who was touching his neck with such a cold, cold bony hand. He looked around, started, tumbled head over heels like an acrobat, reached the safety of the furthest corner of the cottage, then picked up a heavy stone which he could use as a weapon. His hair, if it had not been so crabbed, knotted and dirty would have been standing on end.

'Who are you?' hissed Togura, menacing the glimmering, skeletal figure which confronted him.

It addressed him in a foreign tongue. Its voice was old and watery. He could see through its pearl-white armour, through the shadowy outlines of its flesh, through the harder white of its bones, and out to the walls of the cottage beyond.

'What are you?' said Togura, attacking this phosphorescent manifestation with questions. 'Where do you come from? What are you saying? How? Why?'

The phosphorescent apparition did not flinch, diminish or withdraw. It was not an ilps. It might well be a ghost.

'Vara vinklet venvindaanaas telyauga zon makovara,' said the spirit-thing.

'Up yours too,' said Togura, recklessly.

The spirit-thing beckoned to him. He could see, quite clearly the bones of its hand articulating within its spectral flesh.

'No,' said Togura. 'I'm not going with you. So cut it off and pickle it.'

The spirit-thing did not seem to understand his refusal, or his gratuitous obscenity. Its voice became louder and more demanding. It took a step toward him.

'Okay, okay,' said Togura. 'I'm coming.'

He discarded the stone, chose a short stabbing spear from his meagre bundle of possessions, and followed the phantom out of the cottage and into the night.

The sky was pitchblende black, but for the light, as cold and pallid as the frigid starshine of glow-worms, which flickered around the horned cairn. That ancient burial mound, a barrow raised by forgotten peoples in the long ago—time out of mind!—seemed to be burning with cold, cold flames, which failed to consume its substance.

A door had opened in the nearest flank of that cold-burning tumulus. Togura could see down a curving gem-bright hallway, leading down into unknown depths. He caught a whiff of roasting rotch, heard the chimes of an uncanny music, and the shouts of bright brave voices glittering with laughter.

The phantom entered the hallway then paused, and gestured with a hand now positively imperious.

'Come!' said that gesture.

And Togura Poulaan knew he was confronted with a challenge fit for a hero. To dare the unknown! To brave the perils of the land of death or faery! To rouse great warriors from their sleep!

Or, perhaps—and this was experience talking—to be slaughtered without warning, and eaten.

The phantom, growing impatient, advanced to claim Togura. He hurled his spear at it, saw it miss, then turned and fled to the night. He ran till exhaustion checked him, and then, unable to run any more, he walked. Dawn came, but he did not stop; he walked through the day to dusk, and into the night beyond.

During the course of his flight he lost his one and only coin. He was now penniless, but that, for the moment, was the least of his worries.

$$\star$$

CHAPTER
17

Togura Poulaan was cold, wet and hungry, but his spirits were high, for he could see D'Waith in the distance. It was a small walled city set on a hill about half a league from the sea. He could not make a beeline for it, as swathes of barbarian thorn blocked the most direct route; instead, he was forced to follow the coastline.

The weather was the worst he had seen so far on his journey. He was astonished to see a boat on the sea, and was not surprised, shortly afterwards, not to see it. He stumbled forward through the wind, which hazed and harassed him. He was cold to his bone marrow.

'Civilisation,' he said, promising himself a hot fire, a mug of ale and a meal of something good and nourishing.

Hope kept him going.

As he staggered on, buffeted by the wind, he passed an old herbalist who was gathering gypsyworst, horehound, vetch, chickweed, bistort, bracken and sea-cranny. The old man bent to his work, regardless of the weather, ignoring him.

'He must be mad,' said Togura.

This clinical judgment, though made by a rank amateur, was entirely accurate.

The weather, if anything, was getting worse. The tumbled sea was wrought into great spumes and fraughts by the gale. The avalanching waters, afroth with yellowish foam, sent sleets of water spuming over Togura's shore path.

Ahead, Togura could see D'Waith's marginal harbour, where seven ships were rocking at anchor, a beleaguered hebdomad which, until a disaster earlier in the day, had been an octet. The waves were roaring in over the mole which attempted to guard the anchorage: the tides were even threatening some of the low-slung buildings scattered around the foreshore. There would—surely—be a road from here to the city on the hill.

'If I'd built D'Waith, I'd have built it by the harbour,' muttered Togura.

This being so, it was fortunate that he had not built D'Waith, as the boggy ground would have swallowed it. He found out just how boggy it was as he sank to his waist in the marshy ground. He struggled to firmer ground and plugged on relentlessly until he came to the nearest building. A wave from the sea foamed around the building and tugged eagerly at his ankles.

Soaking wet, shivering, stung by the pelting rain and driven by the wind, Togura hobbled to the door. He opened it. The door swung inwards, opening to a roar of conversation, laughter and thumping tankards. Togura, peering into the gloom of beards, voices and storm lanterns, wondered if he was hallucinating. Three fires were blazing in three separate fireplaces; three rousing drinking songs were competing against each other; gusts of noise, heat and communal stench billowed out, together with smells of drink and food which set his reeling with giddy hunger.

'Come in!' roared the landlord, who had the head and the horns of a bull.

Embarrassed, Togura hesitated. He could imagine what he looked like, soaking wet from head to toe, mud from waist to foot, his hair in tangled dreadlocks, his body clad in mouldy old sealskins, an unkempt feathery moustache clinging to his upper lip just beneath his notched nose, and an unkempt straggly growth—a body's excuse for a beard —sprouting from his chin.

'Come in before I break you in half,' bellowed the landlord. 'In boy, and shut the door.'

A wave, chasing round Togura's feet, swarmed through the door to join the waters inside, which were already knee-deep. He went in, closed the door with effort, descended a couple of steps to the floor level, and stood there in the knee-deep water, gawping.

'Here!' yelled the landlord, thumping the bar. 'You paralysed, boy?'

Togura waded to the bar, which was a vast slab of battle-scarred oak. Behind it stood the landlord, a towering figure who really did have the body of a man but the head of a bull. His eyes were fierce, burning, red. His horns, their ivory polished to the brightness of the moon, grazed the ceiling. There was a heavy gold ring in his nose. Ranked up behind him were casks, barrels, stone jars, stone bottles, wineskins and tobacco holders. Helping the landlord at the bar was a motherly woman of middle years who looked perfectly normal except that her hands were the paws of a cat.

As Togura reached the bar, a drunk, bleeding badly from a recent knife fight, embraced him and gave him a kiss. Togura shook him off. The drunk fell backwards to the water, where he floated with a seraphic smile on his face, singing incoherently.

'Here we have us a hungry little man,' said the landlord to Togura. 'Hungry! Pinched, even. Yet honest, all the same. I pick you for an honest man.'

'How can you tell?' said Togura.

'I can't,' said the landlord. 'But I was born and raised politely.' This, apparently, was a joke, for he laughed uproariously, his merriment deafening the storm. The patrons took no notice; they were used to it. 'Come on now, boy. Will you eat? Answer me!'

'I won't deny my hunger,' said Togura. 'But I have no money. Have you any work that needs doing?'

'None, but there's plenty in town. Here, have a bowl of polenta,' said the landlord, shovelling great gollops of steaming porridge into a huge wooden bowl.

'At what obligation?'

'None.'

'What do you mean, none?'

'I mean this is free, gratis, given for nothing. Come on, boy, don't look so startled. Eat! Eat! It's hot. It's good. Oatmeal, maize, chestnuts, barley. Here, have some hot milk with it. Now eat. No, not with your fingers! Were you born in a barn?'

'Yes,' said Togura, in all honesty.

'Then here's a spoon regardless. No slobbering fingers here. This is a respectable house, you know. We have standards to maintain.'

And the landlord laughed again.

'Well thank you,' said Togura, sampling the food.

It was hot, it was good, it tasted like youth and wild honey, like nectar and sunlight, like hot bread and kisses, like pollen and potatoes, like the strength of life itself. The first mouthful cleared his head; the second mouthful warmed him; he took a third, then remembered his own manners.

'Thank you,' said Togura. 'Thank you.'

'Thank me later, boy. Thank me when you come swaggering back to town with gold in your pockets and silver in your socks.'

'That may be never.'

'What a dirge! Come, boy, why so grim? Have you not arms and legs and balls and a cock the girls will greed on? Have you not eyes and ears and nose—well, nose of a sort—and a good stout stomach within?'

'I've had a hard time,' said Togura, a little offended to find this stranger dismissing his rightful claims to pessimism without even hearing them out. 'I've suffered.'

'Suffered? Piffle!'

'I tell you—'

'Don't tell me, boy, eat. Slop down the food, it's good for you. Priorities, boy, priorities! Food first then friends. And a drink withal. That's the making. Dox! Dox, my good man. Buy the young man a drink. A drink for a boy born in a barn, and, by the looks of him, not recovered from the shock. Dox! Don't pretend you can't hear me. You hear me all right, you cheese-faced stoat-shagging tobaccanalian. Come on, Dox, you idle son of a shit-shoving whoremaster, bring out your silver.'

A disfigured man with a clay pipe wedged between his naked gums waded to the counter. He smelt heavily, but not unpleasantly of tobacco.

'Cold potato twice,' he said, laying his bronze on the counter.

'Hard spirit for you, Dox,' said the landlord, passing him a beaker of a clear and odourless fluid, 'but ale for the boy.'

And he drew a tankard of thick, nourishing dark-stained ale and passed it to Togura. It was cold; Togura preferred his beer warm—preferably at blood temperature—but he accepted it with a good grace nevertheless.

'Come,' said Dox.

Togura, food and drink in hand, followed him to a crowded table, where they found buttock-space on a creaking bench jammed with men in rags, furs, flax raincoats, fighting leathers, feather capes, canvas coveralls or businesslike sea gear. While men eyed him and summed him, Togura ate and drank, bewildered by the landlord's hospitality, which was so unlike what he had learnt to expect from the world.

'Who are you?' said Dox, suddenly, without any preliminaries.

Dox, the toothless pipe smoker, had a hoarse and rasping voice, and had an ulcer the size of a fist on one side of his face. He was missing his ears and his nose. Togura, disconcerted by his appearance, and even more disconcerted by the free food and drink, concealed his own identity with an untruth of some cunning.

'They call me the Forester,' he said. 'Before certain misfortunes, I was part of a party searching for Barak the Battleman, also known as Togura Poulaan.'

'Ah! After the reward, no doubt. But you have no sword about you. So how would you take him?'

'I have my hands,' said Togura, restraining his astonishment.

'Hands, yes. Lovely things! Strangulation, hey? Yes, of course. That's the story! Squeeze them till their eyes pop. I love it. Take him when he's sleeping, eh boy? But find him first. The reward's worth having, nay-so? Did you hear Cromel's doubled it?'

'His name isn't Cromel,' said another man, a hard-faced villain with pietra-dura eyes. 'It's Cromdarlarty.'

'No,' said a third, a sallow-faced consumptive windle-straw with a thin, piping voice. 'Cromarty, that's the name. I met him face to face in Keep myself. We argued belly to belly. He told me himself, the reward's now set at a hundred crowns. A hundred crowns for the head.'

'That head's probably done and deep rotted by now,' said another voice, slurring out of an alewashed face which was one part tattoos, one part scars, one part burns and one part syphilis sores.

'What do you mean?' said a big, brawn-voiced one-eyed man with a beard dyed green and yellow.

'I mean that the oath-breaking father-killer is probably dead and buried. What do you think, Forester?'

Togura, spooning down his polenta, said nothing, waiting for Forester to answer.

'Forester!' said Dox, seizing his elbow and banging it on the table. 'Are you deaf?'

'Somewhat,' said Togura, remembering, as he rubbed his elbow, that he was Forester. 'What was the question?'

'He claimed a death for Barak. You agree?'

'The last rumour that came my way,' said Togura, lying as sweetly as a poet, 'held that Barak had been to Estar and back. Lately he happened on the road for Chi'ash-lan, or so it was told, but then I met a man who swore he'd turned for D'Waith.'

'That's wrong,' said a hoar-skinned fellow with sausage-shaped lugs of ulcerated flesh spilling down his cheeks and his neck. 'He's at Larbster Bay for certain. What do you think—'

The rest of the question was drowned as a huge wave, larger than all the rest, pounded into the building. The storm lanterns hanging from the roofbeams were set to swaying. As see-saw shadows and gutteral light swung back and forth across the haggling card games, the helpless drunks, the boozing syndicates, the wrist-wrestling bravos and a gaggle of pipe-smoking ancients, an even larger wave slammed against the seaward wall, bursting shutters open. A torrent of water poured inside, scattering a game of dragon chess. The participants shouted in dismay, but the rest of the tavern broke into drunken cheering.

As hands laboured the shutters home to close out the wind, the door was flung open and a woman entered. She

was tall, she was blonde and she was built like a butcher's
block. The cry went up:

'Mary!' 'It's Mary!' 'Why bless your heart and spit on
it!' 'Mary, my doxy, come kiss me quick.'

'Silence,' she roared.

The building shook with her voice, which could have
shouted the landlord himself right down to nothing. Every
jargoning mouth in the whole building quailed down to
zero. Even the sea seemed muted.

'That's better,' said Mary. 'Now stay your cheek and
rattle your pins. There's pirates wrecked on the coast. West
of us, three leagues. Get up off your shit and get moving.'

With a roar and a whoop, the tavern emptied to the
howling storm. Togura, only half understanding, swilled
down the last of his polenta in three and a half desperate
gulps, drained his tankard, then allowed himself to be carried along with the others. As they staggered through the
brawny weather, he saw that other buildings were also
emptying. The mob, a rough and raggedy beast if ever
there was one, slouched and stumbled through the storm,
heading for the west.

CHAPTER
18

Togura Poulaan was once more cold, wet and hungry. As he made his way back to the tavern, the thought of its warmth, its drink and its food was increasingly appealing. Nevertheless, he had his misgivings. It was dusk, and Togura did not think the tavern a good place to be at nightfall, even though he was no longer alone.

Togura's new companion was Gelzeda Zurdok, a merchant from Androlmarphos, which was a distant city in the south of Argan, one of those fabulous foreign places which Sung knew only by rumour. Togura and his new acquaintance made an odd couple, for Togura was still in his barefoot rags, while Zurdok, on the other hand, was a mature, bearded man, richly dressed from his swaggering seaboots upwards.

Whistling lightly, Zurdok led the way. Togura was still unarmed, but Zurdok wore an ornate swordbelt which sustained a cutlass, a throwing knife, a dirk and an apple corer.

'Why did they let you keep your weapons?' said Togura. It was a question which had only just occurred to him.

'I was on parole,' said Zurdok. 'We merchants of An-drolmarphos have the highest reputation when it comes to probity. When I told the pirates I'd make no trouble, they took me at my word.'

'That was kind of them.'

'I'm rich. The ransom was going to make their kindness worth their while. Believe me, they knew it, too. Every pirate on the twenty-seven seas knows the wealth of Tezelja Burnok.'

'I thought you said your name was Gelzeda Zurdok,' said Togura.

'So it is, my son, Gelzeda Zurdok. A good name, too, isn't it? My credit's good from Androlmarphos to Selzirk. And beyond.'

'But just now you called yourself—'

'What?'

'I can't remember.'

'No, boy, I don't think I called myself that. Gelzeda Zurdok's the name, always has been, always will. If you start hearing different, wash the wind out of your ears. That's the tavern, I take it?'

'That's right,' said Togura. 'That's the tavern.'

Bending his steps toward it, Zurdok resumed his whistling. The wind, which had weakened dramatically, was blathering away in the background; the rain had eased to a drizzle, and the sea to a sullen chop. Occasionally a wave larger than the rest sent a little bit of water slouching up to the tavern walls, but it seemed the storm was over.

As they neared the tavern, picking their way with care between the boggier bits of ground, a blue-feathered mocking gull, a bird of ill omen, went caterwauling overhead. Togura spat, and made a warding gesture in the direction of the retreating gull, but Zurdok did not seem to notice. Togura had already tried to dissuade Zurdok from seeking refuge in the tavern. He had failed, but now he tried again.

'I don't know that the tavern is quite the place for us,' said Togura.

'Why not?'

'It's full of thieves, pimps, card sharps and drunks.'

'Low types like us, joked Zurdok. 'They'll make us feel at home.'

'They'll more likely draw cuts for the privilege of slicing and dicing us. It was bad enough by day. It's no place to venture at nightfall.'

'It's not dark yet, boy,' said Zurdok. 'So we'll risk a look at the place, at least.'

For a man who had recently come close to death, Zurdok was in exceptionally high spirits, all smiles and whistles. Then, as they approached the tavern from the blind side, the whistling abruptly stopped. They heard hoarse shouts and a cry of pain. A duel? A brawl?

'This may be one of those times,' said Togura, 'when it's best to leave before arriving.'

'Gather your courage,' said Zurdok. 'And follow me.'

They ducked round to the doorway side of the tavern. The first thing Togura saw was a man lying dead on the ground. The landlord was being held at bay by half a dozen masked men armed with staves, flails and hatchets. He was armed with a whip and a pitchfork. His horns were stained with bright fresh blood.

'Back, you braggarts!' roared the landlord. 'Back, before I scupper the lot of you.'

'You're the one who's scuppered,' shouted a bald man with golden roses tattooed on his naked pate. 'Here's reinforcements!' He appealed to Togura and Zurdok: 'Will you join us for the monster's gold? His death's a fortune for each of us. Will you join us?'

'Yes,' said Zurdok, striding forward.

'Good,' said the man of the golden roses.

And Zurdok booted him in the crutch then wrecked him with three well-placed blows too swift for Togura to follow. As the others gasped alarm, Zurdok's fingers flickered. A man went down with a throwing knife in his throat. The landlord hurled his pitchfork and slashed away with his whip. Zurdok drew his cutlass and laid about him. Closing with his nearest victim, the landlord gored him through the heart.

And suddenly there were four men freshly dead and two men running for their lives. The action had been so swift that Togura had scarcely had time to realise it had started. The landlord shook himself free from the body of the man he had gored.

'You!' said the landlord, in surprise.

'Me!' said Zurdok.

And the two embraced.

'I thought you'd setsko and amanacain,' said the landlord.

'Me? Log Jaris, you'd fana-ma-skote.'

There was a lot more of this swift, jabbering argot, which Togura found impossible to follow. The language the two men were speaking was basically Galish, but it was so full of slang and foreign lingo that he found it incomprehensible.

'Well,' said the landlord at last, breaking off the conversation, 'I'm sure we can bed down a boy and a pirate. So come in, the two of you.'

'Pirate?' said Togura, looking round.

'He's the pirate!' said the landlord, laughing as he pointed to Zurdok.

'He's no pirate,' protested Togura. 'He's Gelzeda Zurdok, merchant of Androlmarphos. He was being held prisoner on the pirate ship which was wrecked.'

'And you helped him escape from the frenzied mob.'

'Yes!' said Togura, who was proud of his effort, which had taken a lot of quick thinking and a nimble bit of bluff.

'Well, well,' said the landlord. 'What a brave little boy. Come on, let's no more linger. Inside!'

And in they went.

The landlord's woman, she of the cat's paws, was standing behind the bar, mopping the counter. She greeted them with a placid smile, then carried on sponging up the blood which had been spilt so liberally on the counter. There were at least five sodden bodies floating in the water.

'Love,' said the landlord to the woman. 'Fetch us two bailing boys from the Nun's Backside. And send a messenger to old Karold; tell him there's butcher's meat here for the taking.'

'Shall I set up first for the evening trade?' asked the woman, her voice smooth and mellow.

'There'll be no evening trade tonight,' said the landlord. 'They'll be whooping it up at the wreck, burning their prisoners alive. Come, boys, let's have an ale.'

The three sat themselves down at a table with bread and tankards, then the landlord talked ninety to the dozen with Gelzeda Zurdok. Togura, unable to follow their quick-weaving cant, felt excluded and insulted. Finally he could stand it no more.

What's that language you're talking?' he demanded.

'Galish,' said the landlord easily. 'Galish as she is spoke in the Greater Teeth.'

'The Greater Teeth? But only pirates live there!'

'Then what else would we be? I told you already, the man you saved from the wreck is a pirate. No—don't give me that merchant nonsense again. What merchant from Androlmarphos would walk with a sea swagger as he does? Besides, boy, if you knew your Androlmarphos you'd know that the men there have a fashion for clean shaving. They walk their lives beardless—not like Draven here.'

'Draven?' said Togura, staring at the man he knew as Gelzeda Zurdok. He'd heard that name before. The more notable sea bandits were known by name even in the households of Keep. 'Draven the Womanrider?'

'No, boy!' shouted Gelzeda Zurdok, slamming the table with the flat of his hand. 'Do I look like him? Do I speak like him? Do I stink like him? No and no, and again no. Don't confuse me with the most notorious coward of the twenty-seven seas. I'm not the Womanrider. I'm not Draven the leper, either, or Battleaxe Draven. I'm Bluewater Draven, and you'd better remember it.'

'Peace,' said the landlord, with a smile. 'Peace, the pair of you.'

'I wasn't arguing!' said Togura.

'Then peace regardless,' said the landlord. 'He tells the truth. An unusual experience for him, but he tells it. He is, in truth, Bluewater Draven of the Greater Teeth. His ship, which was wrecked today, was one of three on passage to Ork, an island far distant which you're not likely to have heard of. They were on a mission which does not bear naming at the moment.'

'How do you know all this? said Togura.

'We've been talking, haven't we? Why so fierce, youngster?'

'Because I've been cheated and tricked and lied to. Because I risked my life to save him and because I thought him an honest stranger. Because he conned me and duped me and gives me no thanks. Look at him smirking!'

'Thanks is not in his nature,' said the landlord, 'but he can surely redeem his debt to you all the same. As I was telling you, his ship was one of three. They had a rendezvous point for gathering in case they were separated in the Penvash Channel—which is that body of water at our doorstep, in case you didn't know.'

'I know,' said Togura, who hadn't until that moment.

'If one or both remaining ships survive, they'll search for Draven's vessel. In all probability, they'll put a boat ashore to make discretions in D'Waith.'

'Discretions?'

'They'll ask after the lotch, but carefully,' said the landlord patiently.

'The lotch?'

'The missing one, the retarded one, the latecomer,' said the landlord, supplying the meaning of the cant word. 'If they varry—'

'Varry?'

'Enough of this language lesson!' said Draven impatiently. 'Come on, let's pay off the boy.'

'I don't want to be paid off, I want an apology,' said Togura.

'What an innocent little mannikin,' said the landlord, with a laugh which—and this was unusual for him—had something of a jeer about it. 'Apologies? From a pirate? You'd be searching! There now, don't take it hard. You saved a life. That's something for a day's work. You've got Bluewater Draven in your debt, so take what's offering. Take his gold or his services. He can ship you to Ork, if you're wanting.'

'Can I think about it?' said Togura, seeing that argument was going to get him nowhere.

'Thinking's free,' said Draven. 'But have a decision by tomorrow's daylight.'

At that moment two boys arrived, with buckets, and began to bail out the tavern. Shortly afterwards, a butcher from D'Waith arrived to take away the dead bodies to be made into sausage meat. Then some jubilant wreckers entered, bearing trophies—the heads of five sea rovers—and pirate gold. As the tavern began to get lively, despite the landlord's expectations, talk of sensitive matters ended.

From the tavern talk, Togura was able to complete his picture of what had happened while he had been absent from civilisation. On the day on which the Warguild had attacked the wedding at the Suet's Grand Hall, Baron Chan Poulaan had gone missing. Rumour had it that Togura Poulaan, also known as Barak the Battleman, had pitched his father into a mining pit, thus murdering him.

Togura's half brother, Cromarty, had assumed control of the family estate near Keep, and had offered a reward for Togura's head. Rumour held that Togura, aka Barak, had been sighted in fifty different places during the time he had been hunted—which was now almost a year. He was credited with five rapes, two murders and several acts of vandalism and arson; most recently, or so rumour had it, he had attacked a homestead in the mountains, routing the seven men who tried to defend the place against his depredations.

'Ay, I can credit that,' said a one-legged card sharp and proceeded to give a vivid eyewitness account of how he had confronted Barak half a year ago. 'Chewed off my leg, he did. Turned himself into a great black manul, leapt, fanged me, bit, chewed, swallowed—kneecap, ankle, shin, he ate the lot.'

'Give over, Doss,' said an onlooker. 'You lost that leg ten years ago if it was a day.'

'No,' insisted the card sharp. 'That's not true. Listen, it was up in the mountains. A cold day. I challenged him. One moment he was standing there, as clear as I see you—a great big unruly fellow with a spiked club in his hand—and the next moment he'd turned himself into this gory great cat, as big as a horse if it was larger than a mouse.'

His eyes shone with sincerity; his voice carried the tones of impeccable conviction; it was clear that more than a few believed him.

These being the rumours that Togura did hear—and in a single night, at that—he could only guess at those he didn't hear. Offering a reward for a man's head was a foreign practice previously almost unheard of in Keep; the reward made this manhunt a novelty, and the recent increase in the amount of the reward had made it a topical novelty at that.

With his dreams of retiring into his father's home now shattered, Togura had to think of his own safety. There were no portraits or sketches of him in circulation, so few people outside Keep would know what he looked like. Nevertheless, it would be safest to get out of Sung until this trouble blew over.

By morning, Togura had come to a decision. He asked Draven to take him to Larbster Bay; from there, he would make his way along the Salt Road to Estar. Once he reached Estar, he would be faced with another decision. There were two possibilities. Either he could stay in Estar and work at some honest trade, hoping for Cromarty to get himself killed in a duel or a feud, thus opening the way for Togura to return home; or, alternatively, he could approach Prince Comedo of Estar and ask for permission to dare the terrors of the monster which guarded the bottle which contained the box which contained the index which spoke the Universal Language which would give him control of the odex.

'Can you take me to Larbster Bay?' said Togura to Draven.

'Nothing easier,' said Draven. 'Once a ship calls for us. It's on the way to Ork. Perhaps, of course, there'll be no ship. If so, I'll buy us a passage with the next Galish convoy travelling from D'Waith to Larbster Bay. We'll get you on your journey, youngster. Trust Draven. Thousands do —and no man ever regretted it.'

Togura, judging Draven to be sincere, ate well, drank well, slept well, helped the landlord tend the bar, and waited until they could start their journey.

CHAPTER
19

The seas at the end of summer were in full flood. The tall ship strode the ocean, riding over the scalloping light, urged by a brisk wind which drove it through the dalloping dolloping waves.

The name of the ship was the Warwolf, but her figurehead was no wolf but a dragon. She had been built by the best shipwrights of the Greater Teeth. Her timbers were of winter oak and cedar, but for the masts, which were of kauri from Quilth, and the deck, which had been made of a chance load of mahogany alleged to have originated in Yestron. She had three masts, and sails of green canvas.

Togura Poulaan, taking his ease on a sunny yet sheltered part of the deck, surveyed the work going on near at hand and thanked his stars—which were the two green ones known as the Cat's Eyes—that he was not a pirate. From this vantage point, it looked too much like hard work.

Taking advantage of the fine weather, the weapons muqaddam was supervising the overhaul of armaments and muniments. He was a broad-fisted man with shoulders like an ox and a shadow like a menhir. He was bald but for a little floccus scabbing the centre of his skull. His eyes, squinting out of a sun-weathered face, were as sharp as caltrops. His tongue was as rough as pumice, and he used it industriously.

Glad to be a passenger, Togura closed his eyes and leisured out at full length on the deck. Then cloud quenched the sun; a crisp whippet of wind came cleaning around him, and, chilled and annoyed, he sat up again.

'Come back sun,' said Togura. 'Go away wind.'

The wind, obedient to his commands, veered away to vanishing. But the sun remained hidden by a sulk of cloud. In the sea, something hinted through the waters. Seal? Dolphin? Whale? Rock? Togura narrowed his eyes, trying to see it more clearly. But it had gone. Perhaps it had been nothing to start with or a chance bit of driftwood or float-stone now smothered by a wave.

Togura closed his eyes again, but was abruptly jolted into full alertness when a fight began. Looking round, he saw it was only two young pirates sparring with a lot of brag and paraffle. The weapons muqaddam, seeing their footwork looked sloppy, screamed abuse at them. They took heed, stopped fooling around and became more businesslike. They were rather good.

Togura had always imagined pirates as being lazy, leisurely beasts, loafing through the idle seas, amusing themselves with wine and women until the opportunity for pillage aroused them from their sport. Now, after only a brief acquaintance with the breed, he knew the reality was altogether different.

There was wine abroad, true, but it was rationed—a gill per man per day, which was next to nothing. There were women somewhere below deck—not that Togura had seen them—but the woman ration was stricter still. Most of the day was spent in work, maintenance, exercise and training. The Warwolf was a taut, sober, workmanlike ship, captained by the stern, ascetic Jon Arabin; there was no laya-bout nonsense here.

If Togura had ever had the misfortune to sail on Draven's ship, the Tusk, then he would have found a state of affairs rather closer to his imaginings—which was the main reason why the Tusk had been smashed on the coast of Sung, the crew butchered by the local populace and the wreckage looted, while the Warwolf rode out the storm with match-less aplomb.

As the sun came out again, Togura dozed down to the deck and relaxed. For the moment, he had no worries. This ship, its mission urgent, had no time to call at Larbster Bay on this leg of its journey. Instead, it would take him all the way to the distant island of Ork, then drop him at Larbster on the return voyage. For the time being, all he had to do was eat, sleep, and enjoy the sun at the end of summer.

With all his difficulties thus comfortably postponed, it was pleasing to toy with the idea of being a questing hero. Once he finally got from Larbster Bay to Estar, he would most certainly have a look at the monster in Prince Comedo's Castle Vaunting. He would then be able to decide whether he should attempt to recover the box which held the index.

He remembered back to the days when he had lived in the stronghold of the Wordsmiths in Keep. Brother Troop had talked about the box, which held the index which could control the odex. Asked what the index looked like, he had answered:

'When you open the box, you'll know. Remember, it speaks the Universal Language.'

Togura, daydreaming, imagined himself performing desperate heroics and recovering the vital box. It would open at a Word. And that Word was?

—Konanabarok?

—Yaradoshek?

—Slonshenamenel?

No, it was nothing like that. It was something else, but, for the life of him, he could not remember what. For a moment, he panicked. Then he relaxed. There was no need for him to remember how to command the box. All he had to do was get it to Keep. The Wordsmiths would do the rest.

It would be easy.

Or would it?

After all, there was not just Castle Vaunting's monster to deal with. If he slew the monster, that in itself would not be enough to give him the box which held the index, for the box was at the bottom of a bottle. Togura tried to remember Brother Troop's instructions for getting into the bottle, but could not. All he could remember was Brother Troop saying:

'The box itself lies at the very bottom of the bottle, and is Guarded . . . which means there's death waiting nearby.'

Remembering this talk of death made Togura once more doubt the wisdom of being a questing hero. He decided to procrastinate his decision until he reached Estar, which would not be for many days yet: there was no hurry.

A shadow blocked out the sun. Togura opened his eyes and saw a fair-haired young pirate looking down at him. The pirate, who was unarmed, was wearing a woollen shepherd's rig and rope-soled shoes.

'What are you staring at?' said Togura.

'Nothing that catches my fancy,' said the youth. 'They told me you were a manhunter, so I thought you'd be something special. But you're not.'

Togura wondered whether to take offence, then decided against it. The doughty little pirate was a tough, nuggety piece of work; Togura might have trouble handling him if it came to a scuffle.

'Tell me, for you're the expert,' said Togura, venturing a little flattery, 'what's that island over there?'

And he pointed at a high-rising island some distance off. Its coast was 'walled around with bronze,' as the pirate idiom had it—that is to say, it had a rugged, iron-bound coast.

'That?' said the youth. 'We name him Drum. That's—'

He broke off as the ship shuddered as if something had struck it. There was instant alarm on board. Men rushed to the side and peered overboard. Shouts rang out as deck queried crow's-nest.

'What was it?' said Togura.

'Sharbly we grounded a whale,' came the laconic answer. 'No worry. It's gone, and us, we're not drinking.'

At that moment, the ship lurched hideously. Togura was sent sliding. As he clung to the deck rail, he saw something rising up out of the sea. Up, up it came, ascending in blue-green coils.

'Snake!' said the pirate.

Its jaws leered toward them, as if it would strike, then it dipped down into the sea again. It was indeed like a snake, except that it was three times the length of the ship and had the girth of a bullock.

'There's another!' cried Togura.

There were two—no, three . . . four! five! . . . there were six sea serpents in the waters around them. Togura heard Jon Arabin, the ship's captain, bellowing orders. Shortly he heard wails and screams as the ship girls were brought on deck. Fighting and biting, they were dragged to the stern and thrown overboard. They thrashed round in the water, screaming. Blood foamed on the waves as the sea serpents ravaged them.

'That's murder!' said Togura, shocked.

The young pirate gave a twisted grin.

'Them or us,' he said. 'Which would you prefer?'

'Well . . .'

It was indeed a difficult question.

Jon Arabin gave another order. And the weapons mu-qaddam grabbed Togura and started to drag him to the edge of the deck.

'This is a joke, yes?' said Togura.

The weapons muqaddam made no answer.

'A joke? Understand? said Togura desperately. 'A joke?'

They were now very close to the edge.

'Draven!' screamed Togura.

And started to kick, scratch, struggle and bite. It did him no good. He was hauled to the very edge.

'Draven!' shouted Togura, sighting his friend at last. 'Stop him!'

'Sorry, boy,' said Draven, advancing at a casual saunter. 'This isn't my ship. I've no authority here. So enjoy your swim.'

'I can't swim!' screamed Togura.

A lie—but he thought it worth trying.

He locked his hands round the stern rail, and, struggling vigorously, managed to kick the weapons muqaddam in the guts. His enemy did not even grunt.

'Did you hear me? screamed Togura. 'I can't swim!'

'Bait doesn't have to swim,' said Draven, grabbing hold of Togura's flailing feet. 'Give my regards to the chiefest of serpents.'

'Don't do it. Please!' begged Togura, as he lost his hold on the stern rail. 'Draven, help me!'

'Heave ho!' said Draven, cheerfully.

They gave him the old heave ho, and over he went. Arms and legs flailing, he tumbled through the air. He hit the sea awkwardly with a crash, a shock of cold water, and a blunt, ugly pain, as if someone had rammed his rectum with an iron bar. The impact drove him deep.

Momentarily stunned, lost to all knowledge of his place,

time and name, he struggled for the light. Breaking the surface, he gasped for air. A slip-slop wave slapped him in the face. He remembered what was happening. A shrill whinny of terror escaped him. He thrashed at the water as if having a fit.

'No no no,' moaned Togura, drawing his legs up to try and stop anything from biting them.

Another wave slapped him harshly, cutting off his moans. Blinking away the stinging salt of the sea, squeezing a web of water from his eyes, he dared to look around. He could see no women. No sea serpents.

The big seas hoisted him up then sloped him down again. The Warwolf, bulking away from him, heeled in the wind. He saw its lower timbers were foul with weed, barnacles and sea squirts; it was overdue for careening. Draven waved to him from the stern, then shouted something; the wind blurred away the sense of his words.

'What?' shouted Togura.

Draven shouted more unintelligible words, then pointed at something. What? Trying to see, Togura forgot all about keeping his legs up. They drifted down. The next moment, Togura felt something firm underfoot. Ah, ground! A miracle!

The ground began to rise.

Oh no!

Togura began to cry out with short, panting, uncontrollable, hysterical screams. Up came the green surge in a smooth, hypnotic flow, riding up between his legs and lofting him into the sky. He found himself straddling a sea serpent, which was racing through the sea toward the ship. He began to slip. He grabbed for a handhold, finding nothing but a few barnacles clinging to battle-scarred scales. Taking his weight, the old scales themselves started to scab away, revealing fresh, gleaming, frictionless scales beneath.

As the sea serpent raced toward the ship, Togura slid sideways. He scrabbled desperately for purchase. He had a brief, hallucinatory glimpse of the deck of the ship. It was below him. Men were scattering in all directions. Then the sea serpent crunched down. The stern splintered. Timbers smashed. Togura was thrown through the air.

Togura, bruised to the deck, rolled to his feet in an instant. He stood there, swaying. The ship lurched, the deck canted, and down he went again. He saw a scream wailing between the sea serpent's jaws. Then the scream was gone. The jaws were turning toward him.

Togura accelerated from a crawl to a sprint in one and a half paces. Then he collided with a pirate. Both went down. The sea serpent slavered above them. Blood dripped from its jaws. Togura, paralysed with fear, mewled weakly with terror. But the pirate bravely struggled to his feet, drawing his cutlass. A mistake. The monster snacked on the cold steel, then munched down on the pirate. Togura slithered away, then got to his feet and ran with a blind, lurching gait.

Knocked to the deck by the ship's next ungainly movement, Togura turned to see half a dozen pirates charging the sea serpent, using a spare spar as a battering ram. Wood splintered, bones crunched, and Togura went humbling up the ratlines, climbing for dear life or cheap, life at any price, there was no time for bargaining.

He climbed and climbed until he could climb no more, and then, at a dizzy height, he hooked his arms through rope netting and slumped there, exhausted. The ship, struck by another sea serpent, heeled alarmingly then righted itself; the motion, amplified by the mast, did sickening things to his stomach.

'Enjoy your swim?' said a laconic voice beside him.

Togura opened his eyes to look at his neighbour. It was

the fair-haired young pirate he had conversed with earlier in the day.

'You're a murderous pack of unprincipled bastards,' said Togura savagely.

The youth laughed.

'What did you expect?' he said. 'We're pirates! You got off lucky, though. Bait can be cut, blinded, tortured. Or ship-raped, my hearty. If there's time. This time there wasn't.'

'Does that mean I was bait all along? Did you expect to meet—'

'Not so angry, man. Settle, settle! You, you were our much loved, honoured, respected passenger until we met the monsters. Stall it, man, don't say it—of course we weren't expecting them. None in their right minds—or out of them, for that matter—would sail to a monster's jaws full knowing. My name's Drake. And yours?'

'Togura,' mumbled Togura, his strength for anger fading.

'What?'

'Forester,' said Togura, speaking up loudly, amending his name as he remembered who he was masquerading as.

'Welcome, Forester. Do you—'

The mast lurched alarmingly.

'Dahz!' exclaimed the pirate Drake, using a foreign obscenity.

Togura realised a sea serpent had coiled itself around the base of the mast. Even as he watched, the mast, very slowly, began to bend. Then, with a sudden shatter-crack, it snapped.

They fell.

Togura screamed.

The sea roared up and smashed them.

Engulfed in green, harassed by rope, choking and breathless, Togura struggled for air and daylight. Breaking to the surface of the sea, he snorted water, sucked air, was floundered over by a wave, ducked by another, hauled down by a third, rolled over and over by a fourth, then lifted up by a fifth to an eminence from which he saw the Warwolf, encumbered by a trio of sea serpents, crabbing away through the sea with its broken mast trailing.

'Swim!' yelled a voice.

It was Drake.

Togura saw his young pirate friend, still clinging to the mast. What was better? To cling to the mast until the sea serpents were ready for dessert? Or drown in the bottomless ocean?

'Swim! Now!' shouted Drake, wind and distance rapidly eroding his voice.

Togura struck out for the mast and the ship, but it was hopeless. The sea was rough; a strong, fast current was sweeping him away from the ship. Finally he gave up and trod water, watching the ship, listing badly, dragging itself away from him, still in the grip of three implacable monsters.

Seeing a stray spar surfing through the water, Togura swam for it, reached it, latched on and clung to it for dear life. One end was all munched, crunched and splintered; he shuddered. The ship was now too distant for him to make out any detail of what was happening on board, but he saw black billows of smoke beginning to rise from the vessel. Soon one of the remaining masts was on fire; it was Togura's guess that the ship was doomed.

'Drown down, you buck-rat bastards,' he muttered, cursing the ship and its crew.

By now he was very, very cold; he began to shiver violently and continuously. He would be chilled down to his death unless he could get to land. But there was no land anywhere near. Or was there? The island of Drum was now much closer. The current was taking him toward the shore.

The current was swift, but, even so, it seemed a long time before he could cast off from the spar and strike out for the shore. He swam very slowly. Caught in the surf, he almost drowned, surviving by luck alone. The waves tumbled him onto a pebbly beach. He struggled up the beach and across the driftwood line at high tide mark, then shuffled into a cave and collapsed, exhausted.

CHAPTER
20

Waves thrashed, humped and slubbered, mounted and surmounted, gashed themselves recklessly against the rocks of Drum, sifted through seaweed, chopped each other into foam, then hurled themselves against the beach, tumbling stones, sheals and crab claws over and over in a bounteous explosion of spray. The daylight slowly weathered away.

Exhausted, defeated and badly frightened, Togura Poulaan lay in his cave in a state of collapse. At the beginning of the day, buoyant with confidence, he had been a warm, brave, well-fed questing hero, riding a ship on his way to high adventure. Now he was a cold, hungry, shivering vagrant, a helpless waif of a gadling, marooned on the island of Drum, home of the notorious wizard of Drum, an ill-tempered necromancer known to have the unpleasant habit of feeding strangers to his household dragons.

Togura wanted, very very much, to be home on his father's estate. In bed. With a cup of something hot to warm and cheer him. He did not like it here. He was too cold, too wet, too lonely. It was dangerous. Things would hurt him. He would never get off the island alive. Recovering a little strength, he used it to produce hot tears of grief and regret.

He was eventually roused from his blubbering self-pity by a strange clinking crunching slithering sound which he could hear even above the rouse, souse, suck, slap and gurgitation of the sea. It sounded like four or five men dragging a log across stones. Or, perhaps, like a large animal of peculiar construction making its way across the beach.

Sitting up, Togura faced the cave mouth. The strange noise stopped. A beast peered inside, then withdrew.

—A dragon?

Togura was almost certain he had seen a dragon. He did not know whether to scream, to run, to freeze or to pick up a stick and a stone so as to be prepared to fight for his life.

In the event, he froze.

There was a hiatus, in which Togura heard his own pounding pulse and the sea doing leisurely break-falls on the beach. Then the dragon looked in again. It gave a prolonged gurgling cough as it cleared its throat, then it spoke.

'Hello,' said the dragon, in Galish; the word was clear and distinct, marred only by a superfluous bark at the end of it.

'Piss off!' screamed Togura, hurling a rock.

Fortunately, he missed.

'That's not very polite, you know,' said the dragon, mildly. 'Come outside. Let's have a look at you.'

The cave was large enough to admit the dragon, so Togura saw no percentage in disobeying. Reluctantly, expecting at any moment to be incinerated, he quit the cave. As no immediate disaster befell him, he was able to take stock of the dragon. Entirely green except for its eyes—which were red, with yellow pupils—it stood about as tall as a pony but was three times the length. It had short, stubby wings which were folded against the side of its body.

'You look cold,' said the dragon. 'You need a fire. I'll give you one. I'm an excellent pyrotechnist.'

'What?' said Togura.

'Watch,' said the dragon.

It clawed together some driftwood then breathed out flames which were delicate shades of blue, yellow and green. The wood scorched, charred and flamed. Togura squatted down by the fire.

'Thank you,' he said, belatedly, remembering his manners.

'It was nothing,' said the dragon, in a voice which managed to hint that it was really quite something. 'We sea dragons are very talented, you know.'

'I'm sure you are,' said Togura, hoping that he was engaging in a real conversation and not just being subjected to a before-dinner speech.

'Sea dragons are characterised by versatile genius,' said the dragon, encouraged. 'Not like those ignorant hulking land monsters we are so often confounded with. We are not primitive brutes like the land dragons. No! A thousand times no! Sea dragons are the true lords of the intellect, noted for their wit, intelligence, grace, charm, sagacity and fashion sense, for their matchless command of all the philosophies, for their eloquence, good humor and comradeship, for their surpassing physical beauty, their wise counsel, their profound logic and their highly developed artistic sensitivity.'

'And for their modesty?' asked Togura—and instantly wished he had bitten off his tongue.

'That too,' acknowledged the sea dragon, failing to realise that his comment was somewhat barbed. 'Considering the true extent of our genius, considering the power of our swift-speeding inquiring minds armoured by their world-famous panoply of knowledge, we're remarkably modest, believe you me.'

'I do, I do,' said Togura, earnestly.

'Now warm yourself by the fire, young human,' said the sea dragon, 'while I go off to get instructions. Don't worry! I won't be long!'

It waddled down the beach, its tail dragging across the shingle, then spread its wings—which, as it was a sea dragon, were water wings, not capable of flight—and plunged into the water. Swimming swiftly and gracefully through the lumbering seas, it rounded a headland and was lost from sight.

It had gone to report to its master—the wizard of Drum!

Togura knew what he had to do. He did it. He made himself scarce, and, for the next five days, used all his native cunning—plus a lot which had been grafted on in recent months—to avoid and evade his pursuers. But, in the end, he was cornered by a number of dragons—all very pleased with themselves, and saying so at great length—and, after a lot of spurious speechifying, the dragons led him off to the grim, castellated stronghold of the wizard of Drum.

☆

CHAPTER
21

As Togura Poulaan was marched into the shadows of the castle of the wizard of Drum, the iron-clad gates creaked open. Yawning darkness hid the nameless horrors beyond.

'Come on,' said the leading dragon, as Togura hesitated.

The command ended with a short bark, followed by a hiss of smoke, steam and pulsating flame. Reluctantly, Togura shuffled forward. He was sure his death awaited him.

Darkness gave way to the daylight of a big, bare, high-walled courtyard.

'Stand here,' said the leading dragon.

Togura obeyed. The dragons formed a circle, with Togura in the middle. They looked eager. Expectant. Something was about to happen. Togura closed his eyes. One of the dragons started to sharpen its claws against the courtyard stones with a slick, evil, sizzling sound which reminded him unpleasantly of a butcher's shop. The leading dragon cleared its throat.

'This,' it said, 'is the dragon hof. Here we gather each evening to eat, drink and recite poetry.'

There was a pause. Togura opened his eyes. All the

dragons were watching him, as if they expected something from him.

'That sounds very nice,' said Togura cautiously. 'Very civilised. Dragons do seem to be very civilised.' This was going down well, so he elaborated. 'I only wish I had time to know you better. Time to appreciate your full conquest of the higher intellectual dimensions.'

'Time to hear some of my poetry, perhaps?' said the leading dragon, eagerly.

'That too,' said Togura.

'Then we shall oblige.'

And, to Togura's dismay and astonishment, the leading dragon began to recite its poetry. At great length. It was windy, ostentatious and stunningly boring. Nevertheless, he applauded politely.

The other dragons, jealous of the applause, demanded to be given their own chances to recite. Togura, faint with hunger, listened to their angry, arrogant, hogen-mogen voices disputing precedence. Each wanted to be first to recite. They barked, snapped, spat smoke, and suddenly fell to fighting. Togura, ringed round with fighting dragons, screamed at them:

'Stop! Stop! Stop!'

It did no good whatsoever.

Then a voice roared:

'Begenoth!'

The quarrelling dragons instantly quailed down to silence.

'Shavaunt!' shouted the voice.

And the dragons turned and fled.

Togura was alone.

'Now then,' said the dragon commander, entering the courtyard. 'What started all that off?'

The dragon commander was an old, old man with a dirty grey beard, who walked with the aid of a shepherd's crook.

Despite his age, his eyes were bright, his voice was firm, and he looked fit and healthy.

'Well, boy?' asked the dragon commander.

'I . . . I asked if I could hear some of their poetry.'

'You what!?'

'Only some poetry, that's all. I just said I wished I had time to hear some.'

'No, boy, no, a thousand times no, that is one thing you must never ever do when you're face to face with a sea dragon. You must never ever—not on any account—encourage their artistic pretensions. Art, you see, is purely their excuse for being the most lazy, idle, shiftless, foolish, irresponsible, degenerate pack of gluttonous sex-obsessed drunkards this side of the east ditch of Galsh Ebrek.'

'I'm sorry, sir, I didn't know.'

'This time, you're excused,' said the dragon commander. 'Come this way, boy.'

And he led Togura along halls and passageways, up and down staircases, through doors, gates and gloomy portals, past statues, weapon racks and antiquated skeletons, and, at last, into a comfortable room with wall-to-wall carpeting, leather furniture, two cats, a hubble-bubble pipe and large leaded windows where the glass was patterned in circles, squares and diamonds.

'Sit, boy, sit,' said the dragon commander, motioning Togura to a chair. 'Good. Now tell me what you've been doing with yourself since you left Sung.'

'Sung?'

'Your homeland, boy. To be specific, Keep.'

'How did you know that?' said Togura, in amazement.

'I met you there. I introduced myself, didn't I?'

'Did you?'

'Of course I did. I distinctly remember giving you my name—Hostaja Torsen Sken-Pitilkin, wizard of Drum.

Well, boy? Why are you so blank? Senility, is it? Losing your memory already? And you so young? A tragic case!'

'I really don't think—'

'You don't think! Confession time, is it? I'm sure you don't think. I only hope the condition isn't permanent. What did they call you? Let me think. The girl called you Tog. Yet the rumbustical boy called you Spunk Togura. Or did he call you Chids? Anyway, the man—the man called you Master Togura. That's for certain. That was before he bedded me down in that shacklety old building—a garrow, I think he called it.'

'Well . . .'

'Come on, boy! Surely you remember. There was a dreadful noise. I complained. I remember that distinctly. You called it music—a mistake, I thought, but I didn't object. I was tired. I'd just flown in from Chi'ash-lan.'

'Ah!' said Togura, suddenly enlightened. 'You were the old man with the bundle of sticks. A great big clutter of sticks like a huge bird's nest. You called it a ship!'

'Yes, boy, and if you'd roused yourself from your slumbers in the early morning, you'd have seen me fly away in it. Why didn't you remember my name? I always introduce myself. I did so then, I'm certain of it. Or was that in the morning? Perhaps I introduced myself in the kitchen, when I scavenged the breakfast that nobody thought to offer me. I had a long argument with the cook. She was drunk.'

'That would be Salomie,' said Togura.

'That's the name! And what are you, boy? Tog, Spunk, Chids? Speak up, boy!'

'Togura Poulaan, if you please. Son of Baron Chan Poulaan.'

'Ah so! You're the one they call Barak the Battleman. There's a price on your head. I could use it. What say you give me your head, boy? I'll split the reward with you. Straight down the middle.'

Togura blanched.

'Come now, boy,' said the wizard of Drum. 'Can't you tell when someone's joking? I wouldn't dismember a guest. Come now, don't say you believe all that slander spawned by King Skan Askander? All that nonsense about using people as dragon-chop and such-such? Boy, you're looking quite faint. When did you last eat?'

'I don't remember,' said Togura.

'Then sit there quietly and I'll get you something. You're looking as bad as I do after a long trip by air. Relax, boy, relax! You're safe on Drum.'

Togura did not feel safe, but he relaxed all the same. In fact, he closed his eyes and went straight off to sleep. The wizard woke him to eat, and, as he ate, his spirits began to revive.

He realised that he had reached a place of refuge.

From the exciting conclusion
of Togura Poulaan's quest,
WIZARD WAR CHRONICLES: THE HERO RETURNS
to be published later this year
by Questar.

When Togura Poulaan finally punched through to the starlight, he heard men outside, talking in low voices, their conversation punctuated occasionally by laughter. Supposing that they would eventually get bored and go away, he waited. Namaji, exhausted by emotional trauma, fell asleep, snoring loudly. Waiting in the darkness, Togura did mental revision, working through all the ways he knew of killing people. He concluded, with regret, that his repertoire was rather limited.

He heard some men saying their goodbyes, and, after that, no voices, no laughter. He enlarged his hole, then hauled himself out onto the roof and dropped down into the darkness. He stood there, listening. He heard insects cricketing away, frogs croaking in the distance, a few muffled snores, and, far away, a horse neighing. It was a dark, cold night, lit by starlight; there was, as yet, no moon. He could have wished for some wind; the night was very still.

Togura began to slip between the hulking shadows of the mud huts, moving lightfoot-brightfoot through the night.

Without warning, a cock crowed close at hand and close at ear:

'Co co rico! Co co rico!'

The noise was as loud as a slap on the ear. Togura started, as if someone had sheathed a blade in his heart. The cock crowed again.

'Who will rid me of this turbulent rooster?' muttered Togura.

He should have known better than to speak. His voice was low, but it set a dog to barking. Other dogs roused to the challenge. As they barked, furiously, sleepers awakened. Mobbed by angry shouts, Togura sprinted for the village wall. He went over it, ran into the darkness and lay flat.

Togura knew there was no point in escaping without a horse, for the village men would quarter the country and ride him down by daylight. He had to have a mount. But there was no point in making immediately for the horse corral, because it was guarded; no doubt the guard would soon be reinforced. He lay quiet and still, a shadow lost in the shadows.

A furious search was soon going on. Togura heard sounds of fighting, then cries of pain from a man. He speculated that a sentry who should have been patrolling the wall had been caught sleeping. He heard a lot of noise from the horse corral. Men with burning brands searched the area near the corral; someone seemed to be searching in amongst the horses. Soon a number of mounted men were circling the village.

Togura, though he was shivering in the cold night air, did not move until all the fuss and excitement had died down a little. Then he crept back to the village wall and followed it round to the gates. Some men, dismounted, were standing there by their horses, arguing. A dog barked loudly as Togura approached; a man cursed it and kicked it to silence. Someone was urinating noisily in the darkness.

As humble as a cockroach, Togura went sneaking to the nearest horsy shadow. Closing with the animal, he ran his hands along its back, locating the saddle. He found the nearside stirrup and got his foot in it. He found the reins, took them in hand, then mounted.

'Wah-Warguild!' screamed Togura, kicking the horse.

His mount reared. A man grabbed Togura's leg. Togura kicked, and was free. Screaming, he urged the horse to a gallop. A warrior threw a spear, which missed. Still screaming, Togura galloped away into the night. His screams, as he had intended, had scattered the other horses, giving him a decent head start.

Navigating by the stars, he headed north. Once he reached the hills, he would kill the horse then trek over the mountains back to Estar. With dismay, he realised the moon was rising.

Sooner than he had thought, the village men managed to secure their horses and join the pursuit. He heard their shouts and hoofbeats behind him. The rising moon betrayed him to all the night.

'Ride, beauty,' urged Togura, slapping the horse.

He galloped the horse until it could gallop no more; fortunately, the riders behind him were having similar problems with their own mounts. The chase continued at a steady trot.

Suddenly, to his dismay, Togura realised there were riders ahead of him. How had that happened?

He was still trying to work out what to do next when the riders up ahead dispersed. They disappeared into a little bit of hummocked land off to his left. He blinked, wondering if they were ghosts, or if he had imagined them all along. No matter. The way ahead was clear.

But behind him he heard hastening hoofbeats, and realised the village warriors were once more trying to close the distance. He urged his horse as best he could, but it faltered, stumbled, then fell, throwing him. He picked himself up and remounted, but by then it was too late. The village riders, fierce, eager, shouting closed in around him.

'Togura!' shouted the headman.

The name was slurred, but Togura knew it for his own. The next moment, the headman slapped him, almost knocking him off the horse. Then there was an argument. Six riders had made the distance. Some, perhaps, wanted to butcher Togura on the spot. The headman finally mastered them to silence, then began to lead the way south. The horses, after all this hard treatment, could only manage a walking pace; they were not bred or fed to ride so far and so fast.

'Perhaps I'd better tell you,' said Togura. 'I saw some other horsemen back there.'

The headman, who did not understand his Galish, swore at him, and slapped him again. Togura, his nose gently bleeding, did not speak again. He had not been on horseback for ages; as a consequence, he was now saddle-sore.

They were some way back toward the village when shadows on shadow horses came screaming out of some hunchbacked wasteland. Arrows sang through the air. Lances rode home. Horses screamed, flailing down to their death. Togura urged his horse away. An enemy rode up alongside him, jumped, grabbed him round the neck, and took him crashing down to the ground. Togura felt a sickening pain in his right leg. The enemy drew a knife and tried to stab him. Togura fought with all his strength. The knife moved steadily, inexorably, toward his throat.

If Togura had been made of sterner stuff, he would have devoted all his energies to the struggle, and consequently would have died upon the spot. However, he didn't. He panicked instead, and screamed:

'Help help help!'

An enemy, whirling out of a skirmish, heard Togura's voice, and hurled a spear in his general direction. The spear slammed home, taking Togura's attacker fair and square between the shoulder blades. Killed by his own side, the attacker collapsed on Togura, who, thinking him still alive, damaged him dreadfully. Togura had just realised the man was dead when a horse, mortally wounded, collapsed on top of him. Suffocating, he fought it. By now he had a knife in his hand. The horse rolled away, staggered to its feet, managed a few steps, then dropped again, and died—this time falling clear of Togura.

He breathed the sweet cool night air in lurching gulps, sweating with effort, trembling with adrenalin, his heart still doing a decathlon. Somewhere out in the night, someone was being killed, and the sound was not pleasant. Someone, close at hand, was groaning hideously. Togura tried to get to his feet. An agonising pain in his right leg persuaded him against such foolishness. After a little experimentation, he realised the leg was broken.

'Things are not improving,' muttered Togura.

Then he heard someone walking through the night with a strange, shuffling gait. He decided it was best to play dead. He lay there with his eyes tightly shut, listening intently. Shufflefoot wandered, paused, wandered, then fell heavily, and did not move again. Slowly, Togura opened his eyes.

Old Scar Face, the moon, floated above him, cool and remote. Somewhere close at hand, someone was crying bitterly. Togura listened, carefully, and ascertained that it wasn't him. Despite his current predicament he was, for once, dry-eyed and clear-headed.

Out in the night, some unknown animal cried.

Togura was still trembling—but now it was not adrenalin which was responsible, but the cold.

He could see that it was going to be another one of those long, long nights.

Togura slept fitfully, dreaming that he was lying out under the sun with a broken leg. He woke to find it was true. The morning was still young but already the day was dominated by unseasonable heat. His mouth was hot, dry, dusty. Flies picked their way over his face. He shook them off.

The air was loud with the buzz of flies. Dead men, dead horses, discarded weapons, a confusion of tracks and bloodstains marked the scene of battle. Togura, careful not to disturb his broken leg, looked around. He counted five dead horses, a dozen dead men, the bodies being spread over quite a considerable area.

Who won?

There was no telling.

Carefully, he examined his broken leg. It was the shin bone which was sore. He slit his trews below the knee so he could examine the break. To his relief, he found the bone had not forced its way through the skin. The area was very, very painful, but there was not much swelling. As broken legs went, this one was not very serious. But there was still no way he could walk on it.

'Togura,' said a familiar, slurred voice.

It was a bit early in the piece to be having hallucinations, so Togura looked around. One of the bodies had moved. It was the village headman, who was lying on the ground a dozen paces away, both wrists bent at a strange angle. Togura could only presume that the headman had broken both wrists in a fall.

'Come and help me,' said Togura, though there was not much hope that the headman would understand his Galish.

The headman, urging himself forward on his elbows, moved half a pace forward then stopped, his face a mask of pain. Obviously he hadn't just broken his wrists. Something else was smashed. Leg? Legs? Pelvis? Spine?

'Togura,' said the headman. 'Dosh.'

'What did "dosh" mean? It meant "go"'. Togura knew that much.

'I can't,' he said, hurt by this totally unreasonable order. 'I've got a broken leg.'

The headman repeated himself.

There was, or so Togura supposed, some sense in the order. The attackers, to judge from their dead, were of the same tribe as the assassin who had tried to kill the headman—Togura could tell that by their hairstyles. They might have been a scouting party, or they might have been part of a much larger war party. If any had got away alive —and quite possibly the enemy had had the better of the battle—then they might come back with reinforcements. The area was unhealthy.

'If I had half a chance of getting anywhere,' said Togura, 'then I'd go. As it is, I'm staying.'

'Dosh,' said the headman, thrusting one of his broken wrists in the direction of the south.

'What do you mean, dosh?' yelled Togura, angry now. 'You're crazy.'

The answer was the same.

'Dosh yourself!' said Togura.

'Togura,' said the headman, his voice intimate, urgent, commanding. 'Togura, dosh.'

They could go on like this all day. It was very frustrating arguing with someone who didn't speak your language.

'All right then!' shouted Togura. 'Dosh dosh dosh dosh!'

His throat was sore. He wished he hadn't shouted so loudly. He saw the headman smile.

'Ssh-schaa,' said the headman; Togura recognised that as an expression of satisfaction.

'This is crazy,' said Togura.

But despite his reservations, he looked around for something he could use to splint his leg. The nearest suitable object was a spear sticking out of the back of one of the enemy dead. Togura wrenched it out, disturbing a hubbub of flies in the process. Using a knife which was his by right of combat, he cut it down to size. He cut into the flesh of a dead horse; he used lumps of horsemeat as padding, and strips of horsehide to tie the splint in place.

He ate some horsemeat, raw, then, as an afterthought, threw a dollop at the headman; it hit his nose and fell to the dust. The headman salvaged it with his mouth, tasted the dust and spat it out.

'Choosy,' said Togura. 'Beggars can't be choosers, you know.'

'Donz-m'dola,' said the headman.

That little phrase had something to do with the idea of getting bigger, or increasing. Togura had a hazy notion that in some contexts it was obscene, but that could hardly be the case here. Realising what the headman meant, Togura cut a sizeable chunk of meat and tossed it so that it fell within mouthreach.

'Zon,' said the headman.

Which meant more.

Togura provided. He ate some more, feeding methodically. When he could eat no more, he decided it was time to go. To give his broken shinbone the smoothest possible ride, he was constrained to travel on his back. He started off, using his hands and his good leg. Raising his buttocks from the ground sent pains shooting along his right leg; his saddle-sick buttocks would have to drag along in the dust.

'Gjonga,' said the headman.

The word, a very formal form of 'goodbye', was unknown to Togura. He did not answer, but concentrated on the task at hand. He scraped along, clumsy as a broken insect. Under the pitiless sun. Under the pitiless sky. Flies were already festering on his horsemeat padding. His broken leg, even though it was splinted, nagged him constantly.

It was hot work. The meat ripened as the sun lazed through the sky. He started to feel nauseous, perhaps from the burden of horsemeat in his stomach, or from the stench of rotting meat wrapped round his leg, or from the constant twinges of pain from the leg—pain which was sharp, stabbing, unrelenting, worse than toothache.

—Pain is the worst thing.

The battlefield was distant now. He could just make out a small clump of shadows far away on the open plain. Carrion birds circled overhead.

—Courage, Togura.

His hands hurt. His buttocks hurt. His legs hurt. Thirst, like a jagged spatula, scraped at the back of his throat. Familiar muscles began to cramp; unfamiliar muscles ached and protested. He was starting to get backache. He was a crippled skeleton. An insect man, a freak of nature. A damaged organism.

The skin was wearing away from his buttocks. And from the palms of his hands. He should have padded himself with something. Strips of horsehide, perhaps. From time to time he had little dizzy spells in which the world blurred and darkened. Drops of sweat crept down from his fore-head.

He needed water. So what was he going to do about it? Dig a well? Do a rain dance? He laughed, hurting himself. He tried to generate saliva, so he could ease the scraping thirst in his throat. No joy. He should have brought some horse meat with him. He could have sucked on it. Before setting out, he should have dragged himself round the dead men and the dead horses, looking for a water skin. Surely there would have been at least one. He was an experienced survivor. He had no excuse for not thinking of these things.

He halted, to take a rest. High overhead, a skylark was singing. He listened intently to its attenuated song. It carried him up, up, up, higher and higher into the dizzy sky. Then vanished, dropping him away to nothing.

He fainted.

He woke when something hurt his leg. Opening his eyes, he saw a big bald-headed bird gashing into his horse-meat splint padding. He waved an arm. It went scuffling into the air, then settled on the ground. Its beady eyes considered him. Then it hopped forward. He dragged himself away, thinking unpleasant thoughts about the carrion birds he had seen circling over the battlefield, and about the headman lying there, utterly defenceless, with two broken wrists. Well, at least the headman would be able to jerk his head around; that would probably be enough to dissuade the birds, at least while they had plenty of quiescent carcases to feed on.

—Onward, Togura.

He dragged himself on, chafing away the last of the clothing protecting his buttocks. The skin began to rub away. He endured.

—Pain is life.

Night came, bringing unrelenting cold. Togura slept a little, then dragged himself on. When the pain was at its worst, he cried out with high, harsh, half-singing exclamations, which sounded almost like broken snatches of song. He allowed himself a little sleep, dreaming of pain only to wake to pain.

—Worse things happen at sea.

He kept the stars of the north dead ahead of him, knowing that the south lay behind his head. The moon rose, making shadowed craters out of the hoof-marks of horses. He was on the right track.

Towards morning, he heard dogs barking in the distance.

—Strength, Togura, strength.

He was taking his journey a step at a time. Pause. Brace. Push. Scrape. Endure the pain. Rest. Think out the next move. Gather courage. Brace. Push. Scrape.

—This is your test.

Rest. And brace. And now—strength!—push. Scrape. Rest. Endure. And once more, Togura, once more. Brace! Push! Scrape!

—And once more.

The night slowly lightened. The sun rose. His blood, pulsing through his ears, sang to him. He felt the steady thud of his heart in his chest. He pushed himself along. Relentlessly. He was a master torturer now, absolutely without pity for the broken organism he was punishing. Brace—push—scrape—

—And rest . . .

Resting, he heard hoofbeats. They came closer and closer, then the horse wheeled, riding in to halt beside him. Looking up he saw, hazily, a man in the saddle. Togura recognised him by his haircut. He was from the home village.

'Dosh,' croaked Togura, pointing north. Then, louder: 'Dosh!'

Then he fainted.